ANONYMOUS REX

A DETECTIVE STORY

ERIC GARCIA

BERKLEY PRIME CRIME, NEW YORK

This is a work of fiction. Names, characters, places, and incidents either are the product of the author's imagination or are used fictitiously, and any resemblance to actual persons, living or dead, business establishments, events, or locales is entirely coincidental.

ANONYMOUS REX

A Berkley Prime Crime Book / published by arrangement with Villard Books, a division of Random House Inc.

PRINTING HISTORY
Villard Books hardcover edition / 2000
Berkley trade paperback edition / March 2001
Berkley Prime Crime mass-market edition / February 2003

Copyright © 2000 by Eric Garcia.
Cover art by Jeff Crosby.
Cover design by Jill Bolton.

All rights reserved.
This book, or parts thereof, may not be reproduced in any form without permission. For information address: The Berkley Publishing Group, a division of Penguin Putnam Inc., 375 Hudson Street, New York, New York 10014.

Visit our website at
www.penguinputnam.com

ISBN: 0-425-18888-4

Berkley Prime Crime Books are published
by The Berkley Publishing Group,
a division of Penguin Putnam Inc.,
375 Hudson Street, New York, New York 10014.
The name BERKLEY PRIME CRIME and the BERKLEY PRIME CRIME design are trademarks belonging to Penguin Putnam Inc.

PRINTED IN THE UNITED STATES OF AMERICA

10 9 8 7 6 5 4 3 2 1

Praise for
ANONYMOUS REX

"First-time novelist Eric Garcia pulls ~~~~~~~~~ the laughs frequent and the plot intriguing. ~~~~~~~~~ chapters, it seems downright logical to believe ~~~~ re surrounded by a cast out of *Jurassic Park.* Apart from showing off a splendidly warped imagination, Garcia provides a solid mystery."   —*People*

"Garcia has come up with an imaginative twist to the detective fiction genre."   —*Daily Variety*

"Audacious and imaginative. You might not believe any of this thirty seconds after you close the covers, but while it's going on you're going to be dazzled by Garcia's energy and chutzpah."   —*Publishers Weekly*

"Garcia plays it almost completely straight, respecting all noir traditions, and comes up with lovely touches."
                                                —*Chicago Tribune*

"A 'noir-asaurus' of a novel, bellowing for attention, the first and only of its breed in the dinosaur detective genre. Garcia has written something so strange, so bizarre, that he's to be admired just for the attempt. And he not only pulls it off, he also actually makes you wonder why someone hasn't thought of it before."   —*The Miami Herald*

"Vincent Rubio, the protagonist of this first-person—er, first-dino narrative is so likeable, the story handled with such deftness, that it actually, incredibly works. Spider Robinson meets Sam Spade . . . sardonic and strong in the hard-boiled tradition, and laced with jokes."
                                          —*Richmond Times-Dispatch*

"*Anonymous Rex* leaps out of its gumshoe formula fast enough to break the genre barrier. Imagine a hard-boiled detective novel crossed with magical realism. Think film noir with great special effects. Think fabulous read. Well paced, well plotted, and charming . . . a gem of modern detective fiction."   —*The Austin Chronicle*

continued . . .

Praise for
CASUAL REX:

"A funny book. I can't remember an author pulling off a more difficult premise, unless it's T. Jefferson Parker."
—*Los Angeles Times*

"Every bit as delightfully strange, richly imagined, and just plain funny [as his debut]."   —*The Seattle Times*

"It's so hard to resist stomping around in dinosaur metaphors in reviewing *Casual Rex*. But the book . . . is too good, too funny and too inventive to get bogged down in Jurassic jargon . . . dripping with tongue-in-jaw wit, snappy action, funny lines, and plot twists. A genre-bending, species-bending, gender-bending romp of a mystery. . . . What's really intriguing is Garcia's commentary about society and historical events as seen through dinosaur eyes. . . . It's obvious Garcia had fun with *Casual Rex*. Readers will too. May be the most entertaining book out this year."   —*The Columbus Dispatch*

"Garcia keeps the jokes coming . . . to present a tale that's slightly cornball, at times hilarious, and unquestionably original . . . will appeal to both mystery and SF readers. Here's a series with dino-sized legs."   —*Publishers Weekly*

"Hugely entertaining. . . . Seamless, wonderfully clever world-building, a little dino-depravity, and an abundance of tongue-in-cheek humor to keep things rolling along."
—*Booklist*

"*X-Files* meets Sam Spade . . . hip, knowing, and often very funny."   —*Library Journal*

"You could call *Casual Rex* dinomite." —*Gotham Magazine*

For my wife, Sabrina,
who is my basil, my cilantro, and my marjoram,
all wrapped into one

And for my parents, Manny and Judi,
whose faith is unending,
and who made me re-wear my socks

"I have never been hardboiled, but I'm trying. I'm trying real hard."

ACKNOWLEDGMENTS

Thanks, first and foremost, to Barbara Zitwer Alicea, the greatest literary agent in the known universe (and an all-around wonderful person), without whom this book would be in a very different form and still collecting dust on a shelf in my home. And T-Rex-sized thanks to Jonathan Karp, my editor at Random House/Villard, who saw something bright and glittering buried in the tar pits of my novel and helped me to drag it out and clean it off.

Thanks, also, to those who read the book at its inception and were never anything but constructive with their criticism, and to friends and family who were always ready with help and support: Steven Solomon, Alan Cook, Ben Rosner, Julie Sheinblatt, Brett Oberst, Michele Kuhns, Rob Kurzban, Crystal Wright, Beverly Erickson, and Howard Erickson.

No doubt about it, I've been hitting the basil hard tonight. Half a sprig at the Tar Pit Club, quarter in the bathroom stall, half heading down the 101 on the drive over, two more waiting here in the car, and only now is the buzz crawling on, a muddled high that's got me jumping at my own tail. Scored it fresh tonight, a whole half-pound from Trader Joe's up on La Brea. Gene, the stock clerk, keeps a hidden stash for his special customers, and though it takes the occasional fin or two to stay firmly entrenched on Gene's good side, you haven't truly done basil until you've done Gene's Special Stash basil. Throws out the kind of buzz where you're wishing the high would come on and you're wishing the high would come on and you're wishing the high would come on and then you're there, and you're wondering how the hell it was possible that you ever *weren't* there.

This camera's hanging heavy about my neck, lens cap off, tugging on me, begging for action. It's a Minolta piece of crap I bought for forty bucks, substandard in all specifications, but I can't do snoop work without a camera, and I didn't pull down enough gigs last month to get my good one out of hock. That's why I need this job. That and the mortgage payment. And the car. And the credit cards.

A pair of headlights breaks the darkness, creeping slowly down the street. Flashers, strictly orange. Rent-a-cops. I slouch in my seat. I'm short. I'm not noticed. The car drives past, taillights drowning the peaceful suburbs in a wash of pale crimson.

Inside that house across the way—that one, there, with the manicured lawn, the faux gas-lamp security lights, the pressed concrete driveway—is this month's potential windfall. In the old days, that'd mean a case capable of bringing in anywhere from twenty to fifty thousand dollars by the time Ernie and I threw in fees, expenses, and whatever the hell else crossed our minds as we wrote up the bill. Nowadays it means I'll be lucky to clear nine hundred. My head hurts. I fix up another pinch of basil and chew, chew, chew.

Third day of a three-day tail-and-stakeout operation. Sleeping in the car, eating in rat-infested diners, eyes sore from the strain of picking out details at a distance. For an hour and a half, I've been sitting in my car, waiting for the bedroom lights to click on. It's useless taking pictures of a darkened window, and firsthand personal skinny doesn't make the grade—distraught wives don't give a damn about what a PI sees or what a PI hears. We are persona non grata, big time. They want pictures, and lots of 'em. Some want video. Some want audio. All want proof. So even though I personally witnessed Mr. Ohmsmeyer giggling, cuddling, and generally making cutesy-face with a female who was neither his wife nor a member of his immediate family, and even though my gut tells me that he and the un-named floozy have been tearing a sexual cyclone through that house for the last ninety minutes, it means crap to Mrs.

Ohmsmeyer, my client, until I'm able to grab the shindig on a negative. It'd be my pleasure if they'd just turn on the damn lights.

A halogen pops to life in the living room, silhouettes shimmying into place behind gauzy curtains—now we're cooking. A grope to find the door handle, a simple tug, and suddenly I'm out of the car and stumbling toward the house, my costumed human legs betraying me with every step. Funny how the ground's twisting into knots like that. I stop, catch my balance, lose it again. A nearby tree arrests my fall.

I'm not worried about being seen or heard, but passing out on the front yard in a basil-induced stupor could look bad come morning. Steeling myself, muscles flexed, legs bent ever so slightly, I flounder across the lawn, hurdle a small hedge, and hit the dirt. Mud splatters my pants; it will have to remain there. I have no money for dry cleaning.

Window's a low one, bottom of the frame just above my line of sight. Thin curtains, probably a cotton blend, lousy for photographs. The silhouettes are dancing now, shadowy figures moving back-two-three, left-two-three, and from the muffled sounds of grunts and growls, I'd say they're out of guise and ready for a full night of action.

Lens cap off, pulling focus, setting the frame to get a nice, clean shot. But not too clean—no divorce court's gonna grant a big settlement on the basis of an adultery pic with Ansel Adams composition. The illicit has to look illicit. Maybe a smudge on the print, a casual blur, and always, always in black and white.

Another light, this one in the hallway. Now I'm noticing features, and it's quite clear that the two lovebirds have shed their skins. Unfurled tails snake through the air; exposed claws draw furrows along the wallpaper. Passion is driving the couple to carelessness—I can even make out the female's mammalian guise tossed across the back of the sofa, knitted blond hair flung across the throw pillows, limp human arms dangling like ticker tape over the side. And moving through the hallway now, toward the bedroom, a pair of lumbering shapes both too concerned with libido to hide their natural postures. Gotta get to that bedroom window.

I'm able to make it to my feet before falling back down again, at which point I decide that crawling around to the side of the house might be the best option. There's dirt and mud and grime down here, but it beats elevating my head above my knees. Along the way, I pass a beautifully landscaped garden, and promptly throw up on the begonias. I'm beginning to feel much better.

Bedroom window, a large bay jobbie that is fortunately hidden behind the overgrown branches of a nearby oak. The curtains, though closed, have parted slightly, and it is through this crack that I may just get my best shots. A quick peek—

Mr. Ohmsmeyer, certified public accountant and father to three beautiful Iguanodon children, is fully out of his human guise, tail extended into proper mating position, claws retracted for safety's sake, a full set of razor-sharp chompers tasting the pheromone-stained air. He stands over his lover, an Ornithomimus of average proportions: nice egg sac, thin forelegs, rounded beak, adequate tail. I don't see anything outstanding there, can't comprehend whatever urges are driving Mr. Ohmsmeyer to break his sacred vows of marriage, but maybe it's hard for a lifelong bachelor to understand the passions that overcome married men. Then again, I don't have to understand it; I simply have to photograph it.

The shutter's not as whisper-quiet as I'd like, but with all the noises they're about to start making, it won't make a difference. I click away, eager to grab as many photos as possible—Mrs. Ohmsmeyer agreed to pay for whatever film and developing costs might be incurred during the process of my investigation, and if I'm lucky, she won't realize that she's also picking up the tab for some prints of last year's fishing trip up at Beaver Creek.

A steady rhythm is set—one, two, thrust, pause pause pause, four, five, retract, pause, pause, repeat. Mr. O.'s got a rough, hit-a-home-run-with-every-swing style to his lovemaking that I'm used to seeing with adulterers. There's an urgency to the process, and maybe even a little anger in that hip action. His scaled brown hide scratches roughly against the green Ornithomimus, and the fragile four-poster bed rocks and creaks with every insistent thrust.

They continue. I continue. Click click click.

This set of pictures will represent what I hope is the end of a two-week investigation that was neither particularly easy nor interesting. When Mrs. Ohmsmeyer came to me two weeks ago and laid out the situation, I figured it'd be your basic cheat job, boring as all hell but in and out in three days and maybe I could hold off the creditors for a week. And since she was the first lady to walk in my door since the Council rectification came through, I took the gig on the spot. What she didn't tell me, and what I soon found out, was that Mr. Ohmsmeyer presented a new wrinkle to get around in that he had somehow obtained access to a multitude of human guises, and had no shame in changing them as often as possible. Spare guises are permitted in certain situations, of course, but only when ordered from the proper source and with the proper personal ID number. Identity fraud is easy enough in this day and age without dinosaurs changing their appearances willy-nilly. Definite

Council violation right there, no question, but I'm the last person who's gonna bring Ohmsmeyer up on charges in front of that goddamned organization.

So, sure—I could just stake out the house, place my rump in the car, and watch like a hawk, but who knew where the randy bugger would be throwing it down next? Tracked a guy once who liked to have sex on the girders underneath bridges, of all places, and another who only did it in the bathrooms of the International House of Pancakes. So though a stakeout was an option—and the family home was indeed where I finally ended up—there remained the problem of keeping a bead on Mr. O. But once I decided to trust my nose, my most base of instincts, it all fell into place.

He's got an antiseptic scent, almost grainy, with a touch of lavender riding the edges. Very accountant. Strong, too—I picked up a whiff at two hundred yards. So the next time he tried to pull the switcheroo, it went like this: Into a restaurant dressed as Mr. Ohmsmeyer, out of the restaurant two hours later guised up as an old Asian lady with a walker, but no matter—he left great clouds of pheromones lingering behind like a trail of bread crumbs, and I followed that olfactory path as he led his floozy back to this street, this house, and this bedroom window. Gutsy move on his part, trysting on the home front, but Mrs. Ohmsmeyer and the kids are at her sister's place in Bakersfield for the weekend, so he's safe from direct marital discovery.

Third roll of film spent, and it's almost time to close up shop. Just in time, too, as Mr. Ohmsmeyer's nearing the end of his fun and games; I can feel it in the grunts emanating from the bedroom, growing deeper, harsher, louder. Bass echoes through the house, vibrating the window, the two intertwined dinos flexing before my eyes, and the beat intensifies as the female Ornithomimus begins to howl, lips stretching, reaching for the ceiling, legs locked tight around her lover's tail, that sandpaper hide blushing with blood, sliding from green to purple to a deep mahogany glazed over with excess sweat, Mr. O. panting hard, tongue licking the air, steam rising from his ridged back as he turns his head to the side, teeth parting wide, and begins the last rise, preparing to fully consummate his lust—

A clang, behind me. Metallic. Scraping.

I know that sound. I know that clang. I know that familiar ring of metal on metal and I don't like it one bit. Forgetting my earlier lack of coordination, I leap to my feet and crash through the nearest set of hedges—screw Ohmsmeyer, screw the job—branches breaking as I push through, a crazed adventurer scything his way through the underbrush. Wheeling around, almost losing my balance as I make the turn toward the front of the house, I come to a stop midway between a lawn gnome and the most terrifying sight these eyes have ever seen:

Someone is towing my car.

"Hey!" I call. "Hey, you! Yeah, you!"

The short, squat tow truck driver looks up rapidly, his head seemingly independent of his neck, and cocks a thick eyebrow. I can smell his scent from thirty feet away—rotting veggies and ethyl alcohol, a potent mixture that almost makes my eyes water. Too small for a Triceratops, so he must be a Compy, which should make this conversation frustrating, if nothing else. "Me? Me?" he squawks, the clipped screech tearing at my ears.

"Yeah, you. That's my car. This—this here—it's mine."

"This car?"

"Yes," I say, "this car. I'm not illegally parked. You can't tow it."

"Illegally parked? No, you ain't illegally parked."

I nod furiously, hoping nonverbal cues will help. "Yes, yes, right. There's no red curb, no signs—please, unhook my car—"

"This car here?"

"Yes, right. Yes. That car. The Lincoln. Unhook me and I'll be going."

"It ain't yours." He resumes clamping the winch onto the front axle.

Swinging around to the passenger-side window, I reach in the glove compartment—gum, maps, shaker of dried oregano—and pull out the wrinkled registration. "See? My name, right there." I place the document directly under his eyes, and he studies it for quite some time. Most Compys have literacy problems.

"It ain't yours," he repeats.

I have neither the time nor the inclination to engage this dimwitted dinosaur in a philosophical debate as to the nature of ownership, so it looks like a little intimidation might be in order. "You don't wanna do this," I tell him, leaning into a conspiratorial whisper. "I've got some pretty powerful friends." A bald bluff, but what does a Procompsognathus know, anyhow?

He laughs, the little apefucker, a chicken-cluck guffaw, and shakes his head back and forth. I consider a bit of controlled assault and battery, but I've had enough trouble with the law in recent months without having to add another run-in to the list.

"I know 'bout you," says the Compy. "Least, I know all I gotta know."

"What? You've been—look here—I need this car to work—"

Suddenly, the front door to the house across the street opens up, and Mr. Ohmsmeyer, who must have reguised himself in record time, strides purposefully down the front walk. An impressive display of speed, considering it takes most of us at least ten, fifteen minutes to apply even the most basic human makeup and polysuit. For what it's worth, the D-9 clamp riding beneath the guise across the left side of his chest is unbuckled—I can see it even through his guise—but it's nothing a mammal would ever notice. His eyes dart back and forth, nervous, paranoid, searching the darkened street for any sign of his loving spouse. Perhaps he heard my hasty exit from the bushes; perhaps I interrupted his climax.

"The hell's going on here?" he grumbles, and I'm about to answer when the Compy tow truck driver hands me a sheet of paper. It reads BYRON COLLECTIONS AND REPOSSESSIONS in bold twenty-point type, and lists their phone number and some sample rates. I look up, a host of indignant responses foaming to my lips—

To find that the Compy's already in the truck, revving it up, winching my car into place. I leap for the open cab, claws almost springing forth on their own—and the door slams in my face. The sonofabitch is sneering at me through the glass, his angular features almost daring me to leap in front of the truck, to give my life for the life of my automobile, which in Los Angeles is not unheard of. "You pay the bank," he crows through the closed window, "you get the car." And with a shove of the Compy's scrawny arms, the tow truck hops into first gear, dragging my beloved Lincoln Continental Mark V behind it.

I stare down the street for quite some time after the tow truck's taillights have disappeared into the night.

Ohmsmeyer breaks my reverie. He's staring at my legs, at the mud splattered across my pants. A slow wave of anger carves a wake across his forehead. I grin, attempting to head off any ill will. "I don't suppose I could use your phone?"

"You were in my bushes—"

"Actually, I—"

"You were at the window—"

"There's a technical point here I'd like to make—"

"What the hell's that camera for?"

"No, you're—you're missing the point—"

I don't get any farther before I'm doubled over from a swift hit to my belly. It's a featherweight slap, nothing more, but the combination of the sucker punch and five sprigs of basil has got me woozy and ready to lose the second half of my lunch. Backing away, I hold my hands above my head in half-surrender. It helps the nausea dissipate. Hell, I could fight back—even fully guised I could take this accountant, and without the straps and girdles and buckles on, I could whip the tar outta two and a half Iguanodons—but the night's events have lost their charm, and I'd like to call an end to the festivities.

"Who the hell do you think you are?" he asks, standing over me, ready to deliver another glancing blow. "I can smell you from here. Raptor, right? I've got a good mind to report you to the Council."

"You wouldn't be the first," I say, straightening up again, able to look the fellow in the eye. What the hell—photos'll be developed tomorrow, I might as well give the poor sap a head start on legal matters.

I put out my hand, and to my surprise, the Iguanodon takes it, shakes it. "My name is Vincent Rubio," I say, "and I'm a private investigator working for your wife. And if I were you, Mr. Ohmsmeyer, I'd start looking for a good divorce lawyer."

Silence, as the dinosaur realizes he's been caught, and caught by the best. I shrug, issue a tight smile. But as his brow furrows, I notice that this is not the proper facial expression to register fear, anger, betrayal, or any of the other emotions I expected. This guy's just . . . confused.

"Ohmsmeyer?" he says, comprehension slow to dawn. "Oh, you want Ohmsmeyer? He lives next door."

It is a lovely night out. I choose to walk home. Perhaps I will be mugged.

The window still says WATSON AND RUBIO, PRIVATE INVESTIGATIONS, even though Ernie's been dead for nine months. I don't care. I'm not changing it. Some jerk from the building came by to scrape off the Watson a few weeks after Ernie bid the world farewell, but I ran him off with a broom and a broken rum bottle. Good thing alcohol doesn't affect me, or I'd have been even more upset—it was expensive rum.

The office has that musty-carpet, old-lady, forgot-to-put-the-laundry-in-the-dryer odor that I'm used to smelling every time I return from a marathon stakeout session, which is surprising, considering they repossessed the carpeting two months ago. Still, no matter how well I disinfect before I leave for a trip, those damn bacteria find a way to congregate, divide, and contaminate every square inch of this place, and someday I'm gonna get those little suckers. It hasn't reached the stage of personal vendetta yet, as it's difficult to bear a grudge against one-celled organisms, but I'm trying hard to take it to that next level.

What's more, I forgot to take out the trash before I left, and the place is as cold as a Mesozoic glacier. Seems I left the air on the entire goddamned time, and what that's gonna do to my electric bills I don't even want to think about. I'm just lucky they didn't cut the power altogether; the last time that happened my refrigerator cut out, and the basil turned sour, though I was already on such a high when I started chewing that I didn't realize it until too late. I still get the willies when I think about the nasty trip that brought on.

Speaking of bills, looks like I've become the lucky winner of at least two dozen, each of which is promptly added to the burgeoning heap on the office floor. There's the odd mailer, the coupon for four-room carpet steam cleaning, but that pile's mostly filled with irate missives printed on bright pink slips of paper, wordy legal documents threatening my financial well-being. I'm well past the range of Please Remit Promptly and in-house collection notices. We're talking attorneys and anger here, and it takes a great deal of concentration to pay them no mind. The only good thing about crappy credit is I've stopped receiving countless offers for preapproved Platinum Cards. Or Gold Cards. Or any cards whatsoever.

A blinking light. The office answering machine, once upon a time a useful, even cherished appliance, now taunting me from across the room. I have eight—no, nine—no, ten!—messages and each flash of red tells me I am screwed—blink—screwed—blink—screwed. I suppose I could yank the plug out of the wall, pull off a nice bit of digital euthanasia, but as Ernie always told me, turning away from your demons doesn't make them go away—it only makes it easier for them to bite you in the back.

Unsnapping the buttons hidden beneath the base of my wrist, I take off my guise gloves and allow my claws to snap into place. My long underclaw has begun to turn downward at a distressing angle, and I suppose I should see a manicurist about this, but their fees have become unreasonable recently, and they refuse to barter with me for free investigative work. I reach out and tentatively press Play.

Beep: "Mr. Rubio, this is Simon Dunstan at First National Mortgage. I've sent you a copy of the foreclosure documents from our legal department—" Erase. A trickle of pain lances out across my temple. Instinctively, I walk to the small kitchen set off in the front corner of the office. The refrigerator seems to open by itself, a nice clump of basil waiting for me on the top shelf. I chew.

Beep: "Hey, Vinnie. Charlie." Charlie? I don't know a Charlie. "Remember me?" Actually, no. "We met at the Fossil Fuels Club in Santa Monica, last New Year's." Some vague memory of lights and music and the purest pine needles at which my taste buds have ever had the pleasure to erupt floats through my head. This Charlie—another Velociraptor, maybe? And his job . . . he was a—a— "I work for the *Sentinel,* 'member?" Oh, right. The reporter. As I recall, he left with my date.

"Anyway," he continues, taking up valuable digital space in my answering machine's memory cache, "I thought maybe since we were old buddies and all, you could give me a little scoop on your ouster from the Council. I mean, now that the rectification came out—old time's sake, right buddy?" Bad enough to be a moron, but worse yet to be a dangerous moron. Mentioning the Council or any dinosaur-related topics in a setting where a human could accidentally hear is a strict no-no. I punch Erase and massage my temples. This migraine is taking its own sweet time showing up on my welcome mat, but it's those slow-setting ones that really pack a wallop once they start pounding on the front door.

Beep: Click. A hang-up. I love those—the best kind of message is none at all. They are perfectly, undeniably unreturnable.

Beep: "Hello. Please call American Express at—" Okay, a recording, that's not so bad. They don't really come after you until long after they've exhausted the one-on-one option. Erase.

Beep: "My name is Julie, I'm calling from American Express, looking for a Mr. Vincent Rubio. Please call me as soon as possible—" Damn. Erase.

It goes on like that for three or four more messages, terse, succinct speeches swarming with undercurrents of intimidation. I'm about to throw myself down on the springless sofa in the corner and wrap a ratty pillow around my head like a giant pair of earmuffs when a familiar voice cuts through the litany of vitriol.

Beep: "Vincent, it's Sally. From TruTel." Sally! One of the very few humans I've ever come to grudgingly like, and though she's hampered by her pitiful genetic structure, she's pretty hip to the whole scene. It's not that she knows about us—none of them have the faintest idea of our existence—but she's still one of the less offensive Neanderthals with whom I've had to interact. "Been a long time, huh? I've got a message . . . a request, I guess, from Mr. Teitelbaum, and he'd—he'd like to see you in the office. Tomorrow." Her register drops, decibels low, clearly whispering into the phone. "I think it's a job, Vincent. I think he's got a case for you."

There's something to think about there, something inherently good about that last bit of news, but too much of my mind is currently taken up with fighting the pain that's decided to take an extended vacation on my synapses. I save the rest of the messages for a time when I'll have either less of an impending headache or a higher blood basil content and stumble toward the sofa. The pain has just begun to radiate out from within the center of my head, taking big, bouncy steps toward my frontal lobes. There's a swinging party going down in my brain, six rock bands and three dance floors, and I'm the only one who hasn't been invited. Standing room only, kids, and stop pounding on the walls. It is time to lie down. It is time to go to sleep.

I dream of a time when I used to be on the Council, of a time when Raymond McBride was just the name of just another dead industrialist, of a time when Ernie hadn't yet been squashed by a runaway taxicab, of a time before I was hooked on the basil and before I was blacklisted from every PI job in town. I dream of a time of productivity, of meaning, of having a reason to get up and greet each morning. I dream of the Vincent Rubio of old.

And then the scene changes, the honeydew days and butterfly skies giving way to a crimson-coated battle working its way through the entire modern dinosaur population, of Stegosaurs and Brontos slugging it out, of Trike horns sliding into Iguanodon sides, of Compys huddling in dark alleys, whining, petrified, and of a woman—a human—standing in the middle of it all, her hair full and wild, her eyes alight with passion and excitement, her fists clenched in titillation of the glorious, blazing corona of violence and fury surrounding her frail body.

I dream that I approach the woman and ask her if she would like me to take her out of this civil war, to take her away from this scene, and that the woman laughs and kisses me on the nose, as if I am a favorite pet or a teddy bear.

I dream that the woman sharpens her fingernails with an emery board, rears back on her haunches, and joins the fray, launching herself into the pile of writhing dinosaur flesh.

2

Teitelbaum is waiting for me the next morning, just as I knew he would be; I can see his hulking silhouette through the glass bricks that make up his outer office wall. He never leaves that oak desk of his, even in the most dire of emergencies—no matter the crisis, the entire employee base is always compelled to convene in that tacky room, filled with the worst that airport gift shops around the world have to offer: a coconut with the Hawaiian islands painted on it. A hand towel bearing the machine-stitched inscription I GOT CLEANED OUT IN VEGAS. An ice cube tray with molds in the shape of the Australian continent. And since there are only two available guest chairs, most of the office staff is forced to sit on the floors, lean against the walls, or try to stand upright during his legendary epic-length speeches. It's all so perfectly demeaning, and I'm sure that's just the way Teitelbaum wants it.

I also wouldn't be surprised to find out that he's permanently wedged into his high-backed leather chair, the big . . . big . . . fatso. But that's neither here nor there, and it's patently unfair of me to criticize a Tyrannosaurus Rex on his weight problems. I'm sure that there's some muscle fiber buried underneath all that flab, and everyone knows that muscle weighs more than fat. Or is it that water weighs less than muscle? Oh, hell—any way you look at it, Teitelbaum's a big ol' chub, and I don't mind saying it twice. Chub!

I've got half a buzz going on, as I figured it wasn't morally right or mentally sound to show up either stone-cold sober or high off my gourd, and this low-grade high suits me quite nicely. The outside world flows by at three-quarter speed, just the proper rate for me to take in all relevant details, omitting and/or ignoring any feelings of hostility. The secretaries in the outer office look up in astonishment as I pass, and I can hear my name echoing in low whispers about the cubicles. I don't mind. It's all swell.

TruTel is the largest private investigation firm in Los Angeles—second largest in California—and, until I fucked up royally, a regular employer of my services. In the days when Ernie was around, we'd often be called in to help on any case that needed an extra helping of tight, confidential snoop work. We got a few jobs that skirted the boundaries of the law, gigs that the company couldn't put on the books, and it paid out real nice. Of course, if you deal with TruTel, you have to deal with Teitelbaum, and that's another matter entirely. He loves to throw out cases to PIs and watch us claw at one another like gamecocks for the right to earn a minuscule commission, but if you want to make your way in this business, sometimes you've even gotta bend over and smile for a T-Rex.

Time to brave the sanctum sanctorum.

"Morning, Mr. Teitelbaum," I say as I enter his office with a false bound in my step and lilt to my voice. "You're looking . . . good. Lost some weight." My legs are in control, my feet are in control, my body is in control.

"You look like crap," Teitelbaum grunts, and motions for me to sit down. I gladly take him up on the offer.

From some of the gossip I heard out in the lobby, the big cheese here at TruTel, whose human guise is a cross between Oliver Hardy and a sentient mound of sweat, has spent the better part of a week engrossed in a new toy that was delivered more than eight days ago, but that he is unable to operate as of yet: Sitting on a corner of Teitelbaum's desk is one of those devices with four metal balls attached to an overhead beam by four strands of fishing line. By pulling out an outside ball and letting it drop against the others, one can witness the miracle of Newtonian physics as the spheres click and clack back and forth for hours on end. Teitelbaum, though, who has most likely never heard of Newton, and perhaps never even heard of physics, is still hard at work trying to figure out the exact machinations of his new plaything. He grumbles at it. He breathes on it. He bats it around with a rough, clumsy swat, his puny arms barely able to reach across the desk.

"'Scuse me—" I say, interrupting this most scientific of procedures. "May I?" Without waiting for a response, I reach out, grasp one of the silver spheres, and drop it into action. The gadget lets loose with a steady clack-clack-clack, echoing about the stillness of the office.

Teitelbaum stares at the balls in awe, clack-clack-clack, his gargantuan jaw gaping wide open, clack-clack-clack. He had a sheep for breakfast; I can make out the fur on his molars. Eventually, the fool regains his composure, even though it's clear he's dying to ask me what miraculous magic I used to start the machine in motion.

"Brought it in from Beijing Airport," he says, evading the issue of his ignorance altogether. "Cathy had some

business up Hunan way." Big ol' lie. Cathy is one of Teitelbaum's secretaries, and the only business she ever has—
ever, ever, ever—is traveling the world fetching gift-shop
trinkets for Mr. Teitelbaum so that he can feel worldly and
accomplished without actually having to leave the safety,
comfort, and padding of his office chair. And since Teitelbaum puts all of the plane tickets under his name, the poor
girl doesn't even rack up any frequent-flyer miles. Cathy's
current annual salary (I know, because I snuck a peek at the
finance report some years back) is slightly over thirty thousand dollars, and since she's out of town more than five-
sixths of the year, Teitelbaum had to hire an additional
secretary—that's where Sally comes in—to do all of the
actual paperwork that floats in and out of his grimy hands.
As a result, Teitelbaum's secretarial bill comes to more
than sixty thousand dollars a year, all charged to the firm,
which means that his PI hacks have to work that many
more hours to pay for the extra overhead. And all so the
former homecoming king of Hamilton High can buy sou-
venirs that he's too stupid to operate. Lord, I hate Tyran-
nosaurs.

"It's very nice," I assure him. "Shiny." I am glad he's too
dumb to know when I am mocking him.

"Got one question for you, Rubio," Teitelbaum growls,
leaning back in his chair, his meaty flanks spreading out,
spilling over the sides. "You drunk?"

"That's blunt."

"It is. Are you drunk? Are you still hitting the basil?"

"No."

He grunts, sniffs, tries to look me in the eyes. I avert.
"Take out your contacts," he says. "Lemme see your real
eyes."

I pull back from the desk, begin to stand. "I don't have to
listen to this—"

"Siddown, Rubio, siddown. I don't give a good god-damn if you're drunk or not, but you don't got a choice other than to listen to me. I know people at credit departments. I know people at the bank. You got no money left." He seems to relish this little speech; I am not surprised.

"Is there a point?" I ask.

"Point is, I don't gotta have you in here at all!"

"Tell you the truth," I say, "I was a little surprised—"

"You talk too much. Maybe I've got some money for you. Maybe. Maybe I can throw a job your way, God knows why. If—and this is a big if, Rubio—if you're ready for it. If you're not gonna screw it up and screw me over like last time."

On Teitelbaum's desk, a shudder passes through the balls, a metallic buzz, as they slow and die. Teitelbaum fixes me with a hard stare, and I reach over and start them up again for him, apparently one of my new duties as a potential employee. I just hope that starting and restarting this contraption all day isn't the job he's got in mind. The sad thing is, I might take it.

"I'd be very grateful for the opportunity," I tell Teitelbaum, trying to keep the pushpins out of the syrupy drawl of my obsequiousness.

"Sure you would. Eighty hacks around this city'd be grateful for the opportunity. But I didn't hate that Ernie of yours"—and for Teitelbaum, this is tantamount to a declaration of true love—"so I'm gonna cut you this break. Plus, I got no choice. God help me, I got nineteen idiots who call themselves private investigators in this office, and every one of 'em is tied up in some bullshit case or another, dragging out the clock so they can make a few extra bucks. In comes a case with a time limit, and look where I gotta turn—a drunken has-been with a dead-partner complex."

"Thank you?"

"Look, I need assurances here. The last time you went out on a case, you went over the line—"

"It won't be like last time," I interrupt.

"I gotta have assurances. Assurances that what I say goes. No backing out on orders, no screwing around with the cops. I tell you to drop it, you drop it. Are we on the same page here?"

"It won't be like last time," I repeat.

"I'm sure it won't." Now his tone softens imperceptibly from granite to limestone. "I understand how it was for you. Ernie, killed on the job like that. Work with a guy for ten years—"

"Twelve."

"Twelve years, it gets you. I got that. But it was an accident, nothing more, nothing less. The guy got hit by a taxi-cab, they're all over New York—"

"But Ernie was careful—"

"Don't start that shit again. He was careful, yeah, but not that time. And running around bothering the cops, flapping your lips about crazy conspiracies, doesn't get you any love." He pauses, waits to see if I will speak. I choose not to. "It's over, done with. Kaput." Teitelbaum purses his lips, face screwing up like he's mainlined a lemon. "So what I need to know is, are *you* over it? All of it—Ernie, McBride . . . ?"

"Over it? I mean, I—I'm not—I'm not—they're dead, right? So . . ." No, I want to scream, I'm not over it! How the hell can I be expected to forget about my partner, to let the death of my only friend go down unsolved? I want to tell him that I snooped before and given the chance, I'd snoop again. I want to tell him to damn the Council rectifi-cation and damn whatever blacklist I've been put on, that I'll keep searching for Ernie's killer until my last breath wheezes past my lips.

But that was the Vincent Rubio of the last nine months, and anger and resentment haven't gotten that Vincent anything other than sixteen pounds of collection notices, imminent foreclosure, and a costly basil habit. I've got no money, I've got no time, and I've got nobody left to turn to. So I brighten up my best grin and say, "Sure. Sure, I'm over it."

The Tyrannosaur silences the clack-clack-clack of the metal balls with one withered finger and stares me down. "Good. Fine." Silence hisses through the room. "On a related note, you hear about any Council fines?"

"I'm not on the Council anymore, sir." And when I was, Teitelbaum was always pressing me for information. He took it as a major slight that an employee of his held a seat on the Southern California Council, that I had the ability to form policy that would affect his daily life. It was one of those little tidbits that kept me going. "They . . . they voted me out after the New York incidents."

He nods. "I know you're off, they had me testify at the meetings. But you still got friends—"

"Not really," I say. "Not anymore."

"Goddamn it, Rubio, you must have heard something about the fines."

I shrug, shake my head. "The fines . . ."

"On McBride—"

"He's dead."

"On his estate. 'Cause of the human thing."

"The human thing," I echo. I know exactly what he's talking about, but refuse to let on.

"Come on, Rubio," he says, "you were on the Council, you knew what was going on. McBride, having an affair with that . . . that . . ."—his shoulders, if you could call them that, shivering in disgust—"that *human*."

He's right as rain, but I can't let him know that. Raymond McBride, a Carnotaurus who had burst onto the dino scene out of midwestern obscurity and then risen to great financial standing in a few short years, had indeed engaged in multiple affairs with a series of human women. This is not conjecture; it is fact. We know this from an array of sworn statements given to Council members at official auxiliary hearings, along with ample physical evidence in the form of clandestine photographs clicked off by J&T Enterprises, the largest PI firm in New York and, coincidentally, TruTel's East Coast sister company.

A consummate playboy, McBride had always been known for wooing the females of our species with incredible success despite his intact and lengthy marriage, and the resultant branches of his family tree have been rumored to spread from coast to coast, possibly into Europe. He owned an apartment on Park Avenue, a house on Long Island, and a "cottage" out here in the Pacific Palisades, not to mention the twin casinos in Vegas and Atlantic City. His features, sharp and classically Carnotaur in nature, were masked daily by a team of professional obscurers who knew how to easily make even the most reptilian of dinosaurs appear perfectly human, a task that takes the rest of us countless hours of pain and frustration. Raymond McBride's life was blessed.

No one knows, then, why he chose to delve into another population pool—perhaps he had grown tired of our kind, weary of the egg-laying and endless waiting for a crack in the shell. It is true that he was childless. Perhaps he wanted to sharpen his carnal skills on a different breed of creature. It is true that he was ambitious. Perhaps, as many are inclined to believe, he had developed Dressler's Syndrome, that he thought of himself as truly human and simply couldn't help but be tempted by the pleasures of mammalian flesh. Or maybe he just thought the chicks were cute. Whatever the case, Raymond McBride had broken cardinal rule number one, established since *Homo habilis* first dragged themselves onto the scene: It is absolutely forbidden to mate with a human.

But now he's dead, murdered in his office almost a full year ago, so what the hell's the use in fining the poor guy?

A knock at the door saves me any more questions about McBride or Council meetings of which I no longer have any knowledge. Teitelbaum coughs out a "What?" and Sally pokes her head into the office. She's a mousy little thing, really. Pointed nose, stringy hair, wan complexion. If I didn't know she was a human—no scent, never seen her at any of the dino haunts throughout the city—I'd peg her as a Compy in two seconds flat.

"London on line three," she squeaks. Sally's a great gal, a real hoot to talk to, but in Teitelbaum's presence she shrinks up like a dry sponge.

"Gatwick Gift Shoppe?" asks Teitelbaum, his hands jittering in childlike anticipation. If he weren't so disgusting, I might find it endearing.

"They found the Tower of London toothpicks you wanted." Sally shoots me a quick smile, turns, hops, and flits out of the room, mission accomplished. A surgical strike into the boss's domain: in—out—six seconds! Good for her. I should be so lucky.

Teitelbaum breathes heavily, a ragged paper-shredding growl that trails off into the wheeze of a deflating balloon, and grabs clumsily at his desk phone. "I want two gross," he says, "and send 'em overnight." End of conversation. I'm sure the Brit on the other end is astounded with American courtesy.

An abrupt change in tone now as Teitelbaum moves into business mode. Extending a teensy costumed arm across the expanse of his desk, grunting with the meager exertion, Teitelbaum grabs at a thin file folder. "Now I ain't saying you're gonna be looking for the Hope Diamond or nothing," he says, and flips the folder into my arms. "Just a little legwork, nothing you can't handle. It ain't much, but it pays."

I scan the pages. "Fire investigation?"

"Nightclub in the Valley, lit up Wednesday morning. One of Burke's places."

"Burke?" I ask.

"Donovan Burke. The club owner. Hell, don't you read the magazines, Rubio?"

I shake my head, unwilling to explain that nowadays the price of a single magazine would surely affix me below poverty level once and for all.

"Burke's a big skiddoo on the nightclub scene," Teitelbaum explains. "Had celebrities in and outta that place every day, mostly dinos, a couple of human clientele. Had the place insured up the wazoo, and now they're gonna have to pay off about two million in fire damages. Insurance company wants us to check it out, make sure Burke didn't blow the place 'cause business was lousy."

"Was it?"

"Was it what?"

"Lousy."

"Christ, Rubio," says Teitelbaum, "how the hell should I know? You're the PI here."

"Anybody in the club at the time?"

"Why don't you read the goddamn folder?" he huffs. "Yeah, yeah, lotta people there. Witnesses galore, party in full swing." He takes another swat at his Newtonian balls, a clear signal that my presence is no longer required. I stand.

"Time table?" I ask, and I know the answer—

"A day shorter than usual." Stock reply. He thinks he's being cute.

I try to make the next question sound casual, though it surely is not. "Pay?"

"Insurance company's willing to fork over five grand and expenses. Company takes three grand, leaves two thousand bucks for you."

I shrug. Seems standard to me, at least when it comes to the poverty-level wages most TruTel employees are forced to live on. "But I've got this problem with the pool in my backyard," Teitelbaum continues, "and I need a little spare cash myself. Let's say we split your commission, fifty-fifty." He attempts to grin, a wide shark-toothed smile that ignites in me the most basic urge to leap across the desk and garrote him with the razor-thin wires of his Newtonian balls.

But what choice do I have? One grand's better than nothing, and now with the Ohmsmeyer job busted like skeet, this might be my only chance to fight off foreclosure and eventual bankruptcy. A semblance of pride is in order. Elongating my neck as far as this guise will let it go, I hold my head aloft, clutch the manila folder to my breast, and strut out of the office.

"Don't screw it up, Rubio," he calls after me. "You wanna work again, you won't do your usual half-assed job."

A hard sprig of basil is between my teeth not twelve steps later, and already I'm putting that tyrant of a T-Rex behind me and feeling better about the assignment. Money in the bank, maybe a little respectability, and it won't be long before the other PI firms are itching to contract some glamorous and expensive work out to Watson and Rubio

Investigations. Yeah, I'm coming back. I'm on my way up. The Raptor is on a roll.

On my way out the front door, I shoot a congratulatory wink toward a temp receptionist taking down dictation in the vestibule. She recoils from my friendly gesture like a startled rattler and I halfway expect her to bare fangs and slither into a niche beneath her desk.

Six leaves of basil are busily working their special brand of magic through the hills and valleys of my metabolism, and that herbal chill is the only thing that's keeping me from running off this crowded city bus with my hands waving wildly above my head like a chimpanzee. This is the first time I've ever been forced into any form of mass public transportation, and if the meager car-rental allowance Teitelbaum granted to this case will snag me anything nicer than a '74 Pinto, it will be the last. I don't know what died on this bus, but from the tidal wave of scents streaming toward me from the back three rows, I imagine that it was large, that it was ugly, and that it had eaten a good deal of curry in its waning moments of life.

The woman next to me has a strip of tin foil wrapped around her head like a sweatband, and though I don't ask her what the foil is for—it's a policy of mine never to question anyone who clearly has a constitutional right to insanity—she nevertheless feels the need to shout at me that her protective headgear keeps the "terrestrial insects" away from her "moist bits." I nod vigorously and turn toward the window, hoping to squeeze my frame through any opening leading to the rational, outside world. But the window is closed. Locked up tight. A wad of pink chewing gum has hardened over the clasp, and I can almost make out the bacteria dancing on the surface, daring me to try my luck and pluck the rigid mess from its place.

But the basil is coming on stronger now, mellowing the scene, and I lean back against the hard vinyl bus bench, hoping to drown out the cacophony of coughs, of sneezes, of endless rants against society and those damn terrestrial insects. My arms drop away from their protective cross across my chest and fall easily to my sides; I can feel a slight grin tugging at the corners of my lips. Smooth.

I don't know how he did it, but Ernie was a regular supporter of public transportation. That's right—every week, usually on Thursday, at least once in the morning and once at night, my Carnotaur partner parked himself on a street bench and waited for the number 409 to show up and ferry him to and from our office on the west side.

"Keeps you in touch with the people," Ernie used to say to me. "In touch with the good folk." And whereas there is not one good folk on this bus I'd be interested in touching, I believe that he believed. I always believed that he believed.

Ernie.

The last time I saw Ernest J. Watson, PI, was the morning of January the eighth, nearly ten months ago. He was walking out the door, and I was doing my best to ignore his exit. We'd just finished up a particularly petty argument—typical nonsense, the kind of tiffs we'd get into three, four times a week, like an old couple spatting over the husband's tendency to chew his ice, or how the wife babbles endlessly about nothing—that sort of married, been-around-the-block kind of crap.

"I'll call you when I get back from New York," he said to me just before he stepped past the threshold to our office, and I grunted in response. That was it—a grunt. The last thing Ernie ever heard from me was an "eh," and it's only my daily herbal intake that keeps that nagging thought safely on the edges of my brain.

It was a case, of course, that demanded his attention, and here I should say it was a case like any other, but it wasn't. It was big. T-Rex big. Correction: It was Carnotaur big.

Raymond McBride—Carnotaur, connoisseur of human female companionship, and grand exalted mogul of the McBride Corporation, a financial conglomerate specializing in stocks, bonds, mergers, acquisitions, and pretty much any venture that brought in cash by the boatload— had been murdered in his Wall Street office on Christmas Eve, and the dino community was in more of an uproar than usual.

Due to some slipshod investigation by the crack team of forensic docs sent to the scene, it was still undetermined as to whether McBride had been killed by a human or by a fellow dino, so the National Council—a representative conglomeration of the 118 regional councils—took it upon themselves to send in a team of investigators from across the country to do some preliminary work on the case. Dino-on-dino murder will always bring up a Council investigation, no matter the circumstances, and it was imperative that the Council learn, as quickly as possible, which species had committed the crime and, more important, against whom they could levy some massive fines. The Council is always on the lookout to make a quick buck.

"They're offering ten grand to every private dick that takes the case," Ernie told me one Friday morning just after New Year's Day. "Council wants this one wrapped up fast, bigwig like McBride. Wanna know if it's a human who offed him."

I shrugged and waved the suggestion away. "Dino killed him," I said. "No mammal's got the guts to take out a guy rich as that."

Ernie grinned at me then—that stiff-lipped grimace that widened his face by a good three inches—and said, "No such thing as killing a rich man, Vincent. Everybody's poor when they're under the claw."

So Ernie left, I grunted, and three days later he was dead. A traffic accident, they told me. A runaway taxicab, they told me. A hit-and-run and that was the end of that, they told me. I didn't believe a word of it.

I flew to New York the next morning with a brown suitcase full of clothes and another full of basil. I remember very little of the trip. Here are the images that have seen fit to fight their way through a memory shot through with gaping holes of basil blackouts:

A county coroner, the one who worked on both McBride and Ernie, suddenly missing in action. On vacation somewhere in the South Pacific. An assistant, a human, who was neither helpful nor cooperative. A fistfight. Blood, perhaps. Security guards.

A bar. Cilantro. A female, maybe a Diplodocus. A motel room, dank and foul.

A police officer, one of the many detectives who investigated the supposed hit-and-run that took Ernie's life, refusing to answer my questions. Refusing to allow me into his house at three o'clock in the morning. His children, crying. A fistfight. Blood, perhaps. The back of a patrol car.

Another bar. Oregano. Another female, definitely Iguanodon. A motel room, still dank, still foul.

A bank debit card linked to one of the many accounts

held by the Southern California Council, in my possession
because I was at that time the Velociraptor representative
and a member in good standing of the most bureaucratic
and hypocritical board of dinosaurs the world has seen
since Oliver Cromwell and his cronies—Brontosaurs, to
the last—ran rampant through the coffers of the British
Empire. A covert withdrawal in the amount of a thousand
dollars. Another in the amount of ten thousand. Bribes, in
the hope that someone—anyone—would give me a clue
about McBride, about Ernie, about their lives and their
deaths. More bribes to cover up the first bribes. Useless answers that brought me nothing. Anger. A fistfight. Blood,
perhaps. A swarm of police officers.

A judge and a hearing and a dismissal. A plane ticket
back to Los Angeles and an armed escort to ensure my de-
parture from the Tri-State area.

Somehow, the Council learned of my creative account-
ing regarding their bank account and the sizable with-
drawals—it wasn't like I was in any state of mind to
properly cover it up—and took a vote to boot me off the
board. To *rectify* the situation, as the official term goes, and
with a single unanimous "Aye" from the Southern California Council members, I had my social standing stripped
away from me in the same week as my sobriety, my spot-
less criminal record, and my best friend. That was the end
of my investigation, and the end of my life as a well-
heeled, middle-class private investigator working the
streets of suburban LA.

If there's one thing I learned from that first week or so
last January, it's simply this: It's a long, slow, grueling
climb to the middle, but the ride down comes at nothing
short of terminal velocity.

The bus rambles on.

* * *

Three hours later, the car I rented from a cut-rate agency sputters to a halt in front of the Evolution Club in Studio City, and I say a silent prayer to the automotive gods that the last two miles have all been downhill. This rusted-out warhorse of a 1983 Toyota Camry conked out on me as I was driving up Laurel Canyon, and it took an hour and a half to find someone who would open the door to a total stranger claiming to need a pair of pliers, a length of yarn, and a wire cutter. Turns out I wasn't the only one who'd ever decided to make some on-the-fly additions to this pitiful automobile—one peek into the Camry's engine is like a look into an alternate reality where children and mental patients are the only ones permitted to become mechanics. Fraying gift ribbon holds together bundles of wires, one of the cylinders still bears the markings of a Campbell's-soup wrapper, and I'm pretty darn sure that paper clips do not make for good spark-plug holders. I simply can't imagine that any of these improvised improvements will hold up for much longer. With luck, I can squeeze a little more money out of Teitelbaum and rent a better car soon, as I can foresee the day in the near future when this little Japanese import will snap beneath the pressure of jerry-built engine parts and stopgap gas hoses and commit hari-kari, happily shuffling off its 'motive coil in favor of a less makeshift existence.

And I refuse to take the bus again.

The Evolution Club—gotta be a dino joint, no two ways about it. We love shit like that, little in-jokes that make us feel oh-so-superior to the two-legged mammals with whom we grudgingly share dominance over the earth. My usual haunt is the Fossil Fuels Club in Santa Monica, but

I've logged in some classically blurry early morning hours at the Dinorama, the Meteor Nightspot, and mid city's very own Tar Pit Club, just to name a few. The last Council estimate laid the dinosaur community out at about 5 percent of the American population, but I have a hunch we own a disproportionate amount of nightclubs in this country. But hey—when you spend the majority of your waking hours walking around in human drag, you're going to need a dino-intensive place to unwind at the end of the day, if only to snap you back into that terrible lizard state of mind.

The rental car complements the new look of the Evolution Club, its crumbling chassis blending nicely with the charred structural supports of the fireswept building. "Maybe I should leave you here, old fella," I say, playfully slapping the car on its trunk. My hand pops through the rust, punching out a rough hole in the metal. I head inside.

The Evolution Club, so far as I can tell from my vantage point on what used to be the main dance floor but is now a twisted mess of splintered laminate, must have been a pretty groovy place once upon a Wednesday morning. Three levels, each with its own separate bar, flow organically out of a pair of sweeping Tara-esque staircases, great marble risers disappearing among the shadows. Glitter balls sparkle like distant, dying stars against the meager daylight that manages to sneak its way in through the cracked walls, and I can make out a fancy illumination system that, if the bulbs were replaced, the lenses mended, and the computer control board cleaned of the omnipresent ash, might rival the best Broadway or Picadilly has to offer. Sprawling graffiti art covers the walls, a fantastic mural celebrating the glamour and the glory of unadulterated hedonism throughout the ages.

A hulking refrigeration system lies in ruin, attached to

the remnants of what looks to be a walk-in herbidor—I can almost smell the fresh-cut basil and marjoram now, and can only imagine the convenience of walking into that cold, sweet room and taking my pick of any and all substances. Looks like the kind of joint I would have been magnetically attracted to in my younger days, and all my organs are grateful at this moment that I never knew of the club's existence.

As I climb the staircase to the second level, a pinch lances out from my tucked-away tail. I shake my rump, but the pain persists, small and sharp, as if a minnow with shark's teeth has found himself at an all-you-can-eat brunch on my tail and refuses to leave the buffet line. It's my darned G-3 clamp—somehow it has shifted to the left, the metal buckle digging into my hide, and there's no way to rectify the situation other than to completely readjust the entire G series. It's a quick process, simple enough, but would necessitate releasing my tail out into the great wide open for a few precious minutes. If any humans were to come in . . .

But who wanders into burned-out nightclubs at noon on a weekday? Just to be safe, I shuffle up the stairs in a hunchback gallop—the clamp pinching and poking and prodding me all the way—and hop into the relative security of a nearby shadow.

A twist here, a turn there, and pop! the G-1 and G-2 clamps spring open, buckles spinning into the air. My tail swings free of its confines and I breathe a sigh of relief as the G-3 releases its hold and clangs to the floor. There's a dull throb coming from my nether region, and I can make out the early stages of a bruise where the clamp had nipped my flesh. Now to buckle up again before—

"Somebody in there?" A voice at the nightclub door.

I freeze up. Sweat springs from my pores, instantly cascading my body with rivulets of saltwater. I curse the evolutionary process that brought sweat glands to my species after so many millennia of blissful aridity.

"Private property, buddy. Police scene."

I can't believe this is happening. My hands, thick and clumsy inside their pseudohuman gloves, fumble with the buckles, forcing them rudely into place.

"Hey you! Yeah, you!" comes the call again, filtered past the roar of alarm rushing like tidewater through my brain.

With skill and dexterity somewhere between that of a world-class Olympic athlete and a moderately fit executive-league softball pitcher, I leap into the air and, in one swift move, tuck my tail between my legs, wrapping it up and around my torso. Clamp G-3 slides into place, followed closely behind by G-2. Working furiously now, dressing myself faster than ever before. Buckles buckling—snaps snapping—buttons, knots, zippers, Velcro—the race is on . . .

"You can't be in here." Halfway up the stairs. "No public. You're gonna have to pack it up, pal."

My G-1 clamp is sticking, refusing to budge. It's an older model, sure, but these things are supposed to last, damn it! The last vestiges of my tail are poking out through my open zipper, and even if the person coming up the stairs doesn't recognize it as the tip of a folded dinosaur tail, it looks darned obscene nevertheless. I've done the public indecency rap before, two days in a Cincinnati lockup—don't ask, don't ask—and have no urge to repeat the incident, thank you very much. I shove and push and mush and tuck and—

"Hey, you—yeah, you, in the corner."

Slowly, reluctantly, I turn, ready to lie, ready to chortle

and say *pardon my weasel* or *must be my shirt. A tail? Dear god, no! It is for to laugh! A tail on someone as undeniably human as I? How absurd!*

And then the clamps give way. With the sound of a hundred claws tearing across a hundred chalk-caked blackboards, my tail rips free from its confines, cleanly splitting my new Dockers pants in half. Shreds of the comfortable cotton/polyester blend waft through the air.

Slowly, almost luxuriously, the last remaining years of my life flash before my eyes. They begin with this intruder screaming like a spook-house dummy, running down the stairs, out of the building, making an emergency appointment with his psychiatrist, and spilling his guts about the half-man, half-beast that *practically attacked him, by God,* inside the smoking remains of a Studio City nightclub. He's institutionalized (just desserts, I say), but that's no matter. Word gets out about my indiscretion, and I end up lonely and penniless, selling pocket lint on the street corner, formally excommunicated by the Council and ostracized by the dino community for letting out the most classified Secret of all the classified Secrets: our existence.

"Jesus, Rubio," comes the voice again. "With a tail like that, you must get all the chicks."

My eyes focus away from their exaggerated, morbid fantasies and return to the second floor of the Evolution Club, where they alight upon a grinning Sergeant Dan Patterson, longtime detective for the Los Angeles Police Department and one of the greatest all-around Brontosaurs I've ever known.

We embrace, my heart swinging down off its crazy reggae backbeat, rat-a-tat-tatting away inside my chest cavity. "I scare you?" Dan asks, a sly grin curving the corners of his wide lips. His scent, a mélange of extra virgin olive oil and crankshaft grease, is weak today, which probably explains why I didn't smell him as he approached.

"Scare me? Hell, man, I'm a Raptor."

"So I'll ask again: I scare you?"

We tag-team on my recalcitrant tail, alternately taking turns shoving the bad boy this way and that. Dan's taut muscles, evident beneath his guise as a middle-aged African-American, ripple with power as we eventually manage to tuck the critter back into its hiding spot, tightening up the G clamps and strapping on the buckles without causing further injury. I've got a spare pair of pants in the Camry, and so long as the ones I'm wearing don't choose to spontaneously dissolve any more than they already have, I should remain decently outfitted for a few more minutes. I have never known Dan Patterson to be a fashion hawk, and he doesn't seem all that concerned about my current state of half-dress.

"Good to see you, my man," Dan says. "It's been too long."

"I meant to call you . . ." I begin, and then trail off into a wan smile.

Dan puts a meaty gloved hand on my shoulder, squeezing tight. "I understand, man, trust me. How you holding up? You finding work?"

"I'm great," I lie. "I'm doing great." If I tell Dan about my financial situation, he'll offer me money—practically force it upon me, if I know the guy—but I don't go in for handouts, even from the closest of Brontosaurs.

"Listen, you get that watch I sent you, the one—"

"Yeah, yeah I got that. Thanks." A while back, Dan came across a watch that Ernie had accidentally left at his place a month or so before he was killed. After my ignoble return from New York, Dan had the watch messengered over to my house, which I took as Dan's way of saying he was there for me without actually having to say it. It was the greatest consolation I received during the entire affair.

"You investigating for the insurance company?" he asks.

I nod. "Teitelbaum sent me."

"No kidding—you're working for TruTel again?"

"This job, at least. Who knows, maybe there's more in it down the road."

"The good old days, huh? Mr. Teitelbaum. . . . Man, there's a T-Rex I've been trying hard to forget." Dan spent a miserable year and a half working as an outside contractor with TruTel—that's how we met—before he quit the freelance life and joined up with the LAPD, and his run-ins with Teitelbaum were the stuff of legend around the office.

We talk a little more of old times—the Strum case, the Kuhns trial, the Hollywood Boulevard hooker fiasco—don't ask, don't ask—and a little of plans for the future. He's interested in catching some time at Expression, that dino nudist colony up in Montana—hundreds of us, roaming free, unencumbered, baring our natural hides to the warmth of the sun—and though that sort of ego massage sounds like a great way to spend some lazy days, I don't want to tell him that I can't afford any lazy days, much less the cost of a good suntan lotion. "Sounds great," I say. "Make some plans, give me a call."

Eventually, after the conversation of two old friends runs its course, I come back to the matter at hand. "What are you doing up here?" I ask. "Isn't this a little out of your jurisdiction?" Dan usually works out of Rampart division; the San Fernando Valley's far outside his stomping grounds.

"They called in our arson unit," Dan explains. "We give crossover help like this, do it all the time. I'm just here to finish securing the scene; seems I didn't do a good-enough job."

"So," I ask, "whaddaya got for me on the fire?"

"Tired of doing the actual investigating, Mr. Private Investigator?"

"Figure if I can get you to do it for me, I can go home and sleep. Been a long week."

Dan pulls out a faded yellow notepad, mumbling to himself as he flips through the pages. "Lessee. . . . Wednesday morning, 'round 'bout three in the A.M., Fire House Eighteen gets word that the Evolution Club on Ventura is goin' up, and fast. Anonymous caller says there's a big ol' blaze."

"Where'd the call come in from?" I ask.

"Outside source, pay phone. Across the street. Three engines dispatched, along with a fleet of special-service vehicles—ambulances, paramedics, that sorta thing."

"That standard protocol? The whole fleet, I mean?" I whip out my own pen and paper, scribbling down whatever tidbits—obviously important or otherwise—I come across. Never know what you're gonna find.

"Nightclub fire, yeah. Usually it ain't the smoke or the flames that does the damage—it's the patrons scrambling to get out. Gets so everyone turns into a herd of spooked Compys, don't care who they trample on." He licks his fingers, skims the pad again. "The engines arrive, start work on the fire. Patrons are streaming out, they're evacuating left and right . . ."

"Fifty, a hundred, what?" In other words, how many damn witnesses am I going to have to interview?

Dan laughs and shakes his head. "You ain't been to a Valley party in a long time, have you?"

"I try to stay on the west side," I say. "Health's bad enough without me killing my lungs down here in the smog bowl."

"Place like this could pack in four hundred on a good

night. Lucky for you—and them, I guess—Wednesday morning's not exactly a club-hopping kinda time. All told, estimates range around one eighty, two hundred."

"Names and numbers?"

"About twenty of 'em."

"Good enough for me."

"Two dead, though—smoke inhalation, we think," says Dan. "One more in critical got caught in the fire—guy who owns the joint, actually."

"Dino, right?"

Dan fixes me with a raised eyebrow. "With a name like the Evolution Club? Come on . . ."

"Kinda shoots down the insurance company's self-inflicted arson theory," I point out. "I mean, if I was gonna torch my own place, I'd sure as hell step out for a bite to eat a good hour before those flames hit."

"You'd think so, right? But my men said it took four of 'em to pry the guy outta the back room. He's half dead, burned like a turkey, and still he's grabbing onto the door frame, putting up a fight. . . . Said they never seen anything like it."

"Like he was protecting something?" I ask.

"Who knows? We didn't find a thing, 'cept a real nice desk chair."

"Lemme guess—he's a Compy, right?"

"Nope—one of your kind. We know them Raptors ain't too bright."

"Least my brain ain't the size of a Ping-Pong ball."

Dan flips me his pad, the papers crackling through the air. "Check it out," he says, pointing to his handwritten notes. "Got these word for word from the attending officer. Witnesses all confirm a loud noise, then smoke. The place starts to clear, the trampling starts, and then a rush of fire from the back just as the firemen arrive."

"Rush of fire, eh? A bomb?"

Dan shakes his head. "We've had inspectors combing the place for the last day, and they can't find explosive traces. But you're on the right track. . . . Here, walk with me." Dan heads down the stairs, and I dutifully follow. The dull ache in my tail is slowly subsiding, and for this I am grateful.

We wend our way past scorched tables and blackened bar stools, every surface covered in a light gray ash. The individual chair backs, I notice, have been carved into the shape of humans at different points along their twisted evolutionary path, each of them wildly caricatured and none of them particularly flattering. *Australopithecus afarensis'* expression of outright stupidity is counterbalanced perfectly by the smug, I'm-running-the-food-chain-now look on the face of *Homo erectus; H. habilis* squats contentedly in a pile of his own feces while the supposedly evolved *H. sapiens* is depicted as a large blubbery mass permanently attached to a big-screen TV. Someone had a bellyful of fun designing this place.

"Look at the spread," says Dan. "Right along the wall here."

I narrow my eyes, squinting in the relative darkness of the club. We're standing far back from the front entrance now, the only available illumination filtering in through a jagged lightning bolt–shaped skylight in the ceiling. But I can see the streaks, vicious skid marks toasted into the walls, and I've been on enough arson jobs to know what it means.

"Blast pattern," I say, and Dan agrees. The long, dark sear tracks emanating like sunbursts from an open doorway lead back to what should be the flash point of the fire. "That the office?" I ask.

"Storage room. Fuse box, too." Dan runs his rough

hands along the wall, the cracked, blistered paint peeling to the ground. "Lotsa boxes in there, most of 'em didn't make it through the fire. I got the boys downtown poking through the stuff as we speak."

A weak scent, a familiar scent, wafts through the air— hits me like rancid roast beef, but I've been on enough of these jobs to know better. "Gasoline," I mumble. "You smell that?"

"Yeah, 'course I do. Our chemical guys found some traces, but that's not surprising. They got a generator one room over in case they lose power, and this place here's where they stored the fuel."

Jotting everything down as quickly as possible, I glance back over my notes. Tight letters, strong loops, tall and thin. "You guys got a scenario mocked up already, don't you?" I ask.

"You betcha. LAPD never sleeps."

"Explains all the sugar intake. Okay, lemme guess at this one." I clear my throat and shoot my cuffs, ready to dazzle, or at least mildly impress. "Fire sparks in storage room, smoldering. Probably electrical, fuse box blowing—that's the first noise the witnesses heard. Catches some boxes on fire, holding maybe skin mags, maybe some of that porn from Taiwan."

"Porn from—you got something you wanna tell me, Rubio?"

"Don't stop me now, I'm rolling. So there go the skin magazines, crackle crackle crackle, and half an hour later, clouds are pouring outta the closed office. We got dinos and humans boogying away, and then someone sees the smoke. Rush, rush, rush, trample, trample, trample, everyone clears out, someone calls the fire department. Still just smoke, but a lot of it now. Firemen arrive, lights flashing, siren blasting, big scene, and just as everyone gets outta the joint, ka-BOOM—fire reaches the spare fuel tanks and the place goes up in flames. Freak accident, end of story, everyone goes home and diddles their spouses, 'cept for the two dead guys and the owner up in the hospital."

Dan applauds, and I bow deeply, feeling my girdle stretch under the pressure. "That's pretty much how we have it," Dan admits. "We checked out Donovan Burke's financial records, by the way—"

"The owner, right?"

"Yeah, some playboy hotshot who flew out west a couple years back, set up shop real quick—he's up in intensive at County. We ran a search on him downtown, 'cause we knew you guys'd be snooping around to make sure it wasn't an inside job, but it came up clean. This place was the hottest spot in the Valley—poor sonofabitch was raking it in night after night. Had to hire an extra girl just to count it all."

I know there's a great mystique, an almost sexual allure, to the lone private eye working his case, sludging through the slime-infested streets, digging past the dirtiest of details to finally find his man—hell, I've gotten dates on that premise alone. And in some respects, I actively enjoy that sort of work. Keeps me sharp, on my claws. But when a job's as seemingly cut-and-dried as this one, I like nothing better than to have all the information handed to me by a good friend in local law enforcement. I mean, they have to do it anyway, so why not share the wealth?

Unfortunately, sometimes they miss things.

"You gonna pack it up?" Dan asks as we walk out of the nightclub, heading to my car and a spare pair of Dockers. "Go back to Teitelbaum, give him the info, and tell him where to stick it?"

"I need to keep this job," I remind him. "And my life. Insulting a T-Rex ain't the way to go about it. Anyway, I'm gonna check out a few more leads."

"Look, I'll give you all the witness reports I got. What's left to check out?"

I need a hat to tip, a trench coat to tug, a cigarette to dangle from my lips. Private investigation without props doesn't make the grade. "You said that the anonymous caller to the fire station reported a big blaze at the Evolution Club, right? Those the exact words—big blaze?"

"So far's I know, yeah."

I tap Dan's shirt pocket, my gloved finger rapping against his notebook. "But none of your witnesses actually saw the flames until *after* the fire engines arrived." I pause a moment . . . waiting . . . waiting . . . and then Dan figures it out.

"We got a time conflict here, don't we?" he says.

"Yep we do," I reply, affecting the widest smile in my repertoire, the one that carves a shining half-moon out of my lips. "And you got a bunch more paperwork to fill out."

Dan shakes his head morosely—forms and filing are not the Brontosaur's forte. But he's a trooper, and I know in my heart of hearts that come morning, he'll be hunched over his typewriter, concentrating on detail like a monk illuminating a precious manuscript. "You wanna come back to the house tonight?" he asks. "I'm gonna grill up a few steaks, maybe go wild and do a little oregano seasoning."

A shake of my head, a shuffle back toward the front of the club. Dinner sounds great—steak sounds better—steak and oregano would just about put me through the roof—but I've got work to do. That, and I need a few more hits of basil, pronto. "Sounds great, but I'll have to take you up another time."

"Hot date, eh?" Dan wriggles his eyebrows lasciviously.

I think of the burned Velociraptor up in the hospital, of his perplexing struggle to remain inside a room blistering with heat, with smoke, with a hundred ways to die. Nobody's *that* attached to a desk chair—even Teitelbaum would manage to wriggle his way up and out of the office with five thousand degrees pressing against his back. It stands to reason, then, that Donovan Burke had a reason to stay in that room—a damned good one—and there's only one dino who can tell me what that reason was.

"The hottest," I tell Dan, and make my way out of the nightclub.

4

Hospitals are a tough gig for anyone, I'll give you that. The last place the sick and dying need to be is around the sick and dying. But for a dino, it's worse. Much worse.

Even after all these millions of years—all these tens of millions of years—of the laboriously slow evolutionary process, we dinos still receive our best information through our schnozzes. Twenty-twenty vision and pin-drop hearing notwithstanding, our main sense is scent, and when we're deprived of the olfactory, it can be quite the debilitating experience. You're not going to find anything on this earth more pathetic than a dino with a head cold. We whine, we sniffle, we complain at the top of our stuffed-up lungs that nothing seems right, that the world has suddenly lost all color, all meaning. The most courageous of us revert into sniveling infancy, toddlers just out of the shell, and those who are pretty sniveling to begin with become downright unapproachable.

A hospital has no smells. None of use, at least, and therein lies the problem. The gallons and gallons of disinfectant slopped along the floors and onto the walls every day make sure that not a solitary odor molecule makes it out of Dodge alive. Sure, it's all in the name of good health, and I can understand where the elimination of bacteria and similar microscopic evildoers might come in handy in fighting off infection and whatnot, but it's a bitch and a half for any dino trying to keep his sanity.

I'm losing it already, and I've barely gotten through the front door.

"I'm here to see Donovan Burke," I tell the thin-lipped nurse, who is busy brooding over a cup of coffee and this morning's—Tuesday's—crossword puzzle.

"You gotta speak up," she says, a stick of gum smacking rhythmically between her short, blunt teeth. Instinctively, I lean in closer to her pistoning jaws, my nostrils flaring, my brain craving a whiff of Bubblicious, Juicy Fruit, Trident—anything to combat this pervading sense of nothingness.

"Donovan Burke," I repeat, pulling back before she notices me sniffing away at her mouth. "That's Donovan with a D."

The nurse—Jean Fitzsimmons, unless she swapped name tags with someone else this morning—sighs as if I have asked her to perform some task beneath her station such as steel-toe boot licking. She allows the newspaper to flutter out of her hands, and her narrow, birdlike fingers set to tapping away on a nearby keyboard. A computer screen fills with patients' names, their respective ailments, and prices that simply can't be correct. One hundred and sixty-eight dollars for a single shot of antibiotics? For that kind of cash, there had better be some serious street pharmaceuticals in that syringe. Nurse Fitzsimmons notices my gawk and pointedly turns the monitor away from my Peeping Vincent peepers.

"He's on the fifth floor, Ward F," she says, her eyes warily combing down and across my body. "Are you family?"

"Private investigator," I reply, whipping out my ID. It's a nice picture of me in my human guise, from a time when I had the cash and the inclination to keep up my appearance—tailored suit, power tie, eyes glistening, and a wide, friendly smile that betrays none of my sharper teeth. "My name's Vincent Rubio."

"I'll have to—"

"Announce me. I know." Standard protocol. Ward F is a special wing, set up by dino administrators and doctors who designed it so that our kind might have a sanctuary within the confines of a working hospital. There are dino health clinics all over the country, of course, but most major hospitals contain special wards in case one of us should be brought in for emergency treatment, as Mr. Burke was last Wednesday morning.

The official story on Ward F is that it is reserved for patients with "special needs," a scope of circumstances ranging from religious preferences to round-the-clock bedside care to standard VIP treatment. This is a broad enough definition that it makes it easy for dino administrators to classify all their nonhumans as "special needs" patients, and thus move them and only them onto the ward. All visitors—doctors included—must be announced to the nurses on staff (dinos in disguise, every one), ostensibly for privacy and security, but in actuality in defense against an accidental sighting. It sounds like a risky system, and every once in a while you'll hear some dino raise the roof about the chances that we take, but the whiners never come up with a better solution than the system we have now. As it is, dinosaurs represent a large proportion of the health care industry; respect for medicine and surgery is something all dino parents try to instill within their children, if only because our ancestors spent so many millions of years dying of insignificant bacterial illnesses and minor infections. And with all these dinos becoming doctors, it's easy for them to fill hospital wards—sometimes entire hospitals—with a primarily dinosaur staff.

"You can go up now," says the nurse, and though I'm glad to scoot away from her scowl, that stale gum sure did smell like the finest ambrosia.

As I ride the elevator to the fifth floor, I can only guess at the commotion taking place up there right now. Nurses are scuttling the patients into safe areas, room doors are being closed and bolted. It's like lockdown at County, but without the convicts and much prettier guards. As an unknown entity, I represent a potential threat, and all signs of dinosaur existence must be hidden as best as possible. Cameras and still shots of my approach are of no use; with costumes as realistic as they are these days, there's only one foolproof way of distinguishing a human from a dino in human garb—our smell.

Dinosaurs spew out pheromones like an out-of-control oil well, gushing out gases 24-7-365. The basic dino scent is a sweet one, at least, a fresh stroke of pine on a crisp autumn morning, with just a hint of sour swamp mist thrown in for good measure. As well, each of us has our own individual scent intertwined with the dino odor, an identifying mark roughly equivalent to human fingerprints. I have been told that mine smells like a fine Cuban stogie, half-chewed, half-smoked. Ernie's was like a ream of carbon paper, fresh off the ditto machine; sometimes I think I can still smell him walking by.

But thanks to the layers of makeup, rubber, and polystyrene with which my species is forced to cover up our natural beauty each and every day, it now often takes close quarters—three, four feet—before a dino can be completely sure with which sentient member of the animal kingdom he is dealing. Thus the precautions on Ward F will continue until I am thoroughly checked out, olfactory and otherwise, by the nursing staff.

The elevator doors slide open. I was right—rooms are locked up tight, silence reigns, and the ward is as empty as the last Bay City Rollers concert I went to. Good show, by the way. A solitary nurse lies in wait behind her station, pretending to read a mass-market paperback. She's in the guise of a well-stacked blonde, and even though I'm not attracted to the human female form, hourglass or otherwise, I can tell through the costume that this dino's got one great infrastructure.

Not wanting to cause any further delay, I glide up to the desk, pirouette, and bare the back of my ears, allowing the nurse to get a good snifferoo of my manly, manly scent. Once, in a drunken stupor, I tried this disco spin on a human woman and got slapped as a result, though to this day I still can't figure out exactly what part of the gesture could be construed as obscene.

"He's clean!" calls the nurse, and the room doors fall open in rapid succession, spreading out like dominoes from the center of the ward. Patients spill into the corridors, grumbling as one about the incessant security checks. Beneath flimsy hospital gowns, I can see tails swishing, spikes glistening, claws scratching, and for a brief moment I fantasize about becoming a patient on Ward F, if only so that I might live for a few days in this milieu of personal freedom.

The nurse notices my wistful look. "You gotta be sick to get in," she says.

"I almost wish I were."

"I could break your arm," she jokes, and I politely decline the offer. It would be wonderful—truly, positively magical—to tear free from my girdles and my clamps and lounge around as the Velociraptor that I am for a few days of blithe self-acceptance, but I have to draw the line somewhere, and that somewhere is physical pain.

"I see it all the time," the nurse continues, reading my thoughts. "Gets so we'll do anything just to be ourselves."

"What would you do?" I ask, flipping on my internal flirtation switch. I have a job to take care of, I know, but Burke's not going anywhere, and he can wait a minute or two while I turn up the charm.

The nurse shrugs and leans into the desk. "What would I do? I don't know," she says, raising her eyebrows suggestively. "Breaking an arm can be pretty painful."

"My thoughts exactly."

She thinks, tosses her faux hair across one shoulder. "I could catch a cold."

"Too easy," I say. "And it won't land you in the hospital."

"A really bad cold?"

"You're on to something."

"My goodness, not a disease!" she yelps in mock terror.

"A minor one, perhaps."

"It would have to be curable."

I nod, draw in closer. "Eminently curable." We're inches apart.

The nurse clears her throat seductively, leans in even farther, and says, "There are some pretty benign social diseases running rampant out there."

After I have secured her home phone number, I head toward Burke's semiprivate suite, fourth door down on my left. All manner of patients, undaunted by my presence, shuffle by wordlessly as I saunter down the hall. There are wounds wrapped in bandages, IV bags attached to arms, tails tied up in traction, and everyone is understandably more preoccupied with their own current state of health than the appearance of yet another stranger on an already crowded hospital ward.

The wipe-off placard on the room door bears the names of Mr. Burke and his temporary roommate, one Felipe Suarez, and I poke my head through the open doorway, making sure to plaster a wide smile onto my face. There are two kinds of witnesses in this world: those who respond to smiles, and those who respond to shakedowns. I'm hoping Burke is the first kind, 'cause I don't like to get physical if I don't have to, and I haven't socked anyone for the last nine months; it'd be nice to keep the streak going. Plus, I'd be violating some pretty serious Emily Post rules by browbeating a hospitalized Velociraptor.

But there's no need to worry about that yet—the beds have been cordoned off by pull-along curtains, my only view into the room blocked by a pair of gauzy white sheets lazily flapping back and forth like flags of surrender in the breeze from an overhead fan. An open closet showcases two empty guises strung up on hangers, a pair of deflated human bodies sagging to the disinfected ground.

"Mr. Burke?" I call.

No answer.

"Mr. Burke?"

"He sleeping," comes a drugged-up, drawn-out voice from the left side of the room.

I quietly tiptoe inside, crawling closer to the covered hospital bed. The small silhouette behind the curtain—Mr. Suarez, I assume—emits a grunt like an old Chevy V-8 straining to turn over as he attempts to prop himself up.

"Any idea when he'll wake?" I ask. There is no sound from Burke's side of the room. Not a peep, not a snore.

"Who wake?"

"Mr. Burke. Any idea when he'll wake up?"

"You got chocolate?"

Of course I don't have chocolate. "Sure I got chocolate."

The shadow coughs, scoots higher in the bed. "C'mere," it says. "You pull back curtain, give me chocolate, we talk."

I can't think of a single dinosaur I know who likes the flavor of chocolate. Our taste buds aren't equipped to handle the rich textures of such rough-and-tumble delicacies, and though we've learned over time to ingest all manner of fatty substances, carob and its cousins have never been high on our acquired taste list. Then again, certain dinos will eat anything. With an inkling of what's in store for me (Lord, I hope I'm wrong), I tentatively pull back the curtain . . .

Suarez is a Compy. I knew it. And now I have to converse with the creature. This should take a good six or seven hours.

"So?" he asks, his withered, frail arms slowly spreading wide. "Where chocolate?"

Suarez is uglier than most Compys I've seen, but it's probably a result of whatever illness he's managed to contract. His hide is a mess of speckled greens and yellows, and I can't decide whether or not it's an improvement over his race's usual feces-pile brown. Multiple pockmarks scar his flexible beak, small rotting blemishes that remind me of the antique, moth-ravaged clothing wasting away in my spare closet. And his voice—that voice!—shades of the tow truck driver, with a side of helium ingestion.

"Hey, where chocolate?" he squawks, and I have to suppress an urge to stifle the bearer of those vocal cords with a pillow. It would be so easy.

"Chocolate comes later," I say, slipping farther away from the bed. "First you tell me about Burke."

"Chocolate first."

"You talk first."

The Compy sulks. I stand my ground. He sulks some more. I whistle. He bangs his feeble fists against the bed railing, and I yawn widely, showcasing my excellent dental hygiene.

"Okay," he says, "what you want to know?"

"What time does Burke wake up?" I ask.

"He not wake up."

"I know he's not awake now. I mean how long does he usually sleep?"

"He always sleep."

Enough of this. I reach into my pocket and pretend to grab something approximately Snickers-sized. Holding my (empty) hand aloft, I shrug at Suarez. "Guess you don't get your chocolate," I say. Man, sometimes you gotta treat these schmucks like babies.

"No no no no no!" he screams, a shrill note climbing higher and louder than the greatest alto castrato of them all could ever hope to achieve. Water glasses should be bursting all around the greater metropolitan area.

Once my eardrums have taken down their storm shutters, I lean over toward Burke's bed and perk up my pinnas. Nothing. Not a twitter. And after that precious bit of cacophony . . . well, maybe he really doesn't wake up.

"Are you saying that Burke is in a coma?" I ask Suarez.

"Yep," he says. "Coma. Coma. Chocolate?"

Ah, hell. . . . Why didn't Dan mention this to me when we were at the club?

"Chocolate?"

With no worries that I'll wake my witness, I step across the room and peek behind Donovan Burke's protective curtain. Bad move. The smell of a human Thanksgiving feast comes on strong, the heady scents of smoked ham and roasted turkey slamming into my sinuses. Then I see the bandages, caked in blood—the flesh, rippled and torn from the flames—the sores, the gashes, pus oozing like custard—my eyes glued to the charred husk that this poor Raptor, so similar to myself in size and shape, has become.

Minutes later I come to, my knees wobbly, my hands trembling. Somehow, I have managed to remain upright, and somehow I have managed to close the curtain. Against the gauze now there is only a still, tired shadow that may or may not be the ravaged, comatose body of Donovan Burke. And though I'm glad to be staring at a blank white canvas once again, I find in myself the perverse desire to rip the sheet aside and soak in another look, as if by burning the effects of such an accident into my brain I could prevent it from ever happening to me. But Suarez's insistent whine pulls me from my reverie.

"Chocolate!"

"Does he . . . does he ever talk?" I ask.

"Oh yeah, he talk sometime," says the Compy. "Real loud. Loud loud."

Then he's not in a coma. I choose not to educate Suarez on the distinction. "What he sa—what *does* he say?" The last thing I want out of this adventure is to fall into Compy-speak.

"He call names," Suarez tells me. "He call out Judith, Judith, and then he moan. Real loud."

"Judith?"

"And he call out J.C.!"

"J.C.? Like the initials?"

"Judith, Judith!" Suarez bursts into laughter, spittle drenching his bedsheets. "J.C.! Judith!"

I run a hand through my faux hair, a gesture I picked up

when I was just a kid still learning how to act like the consummate human. It is a nonverbal signal intended to indicate frustration, or so I have been told, and I've been unable to purge it from my body-language lexicon. "What else does he say? Go on."

"He cry for Mama sometime," Suarez says beneath his breath, as if revealing the secrets of the ages, "and other time he just cry Judith! Judith!"

I figure now's as good a time as any to start writing this stuff down. *Cries out for Judith* goes right on top, if only because the Compy won't shut up about it. *J.C.* is second, *Mama* is third. So sorry, Mama.

"Has he had any visitors?" I ask.

"I have visitors!" Suarez screeches, and proceeds to showcase the array of three-by-five photos that are scattered about his night table. Some are legitimate pictures of other Compys, small, wiry creatures clearly related to Mr. Felipe Suarez, while others are a tad more suspect—snapshots of good-looking Stegosaurs and Brontos, most likely photo-frame models whose pictures have yet to be removed from their holders.

"That's lovely," I say. "Very nice." I close my eyes, and . . . yep, there it is again, another migraine working its way down the tracks. I take a deep breath and speak slowly. "I want to know if he—Mr. Burke—the Raptor in the bed over there—has had any visitors."

"Oh," says Suarez, blinking rapidly. "Oh."

"You understand?"

"Oh. Yes. Yes."

"Yes he has had visitors, or yes you understand?"

"Yes visitors. One. One visitor."

Finally. "Was it a relative? A friend?"

Suarez cocks his head to one side, like a dog wondering

when are you going to throw the damn Frisbee already,
and a smile comes to a slow boil across his beak.

"Who was it?" I ask. "Did you hear a name?"

"Judith!" he cries, breaking into peals of laughter. "Judith, Judith, Judith!"

I storm out, Suarez's singsong ringing in my ears. Whole trip's been a goddamned waste of time, pretty much the end product of any endeavor in which a Compy is involved. I consider asking my newfound nursing friend—her name is Rita, and she's an Allosaur, va-voom!—for Burke's visitor records. I know she'd do it for me, despite its questionable legality, but I don't want to get her into trouble. At least not yet, not without me, and certainly not sober.

But I give her a little head bob, a catch-you-later nod, as I walk by, and she winks back. "You may want to restrict all chocolates from Mr. Suarez's diet," I suggest, residual anger stemming from the Compy's uselessness breaking through my usual reluctance to cause distress to the infirm. "He's lookin' pretty hyper." I step backward into the elevator.

Rita bites her lower lip—ah Lord, she knows the moves, and it's driving me crazy just to look at the doll—and says, "Are those doctor's orders?"

"Better," I reply. "They're Vincent's orders." The doors slide closed and I congratulate myself on being one smooooooth reptile.

Back at the office, I do a fair job bitching at Dan over the phone for not telling me Burke was in such a sorry state and, as a result, generally wasting my afternoon, but my heart's not in it. Despite my dumb little hunches, the Evolution Club fire, tragic though it may be, has all the signs of a true accident, and I'm ready to issue my report, take my thousand bucks from Teitelbaum, and get some much-needed sleep.

"If it makes you feel any better," Dan says, "I got some background info on the guy. Just picked it up from records. I could fax it over to you."

"Anything interesting?" I ask.

"Birth date, work history, that sorta thing. Nah, nothing interesting."

"Send it over anyway," I say. "Makes the client happy." For the two minutes it takes me to scan the fax, Teitelbaum can charge ten extra minutes to the insurance company; daily rates work on a prorated basis, and the fees are jacked to the sky.

The documents arrive a few moments later, spilling out of the fax machine on six of the eighteen sheets of paper I have left to my name. Most of the furniture has been re-possessed, as have the desks, cabinets, and venetian blinds, but I've still got one phone line and one fax machine, remnants of the days when I paid for things in cold, hard cash.

It's the usual claptrap, useless information from which I can glean little or nothing I didn't already know. Donovan Burke, born back east, blah blah blah, parents deceased, blah blah blah, never married, no children, etc., etc., nightclub manager, yadda yadda, last job before Evolution Club was in New York working for—

Oh, my. Now this is interesting.

Last job before Evolution Club was in New York working for the late Raymond McBride. Seems Mr. Burke ran a club for McBride on the Upper West Side called Pangea, then hopped town two years ago, citing "creative differences" with the playboy owner. Within weeks he had found the backing to set himself up in Studio City, certainly not wasting any time in trying his hand at fame and fortune LA style.

Interesting, yes. Useful? Not really.

What is quite the crotch-grabber is this little tidbit, printed unassumingly at the bottom of the page: McBride's wife was the one who was really involved in the day-to-day affairs of the dino mogul's nightclub investments. McBride's wife was the one who worked so closely with Donovan Burke at Pangea. McBride's wife was the one with whom Burke had had his "creative differences," and McBride's wife was the one who sent him packing over three thousand miles away.

Her name, of course, is Judith.

I give Dan a ring and tell him I got the fax.

"Any help?" he asks.

"Nope," I reply. "None at all. Thanks anyway."

My next call is to TruTel's travel agent, and within three hours I'm winging it across the country on a $499 round-trip red-eye, destination Wall Street. Start spreading the news.

5

The flight is wholly uneventful, but when we land, the human passengers choose to applaud nevertheless, as if they were expecting a different conclusion to the evening's festivities. I have never understood this; the only cause I have ever had to applaud while aboard an airplane was when the flight attendant mistakenly gave me two packs of roasted peanuts instead of my rationed single pack. In retrospect, I should have remained quiet, as my clapping alerted the stewardess to her error, and she took away my extra helping.

Teitelbaum would have me killed and mounted on his wall if he knew my true intentions in coming to the city. I let him know that some leads were pointing back toward New York, requested a company credit card (with a five-thousand-dollar limit, no joke!), and he proceeded to grill me over the phone.

"You gonna stick to this case?"

"Of course," I reassured him. "That's why I'm going out there. For the insurance company."

"No screwing around with that dead partner of yours?"

"Right," I said. "None of that."

But if the case leads to McBride, then naturally, I may have to ask questions regarding McBride's death, and if I have to ask questions about McBride's death, I may stumble across information about one of the initial private investigators on the case, my "dead partner" Ernie. Of course, I don't have to let Teitelbaum know any of it. All he has to know is that the insurance company is forking over even more money for an inflated expense account that now includes a stay in the second most extravagant city in America. Next time I'll just have to hope someone gets killed in Vegas.

I have chosen not to rent a car in the city, a decision that, according to my cabbie, was a wise move. There is a special art to driving through New York, he tells me through an indistinguishable accent, and I gather that the uninitiated should not attempt an excursion on their own. Although the cab driver is a human, he nevertheless has his own special scent, though it is not the fresh stroke of pine on a crisp autumn morning, to say the least.

"Where you want go?" he asks me, and suddenly I feel like I'm dealing with Suarez again. Can no one other than myself speak the language? But he's just a human—a foreigner, probably—and he speaks my native tongue better than I speak his (unless he's from Holland, as my Dutch is practically fluent).

"McBride Building," I say, and he tears into traffic, instantly accelerating to at least ninety miles an hour before he slams on the brakes half a block later. It's a good thing I haven't eaten in a while. We're in Manhattan before he speaks again.

"You business at McBride?" he asks, glancing at me all too often in the rearview mirror. I'd rather he pay a little more attention to the actual operation of his automobile.

"I have some business at the building," I say. "This afternoon."

"He big man, McBride."

"Big man," I echo lamely.

As the cab stutters and stops along the street, flashbacks of my last visit to New York stream before my eyes, a blur of police stations and witnesses, missing evidence and rude rebuffs. And more than a few shopping market produce aisles. New York, if I remember correctly, has some particularly potent marjoram, but their supply of fenugreek is sorely lacking.

With any hard-core investigation comes the requisite accoutrements of the office, and due to my recent financial troubles, I'm light on the proper attire. I consider instructing my cabbie to pull over at the nearest department store, where I could promptly use the TruTel credit card to purchase the needed items, but I doubt such mass-produced items would lend the proper authenticity.

On the corner of Fifty-first and Lexington, I stop the cab at an honest-to-goodness New York millinery and buy a tan and black porkpie hat.

On Thirty-ninth, I buy a trench coat. I get a good deal because it is eighty-three degrees in Manhattan today.

Just below Canal, I buy a package of unfiltered cigarettes, though I do not buy a lighter or matches. These cigs are for dangling, and dangling only.

All decked out now, I renew my request to go to the McBride Building, and we turn in to the financial heart of the city. Minutes later, my destination appears, poking roughly out of the artificial horizon.

The McBride Building, towering symbol of capitalism for the last ten years, stands eighty stories high and a full city block wide, muscling its way through the skyline like an overeager bodybuilder. Reflective glass lines this architectural masterpiece, bright silvery mirrors that suck in the streets of the city and spit them back out again, only in richer, more vibrant colors.

Yeah, okay, it's pretty enough, in a slick/gaudy sorta fashion, though I can't extinguish the thought that in many ways it resembles a monstrous silver-plated condom. I hope this renegade image does not haunt me throughout my interview with Mrs. McBride—that is, if I'm able to arrange one.

Inside, the reflective motif continues, mirrors helping me to follow myself wherever I go. I get a few glimpses of my new look; the trench coat works for me, despite the tropical temperatures that have enveloped the city, and the hat hangs heavily on my head, as if constantly threatening to topple. Humans and dinos whiz by, a blur of smells swinging across the odor spectrum. I catch snatches of conversation, snippets about buyouts and mergers and the pennant race. A bold granite reception booth takes up much of the lobby; through the throng of business-creatures, I can discern the outline of a harried secretary.

"Good morning," I say, hoisting my burgundy garment bag higher onto my shoulder. "I was wondering if Mrs. McBride was available."

With one short, sassy smile, the McBride Building's lobby receptionist proves herself to be both more pleasant and infinitely more frightening than my previous secretarial nemesis, Nurse Fitzsimmons. "You want to see Judith McBride?" she says, the sarcasm crouching behind her teeth, scratching at the enamel, just waiting to spring and pounce.

"As soon as possible," I say.

"And you would have an appointment?"

She knows that I don't. I have a garment bag slung over my shoulder, for god's sake. "Yes, yes, certainly."

"Your name?"

Oh, what the heck. "My name is Donovan Burke."

Do her eyebrows twitch? Do her ears perk up? Or is that my mind singing those golden oldies of paranoia once again? I want to ask her if she knew Ernie, if she ever saw him around, but I silence my tongue before it can do any damage.

The receptionist lifts the reflective handset of her phone and taps out an extension number. "Shirley?" she says. "Guy down here says he has an appointment with Mrs. McBride. No. No. I don't know. He has a suitcase."

"It's a garment bag. I just flew in from the Coast," I mutter. "The other coast." This thing is getting heavier by the millisecond.

"Right, right," says the receptionist, making sure to keep an eye on me as I struggle with my luggage. "Says his name is Donny Burke."

"Donovan Burke. Donovan."

"Oh," she says. "Sorry."

"I get it all the time."

"Donovan Burke," she clarifies for Shirley, and then we both wait for a moment while Shirley checks the appointment book for a name that all three of us know won't be in there. The receptionist beams a capped-tooth tiger smile at me; if she has a Wacko Alert button behind that desk, her hand's getting closer and closer to it.

"I'm sorry, sir," she tells me a few seconds later, "but we don't show an appointment for you." She pointedly hangs the phone on its cradle.

I open my eyes as wide as they will possibly go, affecting my best look of shock and surprise. Then I nod gravely, as if expecting such a turn of events. "Judi, Judi, Judi . . . Judith and I, we've . . . we've had our rough spots. But if you could have Shirley—is that her name,

Shirley?—tell Mrs. McBride that I'm in the building, I can assure you that the good lady will see me. We go back."

Another fake smile, another laser look of death. Reluctantly, she lifts the phone. "Shirley, it's me again . . ."

I am shuttled off to wait in a corner while Shirley and the receptionist chat it out. This time, within minutes—seconds, even!—I am approached by the suddenly respectful secretary and told that Mrs. McBride will see me now, sorry for the inconvenience, I will find her offices on the seventy-eighth floor.

High-speed elevator. Love these things. Good thing I don't have eustachian tubes.

On the forty-sixth floor, two dinos in the guise of beefy human secret service guards—black suits, ear mikes, and all—enter the elevator, coming around to flank me on either side. They radiate physical power, and I would not be surprised if either had brought along some sand for the express purpose of kicking it in my face. I suppress a strong urge to engage in isometrics.

"Morning, fellas," I say, tipping my hat. The move tickles me somewhere deep within my archetypal detective conscious, and I resolve to do a lot more hat-tipping.

They do not respond.

"Looking very spiffy in your costumes. Good choices, all around."

Again, no response. Their pheromones—the dark, heavy scent of fermenting oats, brewing yeasts—have already gained control of the elevator, taking as their hostage my own delightful odor.

"If I had to guess," I continue, turning to the behemoth to my left, "and let me warn you, I'm good at this—I'd say that you're an . . . Allosaur, and this li'l tyke over here is a Camptosaur. Am I right or am I right?"

"Quiet." The command is soft. I obey it instantly.

A good word to describe Judith McBride's office—which encompasses the whole of the building's seventy-eighth floor—is "plush." Word of the day, no doubt about it. Plush carpets, plush fabrics, a plush view of the Hudson and distant Staten Island out the floor-to-ceiling windows that comprise the entirety of the structure's exterior walls. If I go to the bathroom, I am sure to discover that they will have found a way to make tap water plush as well, probably via NutraSweet.

"Nice digs," I say to my muscle-bound friends. "A lot like my office, actually . . . in the sense that mine is square, too."

They are not amused. I am not surprised.

"Mr. Burke?" It is Shirley, the infamous Shirley, calling me toward the main office double doors. "Mrs. McBride is waiting."

The guards move to flank the office doors as I enter the inner sanctum, drawing the wide brim of my hat down and across my eyes. The goal is to start out low-key and slowly whip the interview into a nice cappuccino froth, maybe work in a few questions about Ernie for a topping. Light levels are dim, the slatted vertical window shades casting dark prison bars across the carpet. Fortunately, the mirror theme has not been duplicated in this room, so to those random thoughts of *condom building, condom building* I can say adios. Instead, all manner of paintings, sculptures, and objets d'art fill the available wall space, and if I knew anything about the illustrative humanities, I would probably be astounded at the breadth of Mrs. McBride's collection. Might be some Picassos, maybe a few Modiglianis, but as it is, I'm more impressed by the wet bar set off in the far corner.

"I don't have a wet bar in my office," I say to no one in particular. The doors close softly behind me.

"Donovan?" A shadow detaches itself from behind the desk, stands rigidly behind a chair. "Is that really you?" Her voice carries the affected aristocratic lilt of someone who wishes to give the impression of being money-born, of having come from great status through the accident of birth rather than having achieved it.

"Morning, Mrs. McBride."

"My lord . . . Donovan, you . . . you look well." She hasn't moved.

"You seem surprised."

"Of course I'm surprised. I heard about the fire, and . . ." Mrs. McBride is on the move now, arms outstretched, sunlight strobing across her face, coming in for a hug, mayday, mayday.

We embrace, and the guilt sets in. I stiffen. She pulls back and takes a good look at me, soaking in my frame, my features.

She says, "You changed guises."

"In a manner of speaking."

"Black market?"

"What the Council doesn't know . . ." I mutter with practiced indifference.

"I like the old one better," she says. "This one is too . . . too Bogart."

The grin explodes onto my face; I can't help it. Bogart! Wonderful! Not exactly the look I was going for, but darned close enough. But now she's backing away, shooting me sidelong glances, and I have to let the proverbial cat out of the Ziploc.

Slowly, calmly, I spill it all. "Mrs. McBride, I didn't mean to worry you . . . I'm not Donovan Burke." I steel myself for the impending outrage.

None comes. Instead, Judith McBride nods mutely, anxiety welling in those big brown eyes. "Are you the one?" she says, feet backing her body away in a jittery waltz. "Are you the one who killed Raymond?"

Wonderful. Now she thinks I'm her husband's murderer. If she screams, it's all over—I wouldn't lay odds against the notion that those two slabs of dino meat from the elevator are still waiting just outside the door, eager to burst in, beat me into burger, and toss me seventy-eight stories to the bustling street below. I can only hope that my blood and brain matter splatter into a pattern of enough artistic merit to properly complement the building's architecture. Then again, if we can avoid the situation altogether . . .

I gently open my hands to display their lack of weapons. "I'm not a killer, Mrs. McBride. That's not why I'm here."

Relief slides across her features. "I have jewels," she says. "In a safe. I can open it for you."

"I don't want your jewels," I say.

"Money, then—"

"I don't want your money, either." I reach into my jacket; she stiffens, closes her eyes, ready for the bullet or the knife that will send her to meet her husband in dino Valhalla. Why hasn't she screamed yet? No matter. I pull out my ID and toss it at her feet. "My name's Vincent Rubio. I'm a private investigator from Los Angeles."

Anger, frustration, embarrassment—these are but a sampling of the emotions that flit across Judith McBride's face like so many misshapen masks. "You lied to the receptionist," she says.

I nod. "Accurate."

Her composure coming back now, color returning to that middle-aged face. Wrinkles crease her size-seven crow's-feet. She says, "I know people. I could have your license taken away."

"Probably true."

"I could have you thrown out of here in two seconds."

"Definitely true."

"And what makes you think that I won't?"

I shrug. "You tell me."

"I suppose you think that I would be intrigued by all this. That I want to know why you would come in here pretending to be an old business acquaintance."

"Not necessarily," I reply, bending at the waist to retrieve my ID from the shaggy carpet. "Maybe you just don't get a chance to talk much. Maybe you need a chat buddy."

She smiles, a nice turn of her lips that erases ten years from her features. "Do you enjoy detective work, Mr. Rubio?"

"It has its moments," I say.

"Such as?"

"Such as getting to hug beautiful women who think you're someone else." Banter, banter, banter. I love this stuff. It's a game, a contest, and I never lose.

"You read a lot of Hammett, don't you?" she asks.

"Never heard of the guy."

"Rubio . . . Rubio . . ." Mrs. McBride lowers herself into the desk chair. "Sounds familiar." Her fingers twitch, head cocked to one side, as she tries to drag some recollection of my name through the morass of memories surrounding her husband's murder.

"I tried to question you about nine months back."

"About Raymond?"

"About Raymond, and about my partner."

"And what happened?"

"I think I couldn't get an appointment."

"You think?"

"It was a rough week," I explain.

She nods, eyes aslant, and asks, "Who was your partner?"

"His name was Ernie Watson. He was looking into your husband's death when he was killed. Name ring a bell?"

She shakes her head. "Watson . . . Watson . . . I don't believe so."

"Raptor, about five nine, smelled like ditto paper?" I'm starting off on the wrong foot, Ernie's memory taking over my lips, my tongue, asking the questions by themselves, and it takes a Tyrannosean effort to still my tongue.

"I'm sorry, Mr. Rubio. There's nothing more I can say."

We silently examine each other for a moment, feeling out our respective positions. Her scent is strong. Complex. I smell rose petals drifting through a cornfield, chlorine tablets in an orange grove. And there's something else in there that I cannot place, an almost metallic smell that dissolves in and out of her natural odor, tinting it in some implacable direction.

Judith McBride's human guise is attractive enough, pleasant without being too overwhelmingly gorgeous. As a rule, we dinos try not to draw attention to our faux forms by constructing costumes that might prove too enticing to the average human; the potential pitfalls are numerous. I dated an Ornithomimus once who insisted on wearing a knockout disguise—we're talking a 314 on a 10-point scale, curves like a glassblower's experiment gone wrong—and, as a result, ended up as one of the most sought-after bathing suit models in the world. But when a zipper malfunctioned on a bikini shoot in Fiji, the dino community nearly had a full-scale crisis on its hands. Fortunately, the photographer was one of us, and he cleared the set before anyone not of our ilk could notice. The photo shoot continued as scheduled, the incriminating negatives destroyed before they even made it into a darkroom, and the world never knew that beneath that fetching left ankle, so carefully hidden by rocks, seawater, and kelp, was a green three-toed foot scratching wildly at the sand.

"So," says Judith, "I assume this time you came back to talk about my husband's murder."

"And other matters." No need to bring up Donovan Burke at this point. If she wants to talk about McBride's death, I'm more than happy to listen.

"I've already spoken with the police," she says. "Hundreds of times. And a veritable squadron of private detectives, like you, hired by this company or that company. I've signed on my own private investigators, as well."

"And?"

"And they came up empty-handed. All of them."

"What did you tell them?"

She keeps the game alive. "Don't you read the papers?"

"Can't trust everything you read. Why don't you tell me what you told the cops?"

Mrs. McBride inhales deeply and adjusts herself in the wide-backed chair before beginning. "I told them the same thing I told everyone else. That on Christmas morning, I came up to Raymond's office to wrap packages with him. That I found my husband lying facedown, blood pooling, staining the carpet. That I ran, screaming, out of the building. That I woke up an hour later at the police station, unsure of how I got there or what had happened. That I cried for six months straight and only now can I find the strength to reserve it for when I am alone in my bed at night." Her nose twitches; she stops, takes a breath, and holds my gaze. "Does that just about cover your questions, Mr. Rubio?"

This is certainly a moment for condolences if I've ever seen one. I remove my hat, finding yet another use for my newfound accessory, and say, "I'm very sorry about your husband, ma'am. I know how difficult this can be."

She accepts with a curt nod, and I cover my head back up. "They scoured the office," she continues, "they scoured our house. I gave them full run of our financial records—well, most of them, anyway—and still, nothing."

"The investigation . . . stalled, as it were?"

"Dead," she says. "As it were."

"What about the coroner's report?" I ask.

"What about it?"

"Do you have a copy?"

Judith shakes her head, ruffles her blouse. "I assume they have a copy down at the police station."

"I'd hope so. Do you remember anything from the report?"

"Such as?"

"Such as whether or not they decided your husband was killed by another dino." This information was never released to the Council—they were "working on it" last I heard before they ousted me from their ranks—and I'm wondering if the geniuses down in forensics were able to piece the info together sometime within the last nine months.

"I don't know what they decided," she says, "but I don't believe that it was a dino attack."

"You think or you know?"

"No one knows, but I am quite positive."

"What makes you so sure?"

"I was told his death was a result of firearms. Does that satisfy you?"

I shrug. "We've been known to carry guns. Capone and Eliot Ness were just two Diplodoci with a grudge to settle, you know that."

"Then allow me a gut instinct. I imagine that those in your profession work off of hunches quite often, yes?"

"When they're justified," I say, "a hunch is indeed a powerful tool."

"Believe what you will, Mr. Rubio." A glance toward a nearby mirror, a primping of the hair. Judith McBride would like to be done with me. "I have a lunch date at noon, did I mention that?"

"Almost done here," I assure her. "A few more moments, please. Did your husband have any enemies? Dinos or otherwise?" I hate this question. Anyone with that much money is bound to have a few, if only for the fact that deep, deep down, no one likes anyone with that much cash.

"Of course he had enemies," Mrs. McBride says. "He was very successful. In this town, that can be dangerous."

Time to pose. I take out a cigarette, flip it toward my waiting mouth. As it flies, slo-mo, spinning toward my lips like an out-of-control bandleader's baton, I realize that for all my fantasizing, I haven't yet practiced this move. The first shot bonks into my nose, and the cigarette drops to the floor. Decidedly nontheatrical. I grin sheepishly and pick it up.

Mrs. McBride frowns. "We don't allow smoking in the McBride Building, Mr. Rubio. An old rule of my husband's that I have seen fit to carry on."

"I'm not going to smoke," I say. Another flip, and this time I catch the cigarette on the edge of my lip. Perfect. I let it dangle. Perfect still.

Mrs. McBride laughs, and another ten years of wrinkles and blemishes vanish into that grin. If I can keep this woman happy, she'll regress into a past life. But that's not my job.

"Tell me about Donovan Burke," I say, and her smile

drops away. I watch as she struggles with it, strains at it, pulls and prods and coerces it, but the grin is gone.

"There's nothing to tell."

"I'm not asking for life history, here. I'm just curious about your relationship." I remove a brand-new notepad from my brand-new trench coat and open up a package of brand-new pens. Cigarette still in place, I am ready for action.

"Our relationship?" says Mrs. McBride.

"You and Mr. Burke."

"Do you mean to imply—"

"I don't mean to imply anything."

Judith sighs, a faint huff of air that ends with a tight gerbil squeak. I get a lot of sighs from my witnesses. "He was an employee of my husband's. Came over to the house for dinner parties, mainly. Once or twice we attended functions with Donovan and Jaycee, sat with them at dinner, that sort of thing."

"Jaycee?" Here's a new name.

"Donovan's fiancée. You did say you were a private investigator, didn't you?"

"Fiancée . . . yes . . ." This must be the J.C. that Burke called out to from within the depths of his coma. J.C., Jaycee . . . close enough. Dan's background sheet on Burke hadn't mentioned any of this. The more contact I have with my pal on the police force, the more I realize what a font of noninformation he has become.

"Jaycee Holden," says Mrs. McBride. "Lovely girl, just darling. She was a Council member, you know."

"Upstate or Metro?"

"Metro." She fishes around the desk for a photo; finding one, she turns it into my line of sight. "This was taken three or four years ago at a fund-raiser. It was for a hospital here in the city. Raymond and I had donated a child care center."

"Of course you had." I draw the picture in closer, then hold it at arm's length to wipe away the fuzzies. My eyes aren't what they used to be, and the sprig of basil I downed on the way over has just begun to take effect, exacerbating the problem.

There's Judith, decked out in a light blue dress that would put the sky itself to shame, pearls dancing like clouds about her neck. Raymond McBride, dutiful hubby, is flanked to her right, looking sharp—black tie, diamond studs and cuff links, cummerbund canted like the *Titanic*. These two are instantly familiar; even if I had never met Judith in person, I have scanned my way through enough supermarket tabloids in my time (only while waiting in line, I swear it!) to recognize the wealthy couple in their human guises.

I have never laid eyes on either of their dining partners before, photo reproduction or otherwise, but it is clear that they are deeply in love, or at least in a physical approximation of it. Intense swells of desire stream out from the picture like radiation waves; the glossy surface of the photo steams up the surrounding air. Donovan, the dapper young Raptor, looks a whole heck of a lot better than he did at the hospital, I can tell you that, and my heart dutifully pounds out "Taps" in mourning for my kindred soul. As for his date on that fine evening somewhere in the unreturnable past, she is quite the healthy filly, with a strong back and wide hips. Of course, this could just be a trademark of the guise she's in—like the way that most Nakitara guises have a birthmark on their butts—but I can sense that beneath the costume, her actual body conforms nicely to the polysuit. Auburn hair, shoulder length, frames a face that is cute enough for a guise, nothing to cry over one way or the other.

"Nice couple," I say. "Marriage is so cute."

Mrs. McBride replaces the picture. "Certainly." Then, as if it were an afterthought, though it clearly is not—"Are you married, Mr. Rubio?"

"Lifelong bachelor."

"Does that mean you've been a bachelor all your life or you plan on being a bachelor for the rest of it?"

"The first one, I hope. I'd like to find me a nice female Raptor one of these days. Like Ms. Holden there."

"If you want a Raptor," says Mrs. McBride, her lips twitching as if she'd just ingested a bit of sour wine, "Jaycee Holden wouldn't be your girl. She's a Coleophysis."

This just keeps getting better. "I thought you said they were engaged."

"They were."

"They didn't want kids, then?"

"They did."

I blink. I have forgotten to write all this down—it's bound to come back to haunt me later—but now I'm intrigued. Casually dating members of other dino-races is common, as is marriage if the couple isn't interested in reproducing and furthering the species. But the simple fact is this: mixed dino marriages cannot successfully produce children, and there's no ten ways about it.

This limitation on our reproductive abilities is not a social constraint as it is in the human world, where people argue about the matter to no end—on national television, no less. We are not, as a species, that insufferably priggish. With us it's a simple matter of physiology: A Velociraptor daddy plus a Velociraptor mommy make a litter of Veloci-

raptor babies, while a Velociraptor male plus a Coleophysis female, while it may make for a fun night, will never,
ever make a baby Velociphysis. Except . . . except . . .

"Dr. Emil Vallardo?" I ask.

Mrs. McBride is impressed. "You know of his work?"

"I'm on the Southern California Council," I explain.
"That is . . . I used to be—"

"Used to be?"

"Rectification."

"Ah. I see."

"It's not what you think," I explain. "I misused some
funds, abused a little power." Actually, I misused about
twenty thousand worth of funds and a good deal more than
that in power, intimidation, and throwing around the repu-
tation of the Council like it was my own weight. But it was
all in the name of Ernie, and I'd do it again in a blink.

"So yes," I continue. "I know Vallardo's work."

"He's a good man," she says, and I shrug. The last thing
I want to do is get into a philosophical discussion on the
nature of interracial children; this is the kind of topic that
kills dinner parties in seconds flat, and I can't imagine
what it would do to an interview.

"About Mr. Burke—I gather it didn't work out. With him
and his fiancée."

After a time, she answers. "No, it didn't. Donovan and
Jaycee were no longer a couple well before he left for California."

"Did they break it off because of Dr. Vallardo?"

"I really don't know—I don't think so," she says. "He
was there to help them."

"Did he?"

"Help them? I'm not sure. I don't think so. Donovan and
Jaycee were very much in love, but infertility can change a
couple in ways you can't imagine."

I spin the subject. "Why did Mr. Burke go to California?"

"Again, I don't know."

"Did he have personal problems? Was he into drugs? Gambling?"

Judith sighs again, and I wonder if she's preparing to end our talk. "You ascribe to me a great deal of knowledge, Mr. Rubio. I am rarely able to catalog the ins and outs of my own life—how am I expected to know the details of Donovan's?"

"You were his boss, as I understand it. Bosses notice things."

"I try not to meddle in the personal affairs of my employees."

I should have her give Teitelbaum a call. "I understand there were some . . . creative differences?"

"If you're referring to my working relationship with Mr. Burke, yes, we had some hard times at the Pangea. I felt it was my duty to guard my husband's interests in the nightclub." She's getting uppity now, and I'm back on solid ground. Self-righteous I know how to deal with.

"So you let him go."

"We came to an agreement."

"An agreement that you would let him go."

Judith McBride purses her lips, and the age comes flooding back, wrinkles spotting her cheeks and forehead like engraved cobwebs. Impressive move—she must have one of those new Erickson guises from Sweden, the ones with specialized capillaries for Super Flush Action. "Yes," she says finally. "I fired him."

"I don't mean to upset you."

"You're not."

"Was it an amicable parting?"

"As amicable as a firing can be," she says. "He understood."

Where to go with this next one . . . ? I buzz my lips, pushing them in, out, making noises like an out-of-control popcorn machine. Better to be direct. "Did you and your husband help to set him up in Los Angeles?"

"Whatever would give you that idea?" she asks, a little perturbed.

"He found funding for the Evolution Club awfully quickly."

"Donovan," says Mrs. McBride, "has always been an excellent salesman. He could find funding for a deep-sea fishing company in Kansas." She waves a dainty hand at the multitude of work littering the desk. "I would love to answer more questions, Mr. Rubio, but it's getting late, and as you can see, I still have much to do before lunch. My husband's death has left me in charge of his little empire, and decisions don't get made by themselves."

That's a cue if ever I heard one. I scoot my chair backward, pulling heavy furrows through the shag piling. I used to have a rug like this in my office, long before I was ever faced with the reality that the bank could actually repossess carpeting.

"I may need to question you again," I point out.

"As long as you make an appointment this time," says Mrs. McBride, and I promise her that I will.

At the door, I spin around, having forgotten one last question. "I was wondering if you could tell me where to find Jaycee Holden. I'd like to talk to her."

Mrs. McBride laughs again, but this one does little to erase the signs of aging. If anything, it adds half a decade. "That's a dead-end road, Mr. Rubio," she says.

"Is that a fact?"

"Yes, it is. Don't waste your time."

I shuffle my feet, turn back toward the door. I don't enjoy being told what to do. "If you don't want to tell me where she is, that's fine." I've had my share of reluctant witnesses, though they rarely remain lockjawed for long. "I'm sure I can locate the information elsewhere."

"It's not that I don't want to tell you where she is," Mrs. McBride says. "It's that I can't tell you where she is. I don't know. Nobody does."

This is where the dramatic music comes in.

"She's missing?" I ask.

"For the last few years. She disappeared a month or so after she and Donovan broke it off." She pauses then, a hiccup in her voice. "Lovely girl. Really lovely."

"Well, maybe I can track her down. I'm supposed to be good at that sort of thing. What was her scent?"

"Her scent?"

"Her smell, her pheromones. You'd be surprised how many missing dinos I've nabbed 'cause of their scent. You can guise yourself up however you like, but the smell stays with you. One guy sprayed a stench so strong I tracked him to within a five-block radius ten seconds after I turned off the freeway."

"I . . . I don't know how to explain it," says Mrs. McBride. "It was difficult to describe. Jasmine, wheat, honey, a bit of everything, really."

Not useful. "Last known whereabouts?" I ask.

"Grand Central Station," says Mrs. McBride.

"That's not a home address, I take it."

"She and Donovan had just finished an unsuccessful reconciliation lunch, and he walked her down to the station. Keep in mind this was a while ago . . . I may not be getting this right. From what I remember, Donovan told me that he watched her step off of the escalator and onto an eastbound train platform. They waved good-bye, and a moment later she disappeared into the crowd. Like sugar dissolving in water, he said. There one second, gone the next."

"And that's the last anyone's ever heard of Jaycee Holden?" I ask.

She nods.

Curiouser and curiouser. I thank Judith McBride for her time, her willingness to divulge information, and she sees me out of the office. Do I shake her hand? Do I touch her at all? My usual routine allows for a handshake, but I'm out of my element in all this opulence. She helps me to make up my mind by extending her hand; I grab it, pump, and scurry into the elevator.

I am not shocked when the two bodyguards join me on the sixty-third floor, but this time I'm too busy thinking about my next move to pay much attention to their hulking forms and pungent aroma. They follow me, tracking my every footstep, until I retrieve my garment bag from the information counter and exit the McBride Building through the lobby's revolving door.

Out on the street, I futilely try to hail a cab. I shout, I wave, I yell, and they zip by. Does a light mean they're on duty or off duty? No matter—they're equal opportunity ignorers, and I continue to wait at the curb. I wave money over my head—a twenty, a fifty. The yellow blurs still zoom past. It takes a Bruce Jenner leap into the air to finally catch one's attention, and after I perilously cross two lanes of traffic to enter the taxi, I'm surprised to find that though I have a different cabbie, he miraculously carries the same smell as my old one. Perhaps they, too, constitute a separate species.

We head for City Hall.

Public records are a pain in the ass. I'd much rather skirt the boundaries of the law and sneak a peek at some private files than wait in interminable lines in order to talk to a snotty clerk (do they teach these attitudes in receptionist classes?) who may or may not decide to give me the information I need, depending on whether or not he's eaten lunch yet and what phase the moon is in. Give me a locked door and a credit card over the Freedom of Information Act any day. I enjoy my little chicanery; if I wasn't a detective, I'd probably be a fossil-maker, spending day after day in one of the many laboratories scattered deep beneath the Museum of Natural History, coming up with new ways to fake our "extinction" sixty-five million years ago. My maternal great-great-great-uncle was the creator of the first fossilized Iguanodon shoulder blade, placed carefully in a shallow layer of mud in the wilds of Patagonia, and I couldn't be prouder to have him as a part of my lineage. Deception is fun; human deception is a spectator sport.

So maybe later on today I can get in some real snoopwork, but for the moment, I'm stuck sitting in a hard-backed chair originally constructed for the Inquisition, squinting in the darkness of the Records Room at City Hall, and I couldn't be grumpier about it.

Approximately three years ago, Jaycee Holden, according to the documents I am able to procure after five hours of waiting, waiting, and more waiting, pulled a move Houdini would have been proud of. Her name, previously scattered about on credit reports, lease agreements, power bills, court files, Council rosters, and even a few newspaper articles, ceased to appear on any and all documents mere days after she stepped onto that eastbound platform at Grand Central. No funeral was held for the missing Coleophysis, as there was no body, and no actual proof that she was even dead. There was no family to speak of, no one to yell and scream at the authorities to get off their duffs and do something—both parents were deceased, no siblings. Jaycee Holden was an attractive, vivacious young woman who could nevertheless most easily be defined by her association with the Council and her impending marriage to Donovan; such a lifestyle does not readily provide clues to one's disappearance. According to a one-column newspaper article I found in the back of the *Times,* a small but dedicated effort had been made by Donovan and some friends to search for her as a missing person—flyers, milk cartons, etc.—but it was called off after the private investigators they hired came back with a large bill and nothing to show for it.

People vanish. It happens. But no one vanishes this completely. I've tracked missing dinos and humans all my working life, and the one common thread I've found is that no matter how thoroughly their previous existence has been eradicated, the paper trail that has followed them all their lives still clings like barnacles to their personas. Junk mail, for example, will continue to arrive at their residences, imploring them to take advantage of This Amazing Credit Card Offer. Unrelenting TV telethon volunteers will call their last known phone numbers, begging for money to help the children, it's all for the children. And so on. In today's world, where computers can store your personal statistics until long after the last of your great-great-great-grandchildren have taken up residence in the neighborhood retirement home, no one can just dissolve away anymore. No one.

Jaycee Holden dissolved away. Like Judith said, sugar into water. Her name has been stricken from mailing lists, removed from solicitors' files. If I had any idea how to access the Internet, I'm sure I would find that Jaycee Holden had long ago taken the closest off-ramp from the information superhighway. She became a virtual nonentity after that unseasonably warm February afternoon, almost as if she had somehow taken all vestiges of her life with her on her journey into nowhere.

I've heard of stranger things.

On the other hand, McBride's life is all laid out in public record—newspapers, magazines, the works. At least, the last fifteen years of his life; before then, there is a gaping void, but that's not surprising. Most articles about the deceased dino mention that he and his wife were originally from Kansas, but none of them elaborated on his life there other than to say he was orphaned at an early age and was raised by a family friend. At some point, he met his lovely wife Judith, they moved to New York, entered the social and business scene, built up a Fortune 500 company specializing in bonds, acquisitions, and the occasional hotspot nightclub, and Wham! a mogul is born. From there on in it's all society pages and financial records, both of which have the capacity to bore me to tears within minutes.

I'm heading out of the Records Room at City Hall, eager

to grab a quick bite of dinner at one of New York's luxurious falafel carts, when I come across a set of stairs leading down to the county morgue. I know this place—know it too well, perhaps. Nine months ago, this was the spot of my first altercation with the denizens of New York. I suppose I made some sort of habit out of pestering the coroner's assistant for information on Ernie's death, though all I ever got for my trouble was a rude rebuff and a roughing up by the security guards. I believe there were some threats involved, and perhaps a physical altercation of some sort. And though the exact details of those days are hazy—that was around the time when I began the One True Binge, and my body was filled with so much basil I was practically a walking greenhouse—I'm straighter now than I was then. Only two sprigs of the stuff today, and one teaspoon of oregano, and I'm ready to ask pertinent, probing questions in a nonthreatening manner.

"No, no, no—not you again—" whimpers the coroner's assistant, backing away as I stroll through the swinging double doors of the morgue. "I'll call the guards, so help me, I'll do it."

"Good to see you," I say, holding my hands out in an open, peaceful gesture that works best with canines and some of your dumber humans. No significant odors coming my way, which means this kid's no dino—with this kind of fear, the kind that's turning his frail body into a mini-earthquake, any one of our kind would be shooting off pheromones like a schnauzer in heat.

"You've got—I've got a number to call, I can have you thrown out—"

"Am I hurting you?"

"Don't—please—"

I slow down, spell it out for him: "Am—I—hurting—you?"

"No."

"No, I'm not," I say. "Am I threatening you?"

"No. Not yet."

"Correct. And I won't. I'm here on official business this time, up and up." I take out the TruTel identification card that I snatched off a receptionist's desk and toss it to the assistant. He falters backward, as if I've just lobbed a grenade in his direction, but eventually he leans over the desk and stares at the card, fingers hovering just above the surface. He seems mollified. Petulant, but mollified.

"You broke my nose," he says. "They had to reset it."

"It looks better," I lie. I can't remember what the old one looked like.

"My girlfriend likes it. She says it makes me look tough."

"Very tough." I certainly don't recall a skirmish involving enough force to break bones, but anything can happen on a basil bender. "No rough stuff this time. Promise. To be honest, I'm looking for your boss again. He can't still be on a vacation." Last time, he split town after Ernie died and stayed split until well after I was thrown out of New York.

"No . . . but he's very busy."

"As are we all. Please, tell him that a private detective would like a few moments of his time, nothing more." I'm trying to be as polite as possible, and the effort is making my teeth itch.

The assistant mulls it over for a while, then wordlessly turns and disappears into a door behind the counter. I'd like to snoop around, open a few file cabinets, but the door swings open once again, as the coroner—bloodstained smock, formaldehyde scent mixing with what must be a natural odor of polished pine and chili paste—steps into the lobby.

"I got a suicide pact back there, three kids up at City

College who decided to off themselves by sucking down a couple gallons of JD. It ain't pretty, and it's a rush job."

"I'll speak to the point, then. My name's Vincent Rubio—"

"I know who you are. You're the guy who roughed up Wally last January." Wally looks on from across the room, cringing when his name is mentioned. "Sometimes the kid needs a pop in the head, but I like to be the one doing the popping, you understand?"

"Understood," I answer. "And I've apologized for that. What I'm looking for now are the reports on Raymond McBride and Ernie Watson, both deceased approximately nine months ago. I understand you performed both autopsies—"

"I thought the case was closed."

"It was."

"It *was*?"

"It is. This is unrelated."

The coroner takes a glance at Wally, at the ceiling, at the floor. Decision time. Finally, he motions for me to follow him. We head through the cadaver room and back to his office, a utilitarian space sporting only a small desk, a chair, and three large file cabinets. I stand at the doorway as he unlocks one of the cabinets, blocking its contents from my view. "Close the door, would ya?" he asks, and I dutifully do so. "Don't want the kid to listen in. Like a son to me, but a mammal's still a mammal, if you get my drift."

Two file folders sit on the desk, and the coroner—Dr. Kevin Nadel, from the nameplate on the door—flips through them rapidly. "McBride. Right, it's the same thing I gave everyone else. I counted twenty-eight gunshot wounds to the body, in a number of different places." Small blue spots mark the surface of a smooth human outline, random polka dots spread across the head, the torso, the legs, seemingly without pattern.

I point to a series of numbers scribbled on the autopsy report. "What do those marks mean?"

"Ammunition caliber. Four of the shots were approximately twenty-two-caliber-sized, eight were from a forty-five, three buckshot wounds from a shotgun, two were from a nine-millimeter, and eleven are similar to wounds consistent with an automatic machine gun of some sort."

"Wait a second," I say. "You mean to tell me that McBride was shot twenty-eight different times with five different weapons? That's insane."

"What's insane is not my business. They bring me dead guys, I open 'em up and take a peek and tell 'em what I find." He removes a photograph from the folder and hands it over.

It's McBride, all right, but much less alive than he usually seems in the tabloids. There he is, lying on the floor of his office, splayed out in a spread eagle, and though it's a black-and-white picture, I can make out the individual bloodstains on the floor, on the seat, on the walls. Wounds dot McBride's body, and much like Nadel is saying, they are of varying shapes and sizes, though all look to be projectile-based. A gunshot wound is a gunshot wound, and despite the different ammo sizes, they tend to look alike in these types of pics. I've seen more than my share of similar ones, believe me.

I hand the photo back. "Go on."

"As for your second body . . . I don't recall the case personally, but my notes here say I came to a conclusion that Mr. Watson's death was of an accidental nature, caused by massive head trauma consistent with an auto collision."

"And you have no reason to doubt that?" I ask.

"Should I? As I understand it, there were witnesses on the street who saw the collision. Hit-and-run, I believe."

I say, "I knew Ernie. Mr. Watson. He wasn't the type to—it didn't make any sense, him getting it like that—"

"That's why they call them accidents, Mr. Rubio."

No argument to that, though even after nine long months of investigation, perspiration, and exasperation, Ernie's death still sits strange in my belly. "This is important to me," I tell the coroner. "It's not just business. This man— he was my partner. He was my friend."

"I understand . . ."

"If you're worried about talking to me—"

"I'm not—"

"But if you are, if you're worried for your safety, I can protect you. I can put you in a safe place." This isn't complete crap on my part—TruTel has been known to foot the bill for safe houses if a witness is willing to come forth with information that might bust a case wide open.

And for a moment, it seems like Dr. Nadel is about to say something else. His lips part, he leans forward, and a shine comes to his eyes, the gleam that's always there just before a witness decides to lay it all out for me—and then . . . nothing. "I can't help you any more," he says, eyes downcast. The folders are summarily replaced in the file cabinets and locked up tight. "I'm sorry."

I show myself out.

On those occasions when my brain ceases to function properly—whether I'm daydreaming, sleep-deprived, or, as more recently is the case, drunk off some noxious herb, the rest of my body is more than glad to assume command and direct me wherever it thinks I need to go. Which, I imagine, is how I wind up in Alphabet City, an area of

Manhattan near Greenwich Village that is neither quite as trendy nor beneficial to one's health. After I leave the morgue I find myself thinking about McBride, thinking about Burke—thinking about Ernie—and suddenly I'm on autopilot, my feet landing me just outside a dark building with crumbling plaster and a paint-chipped façade. Ah, a familiar locale.

The Worm Hole is a bar-cum-nightclub on Avenue D, owned by Gino and Alan Conti, a couple of Allosaurs who have been known to do some work for the dino Mafia. The front room of the bar is run primarily for mammals, as far as I know, and there's always a steady stream of pitiful clientele, professional drinkers who start tossing it back at noon and don't pass out until nine the next morning.

But past the seedy rest rooms with the DON'T PISS ON THE SEAT signs, behind a false wall covered in graffiti, through a metal door barred with two dead bolts, a chain latch, and a Brontosaur named Skeech, is one of the finest dino bars this side of the Hudson, a joint where a chap can score any sort of vice, herbal or otherwise. I believe I spent a good deal of foggy time here toward the end of my last New York trip, though as I walk inside and take a seat, I realize that I don't recognize a soul in the place. Most are guised up, indistinguishable from mammals on the face of it, but a few brave souls have bared their natural heads and teeth, possibly as a warning to others to stay away and leave them alone.

"Basil, two leaves," I tell the waitress, a Diplodocus who's cut herself a slit down the back of her guise so that her tail sticks out, waving lazily behind her on the floor, sweeping aside the dirt like a broom. The combination of human guise and dino tail is both alluring and forbidden, and, as such, enticing to most of the drugged-out patrons who frequent the bar this time of night. As she passes a group of Raptors, they cackle and reach out to stroke her bare hide, but a slight flick of the tail, a warning whap! with the tip, sends the boys skittering back to their best behavior.

"Vincent? Holy fucking shit, is that Vincent Rubio?" A female, clearly surprised and pleased to see me. Footsteps, and a shadow falls over the table. I convince my head to look up.

"Jesus Christ, it is!" she crows, and even if it weren't for the constant cursing, I would have recognized Glenda Wetzel by her scent, a pleasant mixture of carnations and old baseball gloves. Glenda's a great gal, and it's not that I don't want to see her; it's that right now, I'm not all that interested in seeing anybody.

"Hey Glen," I reply, standing up for the embrace, falling right back into the seat. I motion for her to do likewise.

She pulls out a chair and sits before I get a chance to offer. "Shit, it's been, what . . . a year?"

"Nine months."

"Nine months . . . goddamn. You look good."

"I don't." I'm not in the mood to play make-believe.

"Okay, you don't. But you smell really friggin' good, I'll tell you that much."

We play with idle chitchat until the basil arrives— Glenda giving me worried, sidelong glances as I munch both leaves at once, ingesting the compound in wholesale amounts—and Glenda orders up a half teaspoon of crushed thyme.

"Thyme never did much for me," I say.

"Me neither," she admits. "But everybody's gotta cultivate some habit."

Glenda's a fellow private investigator, a working stiff shelling out her time for J&T Enterprises, TruTel's sister

office here in Manhattan. Her boss, Jorgenson, is Teitelbaum's direct analogue, right down to the high blood pressure and subpar social skills. The folks at J&T were the
ones who initially investigated the McBride matter for the
New York Metropolitan Council, snapping off those infamous photos that were passed around our own Southern
California Council meeting like centerfolds in a junior-
high locker room. I can still see them now—McBride, in
guise, actively mating with a human female, and, from the
look on his costumed face, enjoying it immensely. The
woman's face had been obscured by a technical photo-
graphic process known as Blacking It Out with a Permanent Marker, but body language served to display her
emotions quite clearly.

"Shit," says Glenda, easily the most foul-mouthed
Hadrosaur I've ever met, "I can't believe this . . . I mean
with the last time . . ."

"I know."

". . . after the cops had you thrown on that plane back to
LA—"

"Let's not relive it, okay, Glen?"

She nods, abashed. "Right. Right." And her eyes light up
again. "Goddamn, it's good to see you! What shitbag you
staying in?"

"The Plaza," I tell her, giving my eyebrows a raise. I
have yet to check in or make an actual reservation, but I'm
sure I can swing a room.

"Look at this guy, he got an expense account, eh?"

"For as long as it lasts." The basil is starting to hit me
now, and my nostrils flare out of their own accord. Mood
elevating, spirits rising. Glenda's pheromones invade my
senses, and I wonder why I never before asked the lady
out. She's a Hadrosaur, true, and they're not usually my

type, but . . . "Gosh," I gush, "you really smell good. Healthy. Real . . . real healthy."

Laughing, Glenda moves the small ceramic bowl peppered with basil crumbs away from my seat. "That's enough of that shit," she says. "What case you working on?"

"Fire. Out in LA." My words are coming slower now, syllables showing up late at the station though my thought process is right on schedule.

"And some leads brought you back here?"

"McBride. Again."

Her eyes open in surprise. "Oh yeah? Good fucking luck, buddy. Tough nut to crack, right there."

It takes a special concentration of effort to fight past the vines that are growing, spreading, thickening my mouth, but I'm able to stammer out, "You know . . . you know the . . . McBride case?"

"Do I know McBride?" she drawls. "I worked on that goddamn friggin' bastard shitpile of a case for a friggin' month."

"Must have been . . . fascinating."

"Fuck no. Boring as all hell. You ever run surveillance on a goddamn sixth-floor walk-up before?"

"A . . . walk-up?" I don't think these things exist in LA.

"Over a business, no friggin' elevators," she explains. Now I know these things don't exist in LA. Even the poor would faint at the thought. Any distance over twenty feet, vertical or otherwise, must be driven. Preferably with air conditioning. If we want our exercise, we'll use a Stairmaster, thank you very much.

"I mean, the work's okay," she continues. "But lemme tell you—you get pretty goddamned sick of stale air and friggin' take-out food after about the fifth day. And the

ANONYMOUS REX   95

friggin' goddamned bugs, crawlin' on the floor, on my friggin' food . . ."

"McBride was . . . having affairs . . . in a tenement?" I ask. Can't be—the man had millions, maybe billions.

She shakes her head, picks her nose. This is one classy lady. "Wouldn't call it a tenement, just a shitbag building. Just across the way, in the East Village—it ain't on skid row or anything, just not kept up so nice. Anyway, we was across the street, snapping photos all friggin' day—the building they were screwing in was a little better. The bimbo's place, I think. I bet they had a friggin' exterminator. Goddamn roaches . . ."

Eventually, I work my mouth around enough syllables to steer the conversation toward the human with whom McBride had been photographed in flagrante delicto. I ask for a name. "I give it to you, you can't let it out," she says. "It's my ass on the line. So I didn't tell you this, right?"

"Cross my heart and hope to fossilize."

"We know the little pervert slept all over the city— musta had a frigid wife or something—but that bimbo we caught him with is a real wang-doozer." Is this a curse word with which I am unfamiliar? "Human bombshell, tits out to here, legs like stilts." Why is it that I'm more embarrassed hearing this language than she is using it?

"Her name's Sarah," she continues. "How many friggin' times did I have to hear that on the bug? Oh, Sarah, you're beautiful, Sarah. You're amazing, Sarah. Do it, Sarah, do it. Makes me friggin' ill, something that unnatural. I almost puked once, I tell you."

"Sarah . . . ?" I'm searching for a last name.

"Acton . . . Archton . . . something like that." The Hadrosaur with the muddy mouth shrugs it off and tosses back the last of her thyme. It goes down rough; a few hearty coughs, and she comes up for air. "Screw it. I don't remember exactly, but she sings at a joint up near Times Square. Real friggin' songbird, that one."

In an instant, I'm alert, all traces of basil temporarily banished to some forgotten part of my brain that doesn't deal with speech or decision. "Is she singing tonight?"

"Whadda I look like, her freaking manager?"

"Do you *think* she's singing tonight?"

"Yeah, sure, I guess. It's been a few months since I seen the file, but I think it's a pretty steady gig. What, you wanna go see the human? What the hell for?"

The basil floods back, a mellow rush that melds with my excitement at finding a new witness, a way around the roadblock of missing evidence and cagey answers, a path to McBride, and a path to Ernie.

I lick the bowl of all its remaining morsels and tell Glenda simply, "I wanna hear a song."

7

Two-legged mammals are bad enough by themselves—rude, egocentric, generally sporting bad hygiene—but an entire pack of the filthy apes gives me the willies. It's a visceral reaction, a subconscious tug at my gut that I'm sure is somehow representative of my shared genetic dislike and discomfort. My forefathers watched these creatures evolve from nothing more than hairy toads, and it must have pained them to no end to realize that at some time in the future, they would be forced to recognize the existence of this separate but sentient species. Sure, my ancestors could have killed them off, stomped the little Neanderthals into pâté with a few good whacks of a tail, but by that point they'd already decided to try and live in peace with the humans, even to mimic them if the need arose. Bad move.

Because now I find myself sitting in a human nightclub, surrounded by humans, listening to human caterwauls, smelling human perspiration, *touching* bare human flesh, and if another one rubs up against me, I think I may become ill. Smoke wafts through the air in huge spiraling waves, and though I don't mind the occasional whiff of cigarette, I am almost overcome with the odors emanating from an impressive variety of brands, tars, and filters. A primitive lighting system brightens an otherwise dull stage, set off by a small floor riser and maroon velvet curtain.

"When's it start?" I ask Glenda, who's sipping a gin and tonic. Alcohol slips right through our metabolism like a kid on a water slide, but Glenda's always been one for the When in Rome theory. I ordered a glass of ice water as part of my two-drink minimum, for which I paid enough to cover a day and a half of a good basil binge.

"Bartender said she goes on around ten."

"Good," I say. I can't take much more of this. My garment bag, which is holding up nicely despite the marathon I'm putting it through today, sits on the floor by my feet, wallowing in the filth of a floor stained with the residue of alcohol and vomit.

After a few more minutes enduring the close presence of these slow-witted baboons, I cool down as the lights dim and a single spot strikes the stage. A line of bass notes pumps out of a nearby loudspeaker, a jazzy riff that repeats itself over again with a slightly different beat. Then a rat-a-tat high hat joins in with the buzz of a ride cymbal as the curtains swing wide and a soothing male voice announces, "Ladies and gentlemen, we are proud to present the vocal stylings of Miss Sarah Archer." The show has begun.

A gloved hand, emerald to the elbow, emerges from behind the curtain and snakes its way into the spotlight. Behind it, a long, lithe arm attached to a single bare shoulder waves seductively through the air. A shoe is next, three-inch heels on glittering green pumps, and a leg that, by any human standard, is on the close side of perfect. The crowd leans forward as one, and I can feel a collective breath being held, waiting for the eventual exhale. Now, as if she were there all along, a woman has appeared on the stage, a cascade of fiery red hair falling about her shoulders, across her back, framing a delicate body with ample curves in the proper mammalian positions. Hoots and catcalls momentarily muscle their way through the music, but are silenced almost instantly as soon as Sarah Archer opens her mouth to sing.

It's one of those slow jazzy numbers with a name I can never remember, but her voice is a cascade of molasses that falls all over my body, trickling down into my ears, forcing my eyes closed until I can no longer see the human standing on stage and can instead imagine a gorgeous reptilian beauty to match that contralto. The dino flesh beneath my guise rises into anthills of delight as the warm thrill of the song envelops me. She wants a man to touch her like no man has touched her, I am led to understand by the lyrics, and I have no trouble believing that the songbird means it. A moment later, I force my eyes to snap to attention, and the illusion is gone. It's just another human up there.

A step or two off the stage, a stroll out into the nightclub as she sings, and soon Sarah Archer is sitting at our table, staring past Glenda, trying to catch my eye. I look away. She takes my chin, turning my face toward those pouting lips. I mask my revulsion with the best boredom I can muster and take a sip of my ice water. A playful tug on my shirt sleeve, a wink that's more for the audience than for me, and she's off, back to the stage once again to finish it up.

Applause, whistles, the works. Another number follows, more up-tempo, and then another, and soon forty-five minutes have passed before Sarah Archer thanks the audience and departs the stage. There are calls for an encore, lighters held aloft, but the stage lights dim, the houselights come back up, and it's all over for the night. Drunks stagger out, forgetting to tip their waitresses.

"There you go," says Glenda. "I told ya. Don't it make you friggin' sick?"

I push my chair back, catching it an instant before it accidentally tips over. My balance is almost too good now that I'm a few hours off my buzz, and I feel the pressing need to pollute my brain chemistry, and quick. "I need to question the singer."

"Now? I was hoping we'd hit Cilantro, this place I know uptown—leaves like you wouldn't believe—"

"No, I need—I'd like to question her now."

Glenda sighs. No one wears down a stubborn Raptor, and she knows it. "Okay. Maybe I can talk to the manager here, get us backstage—"

"You go on, Glen," I say. "I can take this one alone."

She shakes her head. "Forget about it—I'll join you—"

"I can take this one *alone,*" I repeat, and this time the gal swings with my drift.

"I'll see what I can do."

Forty dollars later, after Glenda has arranged a backstage rendezvous for me and then retired to that uptown cilantro bar for the evening, I stand at the entrance to Sarah Archer's dressing room, a frail wooden door upon which someone has spray-painted a ragged gold star. A crate full of old beer bottles sits against the nearby wall, the stench overpowering in the confined area. I knock on the door.

"Come in." Her spoken voice is distinctly higher than when she sings; she must take great pains to cultivate the inflections of a smoky chanteuse.

I try the door. It sticks. I try again. Still not working, so I bang at the lock with a closed fist. From within the room, I hear a scuffle, a chair falling over. "Sorry," calls Sarah from the other side. "Sorry about that. I'm trying to get them to fix it—"

The door pops open, and just like that we're staring at one another. She's out of her green dress and into a yellow terry-cloth robe, sash pulled tight across her waist. "You were in the audience," she says.

"Second table in. You sang to me."

"I sing to everyone." She shifts her balance, weight resting heavily on one leg. "Do I know you?"

"I doubt it. I'm from Los Angeles."

She laughs. "Is that supposed to impress me?"

"Does it?"

"No."

"Then . . . no." I pull out my best Jack Webb face and hold out my ID card. "Vincent Rubio. I'm a private detective."

Sarah blows a strong gust of air up and through her hair; she's been down this road before. "Sarah Archer. You don't look like a detective, Detective."

"What do I look like?"

She mulls it over. "A house cat." And with that, she turns and slinks into her dressing room, leaving the door ajar. As per the script, I follow.

Closing the door behind me, I ask, "You knew Raymond McBride?"

"You get right down to business."

"Why mince words? How long did you know him?"

"I didn't say I did."

"Did you?"

"Yes," she says. "But I like to do things in order." Sarah

walks to the wet bar set into a niche in the far wall—
why does everyone in this town have a wet bar?—and
pours herself half a tumbler of Johnnie Walker Black.
"Drink?"

I decline, as Sarah kicks off her slippers—lime green, no
more than size four—and curls up on a plush green sofa.
There are small tears in the cushions, minor eruptions of
foam stuffing, but, as a whole, the furniture is in decent
condition. A single dressing mirror with three broken
lights teeters above a simple wooden makeup table. Po-
laroids of the singer wearing an array of different hair-
styles are tacked to the wall. "Did you enjoy the show?"
she asks me.

"Entertaining. You have a beautiful voice."

A smirk, a sip of her drink. She tosses her hair, presum-
ably in a human attempt to be seductive. "And the rest of
me?"

"The rest of you has a beautiful voice, too."

"That's cute."

Now it's my turn to smirk. "McBride. How long did you
know him?"

A pout from Ms. Archer; I can tell she wants to carry on
the banter, and though I'm not usually one to shirk away
from a good game of verbal volleyball, I'd like to expedite
matters. Already I can feel my allergies acting up from all
the mammal sweat dampening the nightclub air. "About
two, three years, I guess."

"How did you meet?"

"At a fund-raiser."

"For . . . ?"

"I have no idea. Cancer, leukemia, the arts, I really don't
know."

I mutter noncommittally. "And you were his . . . mistress?"

The shock I expected at my blunt question does not materialize. "I prefer the term *lover*."

"You know he was married."

Sarah flinches, eyes narrowing. She crunches on a piece of ice, lips pursing tight. "Yes, I knew he was married."

"Then you were McBride's mistress. When did you two start screwing?"

"That's a charming phrase, Mr. Rubio."

"I'm a detective, not a poet."

"And you could use a course in manners. This is my dressing room at my place of business. I am more than glad to invite you in for a drink and a chat, but if the conversation is going to take on overtones of . . . of vulgarity, then I may have to ask you to leave."

Pushed it too far—I have a tendency to do this. Come to think of it, this is precisely what got me thrown out of New York and the rest of society nine months ago. I back off, and, as a show of my willingness to exercise social graces, I remove my hat and place it on a nearby table.

Sarah smiles, and all is right once again. Her drink has fallen to dangerously low levels, and she licks the rim of the glass with a long, strong tongue snaking out between a set of blazingly white teeth. Patting the sofa cushion next to her, she says, "Come, sit. I can't stand talking to a man unless I can look into his eyes."

A knot has formed in my throat, and I'm hoping she'll offer me another drink so that I may wash it down. "I can see you fine from here," I say.

"But I can't see you. Nearsighted."

Reluctantly, I place myself on the couch as far away from the witness as possible, but Sarah Archer clearly has other ideas. She swings her legs up and around, depositing them in my lap. Her pedicure is recent, her toenails a bright purple hue. "Now, you must understand, this is difficult for me, talking about Raymond. I may not have been his . . . wife . . ."—and once again, that quinine sneer of the lips—"but we were quite close. Even for a 'mistress.'"

"I understand. I don't mean to upset you—"

"Hasn't the case been closed already?"

"So everyone tells me."

"But?"

"But I don't take my cues from everyone."

Pointing her toes at my chest like a ballerina, Sarah says, "Can you imagine what it's like to stand onstage in three-inch heels for an hour? It's hell on the feet, Mr. Rubio."

"I imagine." Time to press on. "Did you ever meet a man named Donovan Burke?"

"This is the point in our relationship where you're supposed to ask me if I want a foot massage."

"Our relationship?"

"Come on. Ask me."

"I'd like to ask you some more pertinent questions," I say.

"And I'll be more than happy to answer them." She stretches her toes, her legs, and her toned calf muscles catch my eye. Not enticing. "Once you agree to massage my feet."

Clearly, I have no choice in the matter. She could, indeed, throw me out at any moment, and extra questions notwithstanding, I would be lying if I said that I was not enjoying the banter of this interview on some level. A vigorous foot rub begins. The dainty feet I hold between my hands are firm, yet smooth, and though my sense of touch is dampened by the gloves I am forced to wear in order to cover my claws, I am unable to detect a single callused inch. "Back to the question at hand—did you ever meet a man named Donovan Burke?"

"I don't believe so. That's good—right there, on the heel—yes, that's it—"

"Did you ever go to the Pangea nightclub?"

"Sure I did—that was Raymond's place." She sits up slightly, bemused grin, as if remembering a long-forgotten fact. "Actually, I sang there once. New Year's Eve, I think. I did a holiday medley."

"Donovan Burke was the manager of the Pangea."

Sarah spits a chunk of ice back into the tumbler, eyes suddenly averted from my gaze. "Right."

"So I'll ask you again—did you ever meet a man named Donovan Burke?"

"I guess . . . I guess I must have."

"You must have."

"If he was the manager, then I must have. But I don't remember. Raymond had a lot of people on payroll. Managers, trainers, bodyguards—even detectives, like you."

I shake my head. "There are no detectives like me."

"I wouldn't be so sure about that. There was another private detective from LA a few months back who was more than happy to give me the time of day—"

Up in half a heartbeat, I'm standing over Sarah Archer, pulse racing, blood running wild laps through my veins. I think I've scared the poor girl, as she sinks down into the sofa like a woman caught in quicksand. "What was his name? Where did you see him? When did you see him?"

"I—I—I don't remember," she stammers.

"Was his name Ernie? Ernie Watson?"

"Maybe—"

"Maybe . . . or yes?"

"It might have been," she says. I've got her backpedaling, nervous, and though I've got no reason to browbeat this witness, at least she's not coming on to me now. "He was about your height. . . . Older, nice-looking."

"How long ago did you see him?"

"It was after Raymond died . . . January?"

Time scale's right—Ernie was killed in early January, only a few days into the McBride case. "What did he ask you about?"

"Not much," says Sarah. "We'd only talked briefly, and he told me he'd call later. He gave me a card, a local number to call him . . ." She leans toward a nearby night-stand—robe falling open slightly, exposing a flash of pale, naked skin—and searches through a small handbag. A moment later, she produces a small business card, and sits upright. The robe closes. I wasn't looking, anyway.

It's a standard business card from J&T, Glenda's firm. Sometimes TruTel employees use J&T as a home base of operations during their stays in New York; Ernie must have done the same. This may mean that his notes, previously unfound, might be discovered with a diligent search. I make a note on my cerebral yellow pad to call Glenda as soon as possible and have her check it out. "Did you ever try the number?" I ask.

"I didn't get the chance," says Sarah. "And I think he was planning on coming back to see me—to ask me more questions, I guess. But I never saw him again."

I am unable to keep a hitch out of my voice, but valiantly attempt to cover it with a cough. "He died," I say simply.

Only concern and surprise on her face. "I'm sorry."

"He was hit by a taxi."

"I'm sorry," she repeats. "At least it was quick."

Our conversation is interrupted by a rapid series of knocks at the door. Sarah looks at me—"Must be the stage manager," she says—I look back—and before either of us can respond, a letter slides under the door, skittering across the wooden floor like an albino spider, bonking into my penny loafers before slowing to a halt. Sarah's name has been scrawled across the top in a shaky, palsied script, as if scribbled there by a third-grader unsure of how to compose his cursive letters.

I reach down to retrieve it, and—

"Don't!" Something in her voice I haven't heard before, something on the other edge of fear. If she were a dino, I'd know immediately—the scent would give it away.

"I was just going to get it for—"

"I've got it," she says. "I'd rather choose when a man bends over for me, thank you." But despite the quip, Sarah's demeanor has taken on a darker tone. Her feet drag behind her as if manacled, and I can see her teeth working over and around her lips, biting down, leaving marks, almost drawing blood. Knees bending slowly, body reluctantly following, she crouches to the floor and gingerly lifts the envelope, running her fingers over the dark black scribbles that spell out her name.

"Something's wrong," I say, half question, half statement.

She shakes her head, grits her teeth. "No . . . no. Everything's okay." Her temples pulse. "I'm very tired, Mr. Rubio. Perhaps we could continue this at some other time."

I offer to make her a drink, to fetch a bottle of wine from the bar out in the nightclub, but she declines. Sarah hasn't moved from her spot near the couch; she's rooted into the parquet, tendrils of apprehension having burrowed deep into the flooring.

"Maybe . . . maybe you should go," she says, and I expect this. I snatch my garment bag from the living room and hoist it over my shoulder, preparing to re-create my role as Vincent the Wandering Raptor, his worldly possessions bundled up and dragging around behind him as he traverses the streets of New York.

"You're right, I should get moving," I say. "Perhaps we can talk again later."

"Perhaps that's best."

"I'm at the Plaza if you need to find me. Late arrival at the hotel was three hours ago. Maybe if I hang out on the streets for a while, I can stay out until early check-in. Won't have to pay for the extra night."

But she's too far gone to trade quips, and I mourn the loss, even if only a temporary one, of a great small-talker.

"I'll see you out," she says, and then makes no effort to move.

"Don't worry, I can do it myself." I open the door—no one in sight. Whoever delivered the letter, most likely a bike messenger flunky who knew nothing of its contents, has disappeared.

"Goodnight," she says, some part of her brain returning to its owner to operate the politeness functions.

"Night. Maybe I'll drop by tomorrow."

"Yes," she says, her mouth back on autopilot. "Tomorrow." The door closes, and I'm back in the dank hallway, rancid beer odors and all.

I need to call Glenda, and I need a strong hit of basil. But there's a tickle in my belly that's growing into a hunch, and if there's one thing Ernie taught me, it's to treat all tickles like hunches and all hunches like fact.

Whatever that letter meant, whatever was inside, deserved a reaction. It got one. Now that reaction deserves some action of its own:

If my instincts are correct—a pretty big gamble nowadays, but instinct's all I've got left—it won't be more than five minutes before Ms. Sarah Archer skedaddles her way out of that dressing room, down the hallway, through the stage door, and into the night.

And I'll be right behind her.

If I can get a cab to pull over.

Ernie was like this: a Swiss watch with six gears slightly out of whack. You couldn't stop the guy; he always had an answer. You'd tell him, "We can't go run surveillance, the car's dead," and he'd say, "We'll get a jump start." And you'd say, "The spare battery's dead too," and he'd say, "We'll buy a new one." Now you know you're stuck in the game with him, and this isn't the banter game—it's the Q&A game, and the stakes are always higher. Once you get it started, the only thing left to do is play it out, even though you know you're going to lose. "We don't have the money for a spare battery," you'd say to him, and he'd come back with, "We'll borrow one from a store." And by the time you were done, you'd stolen a car, run your surveillance for the night, outrun local law enforcement, and replaced the car back in its original spot, usually with a full tank of gas. At the very least, Ernie was polite.

We were a great team, Ernie and me, and though our styles might have been different, we complemented each other perfectly as partners. Whereas Ernie could run a tail on the slipperiest of ghosts but had a habit of infuriating witnesses to the point where they'd clam up like a . . . well, like a clam, I preferred the more genteel side of investigation, calmly herding suspects just where I wanted them, convincing them to confess hours before they even realized they'd slipped up. Ernie wore whatever the heck fell out of his overstuffed closet first; I was a Brooks Brothers man. I wore no cologne; Ernie practically showered in the stuff, as he was a Carnotaur and felt some shame about his own scent. An excellent guiser, Ernie could go from dino to human in minutes flat and back again, and more than once he startled himself in the bathroom mirror. Ernie was fat, I was thin, Ernie was a smiler, I was a frowner, Ernie was an optimist, I was a pessimist, Ernie was Ernie, and he could be a real shit sometimes. But he was my Ernie, and he was my partner, and now it's all for naught.

But the big guy's still watching over my shoulder, every day, every case, and no matter how ingrained the PI practices have become within me, they still bear that indelible stamp marked ERNIE WAS HERE. It's a shame that he can't be beside me, especially now, as I'm quickly losing sight of Sarah Archer's taxi.

"Make a right up here," I urge my cabbie. This one smells heavily of curry.

"Here?" He's about to turn down a main road, whereas Sarah's cab had swung into a dark alley.

"No, no—up a little farther."

"Where other taxi go?"

"Yes, yes, where that other taxi went."

"You want follow taxi?"

"Please." I hadn't wanted to hop in the car and tell the driver to *follow that cab!* due to my usual cliché restraint, so I have been forced, for the last five miles, to give up-to-the-second directions like a talking Thomas Bros. map.

Fortunately, my cabbie is an excellent listener, almost to a fault. Twice now I've accidentally directed him the wrong way down one-way streets, and he's been too intent on following my instructions like an automaton to pay attention to little things like traffic rules. Hey, this isn't my city, I'm doing the best I can.

"Where are we?" I ask.

"Hmm?"

"Where are we?"

"Yes, yes. Excellent food!"

Even if the cabbie's English ain't so hot, at least he's now figured out that I want the other taxi followed, and at a distance. For a little while, at least, I can sit back, relax, and—

The cab stops.

"Thirty-three fifty," he says.

I peek out the windshield, making sure to keep my head down. A hundred feet away, Sarah climbs out of her taxi and jogs hurriedly across the street. I toss a fifty to the surprised driver—one of the only two I have left, and I don't have time to get change—and, impressed with my tip, he proposes to take me to a place he knows downtown where I can spend my money and find fine female companionship in return. I politely decline the offer and take off down the road.

Sarah is swift, slipping through the shadows of the street with surprising delicacy. I feel like a donkey in comparison, every misstep braying and betraying my presence. I try to remain at least fifty yards behind her at all times, occasionally dropping below garbage bins or scooting behind corners to remain unseen.

Looking around, I can't find a single street name or number; it's as if a confused Pied Piper had strolled through the neighborhood, his sheet music all mixed up, his new tune convincing not rats but street signs to pluck themselves out of their concrete beds and follow him to a happier, less graffiti-intensive land. I do know one thing: Sarah and I are not the only ones on the street. We may, though, be the only nonfelons.

After a few more twists and turns through downtown Crazyville, we arrive in front of what I would assume to be an old warehouse, but for a faded sign that reads CHILD CARE CLINIC in bold, crooked letters. Two shuttered docking bays stand on either side of a covered entrance, and it is this poorly lit door to which Sarah heads. Ducking down behind a mailbox littered with graffiti tags and gang slogans, I am pleased to find out that Reina is Julio's girl, at least as of 9/18/94. I hope all is still well for the couple.

The prospect of dealing with the denizens of yet another hospital is as unappetizing as the Tar Pit Club's infamous Fish and Peppermint Soufflé, but my job necessitates that I suck it up and deal. The clinic door opens for Sarah—I can't tell whether she has a key or someone within the building has emerged to unlock it for her—and she slips inside. After counting ten-Mississippi, I hop across the street and sidle up to the entrance, my eyes pulling Felix the Cat tick-tocks across their sockets, checking out the clinic, checking out the road, checking out the shadows and the darkness beyond.

The door is closed, bolted up tight, and a quick perusal of the clinic's safety precautions tells me that a credit card jiggle isn't going to be my ticket in this time. The direct approach is out as well, though in some respects it would be better for all concerned if I could simply rap away on the clinic door, announce my presence to whomever might answer, and ask if they wouldn't mind terribly if I sat in on their private get-together, maybe take a few notes, record a few conversations, just for posterity's sake. Unfortunately, I doubt I'd get the real skinny on the action using this tack.

The rolling sheets of aluminum that serve as bay doors are padlocked in place, and though I could probably pick them in less time than it takes a hummingbird to sneeze, opening those metallic monstrosities would all but announce my presence over the PA system. Time to look for a back entrance. I slip around the side of the building.

But now, on the hunt, things change:

It is midnight, and something is amiss. Everything has intensified—the smell of decay, the rough gristle of the clinic's concrete walls. The night has grown darker, the graffiti more obscene, and I can taste the sharp sting of metal in the back of my throat. Ernie always taught me to use my instincts, the primal base of my knowledge, to guide my actions in any and all situations. That primal base is telling me to run. To get out.

I press on.

There are noises in any city—the catcalls of the homeless, the cries of lost animals, the moans of a breeze whipping through concrete canyons. But now I am hearing clicks and swishes, the buzzing of lips, the tongue-tooth pop of a guttural stop. I am hearing whispers and I am hearing voices, and I do not know how much of it is real and how much of it is imagined, and I do not know why I have become so apprehensive in a matter of minutes, whipping around at every faint breath of wind on the back of my neck.

Then it comes to me—

Somewhere nearby, there is a backyard barbecue burning away. Odd neighborhood for a family cookout. Odd time of night, too. But I can smell it, smell it strong—the coal, the lighter fluid, the fatty juices stoking the fire, flaming it out, egging it to new heights. And something else in there. Something . . . wrong. Something on the edges of my perception, coming into play, revving up, making a move, jockeying for the pole position . . .

Plastic. Burning, sickly sweet.

I duck.

A spiked tail slams into the wall above my head. Concrete flecks shoot out like shrapnel, and I stumble backward into darkness. What the—

Left arm—fire—a streak of pain, lancing down my shoulder—a ragged intake of breath, not mine, drawing near—I spin and leap away, shoulder screaming, instincts humming.

Sugar-water scent mixed with that burning plastic, sugar in the air, and it is blood that I smell—mine, mine, all mine—streaming down my arm as I back into the wall. There is something back here with me, something on the prowl. My guise is ripped, latex torn to shreds.

A snort—a roar—I brace for the attack—and in the black pit of this alley I can make out the tail, lined with glistening spikes—the claws, filed to razor-edges—the teeth, hundreds of them filling a mouth impossibly wide, impossibly deep. Eight feet, nine feet, ten feet high—taller than any dino has grown in the last million years. This is not a Stegosaur. This is not a Raptor. This is not a T-Rex, and this is not a Diplodocus. This is not any of the sixteen species of dinosaur whose ancestors survived through the Great Showers and evolved into our kind sometime during the last sixty-five million years.

But it is kicking my ass.

With the shriek of a railroad train lying hard on the brakes, it lunges, firm flesh and sharp spikes hurtling toward my body. Shadows—outlines—shift in the darkness, and I take a gamble, leaping right. It pays off.

The . . . *thing* I am fighting—evading—bangs against the clinic wall, a satisfying crunch of bone on concrete.

Have to fight back, defend myself. Free up my weapons, let it loose. Let it all hang out.

Shoulder throbbing, I tear away at my guise, girdles belted down tight to prevent mishaps like the one at the Evolution Club. I struggle with the G series, ripping off buttons, destroying zippers. No time to save the wrapping paper. My tail flops out, a wide slab of muscle covered in a thick layer of green leather hide—no spikes, but excellent for hopping, tripping, parrying, countering all attacks.

That scent, that *wrongness*—the smell of burning plastic, of industrial waste, of creation gone awry—intensifies. Anger, frustration pour from my opponent's pores as he/she/it rises to full height and roars out a challenge.

Fight or flight, fight or flight. Adrenaline is the drug of choice.

G series gone. Tail out, legs uncovered.

E series off. My retractable claws, once aching to be clipped, zing out of their slots and curve ever so slightly down and across my hands, obsidian knives glinting in the moonlight.

P-1 and P-2 discarded. With a wail of my own that would send small villages into paroxysms of panic, I tear away at my mask, ripping the rubber from my head. Bones, softened, set into place, as my snout, tucked for so long beneath its polystyrene confines, flips into position.

M series remaining. With a violent spit, I disgorge my bridge, my caps, my mouthpiece, and they clatter to the filthy ground. It has been three months since I have uncovered my real teeth, those fifty-eight sharp syringes, and it feels so good to snap at the air, to break it in half with a vicious chomp.

The thing pauses. I roar in delight. Bring it on, big boy! Bring it on!

Thinking is muddled, primal instinct all I have.

Plastic, burning still, growing, growing, drafts of rage and confusion—

A staredown, a smelldown—

Growling. Watching. Grumbling. Waiting.

To move is to lose. To move is to die.

A flinch—left—screaming, roaring—my claws whip out, reaching for flesh, grasping for muscle, for tendons, for bones—legs pounding the pavement, grappling for purchase—streams of crimson flowing, gushing, can't feel a thing—mouth working, jaws slamming, snapping down on open air, inching, inching toward a throat—

Blood smell, sugar smell—my own, not my own—flying through the air, but there is no pain, there is no fear, there is just the *thing,* this mélange, with a tail and claws and teeth that do not—cannot—go together.

I lash out with my tail, whipping it up and under my feet, leaping into the air, hoping to bring the beast to the ground, and it feels so good, so right to be locked in mortal combat. Through the part of me that is in every other dino, our shared, archetypal memory, I am momentarily flung to the shores of an ancient river, the air thick with moisture and the wings of Pteros, buzzing with insects long since fossilized, the soil littered with the bones of a thousand conquests. And I know that this creature I am fighting, whatever its genetic makeup, can feel it too. Clinics and taxicabs and warehouses are a hundred million years in the future as we grunt and grab, muscles straining.

A break—I retreat, backpedaling hard, blood loss coming under control. Waves of black gauze shimmer across my field of vision, the world rippling with speedboat wake.

Shoulder wound, leg wound, tail wound, neck wound—
some deep, some glancing, all stinging.

It slinks into the shadows—to recuperate, perhaps, or to
rethink its attack. I will not have much time before it reac-
quires the taste for my blood. I can only hope that its
strength, like mine, is running low, approaching the E mark
on its internal gauge.

"Enough," I pant, breath coming in ragged heaves.
"Tired."

A rabid-dog bark in return, drool trilling the growl into a
sizzling roll. Could it be trying to respond?

"English?" I have no idea what this thing speaks, and I
don't want to assume anything.

No response. At least, not an understandable one.
Breathing, growling, lateral movement in the shadows.

Cautiously—even as I fight against the urge—I raise my
arms, claws half-retracted, baring my breast, a nonverbal
question, can we call a truce?—traces of my settle-out-of-
court upbringing in this human world.

I am vulnerable.

I am wide open to attack.

I am a fool.

The creature leaps high into the air—it is laughing behind that roar, chuckling as it shrieks—and I shrink back—
my arms moving into a protective cross, claws
outstretched—and the beast falls, teeth glistening, tail aiming, saliva dripping, burning holes in the pavement. My
eyes closing, squinting, the end coming near—our eyes
locking, our gazes meeting—

And my upthrust claws tear into its belly.

Blood drenches my arm and the howl of a thousand
dying wolves shreds the night. My fingers grasp viscera,
my claws snip through cavities, and the thing I am fighting

wriggles its body like an eel impaled on a slow-roasting skewer.

It flings itself backward, down into a gutter, and my arm, still attached—claws digging farther, digging up, aiming, target-locked—drags me along for the ride. We tumble through the alley, blood streaming in rivulets across the pavement and into storm drains, heading out to sea. Our faces are inches apart, and even as my body is fighting, tearing away, I am looking into those muddy yellow eyes, eyes shocked with lightning-bolt streaks of crimson, searching for an essence, a clue as to its origin. But all I can see is pain, anger, frustration, and confusion. It was not supposed to lose. It was not supposed to end like this.

Blood gurgling up its throat, choking out all sounds, the creature plants its legs and tail against the curb and pushes—jumping—falling—flinging its ravaged body up, up, and away from my arm. I can hear the ripping of tissue as my claws come away grasping an indistinguishable organ.

I am bleeding, no doubt, but the creature that now stands a few yards away has cornered the market on blood loss. My claws and teeth have torn gaping holes in its hide, and I can see its entrails leaking out of that belly wound, flopping like pasta to the pavement. It stumbles backward, not out of fear or caution, but weakness, its legs trembling, barely able to hold its improbably massive body upright.

Flashing in its eyes, then, what I could not see before, hiding behind those distorted, contorted features—beyond the pain, the anger, and the confusion. There is a sadness there, a cry to be let free. To end it all. To not exist any longer. *Thank you,* this gaze says to me. *Thank you for my ticket out.*

With one final wheeze, the beast pitches over and lands

on the ground with an unappetizing squish. The plastic is no longer burning.

It is ten past midnight, and I cannot help but cry out, in my Raptor tones, a song of conquest, the howls welling up within me, filling me like so much carbonation, exploding, foaming, bursting out. There is a rational section returning to my mind that is telling my body to move on and get out, to pick up my belongings and hightail it into the darkness as fast as possible before someone comes to take a look at the prehistoric battle site in this New York City alleyway. But it is a ninety-eight-pound weakling, that rational part, and it is overpowered by the stronger need to croon out my victory and feast on the flesh of the vanquished.

Mouth creaking wide, tongue prepping teeth, I instinctively lower my snout, aiming for the throat, the meaty muscles around the neck unprotected, easy access, a victor's supper—

Police sirens. Distant, but coming closer. No time to hesitate. My jaws, still operating under last standing orders, chomp closer to the fallen creature's body, and I have to muster my willpower to give it up and back away. That sugar-water smell, the scent of blood, is pulling my desire into knots, lashing away at my primal need. But there will be no taste of flesh for my raging dino-instincts, not tonight. In the morning, I know I will be happy about this. I rarely eat red meat even when I'm not killing my own dinner, and I can't imagine what this creature's raw flesh would do to my stomach. Shades of my life as a relative pacifist are returning to my mind, embarrassed at the carnage, the gore littering the streets.

The sirens grow louder, coming closer. We were not seen; I am sure of that. But I am amazed that someone in this seedy part of town cared enough about their fellow man—or so they thought—to dial up 911 and report the sounds of a *Wild Kingdom* episode emanating from a nearby alley.

So much to do, so little time. Story of my day so far. There is no way to eradicate all traces of the scene; that would take at least twenty minutes, and by my most conservative estimates, I have about four. I'll have to go the quick route, then, a precautionary measure at best. I hope it will do.

I hobble over to my garment bag, the initial burst of adrenaline wearing off, the 12:12 pain train finally arriving at the station. Inside a compartment, hidden beneath a flap, concealed within a pocket obscured by a strip of cloth, I find the small pouch I am searching for. Grasping it as daintily as possible between my teeth, I limp back to the fallen dinosaur and wrap my arms around its torso. I pull.

And nearly give myself a hernia. This thing is heavy, heavier even than its incredible size should allow. The sirens dopple closer, accompanied by the quack of an approaching ambulance. I tug at the creature again, this time throwing my weight into it, and the carcass budges an inch or two. Straining against dead weight, I work my way over to a nearby Dumpster, every foot a Herculean struggle.

There's no way I'll be able to get this thing inside the Dumpster, though it may be the right thing to do. Even if I were somehow able to clean and jerk it over my head—impossible for my frame, even when out of guise—odds are it would come crashing down on me, flattening me into a Wile E. Coyote pancake. Perhaps if I had an hour—or a winch—but I have neither time nor equipment on my side. I can hear brakes screeching, cruiser doors slamming.

My civic duty as a member of our hidden society requires that I move all deceased unguised dinosaurs out of sight, into a safe area where they can be collected by the proper authorities. It does not require that I kill myself trying to carry it out. Into the Dumpster, then, is simply not going to happen. But behind the Dumpster . . . aha! I drag away.

It's a provisional measure at best, as tomorrow's daylight will illuminate the dinosaur's remains for anyone who cares to take a peek around the alley, but the cleanup crew should have arrived by then, erasing any evidence of its existence. I snatch the pouch from between my teeth and tear off its outer layer.

An incredible foulness—rotting carcasses, long-dead citrus fruits—hits me point-blank like a frying pan, slamming my head back into the warm night air. No wonder the cleanup crews have been known to smell this stuff from over twenty miles away—untrained, I could probably pick it up at ten. Holding my breath as best I can, shielding my sensitive snout, I sprinkle the granules inside the pouch onto the dinosaur's carcass.

Its flesh begins to dissolve away.

I would like to stick around and watch my opponent slowly disappear over the next hour or so, muscle and tissue evaporating, steaming into the air, until only a skeletal frame—suitable for display in any of your finer museums—is left. Maybe I'd be able to figure out what the hell it was that had attacked me in the first place, and why a nightclub songbird named Sarah Archer had business inside a dilapidated health clinic that is clearly anything but. But I can hear police-band squawkers and the conversation of officers, and it has come time to take my leave of the scene. I cover the dinosaur's body with a nearby heap of trash, making sure to spread it around, fixing it to look like the rest of the refuse that naturally occurs in the wilds of the city.

Remembering to grab my clamps and girdles, not to mention my garment bag—poor luggage, ripped and torn, used and abused as it has been—I flex my powerful legs and leap atop the Dumpster, tottering on the edge as I regain my balance. Another hop, this time getting my bruised tail in on the action, and I make it to the roof of a low building. With no idea where I am, and no knowledge of NYC landmarks, I take off across the rooftops of the city, not caring where I end up so long as it is far away from the battle scene.

Sometime within the next two minutes, the police will stumble into the alleyway. Perhaps they will not see the remnants of the fight, considerable though they are. Perhaps the shadows will obscure the evidence we have left behind. But the odds are good that they will find the blood, the bits of organ meat, and the odds are good that they will investigate further.

But they will not find anyone or anything to match up with that blood and that organ meat. They'll chat it out, they'll argue theories—cops and their theories, oh my— and then, once they exhaust their verbal energies, they'll run a spot check of the area. It will turn up nothing. Even if an officer should be bright enough to peek behind the Dumpster, he will find only a pile of refuse, a pack of litter that didn't hit the mark. The odor beneath it, so powerful that I can still smell it eighteen rooftops away, will not affect his worn-out snout; humans are unable to detect those tiny microorganisms that so love our decaying flesh.

And maybe there is a dinosaur among those police officers. If this is the case, he'll be unable to escape the smell of that pouch, will understand immediately what it means, and will attempt to wrap things up in the area in as timely a fashion as possible. His job as an officer of the law is important, yes, but all must come in second in the face of duty to the species. Later, once he's alone, he'll call it in to the proper authorities, and they'll go to work.

And if there is no dino cop working this beat tonight? Then we'll just have to hope that a roving cleanup crew, one of the three-dino bands that prowl the streets of the city—twenty-four hours a day, three shifts of eight hours each, no breaks, no holidays, crappy job but somebody's gotta do it—comes across the beast's skeletal remains before a human accidentally stumbles upon them and goes running to the paleontology department at NYU. We cannot afford any more modern fossil finds.

I leap, and I leap, and I leap, giving a workout to whatever frog DNA might have seeped into my genetic code way back when in the primordial ooze. Soon enough, the rooftop quality changes from rotting wood to merely disgusting, yet structurally sound, wood, and I know I'm well on my way to safety. Eventually, I find myself hopping around without having to worry whether or not my landing pad is going to crumble beneath me, and I figure I'm far enough away from that alley to take a break. There's a large road, possibly a highway, maybe ten blocks away. Time to change.

My last jump lands me on a rooftop that is bordered on all sides by a small support wall. Perfect. First job is to dress these wounds. Tossing my garment bag to the ground, I rifle through my clothing and pick out those outfits for which I care the least. I am full on Claiborne for Men, short on Armani—just two shirts, sigh—so Claiborne it is. Wiping the bloodstains from my claws onto the cement underfoot, I tear a few of my cotton button-downs into long, thin bandages and carefully dress my wounds. I leave my linen Henley unmolested, for it is my favorite shirt, and I can't bear parting with it despite the fact that I am in need an extra tourniquet for my tail. It is the only piece of linen I own, and I refuse to destroy it. Linen breathes, I have been told, and I find this an alluring aspect to any fabric.

Wrapped up like a sarcophagus, the bleeding having slowed to a light dribble, I unzip the inner lining to my garment bag and pull out my spare guise, laying the polysuit on the ground before stepping inside. As has been the rule since our species first decided to permanently camouflage ourselves over three million years ago, no one dino is permitted to change his or her human appearance without express consent from the local and national councils. Everyone is allowed a spare guise or two, emergency pairs for when the first line of visual defense is ruptured, but they must be ordered through one of the major guise corporations using an ID number specific to each dino and kept on file in classified record books. Mine is 41392268561, and you can bet I've had it tattooed on my brain since day one.

Still, small changes are permitted, individual quirks that the end user can decide to add or subtract from the guise depending on his or her mood. The guise I am now pulling over my torn, bruised body, for example, is an exact replica of my day-to-day costume in every way but one: This one sports a mustache.

It's a charming bit of facial hair, really, a thin wisp of fur that proclaims my machismo without overstating the point. I purchased it from the Nanjutsu Corporation—Guise Attachment 408, David Niven Mustache #3, $26.95—and attached it permanently to my spare guise as soon as the UPS truck drove away. I was like a kid on Christmas morning, and I wanted to try out my new toy as soon as possible. Slap it on and watch those dates pour in. At least, that's what the advertisement said.

Unfortunately, as Ernie had a habit of erupting into

laughter as if he'd spent the day sucking ether whenever he looked at it, I stopped wearing the entire costume after two days of continual embarrassment. But I've kept the guise around as a spare, a you-never-know pair, and I'm sure glad I've got it now. I toss on one of my few remaining shirts, throw on a pair of pants, and mourn the loss of my hat and trench coat, items I carelessly left behind during my frenzied escape.

I climb off the roof and shimmy down a fire-escape ladder, and as I have no urge to waste another hour trying to hail a cab, it takes me little time to seek out the closest pay phone. It's broken. I walk a block, find another one, also broken. We're gonna play it this way, are we, New York? Eventually I locate a working pay phone, call in my location—street signs, finally, and it seems I've wound up in the Bronx—to the first cab company I can find in the decimated Yellow Pages attached to the booth and wait for my ride. It is nearly one o'clock in the morning now, almost an hour since that spiked tail nearly decapitated me, and I can only hope that the taxi will arrive soon. I am tired.

I stagger into the Plaza Hotel thirty minutes later, my casualty-of-war garment bag draped across my body, and stumble to the reservations desk. All thoughts of the case—of Sarah Archer, of Mrs. McBride, of Donovan Burke and his Evolution Club, and even of Ernie have compressed themselves into the subbasement of my consciousness. There is nothing left of me; I am a husk, a shell, my faculties having long since taken the A train.

"My name is Vincent Rubio," I whisper to the desk clerk, a kid so young he could be here on a work-study program from grade school, "and I want a room."

The clerk, surprised perhaps at my luggage, my weary eyes, my brusque manner, begins a stuttering reply. "Do—do—do you have—"

I know what's coming, head it off. "If you say you don't have a room," I tell him, my brain already sleeping, dreaming, letting the body do all the work, "if you say I need a reservation, if you even think about uttering the words *I am sorry, sir*—I will leap behind that counter and bite your ears off. I will tear out your eyes and feed them to you. I will rip out your nostrils and plug them up your anus, and what's more—what is more—I will make sure you will never, ever, father a child, and I will do so in the most horrible, evil, mind-numbing way that your little mind can imagine. So unless you enjoy hearing yourself shriek in agonizing, blood-curdling, down-on-your-knees pain, I suggest you take my credit card, give me a key, and tell me which elevator to take."

My accommodations in the presidential suite are just lovely.

I f the New York Plaza Hotel is not currently considered one of the finest lodging establishments in the world, I hereby nominate it as such. If it is already on that exclusive list, I suggest that a new category be created called Most Comfortable Berth, and that the king-sized bed—the emperor-sized bed—the dictator-for-life-sized bed—in which I had the great fortune to sleep last night take its rightful place at the very top.

Despite numerous wounds to various parts of my body, I tossed not an inch. Despite a full-tail bruise, the night-sky blues contrasting horribly with my natural green, I turned not a smidgen. Despite a host of images overcrowding my brain like passengers on a stuffed subway train, mental pictures that will provide fodder for years of psychoanalysis, I experienced not one nightmare. There were no unsettling dreams of any kind, let alone of mutant dinosaurs on the prowl, and I ascribe it all to that bed, that wonderful bed, not too firm, not too soft, accepting the contours of my wracked body and mind, cushioning in all the right places.

Now I know why mammals are so keen to get back into the womb.

I order room service because I feel I am owed it after last night's fiasco. Vincent's Rules clearly state that once you have been attacked in an alleyway by a creature that cannot exist according to the laws of nature, the case you are working on triples its budget automatically.

Breakfast—three fried eggs; two strips of bacon; two sausage patties; side of hash browns; side of grits; six buttermilk pancakes; four waffles; a loaf of French toast; three Southern-style biscuits; one chicken-fried steak; bowl of Honey Nut Cheerios; low-fat, nonfat, whole milk; and orange juice—is placed on my nightstand by a room service steward named Miguel, and though I consider asking him to bring up a few garnishes from the kitchen, something in me curdles at the thought of sucking on a sprig of basil this early in the morning. Odd. This, too, shall pass.

A quick check of my voice mail back in LA finds, among the threats and pleadings from various loan departments, two terse messages from Dan Patterson, asking me to call him back when I get a chance. I am reluctant to tell Dan I'm in New York, as I know he'll be hurt that I didn't let him in on my hunch, so I put off the return call until later in the day when I can assuage my guilt with a mouthful of herbs.

I've just hung up and returned to sopping up a hunk of melted butter with a stack of flapjacks when the phone gives a ring.

"Hello?" I mumble through a mouthful of pancakes.

"Is this the . . . detective?" A familiar voice, muffled. Not real familiar, but I know it.

"Sure is. And you are . . . ?"

Silence. I tap the phone to see if it's gone dead. It hasn't.

"I think I might . . ." and the voice trails off.

"You're gonna have to speak up," I say. "Hard to hear." Suddenly I realize that the alignment of my guise is off; the left "ear" and its requisite counterparts are not situated directly over my earhole, leaving the cheekbone of my human face to block the path of any sounds. Must have shifted during sleep. Damn, I was hoping to get moving and on the street without having to reapply the mask epoxy this morning. With a little shifting here and there, I am able to realign my guise for the moment, at least long enough to carry on a conversation.

A whisper now, though audible: "I think I might have something to give you. Some information."

"Now we're getting somewhere. Do I know you?"

"Yes. No—we—we met. Yesterday. At my office."

Dr. Nadel, the coroner. "You remember something?" I ask. Witnesses have this tendency to recollect crucial events well after I've left the scene. It's rather annoying.

He says, "Not on the phone. Not now. Meet me at noon, under the bridge near the south entrance to the Central Park Zoo." It's nearing ten now.

"Listen," I say. "I don't know what you've seen in the flicks, but witnesses can just tell PIs information over the phone—we don't have to meet under a bridge or in an alley, if that's what you're thinking."

"I can't be seen with you. It's not safe."

"Whoa, whoa—on the phone's a lot safer than meeting each other. You worried about people seeing you with me? You think only the good guys go to Central Park?"

"I'll be wearing a different guise. You will, too."

Like hell I will. "I don't have a different—"

"Get one." This cat's scared out of his wits. Gotta play him tight. "You'll want this information, Detective. But I can't afford to be seen with you, so if you want it, you'll find a way."

"Maybe I don't want it that much."

"And maybe you don't want to know how your partner died."

Guy knows the buttons to push, I'll give him that. "All right, all right," I agree. "We'll do it your way. How'm I gonna know who you are—"

But he's gone. Ten minutes later, so am I.

There are a thousand ways to obtain black market guises in any major city, and in New York there are at least twenty times that. The textile district alone has been busted by Council operatives umpteen times for running in illegal polysuits, and mixed in with all the electronic wholesalers and porn stores around Times Square is a thriving illicit attachments industry. Any time of day or night, if you know the right dinos, you can walk into the back room of a knife store or Laundromat and pick up new hair, new thighs, a new pot belly if it strikes your fancy. Unfortunately, I do not know the right dinos. But I have a feeling that Glenda may.

"You know what friggin' time it is?" she asks me after I show up on her doormat.

"It's ten-thirty."

"A.M.?"

"A.M."

"No shit," she says. "Long night, I guess. I hit a few more bars after we split. Lemme tell ya, I had a whole goddamn pot of this herbal tea, outta this friggin' world—"

"I need your help," I interrupt. Great gal, but you gotta staunch that word flow early if you want to get anywhere fast. Quickly, I lay out the situation for her: Need a new guise, need it now, need it quiet.

"Jeez, I ain't the gal to come to with this, Vincent."

"You're it, babe. Everyone else in New York either wants me dead or out of the city. Or both."

Tongue roving through her mouth, poking the insides of her cheeks as she ponders my request. "I know one guy . . ."

"Perfect! Take me there—"

"But he's an Ankie," she warns me. "And I know how you feel about them friggin' Ankies."

"Hey, right now I'd buy a guise from a Compy."

Glenda barks out a sardonic laugh. "His partner's a Compy."

"You're funny."

"I'm serious."

We're coming up on eleven o'clock. I have no choice. "I'll hold my breath. Take me there."

Ankylosaurs are the used-car dealers of the dinosaur world. In fact, they're the used-car dealers of the mammal world, too—most every pre-owned auto broker in California is descended from the small number of Ankies that survived the Great Showers, which gives you some kind of idea of the perils of inbreeding. They also fool around with real estate, theatrical management, large-scale arms manufacturing, and the odd brokering of the Brooklyn Bridge. The key to dealing with Ankies is to keep the nostrils open at all times; they might be glib, but they still leak lies through their pores.

"His name's Manny," Glenda tells me as we round a corner. We're up near Park and Fifty-sixth, and I'm surprised that she's taken me into such an opulent district.

"We in the right area for this?" I ask.

"See that art gallery across the street?"

"That's the place?"

"You got it. Met Manny during a routine surveillance of the leather shop next door. Let us use the back room to run a few wires, so long as we bought some merchandise." It's always a trade-off with Ankies; they don't know the meaning of the word *favor*.

"You bought art?"

Glenda laughs. "Nah, I bought a new set of lips. Thicker—knockoff of the Nanjutsu Rita Hayworth #242. Nobody buys art—all these joints are fronts. Shit, you ever see anybody buy anything in a gallery?"

"Never been in one."

"Well, me neither—not till then. It ain't about the friggin' art—maybe a few mammals pick up some lithographs for the living room now and then, but . . ." We reach the front door of Manny's, a tastefully decorated storefront with floor-to-ceiling windows out front. Through a jumble of colorful sculptures, I can make out a salesman speaking with two customers. Glenda holds open the door for me. "You'll see what I mean."

A horrible accident with a tanker truck carrying a payload of primary colors—that's all I can imagine happened to the inside of this store. Posters, canvases, sculptures, mosaics, all in blazing reds, yellows, and blues, with an occasional dash of neon green thrown in for good measure. It's positively blinding.

Glenda issues a short wave toward the salesman—I assume this is Manny—and he politely excuses himself from the two customers near the cash register. As he walks toward us, arms outstretched, crocodile smile stretching his lips into two tight caterpillars, I can already feel the ooze seeping out of his pores. What's more, I can smell him, and beneath the typical aluminum Ankie scent is the unmistakable odor of petroleum jelly.

"Miss Glenda!" he cries in mock delight. "What a wonderful pleasure it is to see you today." I have a feeling that he's laying the accent on thicker than it really comes—the last bit came out as *wat a waaanderfool pleeassoore eet ees to see yoo toodai*—but I'll refrain from insulting the guy until I know him a little better.

"We were in the neighborhood, thought I'd drop by and show my friend Vincent your beautiful gallery."

"Vincent?" He envelops my right hand in both of his, clutching it tight. "Is that right? *Veeencent?*"

"Right enough." I force myself to grin.

Glenda lowers her voice a notch and says, "We'd like to talk to you about some of those reproductions you sell."

A notched eyebrow, a wink of the inner eyelid, and Manny turns back to the other customers. "Perhaps I will have what you are looking for next week, no? Manny will give you a call." The couple—human—who know a brush-off when they hear one, exit the gallery. Manny locks the door behind them and turns around an OUT FOR LUNCH sign. When he returns, the accent is softer.

"Mammals. They wanted a Kandinsky. What do I know from Kandinsky?"

Are we supposed to answer? Glenda and I opt to shake our heads in sympathy. I steal a glance at my watch, and Manny steals a glance at me.

"You are in a hurry, yes? Come, come, we go to the back."

And to the back we go, passing crate after crate of paintings and lithographs, boxes of abstract sculptures. An EMPLOYEES ONLY sign hangs on a nearby rest room, and it's through this door that Manny leads us, keeping up a furious stream of chatter along the way. ". . . and when there is a new shipment of latex, I say to my workers, we must install it in the costumes right away, as Manny makes the finest guises around, better than the companies, much better than Nakitara, for example, who don't even use mammal polymers—did you know that?—but instead use some type of cattle product. And I suppose cattle is a mammal but at Manny's we use real mammal products, if you understand me, for only the finest merchandise comes from Manny . . ." He drones on.

The rest room door leads to another, and another, and soon we're hopping through a maze of doorways, each bearing its own innocuous sign: STOCK ROOM, RECENT RETURNS, BLANK CANVASES. DANGER, DO NOT OPEN: ACID.

Instinctively, I step back as Manny opens this last door, expecting to be doused with a spray of chemicals; instead, Manny steps into a small warehouse full to bursting with empty human disguises of every shape, color, and texture. Specialized hangers—Styrofoam shapes cut to the appropriate mammalian dimensions—line the walls, each one covered in a limp mockery of the human form. An electric hum fills the air.

On the warehouse floor, a dozen workers sweat it out around sewing machines and pressing irons, carefully hand-stitching the buttons, zippers, and seams that are so integral to a perfect guise. The heat is sweltering, and I find myself pitying the dinosaurs forced to work under these conditions. I can still remember the stories of days long ago when we used to embrace the heat and humidity—to thrive in it, no less—to wake each morning and lick the sweet, steamy air, each particle dripping with succulent moisture—but now, all these easy, breezy, well-ventilated years later, I would wager that any one of us would sooner live in Antarctica than, say, Miami Beach. Then again, I do quite enjoy the taste of emperor penguins, so I am admittedly biased.

"Pay them no mind," Manny says, clearly reading my thoughts. "They are very happy to be working here." Then, to prove his point, he calls out, "My workers, are you not happy to be working for Manny?"

And as one, they call back, "Yes, Manny," in a spaced-out, drugged-up monotone. I imagine that this Ankie buys cheap basil by the ton.

"Now, Mr. Vincent, what are you requiring today?" We step down to the warehouse floor, Manny leading Glenda and me toward a row of guises at the back. "We specialize in handcrafted torso attachments. Perhaps some new biceps—"

"I need a full guise."

"A full guise, yes? This is a very expensive thing. Here at Manny's, we have only the most excellent craftsmen—"

"Cut the line, Manny. Price doesn't matter." I've got Tru-Tel's credit card on me. "So long's you can charge it up as a piece of art."

Manny's smile is genuine this time; he clearly enjoys when others dispense with the precursors and jump head-long into his little pit of chicanery. "Of course, Mr. Vincent. Right this way."

The next twenty minutes are spent leafing through a series of guises, each of which has its pros and cons in terms of functionality and aesthetics. Glenda serves as my personal shopper and fashion critic, dispensing with shoddy designs and faulty tailoring. To be fair, Manny's guises are indeed incredibly well made, and I express my surprise that he never went into legitimate guise work.

"Wait until you see the bill," he tells me through that grin of his.

We eventually settle on the guise of a stout, middle-aged man with a protruding belly and slightly bowed legs, a knockoff of the Nakitara Company's Mr. Johannsen #419 model. Maybe five eight, 180, darned close to average for the age and gender, which is precisely what we are looking for. But at this stage, the costume, drooped across the Styrofoam mannequin like an ill-fitting bedsheet, is nothing but a featureless shell, devoid of hair, color, or distinguishing marks. I have forty-five minutes to make this thing look like a real human before I can don the costume and hoof it into Central Park.

"Maria is a genius at the hair," says Manny. We are standing next to an old, withered Allosaur, her guise skin loose, wrinkled, falling off of her like it does with the Styrofoam cutouts. Manny must not include a free costume as part of his workers' benefits package. "She has been doing the hair for . . . how many years now?"

Maria mumbles something we cannot understand. I am convinced Manny cannot understand it, either. "You hear that?" he says to us. "That is many, many years."

We settle on a light auburn style, with a touch of gray at the temples—"for that distinguished look, yes?"—and a minimum of body hair in order to save precious minutes. I don't plan on using the guise more than this one time, and I doubt I'll be disrobing in Central Park during my rendezvous with the coroner.

Trevor is the "genius" at distinguishing marks, and from him we pick up a facial blemish and a military tattoo on the forearm, faded and blue. Frank, the human skin-tone "genius," gives the guise a once-over with an olive spray brush, coating it somewhere between tanned and swarthy. Maria, who it seems is not only a "genius" at hair but also at prescription eyewear, picks out a set of blue contact lenses to cover my natural verdant irises.

As Glenda and Manny help me disrobe from my usual costume and place it in a fine leather carrying case—"a gift for my good friend Mr. Vincent"—the rest of the experts in the warehouse apply the finishing touches to my custom guise. Birthmark here, wrinkle there. It's a rush job, but it's done, and it should hold up for the next hour or so.

I dress, slipping into the guise like a comfortable pair of pajamas. The inner lining is made from a silk polymer, I am told, and it facilitates the process quite nicely. Before I stepped into the empty skin, I imagined that it would be odd seeing out from new eyeholes, feeling through new gloves. But I find that the experience is comparable to that in the old guise; a human is a human is a human. A mirror is wheeled over to me, and now when I wave, a chubby middle-aged fellow waves back. When I grin, a chubby middle-aged fellow's second chin puffs out. When I dance, I stumble over my own two feet. Perfect.

"You like?" Manny asks me when we're all through.

"You do good work." I produce the TruTel charge card with little more than a glance at the bill—by God, more than a glance would probably kill me—and Manny eagerly runs it through.

"Mr. Vincent, you are a good customer. You come back whenever you want."

Manny kisses our hands, our cheeks, and leads us back out of the warehouse, through the maze of doors, and into the art gallery. The entire process has taken no longer than thirty minutes.

"You want me to come along?" Glenda asks as we prepare to leave.

"Solo deal. I don't wanna spook the guy—he's shaky as it is."

"Maybe if I hang back—"

"Glen, it's okay. Go to work."

On the way out of Manny's, I detect a familiar scent wafting through the air and spin around like a top trying to locate the source. But with all of these pedestrians streaming by, many with their own particular smells, it's impossible to localize. A young man walks confidently into Manny's; it's possible that the odor is coming from him, but I don't recognize the face and I don't have the time to worry about it.

I need quick directions. "Central Park is . . . ?"

"North," says Glenda. "The zoo's about halfway up on the east side. Stick to the right and you can't miss it."

"Damn, I almost forgot—" I turn back to Glenda. "Can you do a little checking up for me?"

"Checking up how?"

"At J&T, on the computer."

Glenda's face falls into a frown. "You gonna get me into some shit, Vincent?"

"Possibly."

"Finally." She claps her hands together, rubbing them in anticipation. "Whaddaya need?"

"Got a lead that said Ernie mighta been keeping his stuff over at J&T when he was here last time. Notes, files, whatever you can find."

"Ernie's a part of this now?"

"He might be. And even if he's not—"

"This is the kind of thing that got you in trouble the last time, you know that?" A mild rebuke, a featherweight slap.

"I know it. Please, a favor. For me. For Meester Veencent."

As soon as I pressure Glenda into agreeing to snoop around her offices and phone me with the information, we bid farewell. I have fifteen minutes to walk into the heart of Central Park thirty blocks away, and I set myself toward the tall trees in the distance. North, I think.

* * *

Noon. The sun is harsh today, and even through the new costume I can feel its rays heating up my delicate hide. One thing I've already noticed about Manny's guise is that the pore structure is weak, trapping a good deal of my natural moisture inside the skin, rather than allowing it to leach into the air. I pray this does not wear out the epoxy.

No Dr. Nadel in sight, though as he's wearing a different costume and I'm wearing a different costume, sight isn't going to be of much help. Fortunately, the guise I chose has extra-wide nostrils, so I'll be able to catch his scent whenever he should show. I believe it was woodsy, maybe . . . oak? I'll know it when I smell it.

On the way to the zoo, I passed an impressive herbilogical exhibit planted in the middle of Central Park, a series of trees and shrubs from different locales, each bearing a small name plaque describing type, flowering habits, and country of origin. Discreetly, I plucked a few leaves here and there for a little experimental ingestion should I need it later in the day; I may never make it to French Guyana, for example, but if I find that their trees pack a wallop, a trip would be in order. I sit on a park bench and catalog the leaves, tucking them inside the breast pocket of a particularly noxious sweater vest Glenda picked out.

Scent of polished pine, riding on a gust of wind—that's Nadel. I glance around, attempting to localize. Punk with mohawk, strutting this way? Nah, human. Father, angry, storming toward me, holding a squirming child by the wrist? He wouldn't bring along a kid, would he? They pass—both human, I realize now—and the scent remains. Weak, but growing stronger. I look farther afield, into the green pastures of the park.

There—the black woman with short hair approximately

a hundred feet away. Brightly colored running shorts, a pink tank top. Thin. And a small folder in her hands. As she comes closer, the smell grows stronger, and as I catch her eyes, there's a moment of unspoken understanding. It's Dr. Nadel.

Not a bad idea for clandestine work, the male/female swap, though I turned down such an offer at Manny's a half-hour ago. Dinos risk enough identity crises without having to worry about transgender mix-ups. Nadel comes closer, not hurrying, not lagging, moving at a steady pace toward the bridge. I expect there will be little in the way of discussion; he will most likely walk by, leave the folder on the bench, where I will retrieve it moments later before walking back into the park. I take a few steps backward, retreating to safety beneath a small bridge.

Another smell, suddenly, overpowering Nadel's pine, and this one is unfamiliar to me. But it's enough to stop me in my tracks, force my eyes to scan the park once again. Nothing has changed—pedestrians walk, children run, jugglers drop their clubs. There it is again—deodorant and chewing gum. It does not belong.

A tandem bicycle enters the scene, two obese blond women somehow remaining upright on the contraption despite an incredibly high center of gravity. They wear identical T-shirts stretched across their bodies that read TOO HOT FOR YOU, and giggle incessantly at some silent joke. They are pedaling quickly, though—almost too quickly even for experienced cyclists—zipping the two-seated bicycle through the park with impressive speed.

The smells intensify and collide with one another, mixing into a soupy mélange that my olfactory organs are unable to separate. Rooted into the spot beneath the bridge, I find myself glancing back and forth between the black woman I know to be Dr. Kevin Nadel and the two heavy girls on the bike, who I don't know to be anything but two heavy girls on a bike.

But I have a hunch.

Before I can convince my legs to leap from their spot, before the thought has even made its way down my spinal cord, the tandem bikers pull up before Dr. Nadel, and, giggling all the way, stop the bike in the middle of the path, blocking his progress. Now I'm starting to get my legs in gear, just coming off the blocks—but even past the din of the zoo, the children, the sounds of Central Park, I can hear buttons snapping and claws sliding into place. The two women have turned around on the bicycle seats, riding sidesaddle, shielding Nadel from my view with their solid bodies. I run.

There's not much commotion—I don't hear raised voices, shouts of protestations. No struggle—isn't that how these things are supposed to go down? There's a zing, a slice, a squish, and a groan, and in less time than it took for the ladies to stop the bike, they've started it up again, reaching cruising speed in seconds. Nadel is on the ground.

As I approach Nadel and kneel over the body, I look up to find that the bike has already slipped down one of the many shaded paths crossing the park, disappearing into the shadows and the crowds. A small river of blood oozes out from a long, thin slice to the black woman's neck, fluid gushing rhythmically with the faltering heartbeat. Scent disappearing, the doctor dying.

One quick slice with one sharp claw; that was all it took. I don't even know which of the "ladies" did it. The guise is holding up well beneath the strain of an injury—I can barely make out the fake skin from the shredded hide below, though perhaps the blood helps to obscure the bond. There's no time left for Nadel to croak out a last confession; the eyes have already glazed over, the mouth opening and closing like a codfish.

The folder is gone.

A crowd has begun to form, more from curiosity than altruism, I am sure, but it remains my duty to ensure the security and eventual removal of the body. I poke my head up and say, "She's all right, little accident. Passed out. Happens all the time."

This mollifies some of the onlookers, and they walk away. Others, perhaps sensing a little more than a fainted jogger, stick around to watch. I catch the eye of a dino in the crowd—young girl, jasmine scent, probably a Diplodocus—and wink slowly.

"Think you can call us somebody to help, young lady?" I ask her pointedly, and she seems to get the idea. The girl runs off at top speed toward a nearby pay phone where I hope she will ring the proper dino authorities.

Meanwhile, I search Nadel's new—and now unused—body, frisking the corpse for any clues or information the two cyclists didn't grab. The search turns up nothing in terms of information, but a full key chain comes out of the running shorts, and I quickly transfer the metallic mass to my own pocket.

I wait around for the ambulance to show up, shielding Nadel from passersby, pretending to speak to the African-American woman lying on the ground as if she were still alive. "You'll feel better with some food in you," I say to the body. "Right as rain in a minute or so."

"Clear out, clear out," instructs the paramedic. He's got two partners, and from the smell of it, they're all Carnotaurs. They huddle around Nadel's prone body, muttering to one another. The protocol here is simple: Get the dino out of sight and into a secured location, away from human eyes. They load Nadel's body onto a stretcher and wheel him/her/it into the back of the ambulance. The crowd, displeased at the lack of gore, disperses.

After we're alone, the lead paramedic turns to me—"You see it?"

"I didn't see it, but I was here."

"You wanna explain that?"

"I don't have time to explain," I say, "but you can call me at my hotel later tonight." I give him my contact information, run down my PI credentials, and discreetly warn him that on the off chance that the guise is registered (mine isn't), it might not match up with the dino inside. Grudgingly, he accepts my word and prepares to leave.

"Oh, and by the way," I say, "you may want to find another coroner to do the autopsy."

"Why?" he asks. "Guy downtown's always done a good job on our kind."

"Yeah, but he's on vacation. Be gone for a while."

No time to change guises; I don't know who sent the two assassins after Nadel, and I don't know if they're after me. Better to remain hidden for the moment. I'm sneaking through the underground service passages at City Hall, trying to find some back entrance into the morgue. If I can get into Nadel's office without being seen . . .

No such luck. I have to brave the front door. Wally, the coroner's assistant, stands behind the desk, and I half-expect him to freak out and call security as soon as I walk in. But I don't look like the guy who assaulted him nine months ago; I'm just another bereaved man with middle-age spread, and his lousy human nose isn't up to the task of uncovering my deception.

"Is . . . is my Myrtle . . . in here?" I choke out.

"I'm sorry?" Wally's already confused—good.

"My Myrtle, she . . . it was a stroke, they said, a . . . a stroke . . ."

"I—I don't know, sir, ah . . . Let me check the books. The last name?"

"Little."

"Myrtle Little?" He doesn't sound the least bit skeptical, and it hurts not to laugh. I hide it in a barking cough, a sob into my hands. Wally looks through the morgue log.

"I don't see anything," he says. "How long ago—"

"A few hours, I don't know. Please—you've got to find her—please—" I'm grabbing onto Wally's white physician's coat now, tugging in a desperate plea for help.

"Maybe you could go back to the hospital—"

"They told me to come down here—"

"They did?"

"Just a moment ago. Please, my Myrtle—"

Wally grabs a phone, dials, and has a short conversation with the person on the other end, a conversation that quickly turns heated. After nearly deafening me with his shouts, Wally slams the receiver on the hook and storms out from behind the desk, face set in a mask of righteous indignation. "I don't know what the hell's going on in this place," he huffs, "but Mr. Little, I'm going to find your wife."

"Thank you, young man," I cry. "Thank you." I keep up a steady flow of tears until Wally's out the door, down the hall, and up the stairs. Then I'm dry as a bone and it's back to business.

The outer door is unlocked, making the first part of this nice and easy. Nadel's office is a different matter, and it's not until I try the very last key on the chain that I find the right one. The place looks the same as when I left it—neat, precise, boring. I put all my faith in the file cabinet, a four-drawer job with a separate key for each compartment; with such precautions, perhaps excitement lies within.

These keys are easy to locate, and the cabinet doors slide open without a sound. In each compartment, hundreds of manila folders are pressed between two aluminum binders, each file labeled with a date of death and organized by last name. I scan through the M and W sections, attempting to locate what I know won't be there: the autopsies for McBride and Ernie. I also know where the folders are—pressed between the sweaty palms of two chubby, giggling cyclists.

I'm about to pack it up, the lack of evidence and wasted time already making me regret this side trip, when I notice a small subcompartment in the back of the bottom drawer, a metallic box covered by a locked lid. It takes another key off the key ring, a small one I almost overlooked, to unlock and open the box, and inside I find not another file, but a red spiral leather-bound notebook, perfect for writing down names and addresses and the like. I eagerly flip through, ready to be astounded, but all I come across are seemingly random numbers and letters. For example: 6800 DREV. 3200 DREV. Not exactly a case breaker.

But beneath this is a passbook to First National Bank, and it seems that Dr. Nadel has been making deposits as of late. To be more precise, he's been making deposits as of December 28, three days after Raymond McBride was found dead in his office, and then sporadically throughout the past year, and it is these numbers that match up with those in the notebook. The 6800, for example, represents $6,800 that was deposited in this account last December, the $3,200 coming a few months afterward. Now the only thing is to figure out the letters. DREV. I don't see any deposit dates directly around the time of Ernie's death—the closest is thirty-nine days after I got the news—though with diligent study, I'm sure a pattern will emerge.

But I'm sure as hell not gonna do my studying here. I pack up my new belongings, lock the file cabinets, and head back into the lobby, up the stairs, and down the hallway just in time to slip into a niche and watch a frazzled Wally entering the morgue to explain to Mr. Little that his dear Myrtle has, in the last ten hours, stepped down off her gurney and walked away, that she has somehow defected from death.

10

An unexpected and sudden lack of basil has left my body herb-free for over three hours, and despite the occasional stab of withdrawal pains radiating from deep within my chest, I am pleased to find the cobwebs in the corners of my mind clearing themselves away. I have no particular desire to remain this level-headed for any longer than necessary, but while it lasts I might as well get in some good and heavy thinking:

Without a doubt, there's Judith and Raymond and Sarah Archer and that thing from the alley—all of this deserves more than a moment's thought—but if I want to get back to the heart of the matter, I've got to begin at the beginning, if only to justify the expense account. I've got to start back at the Evolution Club.

Nightclub owner Donovan Burke was dating Metropolitan Council representative and all-around American gal Jaycee Holden, who then disappeared without a trace on a crowded subway platform, leaving her distraught lover to search fruitlessly for her throughout the northeastern United States. Fact. Donovan Burke then fled New York

City and his failed romance for the quiet, simple, small-town values of Los Angeles, where he set up shop in a nightclub that burned to the ground despite a team of trained firefighters and eight thousand gallons of water. Fact. During this fire, Donovan Burke risked life and limb by staying inside the nightclub even as the flames were licking his body. Fact. And now a bit of conjecture: Donovan Burke, beset by troubles of the heart, was not particularly attached to this world.

A flashback to the conversation with Judith McBride, and her assessment of Donovan and Jaycee's relationship: "Donovan and Jaycee were very much in love," she told me yesterday, "but infertility can change a couple in ways you can't imagine." Perhaps Donovan had given up on the whole shebang. Perhaps he set the fire as a grand suicidal gesture. Perhaps he'd had enough of the guising and the lying and the pain from knowing that he'd never be with the one he loved. Two different worlds and all that jazz.

And here's where the aforementioned clearheadedness comes in handy. Judith McBride told me that the doctor who was treating Donovan and Jaycee, the one who allowed Donovan to hold out hope that they could beat the system that had served us so well for three hundred million years, the geneticist whose experiments might someday indeed make possible a Raptor-Coleo mix, was none other than Dr. Emil Vallardo.

Dr. E. Vallardo.

Dr. E. V.

DREV.

And so it is that an hour later, after a horrendous traffic jam on Park Avenue that made rush hour in Los Angeles look like the open plains of Montana, I find myself in Dr. Emil Vallardo's private office, awaiting the arrival of the doctor himself. Even if my amateur cryptography of

Nadel's notes about DREV are way off, this is as good a place to start as any. Vallardo—the Spin Doctor, as they called him back in Council meetings because of the rumor that he used centrifuges in his race-mixing experiments— may have no pertinent information to bring to the case, but Ernie always taught me that nothing is coincidence. If a name pops up more than once, it's a name that begs to be checked.

Dr. Vallardo is out of the facility right now, or so the receptionist told me, but he'll be back any minute. After a stylish wash and blow-dry of charm by yours truly, the secretary was kind enough to offer me a seat in the doctor's private office, and though I have a strong feeling that Dr. Vallardo won't approve of her decision, I'm much happier planting my rear in this cushioned leather recliner than sweating it out on those hard vinyl benches in the waiting room. At the very least, I can take this time to peruse the multitude of diplomas and certificates lining the wood-paneled walls. Unfortunately, all it serves to do is make me feel intellectually inferior.

Undergraduate work at Cornell. Big deal. I knew a Stegosaur who went to Cornell and now he's working on cars for a living. Okay, he's designing them, but still . . . Medical degree, specializing in obstetrics, from Johns Hopkins. Overrated. Oh, and a Ph.D. from Columbia in genetics. See, the problem is, this guy's got too many letters after his name—Emil Vallardo, M.D., Ph.D., OB-GYN. Doesn't ring half as nice as Vincent Rubio, PI. Mine sounds infinitely cooler, and would certainly make a hipper TV show.

"I so rarely entertain visitors," comes a voice from behind me, tinged with an accent, no doubt, though I can't figure out exactly which one. It's a European bouillabaisse. "The scientific life is a lonely one, yes?"

"Know all about it," I reply.

Dr. Vallardo, a big, beefy beast with a big, beefy grin, envelops my proffered hand in his and pumps my arm like an auto jack. His left hand is not as strong; it trembles madly, a victim perhaps of spot palsy. "Good to meet you," he says, and maybe there's some Dutch in there? His scent, a stew of anisette, pesticides, and cleansing creams, doesn't give me any clues as to his origin. "Would you like a coffee? Soda? Mineral water? Yes, yes?"

I beg off the drinks, though my throat is a little parched. "I'm a private investigator from LA," I tell him, and he nods rapidly, his shoulders hunching into peaked hills. "I have a few questions, won't take long."

"Yes, yes, so Barbara said. I'm more than happy to help out with . . . official matters, as always." The grin spreads wider, and—Lord have mercy—I do believe it is genuine. "Where should we begin?"

"Your work here . . . fascinating. Perhaps we should start with your experiments."

"My experiments." *Which of the millions?* his tone implies.

"Yes. Your *experiments*." Hard accent on the last word.

"Ah, yes. My *experiments*. Yes, yes."

I love speaking in vague generalities. It's much better exercise for the brain than simple, direct conversation. Dr. Vallardo squinches his nose—perhaps taking in a whiff of my old Cuban stogie scent—and plops into the seat behind his desk.

"There is no need to couch our terms. You may speak freely in here, Mr. . . . ."

"Rubio. Vincent Rubio."

"As I was saying, Mr. Rubio, we may be open in this office. Soundproofed, for various reasons. Yes, yes. Even if we were out in the hallway, we might speak freely. All of my support staff are . . . of our kind, and though I will see the occasional human obstetrics patient, most of my clients are dinos as well."

"Your receptionist—"

"Barbara."

"An Ornithomimus?"

He applauds, his cheeks rippling in genuine delight. "Yes! Yes! Very good! How did you know?"

"Part smell, part hunch. Get 'em all the time."

"Aha! Very nice. Very nice. Allow me to venture a guess . . ." He sizes me up, eyes roving, and if he says I'm a Compy, case be damned, I'll have to kill him. "You are no Sauropod, that is evident. Perhaps . . . a Chilantaisaur?"

He's flattering me, while at the same time acknowledging that I am not the grandest thing he's ever seen. Chilantaisaurs were the largest of the large, massive sentient mountains with decidedly little brain matter. One of the few species of dinosaurs to survive the Great Showers but die out before the Age of Man, the last Chilantaisaur passed into the great beyond nearly two million years ago. His name was Walter; at least, Walter is the closest English pronunciation to the series of whoops and roars he would have been known by in days of yore. Walter's remains, preserved these eons by sharp dino archivists, can be found on display in the anteroom of World Council headquarters in Greenland. I was there only two years ago, and let me tell you, that Walter is one fortunate Chilantaisaur to have died out when he did. He would have had a hell of a time outfitting himself in the modern era, let alone finding anything to slim down those hips.

Dr. Vallardo amends his guess, correctly assuming that I am a Raptor. Then, getting back to the subject, he says, "So you want to know about my experiments. You don't happen to be a Council member, do you?"

"I was."

"Yes?" Distrust now, and a whiff of dislike.

"Stress the past tense," I say. "This is unrelated, I assure you. Nothing we discuss will be forwarded to them."

"I see," says Dr. Vallardo, and for the first time, I notice a crack in that cheery façade. Then it's back up again, all smiles and chuckles. "No problem whatsoever. Always happy to oblige. Yes, yes."

I stand, move behind my chair. It's time to check out the laboratory. "Shall we?"

He didn't expect this so soon in the interview. Flustered, he clambers to his feet. Triceratops, as a rule, are not the swiftest of our kind, but Dr. Vallardo is moving more lethargically than his race would indicate. "Is there a problem?" I ask.

"No problem," says Vallardo, his body alternately moving toward the door and toward his intercom. "I am unprepared to leave the office, that is all."

"Unprepared?"

"I have . . . men. Dinos. They follow me."

Oh no. "Are you saying that you're being followed?" The last thing I need is another case with a paranoid schizophrenic for a witness—don't ask, don't ask.

Vallardo chuckles, shakes his head. "I want them to follow me, Mr. Rubio. For lack of a better term, they are my bodyguards."

Since when does a doctor need bodyguards? "Since when does a doctor need bodyguards?"

"Since the Council leaked the first report on my genetics work," he says, more than a hint of condemnation snaking between each word. "Some members of the dino population were not pleased with my results."

Quickly, then, almost as if he doesn't mean to do it, Dr. Vallardo pulls aside the collar of his shirt and bares a long, wide scar, still healing, an obvious claw mark to those who know how to spot these things. "This is the most recent attack," he says. "A female Raptor who screamed that I was a sinner even as she was reaching for the death blow. A sinner, she called me. In this day and age. Yes . . ."

Releasing any Council-gathered information before an official decision has been made, and before the subject of the investigation can be notified, is a strict no-no, and though I had heard that someone on the NYMC was guilty of lip-flapping, I'd had no idea it had come to this. Once again, I assure the Nobel shortlist geneticist that there is no way that the Council will ever release any information he sees fit to give me this day. I do not tell him that this is because I would sooner live the rest of my life as an outcast than rejoin that group of hypocrites.

A few moments after Vallardo buzzes his receptionist, we are joined by two Brontosaurs in human guise, introduced to me as Frank and Peter. Their costumes designate them as twins, and so far as I can tell from their comparable enormity, they may very well have been actual littermates as well. The evolutionary process that shrank the rest of us dinosaurs into somewhat manageable heights— some of us too manageable—didn't have as much an effect on Brontosaurs, resulting in their current status as the largest dinosaurs on earth. It is no wonder that so many of them play for the National Football League.

Our quartet ready, we set out for the laboratory.

Dr. Vallardo's assigned area inside the Cook Medical Center is deceptive in its size, a tricky optical illusion. At first glance, it is nothing more than a pedestrian suite, comprised mainly of the waiting room, a few examining rooms, and his private office. But through a sliding door behind Barbara's counter, down a claustrophobic hallway, and beyond a series of key-coded metallic portals, lies a budget-busting research center that renders obsolete anything I have ever seen on *Star Trek*.

I am appreciably awed, and Dr. Vallardo does not seem surprised. "Yes, yes, I can see you like it," he says. Pulling at my arm now, his own excitement feeding off mine in a synergy of anticipation, Dr. Vallardo draws me farther into the heart of the operation. Frank and Peter, unmoved, follow right behind.

Aside from the buzzing and the beeping and the whooshing, aside from the spinning and the shooting and the swirling, aside from the beakers and the test tubes and the flasks, I am most taken aback by the scientists. Dozens of them, over a hundred, lined up in rows, bent at the waist like plastic straws, eyes attached to microscopes, to petri dishes, to seed samples. Chalk up one work-intensive environment. It's Manny's, only higher-tech and with better air-conditioning.

"This is my laboratory," Dr. Vallardo says expansively, relishing the opportunity to show off his work space. I, for one, am most willing to be awed by any office sixteen thousand times the size of my own. Where does he get the bread to support this kind of an operation?

"It's beautiful," I say.

He leads me down a row of white-coated scientists scurrying like lab rats between their contraptions, experimenting away, taking off but a second to greet their patron, and then back to work, cracking that self-imposed whip. We approach a bespectacled young man, the duck's-ass hairdo on his guise a humorous attempt to evoke nostalgia for the days of James Dean and early Brando. Must be a Fanjutsu model, like the Jayne Mansfield look-alike they rolled out a few years back. Retro is the hip guise look these days; I've been thinking about adding chest hair—Attachment 513, Connery Style #2—and gold chains to mine. It might complement my mustache, which, I might add, I haven't gotten one negative comment on the entire day.

Introductions are made all around, and it takes two minutes to assure Dr. Gordon—the young scientist—that I am not going to leak information to the Council. Obviously, they've all been under a bit of stress as of late.

"Dr. Gordon is working on the protein transfer for the second receptor site," Dr. Vallardo explains, the scientific gibberish twisting my mind like an old dishcloth. "He's figured out a way to use the cytosine from one strand, and—"

"Whoa, whoa, Doc, wait up." My head hurts already, and I've only been down here for a minute.

"Am I going too quickly?" asks the doctor.

"You could say that." The fact that he's going at all is too much for me to handle. "Can I get this in layman's terms?"

"Have you not read my work before?" he says.

"Sorry to say I haven't. I pretty much got the basics down and that's all."

Dr. Vallardo mulls this over, his bushy eyebrows working like squirming larvae atop his brow. "Come, come," he says, some decision clearly made, and we take our leave of the scientist, who is more than happy to get back to work.

Vallardo leads me through the laboratory and down a set of stairs, saying, "I have been known to . . . how do you say it . . . talk over people." He unlocks another sliding door, and it swishes open. "All these years of schooling and seclusion amongst scientists will do that, yes, yes."

"It's not that," I say, though it partially is. "I was looking for an overview of your work, mainly. Broad strokes."

"Yes, yes. Then perhaps this will be more suitable."

The corridor we enter is paneled wall-to-wall, floor-to-ceiling, in rows of fluorescent tubing, each pulsing with a pale purple glow. Dr. Vallardo steps into the middle of the hallway and raises his arms, pirouetting like a ballerina. Frank and Peter join in, and the sight of these two behemoths dancing *The Nutcracker* nearly breaks me down into hysteria.

"Low-level ultraviolet," Dr. Vallardo explains, urging me to follow the leader. "Kills off surface bacteria. We tried stronger doses, but it made everyone rather ill, yes, yes."

How reassuring. I reluctantly raise my arms and sync up with Vallardo, Frank, and Peter in their surreal dance.

After the curtain call, we emerge from the other end of the corridor disinfected and ready for action. "In a moment I will close the door behind us," Dr. Vallardo tells me—I get the idea Frank and Peter have heard it all before—"and the lights will go out. You will be able to see nothing, but do not worry, this is normal, yes. Another door will open, and I will lead you through it. That one, too, will close, and for some time, it will be quite dark, yes? So stay absolutely still and you won't run into anything. Light levels are low, and for a reason."

I nod. "Ready when you are."

With an electric pop, the lights blow out. I hear the swish of yet another sliding door, and feel a strong hand at my elbow. I am led forward a few feet, and can sense a breeze as the door slips closed behind us. We wait.

"You're right, Doc. I can't see a thing." We have stepped out of the Cook Medical Center and into the Black Hole of Calcutta.

"Give it time," Dr. Vallardo says. "You'll see soon enough, yes, yes."

Still nothing. Nothing. Nothing. Oh . . . maybe . . . a grapefruit glow, balancing between yellow and pink, waist level, but far away . . . and there's another one, more of a homestyle orange juice radiance . . . and another, and another. Slowly, hundreds of small, glowing boxes shimmer into existence, eventually making enough of an impression on my optic nerves for me to finally figure out exactly what I'm standing in: an incubation chamber.

"The different lights you see—the varying colors, hues, shades—are all by-products of the chemical and heating factors of each incubator." Dr. Vallardo leads me around the room, showing off his creations. "The blue ones, for example, are for the most recently fertilized eggs. We won't push them up to the yellow and orange lights for another three weeks. Then, of course, after we've ascertained that we have achieved fertilization, we can move them into a warmer environment, yes . . ."

As Dr. Vallardo prattles on, I find myself searching for evidence of a hoax, looking for the strings on the flying magician's back. Despite all I have read about Dr. Vallardo and his work, my first inclination tends toward disbelief. It was all easy enough to accept while sitting in a Council meeting in a basement clear across the country—okay, there's a doctor in New York who says he can mix the different genes of dino races and produce mixed offspring, and what are we going to do about it if it comes to Los Angeles? But back then it was a policy decision, to be based solely on what would be the best course of action to protect the public interest in such a hypothetical situation, but now, inside this chamber, I feel a more visceral reaction, the consequences slamming home deep within my own reproductive organs.

Every incubator contains an egg, no two alike, their size and shape varying from baseball to football to basketball, but each clearly a dino egg nevertheless. A complex series of clamps and rubber padding sporadically spins each egg in its bed, lifting it up, turning it over, and gently placing it down again. A small monitor attached to the top of each incubator reads off what I assume to be vital signs, though I can't imagine that a just-fertilized specimen would have many vital signs from which to take a measurement.

The entire scene is reminiscent of a singularly ridiculous movie that came out in the theaters a few years back and did tremendous business at the box office; the humans went to see it to confirm their worst fears about our kind, and we dinos went to see it to confirm our worst fears that we are indeed the humans' worst fears and that we would be wiped off the face of the planet the minute we should choose to announce our presence, so it's not surprising that the movie sucked up a lot of money all around. The basic concept of the film, as far as I can remember, involved a human scientist using fossilized DNA—ha!—to create a whole mess of dinosaurs and keep us captive on an island somewhere in the South Pacific, ostensibly to create an amusement park, only we manage to get loose and kill all the humans in sight without forethought as to why or what they would taste like.

Rubbish, the whole thing, especially the way we poor Raptors were portrayed. We can be dangerous, yes, but we do not kill indiscriminately, and I've never known a one of us to kill a human for no good reason. Then again, dragging us up from the depths of a test tube and locking us in cages like wild beasts might be good reason at that.

I realize it's all just fun and games, celluloid fantasies for a mindless human population who could never in their wildest dreams imagine seeing a real live dinosaur, let alone believe that one could run a criminal investigation, process film, serve drinks at the Dine-O-Mat, or head up the world's leading generic drug corporation, but it doesn't make the whole matter any less offensive.

But there I go again, getting worked up, when my whole

point is that the one thing—the only thing—the film got right was the incredible financial burden one would have to work under in order to run about splicing DNA, messing with the whole genetic code, all to bring even a single dinosaur egg through incubation. Since the guy in the movie had business contacts up the wazoo, and as the setup Dr. Vallardo has down here is a heck of a lot more incredible in its scope and depth, I find myself wondering once again where he finds the money for his research. This time, I ask him.

"Private donors, mostly," he says. "I cannot use hospital funds, of course, as many of the trustees are human, yes, but I have been able to secure the work space from a few friends of mine on the board."

"Private donors such as . . . ?"

Dr. Vallardo shakes his finger at me. "Then they would not be so private, yes?"

"May I conjecture?"

"Another hunch?"

"Educated guess."

He shrugs, turns to inspect an egg. "I cannot stop you from guessing, can I?"

Nope. "Was Donovan Burke a contributor?"

"Who?"

"Donovan—Burke." I am sure to enunciate.

He shrugs. "The name does not sound familiar. I have many contributors, most in small donations, too many to remember by name."

"He was also a patient of yours about two years ago," I say. "A male Raptor."

Dr. Vallardo makes a good show of trying to recall a name from his past, eyes glancing up, fingers scratching chin, but I don't buy it for a second. "No," he says, shaking his head, "I do not recall a patient by that name."

"His fiancée was a Coleophysis, name of Jaycee Holden."

Again, the head shake, and again, I don't believe him. "They came in for treatments, you say?"

"I didn't say, but yes, they did."

"Yes, yes . . . I have no recollection. There are so many."

"Probably not big contributors, then."

"Probably not."

"What about Dr. Nadel?"

"Kevin Nadel?"

Ring out the bells—the doctor's admitting to something. "Yes, the county coroner. Was he a contributor?"

"I don't believe so."

"But you know him."

"We went to medical school together, yes? An old friend. But he works for the government—there is little money to be made."

"So maybe you gave him some cash."

"I do not loan money to friends."

"Maybe it wasn't a loan."

"Are you trying to make a point?" he asks, and I decide to let the matter slide before he gets the two Brontos to shove me into a glass box and toss me from the building.

"Let's move on," I say. Time for the big show, everybody take your places. "Was Raymond McBride a contributor?"

Fortunately, Dr. Vallardo had removed his hands from the bowling-ball–sized egg he had been handling, or that particular experiment might have ended with a crush of shell and a splatter of yolk. He calls over to his body-guards, busy inspecting the smaller eggs—"Frank, Peter, could you wait outside?"

The twin Brontosaurs oblige, slipping out through the double-lock doors. Dr. Vallardo waits until they leave, and then turns back, his face straining to hold its good cheer.

"You have spoken with him?" he asks, and from across the room I can hear his teeth grinding. "Before he passed on, that is?"

I expected a reaction, but not one this juicy. I'll have to squeeze it, work out the pulp. "I've spoken with his wife," I say, mustering all the insinuation I can. "We had a long talk. She told me a lot."

He's not falling for it.

"Mr. McBride, rest his soul, was a contributor, yes. A rather public one, in fact. He supported my work fully, yes, yes."

"Fully. . . . So are we talking thousands? Hundreds of thousands? Millions?"

"I'm afraid I can't release that."

"Even if I ask real nice?"

"Even if you beg."

Face-off. Don't flinch. Contest of the wills. This is the way I prefer my battles. Staring contest—first one to blink loses.

Darn. Not fair—I have congenital eye dryness. Okay, so at least I've confirmed that McBride was a contributor, even if I don't have the exact amounts.

"Why would Raymond McBride fund the efforts of a scientist whose work holds nothing for him?" I ask. "Both he and Mrs. McBride are Carnotaurs. They had no need of your treatments."

"How can I comment on a dead man's thoughts?" he says. "Perhaps he wanted to help dinosaur society as a whole, yes, yes."

"Do you think Raymond McBride was murdered by someone who didn't approve of his funding your projects?"

"I have no idea why Mr. McBride was murdered. If I did, I would have gone to the police, yes."

"But is it *possible*," I say, too many recent nights of late night television due to daytime unemployment forcing this Court TV blather out of my mouth, "that Mr. McBride was murdered because of his involvement with your work?"

A deep sigh—I find that I am getting more and more of these from witnesses recently—and he says, "Anything is possible, Mr. Rubio. Anything." This whole time, Vallardo's smile hasn't slipped. It's a costume grin that's getting to me, and I wouldn't be surprised to find out that it's a new guise attachment from the Nanjutsu Corporation—Attachment 418, Perpetual Cheer. There's a wall somewhere in this doctor's brain, strong and thick, and it's going to be a bitch to sledgehammer that baby down. But maybe, just maybe, I can go around it.

I move across the room, forcing my steps into a carefree saunter, casually inspecting the incubators as I go. *No problems here,* this walk is supposed to announce, *everyone relax.* As I delve deeper into the chamber, I find a section of eggs clearly more developed than the rest. They are the senior class of Dr. Vallardo's incubation room, the ones who drive the cool cars and get all the chicks, light pods in their boxes suffusing them with a deep red glow, bordering on brown. Crayola would call it Burnt Umber and be done with it.

"What's this one?" I ask, pointing to an oblong shell. "It's bigger than the others."

With a beam of fatherly pride, Dr. Vallardo snaps on a set of rubber gloves and gently strokes the egg's delicate casing. "This is Philip," he says, his voice a soft coo. "Philip has come farther along than any of our others."

"But he hasn't even hatched yet."

"Of course not," says Dr. Vallardo, still massaging Philip's shell. "We're nowhere near that stage."

"But I heard—"

"—an incorrect report," he finishes for me. "You must be referring to the rumor that I brought an egg to term, yes? As of yet, I have not been quite that fortunate. Innuendo goes a long way."

Sure does. At the Council meeting, they had reported it as fact: Dr. Emil Vallardo had created a live mixed child, though its component parts were unknown. I usually have little cause to doubt Council reports, but if Dr. Vallardo had indeed brought a mixed child to term, why wouldn't he take the credit for something he's been trying for decades to accomplish?

"How long before Philip here comes out of his shell?" I ask.

"If he comes out at all," Vallardo says, "the struggle won't begin for another three weeks or so. He's almost fully formed, but now he needs his strength, yes." Then, turning on a secondary light, a regular twenty-five-watt bulb recessed into the incubator's side, he asks me, "Would you like to see him?"

All in the name of science. "Please."

Dr. Vallardo delicately maneuvers the delicate egg toward the bulb—that left hand of his still trembling—handling it like a young child given permission to hold his mother's favorite porcelain doll. The shell is thinner than I had assumed, and as it comes to rest against the light, a shadowy silhouette appears, floating comfortably in the center of the egg, surrounded by a chalky milkshake plasma.

"If you look closely over here"—he points to the larger, more rounded side of the egg—"you can see the ridged frill around Philip's head, yes."

"Looks like a Trike top."

"Yes, yes, Philip is the product of a Triceratops father and a Diplodocus mother."

Trike father—could this be his child? Physician, help thyself conceive? "Are you married?" I ask.

"I know what you're thinking, Mr. Rubio, and no, the egg is not mine. But it is my brother's. Philip will be my nephew, yes, yes."

Whatever his lineage, Philip is going to be one big boy if he ever breaks out of that shell. Trikes are large enough already without Diplodocus genes amplifying things. Or maybe it doesn't work that way. I have no idea, and to be honest, I don't want to get embroiled in a two-day conference on the matter, either.

But I can see those Diplodod lines in young (very young) Philip, the soft curves of the back, the rounded head, melding and merging with the Triceratopical bony plates that are already beginning to form on Philip's not-yet-infant hide. The tail, too short for a Diplodocus, too long for a Triceratops, is coiled like a Slinky beneath the fetal body, ready to unfurl sometime within the next three weeks. The legs, too, are both long and stocky, a perfect blend of the two creatures, and I find myself wondering what kind of life Philip will lead if he makes it into the world alive: Will he be heralded as a wonder or as a freak?

Which reminds me—"Dr. Vallardo," I say, drawing him closer, making my tone as conversational and nonconfrontational as possible, "are you the only one engaged in this type of research?"

Now he's truly confused; this is no put-on. "As far as I know. Yes, yes, I would say I am the only one."

"No rumors, no reports of renegade scientists, working outside the boundaries of accepted science?" I'm sounding kooky, looney-tunes, and I know it. There is, though, a point in the near future.

Dr. Vallardo shakes his head vehemently, spittle

grenades launching themselves around the lab. "I assure you, I would know of any such research."

"What about random mutation? Could it produce . . . well, something like Philip here?"

A chuckle. "Impossible. Mutations are indeed what drive evolution, Mr. Rubio, but they may not circumvent nature."

"That's your job, right?" Dr. Vallardo says nothing, and now it's time to go fishing. "What if I told you," I begin, stepping out onto the thin ice, ready to test the waters, "that some friends on the New York Council told me of some reports of mixed . . . creatures . . . on the streets of New York. Sightings—"

"What kinds of sightings?" he asks, the quick query betraying his interest.

"We've had a few different reports," I lie. "One woman claimed to have seen an Allosaur with a Hadro bill."

No response from the doctor. I move on.

"Another Council member was told—get this—of a fully grown Bronto with Ankylosaur spikes. Silly, isn't it?"

"Yes, yes, quite."

"Then the last one—really, I shouldn't even waste your time with this—"

"No, no," he says, and I'm thrilled I finally got him to say something other than yes, yes. "Go on."

"It's a bit muddled, actually. I spoke with the poor guy myself, and lemme tell you, I've never seen a Raptor this pale before. Frightened right outta his guise. Seems he'd been in a fight, attacked, no less, by a dino—and let me point out that this is how he put it, not my terms, mind you—a dino straight from the depths of hell."

"Oh my," says Dr. Vallardo.

"Oh my, indeed. Most likely a fruitcake, but lemme give

you the whole bit. He said this thing had the tail of a Stegosaur—big ol' spikes and all—the claws of a Raptor— I'd take off my gloves for a visual demonstration, but you get the idea—the teeth of a Tyrannosaur—many, and large—and the length of a Diplodocus. That would be long, of course. Now have you ever heard anything so insane? My guess is he'd been tossing back a few at the local basil bar."

I am laughing. Dr. Vallardo is not. "Where was it?" he asks.

"The attack?"

"The attack, the creature."

"Does that make a difference?"

"No—no—of course not," he stammers, and I can feel myself slipping around that mental wall already. "Curiosity."

"Said there was an alley, lots of graffiti there. One of the poorer areas of town, I guess."

"The Bronx?" says Dr. Vallardo, a mixture of hope and denial creasing the wrinkles around his eyes. Aha—maybe now I have a borough in which to search for that health clinic.

"The Bronx," I say, "Brooklyn, Queens, I don't even think the guy knew where he was. You've seen one blurry alleyway . . ."

"Yes, yes. You are probably right. He must have been drunk."

"Wasted outta his mind, that's my guess. He sounded pretty convincing, though, describing the ugly thing. Wooo, Creature from the Black Lagoon." Interesting note here: The more often I poke fun at that thing from the alley, the more upset Dr. Vallardo seems to become. There's a definite causal relationship between my jabs and his blood pressure. I try a new one: "Betcha if we ever found the thing we could get a lotta money for it from the traveling circus."

I may be pushing it now; Dr. Vallardo's guise skin is turning blue, which means the geneticist is practically purple beneath that costume. Neat trick, but I'd better calm him down before a stroke pops him out of the world and out of my case. "Hey, what the heck, you say it can't be, it can't be. You say there's no mutant dino-creatures roaming New York City, then there ain't any mutant dino-creatures roaming New York City. You're the doctor in the know, right? The man with the genetic plan."

He blinks, slowly getting himself under control. The blue tint leaves the guise, which eventually returns to a medically acceptable shade of beige. "Um . . . yes. Yes." He's winded from the effort.

Now I remember why I used to love this job.

Dr. Vallardo suggests we take our leave of the incubation chamber—". . . the eggs need their rest, yes . . ."—and I am more than willing to follow him back upstairs. My fishing expedition has paid off well; I've got a few more minnows in my boat than I did at the start, and though I don't know how Dr. Vallardo fits onto the fisherman's platter, at least now I'm pretty sure he's one of the side dishes.

As I prepare to take my leave, I toss out a few more questions about Dr. Vallardo's work, scientific points he can clarify with a host of technical mumbo jumbo that will leave him in a good mood once I have departed. I may wish to return to the geneticist's laboratory in the near future, and if I expect to be allowed easy access once again, I can't have him calling Council headquarters to complain about my visit as soon as I take off.

"It has truly been an honor," I fawn, "a big honor. Big."

"Please, it was nothing, yes."

"No, really, quite the experience. I understand much more now." I tap my notebook, making a big show of waving it around the office. Little does he know it contains nothing but a few notes on the Evolution Club fire, the words *Judith, J. C.,* and *Mama,* and a couple of partially erased erotic sketches I made of the stewardess on the flight over.

We say good-bye and part ways. But I am no more than three steps down the hall when I hear him jogging up to me—the sound as ugly as the sight must be—and feel a rough hand upon my shoulder.

"What happened to your friend?" he asks me, and for a moment I have absolutely no idea what he's talking about.

"The one who was attacked?" I say.

"Yes, what happened to him?"

"As far as I know, he's seeing a therapist."

"Ah. Yes, yes . . ." We stand in the hallway, both of us silent. He's gearing up for something, but I refuse to speak until he does. Then, preceded by a throat-clearing grunt, comes the question Dr. Vallardo truly wanted to ask— "And the . . . creature? The dino mix?"

"Yes . . . ?" I know what he wants.

"What . . . what happened to it?"

I could lie and say it limped into the night, bleeding but otherwise healthy, or claim to have no knowledge of the situation whatsoever, but I am so darned curious to finally see a true emotion on Dr. Vallardo's face that I can't help but tell him the truth.

"You'd have to ask the cleanup crews," I say. "They usually handle the skeletons."

I tell you, it was a Kodak moment.

11

It's nearing rush hour as I leave the Cook Medical Center, and the cabs shoot by, unconcerned with my outstretched arm. What the hell—everyone else in this town is a willing pedestrian, and as I'm feeling paunchy around the midsection, I figure I could stand to do a little bit of walking. I secure directions from a candy striper in the lobby and set out on the road. The journey back to the Plaza will take a little longer this way, sure, but maybe I'll get some time to think about the case, go over it in my head, see if I can spot any inconsistencies. At the very least, I'll save a fin on cab fare.

I have just returned to the beginning, ready to mentally replay the scene at the Evolution Club on the Betamax of my brain, when a sleek Lincoln Town Car pulls up beside me. I would think nothing of this, except for the fact that it continues to stay by my side, puttering along at five miles an hour. It's going to get horrible mileage that way.

There's no way to get a good look at the driver; the windows have been tinted mine-shaft black, far beyond the boundaries of the law and good taste, making identification impossible. I'm getting a bad feeling about this, but I get bad feelings about everything. Maybe his car is breaking down. Maybe he's lost. Maybe the driver simply needs directions, and assumes that since I'm walking, I must be a native. Maybe I'm just paranoid.

I'm not. A moment later, I am flanked by two dinos gussied up in their best Sunday guises. Neither is much larger than I, but the message I'm receiving from their less-than-gentle way of grasping my elbows tells me I should probably listen up.

"You wanna get in the car?" asks the one on my left, reeking of Old Spice and stale helium. Something familiar there.

"Thanks for the offer," I say, "but I was just getting the hang of walking around."

I'm trying to catch the eyes of the other pedestrians on the street in order to send out a warning, a danger signal. But though we're surrounded on all sides by the civic-minded citizens of New York City, not a one looks me in the face; every nose is pointed down, every speed control set to full throttle.

"I think you'll enjoy a nice car ride." This comes from the dino on my right—bigger than his partner, but his scent is nothing more than a weak dose of children's cough medicine. Hardly threatening, kinda fruity.

I glance over again at the Town Car, its tinted windows, its gleaming hubcaps, its brand-new paint job—Intimidation Black, Color 008—and reaffirm my decision to keep walking. A little faster, maybe . . .

Still keeping pace with me, Old Spice places an arm around my shoulder. Were I watching this from a distance, I'd take it as a friendly gesture, a frat-boy hug of camaraderie and good cheer. But that arm is not so benign— he's pulled back one of the latex fingertips on his costume glove, and I can feel the claw beneath poking earnestly at my tender neck. That's why the smell is so familiar—deodorant and chewing gum—these are the goons from the park, the ones who killed Nadel.

"Do a lotta bicycling?" I say.

"I'm gonna ask you one more time real nice," mumbles the assassin, his breath pounding into my ear, "and then I'll have to drop you. Get in the car."

Okay, okay, I get in the car. Ernie's Rule #5: Dead dicks can't investigate.

We drive along for some time in complete silence. The driver, who I cannot see very well due to a gauze partition between the front and rear of the automobile, refuses to turn on the radio. At the very least, they could entertain me with some tunes. The two thugs who muscled me into the Town Car sit to either side of me, and despite the roomy backseat, our shoulders are pressed tightly together.

"My legs are falling asleep," I say.

My dinonappers don't seem to care. We drive on. "You know," I say, "this just struck me—we haven't been formally introduced. Maybe you've got the wrong guy."

"Nah, we got the right guy," says Cough Medicine. "Ain't two dinos named Vincent Rubio who smell like a Cuban cigar."

I squint in confusion, furrowing my brow until the muscles are ready to pop. "Vincent Rubio? See, I knew you had it all mixed up. I'm Vladimir Rubio. From Minsk."

The dumber one appears to mull it over for a moment before Old Spice craps on my party. "Don't listen to the little shit. He's Rubio, all right."

"You got me," I confess, "you got me. So . . . now you boys know my name, but I don't know yours."

"Oh yeah," says Cough Medicine. "I'm Englebert, and this is Harry—"

Old Spice whacks us both in the back of our heads, bringing a burp out of me and a whimper out of Cough Medicine. "The both of you, shut up," he says, and we promptly follow orders.

It is some time before the hard lines of the city give way to the flowing curves of nature, trees and flowers and shrubbery replacing lampposts, traffic lights, and street vendors. The scents change as well, and I am amazed at how empty the air smells, like a one-thousand-piece jigsaw puzzle with six crucial pieces missing. It's been a while since I've been out of a city—LA, New York, or otherwise—and I'm always rendered a little disoriented by the loss of the piquant odor of smog. In some ways, it's a homing beacon, a signal to the land that I love.

As we move into the countryside, Old Spice reaches beneath the seat in front of him and pulls out a paper shopping bag. "Put this over your head," he says, and hands it over, handles first.

"You must be joking."

"I sound like I'm joking?"

"I don't know," I say. "I've only known you about thirty minutes."

"And you ain't gonna know me much longer 'less you put the bag over your head." Obviously, he never learned the maxim that you can catch more flies with honey. My legs are still asleep.

I reluctantly don my improvised headgear, and all those pretty trees disappear. At least I still have my sense of smell.

"Almost forgot," grunts Old Spice. I hear him rummaging through his pockets, change jingling, keys jangling, and a moment later he slaps something in my left hand. I run my fingers over it, trying to make out the shape—long and thin, two sides, both wood, connected to each other by a twisted metal wire, shaped like an alligator's mouth, only without the teeth. One side opens when you squeeze the other side closed . . .

"Clip it on him," Old Spice tells his partner. "Clip it on tight."

With a Medium Brown Bag from Bloomingdale's over my head and a clothespin clamped shut on my nose, we continue to streak through the countryside. Or so I assume. With my two best senses temporarily on injured reserve, we could have doubled back around toward the city for all I know. My sense of time is beginning to fade, as well—the rest of the drive could be an hour or a day, and I'd have no idea. I only hope that once this bag comes off my head, I don't find myself in Georgia, where there may or may not be a warrant out for my arrest—don't ask, don't ask.

My ears have escaped unmolested, though, and after some time, I can hear a buzz-saw snore coming from my left, low but gaining volume. Old Spice is asleep, and about to broadcast it to the world. A little while later, the car slows, and there's the unmistakable clink of three coins sliding into an automatic counter. The car speeds up again.

Ten minutes later, I hear a cow.

Five minutes after that, the pungent aroma of a landfill makes its way past the clothespin barrier, works its way through my nostrils, and slams hard into the olfactory recognition center of my brain. I gasp involuntarily at the eye-watering whiff, and Old Spice wakes from his slumber—his snores transforming into snorts, sneezes, a cavalcade of novelty-store sounds—and languidly reaffixes the clothespin, shutting out the last vestiges of stench.

We're in New Jersey.

Some time later we pull to a stop. This has happened once or twice before, but this time I'm told to get out of the car.

More than happy to oblige, I practically leap out of the backseat, my cramped, tingling legs eager to get in some good stretching.

"Should I take the bag off my head?"

"That would not be wise." Harry grabs my left arm, Englebert my right, as they lead me across a bumpy terrain. My feet send back covert signals—we are walking on a dirt road, littered with loose gravel.

A few minutes later, we break into a clearing. Already I am formulating a plan of attack and escape, should it become necessary. I refuse to die with a Bloomingdale's bag over my head.

"Close your eyes," Harry tells me, and for once I decide not to follow his instructions.

Ouch! Light—bright light—stabbing—eyes on fire, eyes on fire! I slam my lids back down, drawing the shades on my damaged peepers. Harry laughs at me, and Englebert halfheartedly joins in.

"My eyes! What'd you do to my eyes?"

Whap! Another slap on the back of my head. "Quit whining," says Harry. "I took the bag off your head, that's all. It's bright out here, you moron."

Eyes adjusting now, red streaks fading from my corneas. The clearing slowly comes into view, and it's mostly how I pictured it: a rough circle of emptiness hewn out of the surrounding vegetation, the canopy overhead filtering out much of the sunlight, but not enough to give my weary eyes a rest. The one feature I hadn't guessed at is most prominent, though, sitting as it is in the dead center of the clearing: a log cabin, small but sturdy, just like good ol' Abe Lincoln would have made. For all I know, he did.

Harry gives me a little shove, a football pat on my rump. "Go on," he says.

"In there?"

"Yeah, in there."

"Can I take the clothespin off my nose?"

"No."

As I walk toward the cabin, breathing heavily through my mouth, I notice that neither Harry nor Englebert is following me. I'm a good thirty yards ahead of them now, and in theory I could make a break for it—burst across the clearing like a gazelle and crawl madly to safety through the underbrush. Call the cops, alert them to the situation, and live to tell the tale on the talk show of my choosing.

Unfortunately, while I am quite the feisty badger when it comes to burrowing, my speed has always been closer to that of a chubby dachshund than that of a gazelle. Even if I were able to outrun the two lugs behind me, there stands a good chance that they'd be carrying long-range weapons that could drop me in a second no matter how finely tuned my burrowing skills might be. I decide to enter the cabin.

Just my luck, there are no lights inside. Between Vallardo's incubation chamber and the Bloomie's bag, my visual spectrum today has gone from bright to dark to brighter to darker, and my peepers are getting a real workout trying to keep up. I stand in the doorway for a moment, allowing the outside light to stream in, before a female voice—low, insistent—says, "Close the door."

I comply, and find myself in darkness yet again. "Your eyes will adjust," says the voice. "Until that point, I have a few things to say. I ask you to remain quiet until I am done. Is that understood?"

I know a trick question when I hear one. Following orders, I keep my trap shut. "Very good," she says. "This may not be so difficult after all."

Shadows coming into view now—a stove, a chair, a fireplace perhaps, and a long, lithe form standing among it all.

"I understand you are here on business," says the shadow, a thick tail slowly distinguishing itself amid the other silhouettes. "And I can respect that. We all have jobs to do, and we all do them to the best of our abilities. You would be remiss in your duties were you to give your work anything other than the full attention you have bestowed upon it thus far."

And now there's a neck, a long, graceful swan curve—arms, small but toned—almond-shaped eyes riding high above two ripe-plum cheeks. "I also understand that you are from Los Angeles," she says, "and though you may be under the impression that you are used to life in a megalopolis, though you may think you know how to conduct yourself and your business in the big city, I want you to get it through your mind that LA is a playpen compared to the Big Apple. What is acceptable at the mother's breast is not acceptable in the nursery.

"I've brought you out here for your own good, not for mine. In fact, I've already saved your life on two occasions. Disbelieve this if you choose to, but it is the truth."

A Coleophysis, no doubt about it, and a stunner at that. Each of her six toes is the perfect length, the perfect circumference, the webbing between bearing not a blemish. And her tail—that tail! oh!—twice again as thick as mine and forty times as dear. I only wish this damned clothespin were off so that I could breathe deeply of her scent.

She says, "I would be lying if I said that I didn't . . . understand your work. But if you persist with all of these questions, this investigation . . . There is only so much I can do to protect you. Do you understand?"

"I understand your points," I say, my eyes finally finished with their lethargic adjustments, "though I don't necessarily agree with them."

"I didn't think you would."

"I also don't understand why you're dragging me into a cabin in Jersey. You coulda sent a telegram."

"None of this concerns you," says the Coleophysis. "But unlike some others, I don't believe you should get hurt."

"Aside from a scrape with Harry and Englebert back there, I haven't had much danger at all. You know that thug of yours threatened to rip my throat out?"

"They told you their names, did they?" Lips puckered, clearly unhappy.

I shrug. "You don't just pick Englebert outta the air."

"Tell me something," she says, coming closer, hot breath on my throat. "Why do you find it necessary to stir up trouble?"

"Am I stirring? I thought it was more of a shake."

A pause. Will she kiss me or spit at me? Neither—the Coleophysis backs away. "You went to see Dr. Emil Vallardo, is that correct?"

"Considering your goons picked me up outside the medical center, I'd say you know it's correct." Without asking permission—enough with the permission—I squat up and down, up and down, trying to get feeling back in my legs. The Coleo pays my impromptu workout no mind.

"They're not my goons." Then, a moment later: "Dr. Vallardo is a twisted man, Vincent. Brilliant, but twisted. It would be better if you left him to work on his bastardization of nature by himself."

"I gather you don't approve," I say.

"I've seen his work. Firsthand." She pulls up a chair and lowers herself onto the seat. "You've also been bothering Judith McBride."

How does she know all this? Have I been followed since I stepped off the plane? It's distressing to learn that I've been so disoriented by the city that I haven't even been able to spot a tail despite my paranoia. Quick 360s are a regular routine anytime I move through the city; it's an in-grained action for me, like checking the rearview mirror of a car. Heck, I usually check for tails even when I'm in the shower.

"I haven't been bothering," I reply. "I've been interviewing."

A hard stare, and she pulls out a chair for me. "Please, sit." I give up my squats and plop down across the way. I notice that she hasn't mentioned my run-in with the dino-amalgamation in the alley behind the health clinic, but I figure she's either working up to that, or her spies were slacking off on the job that night.

The Coleo takes my hand in hers, and a tingle runs through my guise, up my arm, and stops my heart. Strangely enough, it feels nice. A moment later, it pounds back into action. "The fire at the Evolution Club was a horrible thing," she says to me, and from the glow in her eyes and the soft tones padding each word in cotton, I can tell she really means it. "Dinos died, and that was wrong. Donovan was hurt, and that was horrible. Horrible. And I understand your concern over your partner's death, as well. But it was all an accident. Can you understand that?"

I ask, "Were you there that night? When Ernie died?"

"No."

"What about in LA—at the club?"

"No." And even without my nose to send me clues, I can sense she's telling the truth on both counts. "But I know that what happened was not supposed to happen. Not in the ways it did."

"Fine. What was supposed to happen?"

A head shake, a hand toss—"This is my whole point, Vincent. You have to stop asking questions. You have to leave New York tonight and forget about it."

"I can't do that."

"You have to."

"I understand. I won't."

I can't tell if she's chuckling or crying—her head has fallen into her arms, her body racked with shoulder shudders and full-scale convulsions, easily a sobbing fit or laughing jag—but I take the break in the conversation to stretch again. All this sitting is wearing me out, and my hide is growing clammy beneath my guise.

She arises, her eyes glistening with tears—still no decision on that laughing or crying thing—and shakes her head, forfeiting the conversation. I wouldn't be surprised if there was a sigh in there, too. "I've done all I can," she says. "I can't protect you any more."

"I know," I say, even as part of me wonders why I'm not giving in, going home, and saving my skinny hide. Protection is usually a good thing, and it's only because I feel so close to something so big that I'm still in it at this stage of the game.

The Coleo says, "Is this job more important than your life, Mr. Rubio?"

I think it over, and she lets me take my time. My answer, slow in coming, is out of my mouth before I realize how true it is. "Right now, this job is my life."

She understands, and doesn't press the matter. I am glad. I look at my watch—it's getting late, and now that I'm pretty sure I'm not going to be whacked out in the middle of New Jersey, fatigue has begun to set in. My muscles ache to be released from their confines, already anticipating a nice hot soak back in the hotel bath.

"Are we almost done?" I ask, pointing to my watch. "I hate to be rude, but . . ."

"One more question," says the Coleo. "And then I'll have Harry and Englebert take you back to your hotel."

"Shoot."

"It's a personal question."

"No kisses on the first kidnapping."

"I know you went to the hospital to see Donovan," she says, and the way she says the burned Raptor's name—the tidal swell on the first syllable, the lilt on the next two—tells me she knew him once upon a time.

"I did."

"Tell me . . ." And then a hitch, a snap in her voice. She doesn't want to ask the question, perhaps because she doesn't want to know the answer. "Tell me, how is he doing?"

That pleading look in her eyes, the one that says *tell me everything's okay, tell me he's in no pain,* sets in motion a train of thought I never knew I had on the tracks: She's a Coleophysis—she's been watching me from the shadows—she has experience with Dr. Vallardo—she had her goons clip my nose so that I couldn't imprint her scent on my mind and thus find her again—she has remained out of sight, and wants to continue that way—but most of all, most important, she is still very much in love with Donovan Burke.

Even after all these years.

"He's looking swell," I lie, and the elusive Jaycee Holden smiles. "He's doing just great."

The bag is over my head again, though I've spent the last ten minutes protesting the decision, on the basis that since I already know where we are, there's no use in keeping me blinded in this fashion.

"Orders is orders," grumbles Harry.

"The lady told you to drive me back to the hotel. I was there, I heard her, she said nothing about the bag." Indeed, Jaycee had instructed the two dinos to return me to the

Plaza safe and sound, and as quickly as possible. She emphasized this last part, as if she had some reason to feel they would act otherwise, and the dinos grudgingly acquiesced.

There is a grunt from the driver, whom I have yet to see, and Harry leans forward, mumbling something I cannot understand. Englebert has been closed-lipped the entire time, and his earlier willingness to play along with me has disappeared. I consider piping up again, perhaps asking that the air-conditioning be turned higher, but decide to sit back and play it cool for a while, to use the extra time to sort things out in my head.

I'm running over the connections one by one—Vallardo knew McBride, Nadel, Donovan, Jaycee—Judith McBride knew them all plus Sarah—Sarah slept with McBride and had a short interview with Ernie—Nadel ran autopsies on both McBride and Ernie—Nadel was killed by these two dinos sitting next to me—

And I notice that the surface of the road has changed. We're off the highway, off any form of pavement whatsoever, and onto a soft shoulder. Dirt kicking up behind the tires, car moving slowly now as it digs for purchase.

I put a hand on the bag—"Where are we?"

And my hand is roughly batted away. "None of your freaking business."

Brambles and branches scrape against the side of the car, and despite my lack of knowledge regarding the Tri-State area, I'm quite sure this isn't the way back to Manhattan.

"You fellas made a wrong turn," I say.

"No we didn't—did we, Harry?"

"No."

"I'm pretty sure you did. Ms. Holden told you to take me back to the Plaza, and this isn't Park Ave."

Harry leans close, pressing his forehead up against the

bag, my ear and his lips separated only by a thin sheet of brown paper. "We don't take our orders from that bitch."

I know what this means even before I hear the snap of buttons, the zing of claws extending, locking into place. I know that I will never be brought back to my hotel room. They are planning to kill me, right here and right now.

With a mighty heave from my legs, I launch myself backward, into Englebert, my hands ripping away the bag over my eyes even as they tear away at the buttons that hold my gloves in place—

"Hold him!" Harry screams. "Get the—"

But I'm a slippery little eel, sliding behind the confused Englebert, pushing him in front of me like a shield. My gloves are sticking too well—no time to unsnap them properly—so I let my claws fly free, the sharp edges tearing through the soft latex fingertips, my weapons slicing up and through these useless human hands.

A tail slams into the seat next to me, nearly ripping the cushion in half, and I scoot back against the Town Car door, propping my feet against the window—it's come down to kill or be killed again, and I'm ready to play. Mustering all my strength, I hurl myself into the warm bodies of my attackers. The driver looks back, worried, slowing the car. The scent of battle is overwhelming, a rich blend of fear and anger.

We're balled in a heap of claws and growls, none of us able to free up our limbs, no time or chance to remove our masks, spit out our bridges. Harry's tail is free, but flails about wildly—if he tries to strike me, he'll hit himself as well, so I hold on to his body, scratching away at the eyes, the ears, any soft tissue I can find. Blood and sweat coat the inside of the car—Englebert's tangled up with us as well, and I think his claws might actually be digging into Harry's side—

"Give—give it up—" pants Harry—"you—ain't—gonna win—"

And the rest falls into a roar as I find some hidden reserve of energy, flipping the Brontosaur up and over, slamming him face first into the passenger seat. I reach back with my right claw, muscles taking control, ready to end it here and now—and an electric burst of pain, four sharp syringes of agony, shoots through my rib cage. Behind me, Englebert's claws come away coated with my blood.

I spin, arms outstretched, momentum carrying them in a wide circle—not knowing where the blow will land, not really caring as long as my claws hit something, anything.

They tear through the driver's neck.

The car shoots down the unpaved road as the driver slumps against the steering wheel, his foot a dead weight against the gas pedal. The sound is ferocious now, and I cannot distinguish the growling from the screaming from the roaring from the rumble of the engine as the claws continue to fly and the blood continues to pour and the flesh continues to vanish beneath the furious assault and as I come up for air I get a glimpse out of the windshield of the giant tree ahead of us looming closer with every second and as I fall back into the tangle of shredded human guises and dino flesh—

We crash.

It is a dream of sorts, though I am well aware that I'm lying on the floor of the Town Car, blood covering my body, claw still extended, one arm buried in the ripped passenger seat in front of me. In this . . . hallucination, let's call it, a young human woman approaches the car—the same young woman from the last few dreams, in fact—and stares down at my prone body. I try to wave, try to blink, try to signal that I need help of some sort, but it is of no use. She opens the car door and my head falls out, banging roughly against the door frame. I am unable to move. Apprehension increases.

I am powerless to do anything but watch as this woman, whose features are clear but whose overall face is still obscured by that glowing light that comprises her hair, leans over me like a mother tucking in her child at night. Our eyes meet, and I can see my reflection within them. She smiles, and my nerves subside. Wordlessly, her mouth opens, heading toward mine. A kiss in the making, and I am unable to pucker. Lips parting, tongue snaking out—

And she licks up the blood covering my face, slurping it down with a smirk upon her lips. I scream and, once again, pass out.

The driver is dead. Harry is also dead. Englebert is not, though he is unconscious, and will probably remain that way for a few more hours. All three of them were thrown through the windshield of the car when we hit that big old oak, and I can't thank the Lincoln people enough that they made their front seats sufficiently sturdy to withstand the force of a Velociraptor propelled forward at sixty miles an hour. My guess is that this is not a standard safety test.

I awoke on the rear floor of the Town Car, just as in my dream, covered in blood, some mine, some not, and stumbled out onto the soft ground. It has taken me some time since to regain my bearings. The highway is nearby; I can faintly make out engine noise and horns in the distance. As usual, my first order of business is to clear the scene, and though it takes me some time, I manage to reguise Harry and Englebert, taking great pains to manually retract their claws and replace their gloves. If for some reason Englebert is unable to deal with the situation once he awakens, or should he croak from his considerable injuries, I can't take the risk of a human coming across a bunch of half-guised dead dinosaurs in the middle of New Jersey.

I'm hoping that a quick search of the Town Car will give me some clue as to who ordered the hit on me. But the trunk is empty, the glove compartment similarly so, except for the standard pink slips. Even the registration doesn't help; the owner is listed as Sam Donavano, an unfamiliar name. A quick search of the dead driver produces a wallet and a smattering of identification cards—sure enough, it's Mr. Donavano himself.

My own costume, though ripped, is certainly salvage-able and, as long as I can clean off some of the bodily flu-ids, should suffice on the trip back into the city. I'm able to hold off the more insistent geysers of blood with a tourni-quet made from Harry's shirt, and I'm glad that this time I don't have to waste any of my own clothing for medical supplies. It's going to take some time to pick up a ride back to the city—even if I weren't a little bloody, I'm limping and dragging my poor abused body along like a consum-mate drifter—and the sun is beginning its plunge toward the horizon. Darkness will only help obscure me, though, and obscuration is what I need right now, in spades. I sit down near the oak tree and try to remain awake.

The plan is simple: I will wait for nightfall, and I will re-turn to the city and to the relative safety of my hotel room. Then I will get undressed, lie down on that cloud of a bed, and complete my trifecta of slumber for the day by passing out for a third and final time.

That is, if no one else tries to kill me.

No rest for the wicked. I have no sooner arrived back at the hotel room, removed my guise, taken a much-needed shower, sewn up more gaping holes in the pseudoflesh, reguised, and begun to dress for bed before there is a knock at the door. I waddle over, penguin-like, pulling a pair of pants up and around my hips, and peek through the peephole. Can't be too careful, what with folks trying to kill me and all.

It's the concierge, a pleasant fellow named Alfonse whom I had the pleasure of meeting this morning on my way out of the hotel. I open the door.

"Good evening, Mr. Rubio," he says, bowing slightly at the waist. "I'm sorry to trouble you."

"No trouble." I pause. "Unless you're here to tell me there's trouble."

"Oh no, sir. You have a message, sir."

I glance toward the phone; the message indicator is not lit. Alfonse must understand, as he says, "I chose to deliver it by hand, Mr. Rubio, at the request of the lady who delivered it to me."

A lady, eh? Alfonse places a small pink envelope in my outstretched palm, and I trade him for a five-dollar bill. Pleased, the concierge thanks me, bids me a good evening, and departs. I close the door and sit on the bed.

The envelope is scented with a strong perfume, which tells me right away it's a human that sent it. Sarah.

Dear Mr. Rubio, the letter reads, *I would be grateful if you would accompany me to the theater and dinner this evening. They always give me Halloween off, and rather than play dress-up, I would prefer to spend my night off with someone as interesting as you may prove to be. If you are able to join me, please arrive at the Prince Edward Theater no later than 7:30 P.M. I hope to see you there, and remain Yours Truly, Sarah Archer.*

In my rule book, it's illegal to turn down a dinner offer from a dame, especially when she's also a suspect. But Sarah Archer . . . she's interesting—intriguing even—and I can't help feeling drawn to her in some way, even though the rest of her kind give me the shakes. As it is, logic's been out the window since I got to New York, and though I'm treading in thick water, I choose to go with my instinct.

Downstairs, Alfonse gives me directions to the Prince Edward, which—surprise—consists of him hailing a taxi-cab to take me there. I'm decked out in the one suit I brought with me, a well-made ensemble of black and gray pinstripes, and while it might not have come from the rafters of Rodeo, I think it looks darned nice over my guise. I hand another fiver to Alfonse, he shuts the door, and the cab shoots off toward the heart of the theater dis-trict. I haven't had any time to stock up on basil, and I find that though I'm fresh out, the lack of herbs doesn't inspire in me the panic it once did. I'm sure I'll find a hit some-where, sometime.

"Prince Edward?" the taxi driver asks me. His accent is pure New York, not a trace of foreign inflection.

"Meeting someone there," I explain.

"You seeing that show?"

"That show? The show at the Prince Edward, yes."

"Weird fucking show," says the cabbie, shaking his head back and forth. "That's what they tell me—weird fucking show."

I arrive alive and intact at the Prince Edward ten minutes ahead of schedule, giving me ample time to peruse the crowd. A surprising number of dinos here—at least half the audience is of our kind, I estimate, and that's much higher than the national average of 10 to 12 percent. Odd, but I imagine it's either a fluke of statistics or that the show has been produced by one of our kind.

I wait on the curb like a nervous teenager waiting for his prom date, growing more apprehensive with every passing minute that Sarah will not show. Has she stood me up? The other patrons have filed inside, and I'm sure the show is about to begin. I look around, peer into the darkness for a car, a limousine, any sign of Sarah. Nothing.

"Mr. Rubio?" It's not Sarah's voice, but it's calling my name, and that's a start. I turn to find the ticket taker, the poor thing so hypoglycemic she's almost see-through. "Are you Vincent Rubio?" I tell her that I am, and she says, "Your ladyfriend called, said she's running a little late. Your ticket was at will-call, so . . . here." I am handed a ticket, ushered through the doors, and into my seat—third row, center, between a group of Asian businessmen and an elderly couple who already look bored.

The theater is decked out in jungle paraphernalia, leafy trees and papier-mâché caves plastered onto the walls. Tiger-striped and leopard-spotted fabric drape the stage, ambient roars and elephant trumpets fill the air, and whereas the motif might work in the dinner theaters of rural Santa Barbara, it's downright pathetic here on the Great White Way. The curtains are closed, the audience buzzing, and an illuminated sign, thirty feet long and fifteen feet tall, hangs proudly from the rafters.

It reads: MANIMAL, THE MUSICAL! And I know I'm in for a long, long night.

I have to admit, I was a big fan of *Manimal,* the TV show, back in '83. I got a kick out of watching Dr. Jonathan Chase battle crime, getting all heated up and turning into jungle animals at the drop of a hat, but I must have been the only one, as the show lasted about three months before it was canceled and left in the dumping grounds of low-budget, high-concept television. But even the most die-hard of *Manimal* fans couldn't sit through two and a half hours of a half man/half leopard crime solver singing and dancing his way through a drug-smuggling investigation.

The first song is called "Incredible Leopard Man, I Love You," with lyrics such as *Yes I knew you were part feline / so for you I made a beeline,* and it's at this point of the evening that I decide to turn off my brain, as its services are no longer needed.

Twenty minutes pass, during which time I am treated to two more musical numbers and a four-legged tap dance, when I feel a tap on my shoulder.

"Is this seat taken?" comes a whisper, and I turn, ready to defend the empty seat with all the valor I can muster while wedged into these cushions.

"Actually, it—" And then I see the reams of red hair cascading over bare shoulders, a bright yellow cocktail dress that announces its presence from clear across town, and a familiar figure packed into it all. My heart pounds against the muscles of my chest like King Kong beating his cage. "It's saved for a friend," I say.

Sarah casually lowers herself into the cushioned seat and leans over, whispering into my ear. It tickles. "Would your friend mind if I took her seat?"

"I don't think so," I respond, keeping my voice even as I try to bring my heart rate back to normal. "I really only met her yesterday."

"And she's already a friend?"

I shrug. "She must be. She asked me to the theater."

"She has house seats." She crosses her legs, adjusts the skirt. "What'd I miss?"

Forcing myself into a library whisper, I attempt to catch Sarah up on the main plot points of *Manimal: The Musical*. Trouble is, there aren't many. "Let's see . . . we've got this guy running around, he's human, but he's also a cat. And there are some smugglers."

We silently endure a series of songs about leopards, lions, badgers, drug smuggling (*Buy an ounce or buy a pound / cocaine makes the world go round*), and more leopards, and eventually it all winds up before intermission with a particularly morose Dr. Chase lamenting his woeful state as a creature of two worlds. The audience applauds— Sarah and I mindlessly follow along—and the houselights flick on. Fifteen minutes to get in a good stretch before the second act.

"Would you like a drink?" I ask. "I can bring you something from the bar."

Sarah shakes her head. "They won't let you drink in the theater. I'll come with."

By the time we make our way out of the lower orchestra—human men are leering, soaking in Sarah all the way and though she's not my species I'm still walking tall—the few bars in the Prince Edward are packed with throngs of theatergoers already half in the bag, anxious to get a different perspective on the second half of this opus. Sarah and I step to the end of the line, behind a dino couple guised up as an elderly husband and wife. Their smells—a fireplace, redwood logs burning steadily—are nearly indistinguishable from one another, and though I know it's just an old dino's tale that the scents of a husband and wife become more and more similar over the years, every day I find empirical evidence leading me to believe it.

The elderly couple turn around—they must have picked up on my scent—and nod their heads at me, a friendly how-do-you-do that we dinos occasionally give to others of our kind like a classic car owner honking at a fellow enthusiast who's also driving by in a 1973 Mustang Fastback. But then they see Sarah—and then they smell Sarah, or, more correctly, then they *don't* smell Sarah—and the smiles fade, replaced instantly by grimaces of revulsion.

She's a witness! I want to scream, *Maybe a friend, but nothing more!* Then again, I don't want to protest too much.

"The line is long," I say, searching for something, anything to break the silence.

"Sure is," says Sarah. "If we wait for our drinks, we probably won't make it back to the theater in time to catch the beginning of the second act."

"Yeah. Yeah. Wouldn't want to miss that."

"So you like it?" she asks, seductively twisting her skirt with a petite fist.

"The show? Of course. He's a man, he's an animal . . . he's a Manimal. How can you miss?"

"Ah." She seems disappointed.

"You?"

"Oh, sure. Sure. I mean, what's not to like, right? You've got leopards, and . . ."

"And tigers," I chime in.

"Right. And tigers."

We're lying. Both of us. And we both know it.

Giggling, we run hand in hand across the lobby, down the stairs, and out of the Prince Edward like two school-children playing hooky for the very first time.

An hour later we're still chuckling away, the most infectious part of the laughter having died out fifteen minutes ago. For a while there we were in trouble, one giggling jag setting off the fuse of another, neither of us able to control ourselves long enough to order from the menu at a small Greek tavern we found near the theater. Eventually, I was forced to bite my tongue, cutting off the laughter but nearly replacing it with tears and a trip to the hospital—one of my caps had come loose, and my naturally spiked tooth jammed into my tongue with a force I wasn't expecting. Fortunately, I was able to fake a bathroom emergency, fix my tooth, ensure that my tongue wasn't going to flop out of my mouth and onto Sarah's lap during the course of dinner, and make it back to the table in time for a second run at the menu. Now we wait, we talk, and we drink.

"No, no—" Sarah takes a sip of her wine, her lips leaving a precious red imprint on the glass, "it's not that. I can see where *someone* would like it."

"But not you."

"Not me. Anthropomorphism is nice and all—"

"Big word, ma'am—"

"—but it's hard for me to accept a whole society populated by humanoid felines, operating under some obscure self-imposed rules, running around undetected by the rest of us."

"Not realistic?"

"No, not entertaining."

Our appetizers arrive, and we nibble on hummus, *tzatziki,* and *tarama,* lapping up the dip with wide slabs of pita. Our waiter is as Greek as they come—for this Halloween eve, he has dressed as Zorba in an open-backed vest—and he reads off the day's specials with gusto, each word a meal unto itself. Sarah asks for help with her selection, and I suggest the Greek Platter, figuring I can always pick at whatever she isn't able to eat.

I even go so far as to gingerly pick as much basil and dill from my portions as possible, the action almost automatic, fork dipping and removing before I have a chance to regulate the movement. Whatever we're doing now—Sarah and me—somehow feels right, and this is the first time in a long time that I don't feel the need to chew an herb. For her part, Sarah asks for my helpings of basil to be added to her plate, and since it won't affect her like it would me, I'm glad to oblige.

Squinting into the dim light of the restaurant, Sarah carefully scrutinizes my face, her forehead rumpling into precious little foothills. Her eyes roam my features, dropping around my nose, my lips, my chin.

"Do I have food on my face?" I say, suddenly self-conscious. I rapidly wipe my chin and lips with my napkin, flicking the cloth around and around, hoping to soak up whatever Greek delicacy has managed to moonlight as a facial.

"It's not that," she giggles. "It's . . . I mean . . . the mustache."

"You don't like it?"

Sarah must see my injured look, as she comes back quickly with, "No, no, I like it! I do! It's just that when I saw you . . . what, last night . . . you were clean shaven."

I have no response to this. Costume additions are usually meant to be attached step-by-step in order to give the impression of a natural process—the Nanjutsu Pectoral series, which I considered buying during my vainglorious years, for example, must be slowly built up over a series of months—but mustaches, as far as I know, have always been a one-day journey into machismo.

"It's fake, right?"

"Of course not!" I reply indignantly. "It's just as real as the rest of my body."

Sarah, giggling again, impulsively leans forward and tugs hard on my facial hair. This wouldn't usually hurt, but the light layer of epoxy beneath my mask transfers her yank to my hide beneath, and my "Ouch!" is genuine.

Embarrassed, abashed, Sarah turns away, melting into a sanguine flush. "I'm so sorry," she says. "I really thought . . ."

"We grow hair fast in my family," I say, trying to bring our previous light soufflé tone back into the conversation. "My mother was a terrier."

Sarah laughs at this, and I am pleased to see her chagrin get up and excuse itself from the table. "If you don't like it," I continue, "I can shave it off."

"Really, I like it. Promise." She crosses her heart with a slim finger.

We eat some more. We drink some more. We chat.

"How is the case going?" she asks, refilling her wine glass as she talks.

"Is this a business dinner?"

"Not if you don't want it to be."

Is this a come-on? I play it safe. "No, no, it's fine. Case still wide open. Leads, leads, leads, that's the PI's life. Put it together, hit frappe, and see what spins out."

Sarah finishes off the bottle of wine—good god, can she drink—and orders up another. "You still haven't interviewed me yet," she points out. "Not really."

"It's not polite to grill your date."

"Is this a date?" she asks.

"Not if you don't want it to be."

We smile at the same time, and Sarah leans across the table and pecks me on the forehead. She leans back, dress clinging tightly to her bosom. Soft swells of flesh rise up from the neckline, nipples standing at attention, and I find a strange desire to . . . to touch them? Impossible. I think of the pile of bills waiting for me back in Los Angeles, and the illicit thoughts burst apart and vanish.

"I'd rather we get down to it now," she continues. "Ask me what you need to ask me. I don't want you thinking things about me that aren't true or not thinking things about me that are true."

"You know my case is about Mr. McBride. Raymond. It's not—not really—but close enough."

"I know."

"And you feel comfortable talking about him?" Usually I could give a shit over how witnesses feel—I think of that annoying Compy, Suarez, and my stomach turns in knots—but I allow myself a few special dispensations now and again.

"Ask away," says Sarah. The waiter pops over with a second bottle of wine, and Sarah doesn't bother inspecting the label, sniffing the cork, or tasting the sample before bolting it down by the glassful.

With no notebook handy, I'll have to make do with memory. "How long had you known Mr. McBride? Before . . ."

She appears to think it over. Then—"A few years. Two, maybe three."

"And you met . . . how?"

A wistful look clouds her eyes and her fingers crawl aimlessly about her neckline, drawing my attention down, down, down . . . "At that charity event," she says. "In the country."

"Which country?"

"The country. As in the countryside. Long Island, I think, maybe Connecticut."

Doesn't matter. "And Raymond was hosting?"

"He and his . . . wife"—again, some serious animosity there, the words scorching the surrounding air—"were throwing it at their second home."

The questions come quicker, easier, fluttering off my slightly damaged tongue. "Why were you there?"

"My agent took me. It was a charity event. I was being charitable."

"But you don't remember the charity."

"Correct." She clumsily places a finger on her nose with one hand and points at me with the other. Drunkard move, but cute.

"Fine. So there you are hobnobbing with the rich and famous—"

"Mostly rich. I don't think I saw anyone all that famous."

"Just a phrase. So you meet Raymond that night . . ."

"Daytime," she corrects, and now I'm oh for two. "It was a long affair, if I remember correctly. I arrived in the early afternoon, and didn't leave until the next day. Everyone stayed over at the house."

"You hit it off right away?"

"I wouldn't say right away, but it was obvious something was there. The wife and I got along well that day, actually. By the next morning, we hated each other."

File that. "Did you sleep with Raymond that night?"

I can almost hear the SLAP! and see the welts forming as my offhand question smacks into Sarah's stunned face. I didn't mean it that way. I wasn't thinking. It was stupid, it was dumb, but I'm too aghast at my own words to voice any regret. This is not the first time my runaway mouth has shattered fragile circumstances—once the PI part of me gets turned in a certain direction, the gas gets floored and the power steering goes out, which is great if I'm on a straightaway—but if there's a cliff in front of me, so long Vincent.

Sarah's response is low, pained, the voice of a young girl huddling in a corner who doesn't understand why she's being punished. "Is that how you see me?" she asks.

"No, no, I—"

"Talk to a man once and then sleep with him?"

"That's not what I—"

"Because if you do see me that way, I don't want to disappoint you. You wanna leave the restaurant, go home and lay me, okay, let's go." Anger flooding her eyes now, spilling over onto the table, washing out the restaurant. She leaps to her feet unsteadily and pulls at my arm. "Get on up, boy, and let's go home and see how you can put it to me." Patrons turning, listening, eager to get an earful and enrich their workaday lives. I can almost smell the rancor on her.

I place my hand over hers, trying to restore tranquillity to our once-idyllic table for two. "Please," I say, "I didn't mean it like that." Slow subsidence of the anger waves now, flowing away, back out to sea, look out for the undertow. "Please. I get ahead of myself sometimes. It comes with the job."

Two glasses of wine and a few more dips of *tzatziki* later, Sarah accepts my apologies. "No," she says pointedly, returning to the conversation. "I did not sleep with him that night."

"I gathered that."

"I won't say I didn't find him attractive, though. That strong, weathered face, creased with those deep lines—wrinkles that let you know he'd *been* somewhere. Long, tight muscles, broad shoulders . . . On the outside, Raymond was a very durable man. Not physically, mind you, but mentally. Emotionally."

"And on the inside?"

"You wouldn't see the inside unless you knew him well, and then you learned what made Raymond . . . Raymond. He had some interesting peculiarities, some more endearing than others. I doubt anyone other than myself and maybe his wife knew Raymond as he really, truly was."

Should I tell her that her beloved Raymond was widely known as a philanderer? That he'd seen more mattresses than Inspector Number 7? That while she might have been the last of his lovers, she was surely not his only one? But what would be the point in that, other than to hurt the girl—I've already gotten in my quota of stinging remarks today. Perhaps I am jealous of McBride, of his willingness to flaunt societal constraints, of his desires for the forbidden, which were obviously so much stronger than mine. But this kind of thinking is both destructive and completely moronic, and so I snip it off at the source.

". . . but even if he had been interested at the time," Sarah is saying, "I was in a relationship."

"With whom?"

"With my agent."

"Your agent? Is that wise, mixing business and pleasure?"

"Sometimes it's best," says Sarah, and I'm both glad and

troubled to see she's moved away from anger, back toward seduction. Anger wasn't fun, but easier to handle. "In this case, no, it wasn't wise. We broke up soon after the party, in fact. Which left me out of a relationship and Raymond still in one."

"Judith."

Sarah waves off the name with an annoyed flick of her hand, as if swatting away a bothersome fly. "We didn't call her that. We called her missus, plain and simple. Missus. It was better for me, it was better for Raymond."

"Was he still in love with her?"

In the time it takes Sarah to begin her answer, the waiter arrives with our entrées. My Lemon Chicken is well prepared, but Sarah's Greek Platter looks positively scrumptious. Fortunately, I'm sure she won't finish it all, and then I can peck away.

The waiter trots off, and we hunker down, tearing into our dinners like Compys come upon a fresh kill. I am not surprised at my appetite—it's been over twelve hours since I've had anything substantial, and although my breakfast this morning was a feast fit for the roundest of royals, I'm famished.

What I am surprised at is Sarah's ability to make food disappear off her plate in what has got to be Guinness time. Moussaka, Chicken Olympia, Pastisio, some eggplant dish I've never heard of before—I watch in growing amazement as each forkful enters that darling mouth, only to emerge empty a moment later and return to the plate for more. My word, where does it all go? Under the table? Into a roving dog? But I can see the long lines of her throat swallowing, so I know she's ingesting every bite. How does that platter of food, which probably weighs more than the model herself, vanish into that body? There is some twisted perversion of the laws of nature going down in this Greek tavern, a clash of food and antifood, but I'll be damned if I can figure out how it's working. If I hadn't had the disappearance of Jaycee Holden solved for me today, I'd think that maybe Sarah had eaten her.

I am unable to talk. I can only watch. Wow. Wow.

Ten minutes later, Sarah is finished with dinner and my jaw is agape.

"Hungry?" I ask.

"Not anymore."

I should hope not. Sarah pushes her plate away, and despite the prodigious amounts she's recently ingested, I can't make out a bulge anywhere on that tummy. People like Sarah evoke a lot of hatred from the body-conscious all around the world, but I'm too astounded to feel jealous over metabolic rates. "Where were we?" I ask, honestly forgetting. That display of concentrated consumption put me off my track.

"You asked if Raymond was still in love with the missus," says Sarah, using the title to refer to Judith McBride, "and I hadn't yet answered."

"Well then . . . was he?"

Again, she pauses, though I would think that she'd had enough time to ponder her answer while digesting the whole of Greece. Of course, it probably takes a good portion of one's brain power to shovel it down like that. "Have you ever had an affair, Vincent?"

"With a married woman?"

"Yes, with a married woman."

"I have not." I came close, though. I'd been tailing a Bronto's wife, trying to get the usual incriminating photos, and found that although she was not currently engaged in an extramarital affair, she was most interested to get one started. She'd caught me snapping pictures outside her bedroom window, and the next thing I knew, I was sipping champagne in the Jacuzzi to the strains of vintage Tom Jones. I had to wait until she'd gone back in the house to slip out of her guise and "into some skin more comfortable" before I could make my getaway.

"Married people are just that," Sarah tells me. "Married. You can't ask if a married man who is having an affair is still in love with his wife, because it's a question without a point. It is immaterial whether or not he loves her, because she is his wife, plain and simple."

I pick at my dinner, mulling over her viewpoint and my next question. "How often did you see him?"

"Often."

"Two, three times a week?"

"By the end? More like five or six. He'd try to spend Sundays with the missus, but by that point she wasn't very interested."

"So she knew?"

Sarah snickers derisively as she leans over and plucks a lemon potato off my plate. "Oh, she knew. She's not a dumb lady, I'll give her that much. You'd have to be a real piece of granite not to notice something like that. Working late, every weeknight? Sure, Raymond was a driven man, but no one puts in eighteen-hour days at the office for nine months straight.

"I think the missus got the picture after the first month or so, because Raymond started to loosen up on the telephone. Calling me by my name, not screwing around with code words. Before that it was all cloak-and-dagger, and I could tell when she walked into the room because he'd start calling me Bernie and talking about the great round of golf we'd played the other day. And I hate golf. All my life I've been surrounded by golfers. Please tell me you've never played golf."

"Twice."

"You poor soul."

"Raymond loved that damn game. We'd be in Paris, taking in the spring air, walking through the Arab Quarter, stopping in the shops, talking to the people, and he'd be practicing his swing, wondering what kind of club he'd use if he had to hit a ball over that storefront and into the window of that church. Fourth-tier Eiffel Tower was a nine wood, by the way."

"He took you to Paris, then?"

"Paris, Milan, Tokyo, all the hot spots around the globe. Oh, we were quite the jet-setting couple. Surprised you didn't see us in some social column."

"I don't read much. *TV Guide* sometimes."

"Pictures in all the international magazines, Raymond McBride and his traveling companion. They never mentioned his wife, and they never made a deal over it. That's the one good thing about Europeans—to them, adultery is like cheese. Options are plentiful and varied, only occasionally accompanied by a stench."

The rumors, then, were true: McBride had lost his mind. This well-known Carnotaur had obviously flipped out, flaunting his human girlfriend to the world, even going so far as to let magazines link them romantically. And while the International Councils are not quite as stringent about sexual mores as are the American Councils, cross-mating is still verboten across the globe. All it takes is one slipup from any of us, from the smallest Compy in the smallest district of Liechtenstein, and the last hundred and thirty million years of a persecution-free environment could all be over. Not including the Middle Ages, of course. Dragons, my ass . . .

"Did he offer to marry you?"

"Like I said, he was married to the missus and that's that. I assume they had some sort of arrangement."

"Arrangement?"

"He slept with me, she slept with whomever she slept with." Sarah is glancing about the other tables, looking for more alcohol.

"So you think Jud—Mrs. McBride—was having an affair as well?"

"Think?" Sarah tosses her head, clears some cobwebs, and I have to stop her from motioning toward our waiter-turned-sommelier. " 'Course she was having an affair. She was having an affair before I ever came along, that's for sure."

I should be shocked, I know, but I can't dredge up the proper emotion. "Did you know the guy she was sleeping with?"

A head shake, a nod, and I can't tell if Sarah's answering me or about to drop off into sleep. "Yeah . . ." she murmurs. "That damn . . . nightclub manager."

Score one up for Vincent Rubio. My initial queries into the nature of Donovan and Judith's relationship, questions that clearly had put Judith on edge, will have to be brought up again the next time I see Mrs. McBride. Obliquely, of course, and with all tact, and if that doesn't work, directly and rudely.

"Sarah," I ask, "did you know Donovan Burke?"

"Hm . . . ?"

"Donovan Burke—did you know him? Did you know Jaycee Holden, his girlfriend?"

But Sarah's head is drooping now, tottering in all the cardinal directions, balancing precariously atop that long neck, and no recognizable answer is forthcoming. The wine is finally wielding its power, taking its toll despite the six tons of Greek food mopping it up in her stomach. "He wanted to see his children so badly," Sarah whimpers, on the verge of tears.

"Who wanted to see his children?"

"Raymond. He wanted children more than any other man I've known."

She's rambling now, muttering words I can't make out, but I have to pursue this a little longer. I lift Sarah's head, force her to watch my lips. "Why didn't he have children?" I ask her, making sure to enunciate clearly. "Was it Mrs. McBride? She didn't want kids?"

Sarah flails her arms, tossing my hand from her face. "Not her!" she yells, drawing attention from the general public for the third time this evening. "He wanted to have them with *me*. With me . . ." She trails off, sobs wracking her body.

No wonder she's such a wreck—this poor girl lived the last few years of her life under the delusion that she would eventually carry Raymond McBride's child, never knowing that such a thing was a physical impossibility. Who knows what other lies he told her? And the fact that McBride was so involved in it as well leads me to believe that perhaps he did indeed have Dressler's Syndrome, as many have surmised, that he had truly begun to think of himself as human, unable to distinguish his daily deception from the reality within.

The combination of wine and painful memories has made an emotional invalid out of Sarah Archer, and I feel honor-bound to make sure she returns back home safely. "Let's go," I say, tossing a hundred dollars on the table to cover the cost of dinner, wine, and a sizable tip. With the exception of two twenties tucked into my sock, it's the last bit of cash I have in the world—I should pay with the Tru-Tel credit card, but at this point it's better that we exit, stage left, as soon as possible.

Dragging Sarah up and away from the table isn't as easy as I'd expected; she's not as heavy as the dino-mix I towed behind the Dumpster, but her drunken body machinations give her a lot more heft than her small form should allow. We stumble backward, Sarah slumped atop my lap like an oversized ventriloquist's dummy, and I grunt with exertion.

"Are we having fun yet?" Sarah asks, throwing her arms around my neck and hugging me close. This is easier, at the very least, though her proximity is causing some involuntary reactions that are inappropriate for both the location and the species. The other restaurant patrons are wholly involved in our struggle, having as they do box seats for the main event. I can see their faces grimace along with mine as I half-drag, half-support Sarah as we make our way toward the door. Ten feet away, no more, but it might as well be a mile.

The waiters are approaching, offering their help, holding open doors for us, anxious, I assume, to conclude this evening's entertainment, and I'm more than happy to accept their aid. We emerge from the tavern into the torpid Indian-summer air, the humidity wreaking havoc on my makeup, and I glance about the street for the nearest bench. We wobble over to a bus stop covered in advertisements (which have themselves been covered with graffiti), and I let Sarah plop onto the hard wooden slats. Her skirt hikes up even higher than before, betraying a hint of sun-drenched yellow panties.

"Stay here," I say, pulling her skirt down into a more modest position. "Don't go anywhere."

Sarah grabs my wrist, holds it tight. "Don't leave," she says. "Everyone leaves."

"I need to find us a cab," I tell her.

"Don't leave," she repeats.

Straddling the bus stop, one foot on the bench, one foot in the street, my wrist still enveloped in Sarah's hands, I wave my free arm like an SOS flag, hoping that a taxi will emerge from the darkness and rescue us. Sarah has begun to sing, a muddied conglomeration of words, word fragments, and scatting, her song carrying across the busy city street and into the night. That rich contralto, layered with evident training, is strong through the haze of drink, and I'm surprised at the clarity of the melody despite the fractured lyrics.

Five minutes later, we are still taxi-free, and Sarah's song dribbles to a halt. She releases my wrist and falls silent. The hubbub of traffic drifts away as well, the rest of the world dropping out, vanishing, leaving only a single streetlight illuminating a bus bench, a gorgeous woman, and the Velociraptor standing guard over her.

"Your voice . . ." I whisper. "It's incredible."

Her only response is to look up at me—a feat, considering how that head must be spinning—and smile tightly. The streetlight makes golden droplets from the tears in her eyes, and all I can think to do is kiss them away. I kneel down, my lips nearing her eyes, nearing her cheeks, and suddenly I can taste the saltwater, I can taste the pain, and I can't stop it, I'm no longer in control as my mouth slides across her skin, slipping through the tears, slowly, gaining speed, searching out her lips, the soft flesh sizzling between us, moving, tongues roving, muted moans of need rumbling through our chests, a deep kiss that draws me in and blacks me out—

A taxi pulls up, honking.

"You wanna ride? You—lovebirds! You shaking your hand around before, you wanna ride?"

I may have to kill this man. Sarah and I break apart, the

stars slowly clearing from my vision. Sarah's eyes are still closed, though I suspect it's more from drowsiness than enduring pleasure.

"I don't got all night," calls the cabbie.

"One second!" I shout back.

"You don't gotta yell about it!"

Sarah is too far gone to help along as I lift her off the bench and onto my shoulder like a Neanderthal carrying his devoted wife across the plains. Already, I feel disgusted with my actions. My mouth and a human mouth . . . the possibilities for disease are tremendous.

"You got your hands full there," says the cabbie as I lower Sarah into the backseat. "Quite a hot little number."

I choose not to dignify his crude comment with a response and wriggle in next to Sarah, who has chosen this moment to completely pass out. Not good—I don't know the fair lady's address. A light slap on the face does no good, nor does a rough shake of the shoulders.

As I close the door of the cab, sealing us tight within its restrictive confines, the smell hits me—soft leather and canned dog food, a dino scent if I've ever smelled one. The cabbie turns in his seat, my Robusto-tinted odor hitting him at the same time.

"Hey," he says, "always good to have a fellow dino"— he pronounces it "diner"—"in my cab. Welcome aboard." He thrusts out a meaty paw.

"Shhhhh!" I caution, nodding toward Sarah. I needn't worry—she's kilometers from conscious—but you can never be too sure around humans.

"You mean she . . . No wonder I didn't smell—"

"Yes. Yes."

The cabbie wiggles his eyebrows at me, a lewd leer that says *I know what you're up to, you sly dog, you.* He confirms my suspicions by saying, a moment later, "Well,

well. If you're gonna do it, go all the way, that's what I say."

"That's not it. We're friends."

"Not what it looked like on that bench back there."

"Really, we—"

"Don't worry about me, pal, I won't say a thing. Damn Council fucks think they can run our lives, hell, I can't vote for all but one of 'em, and my guy's always getting pushed around." This moron is under the impression that the Council actually accomplishes things during their interminable weeklong meetings. Must be a Compy.

"No," I say, possibly more for my benefit than for his, "there's nothing going on."

He leans farther over the seat, nearly planting himself in my lap, and drops his voice to a whisper. "I know a buncha guys like you, and I tell you, I wish I had the guts. I see these broads walking around, and I got urges, too, right? Hey, I live dressed up like this most of my life, I get horny to feel the real thing, you know? But I was brought up real strict, I guess. Can't get past it in my head."

He's implying that my moral fiber is not up to snuff. I consider hitting him, taking Sarah out of the cab, calling the Council down on him for some minor infraction that I'll make up if I have to, but the truth is he's right. That one kiss—moment of weakness or not—proves it.

"But if I could get my hands on one of them real human asses . . . every dino's forbidden gamble, right?" He looks over at Sarah, practically slurping her in through his eyes. "And ooh, boy, have you hit the jackpot."

"Look," I say, gathering all the indignation I can from my withered supply, "there is nothing between us. Nothing. Sorry to ruin your wet dream. Can we go now?"

The cabbie narrows his lids, grits his teeth, temples pulsing—is he going to pop me one?—then shrugs, turns back around, and slams the gearshift into drive with a karate chop. "Whatever you say, pal. I don't give a damn what you do. Where to?"

No point in pressing the matter; as long as he doesn't make a further issue out of it, I certainly won't. "The Plaza," I tell him. By the time we reach my hotel, Sarah will be sober enough to give me her address, and I can pay the driver to take her home.

A grunt of derision from the front seat as we leave the curb and merge with traffic. On our way to the Plaza, we pass by the back entrance to the Prince Edward Theater. Tonight's performance must have just ended, for as the theatergoers stream out, they congregate by the stage door where the cast, still guised up in their costumes and makeup, sign autographs for people who have never heard of them before. But as we drive by, I watch children and adults, men and women alike, singing, dancing, laughing, acting out the musical numbers, and I'm pleased to see that someone was obviously enriched by the *Manimal* experience.

I roll down the passenger window and toss my Playbill into the crowd.

13

I am fortunate in that Sarah decided to throw up inside the cab rather than inside my hotel room, as the cabbie had then been forced to clean up the resultant mess instead of me. I am also fortunate that Sarah's regurgitation, a hearty concoction of eggplant, tahini, and voluminous amounts of white wine, has served to partially sober up my little human model, moving her out of falling-down-disintegration mode into a stumbling stupor.

The upshot of all this is that Sarah is able to help support herself as I guide her through the Plaza lobby and toward the elevators. A little rest in the room, that's all, and then it's back to her apartment. She's wobbly, but walking, and that's more than I had expected. There we wait, as the two supposedly express lifts make their way down from the highest floors. An Oriental carpet lies underfoot, a detailed rug that, if destroyed, would clean out my savings account and then some, so I make a silent wish to the nausea gods to spare Sarah from any more mishaps. If they want an offering, I'll gladly shatter a bottle of Maalox next time I'm in a drugstore.

An older couple enters the elevator lobby arm in arm. How cute. Familiar, in some way, though I can't place it. I have seen them before. Hm . . . The piercing looks they launch at me bring it home—this is the snooty dino couple from the bar line at *Manimal: The Musical,* the ones who had practically given themselves nosebleeds climbing up to the moral high ground.

Sarah slips in my arms, and I do my best to tighten my grip around her waist. She flops against my body like a worn rag doll, draping herself across my frame. Struggling to keep her upright, I smile at the couple, chuckling as if to show my good humor over the situation. *Ha ha,* this chuckle is intended to convey. *What a silly misunderstanding. I'll be telling my purebred Raptor kids all about this one some day.* No response from the couple. The ensuing silence is painful, so I break out with, "Enjoy the show?"

It's hard to discern their reactions with those upturned noses.

For some reason, Sarah chooses this moment to speak in complete, coherent sentences. "You have a good time tonight?" she slurs, each word cresting and crashing on syncopated beats. " 'Cause I had a great time."

"Yes, yes, good time. Ha ha, yes, yes."

She tweaks my nose with her thumb and index finger, twisting it harder than I'm sure she means to. The playful gesture brings tears to my eyes. "I mean, I had a *really* great time."

"Great time," I echo, rubbing my nose. I turn toward the couple again, to explain, to shrug, to indicate in some way that this scene, no matter how lascivious it might seem, is not what they think, but the elderly dinos have disappeared.

Sarah grabs at my nose again, and I gently take her hand away, saying, "You need to get some sleep."

"What I need," whispers Sarah, bonking her forehead into mine, "is you."

I pretend not to hear that.

"You you you," repeats Sarah, and this time it's hard to shut out the voice. "I need you." My best response is no response, so I keep my tongue glued to the roof of my mouth while we wait for the elevator, which has obviously entered some type of space-time warp.

The lift finally arrives, and the brass doors slide open. I step back to allow the passengers—a young couple, very much in love, hanging all over each other—out into the lobby. But when I move left, they move left. I move right, and they move right.

It's a mirror. I choose not to think about this. We enter.

The elevator's acceleration nearly throws both Sarah and me to the ground—oh sure, *now* it's express—and once again we clutch each other tightly as we ascend to the top floor.

"Speedy," giggles Sarah, digging into my shoulder for support.

The presidential suite is situated all by itself at the end of a long corridor, set off from the more pedestrian suites in the vicinity. It's a long walk when sober, and I can't begin to imagine what it will be like trying to drag Sarah down there in her condition. Like a weary sailor who knows he has one final leg of his journey before he can return to family, friends, and a home-cooked meal, I wrap Sarah's arm around my neck and set my sails to the wind.

We manage to make it down the hallway with only a few minor slips and spills, Sarah flicking in and out of consciousness like a TV on the fritz. I open the door.

Curse this suite for being so large. I hustle Sarah into the bedroom, using short, quick hops to move across the marble foyer. At this point, my tail would come in darn handy, and I consider loosening it for the short trip. But that would require taking off my pants, and the last thing I need is for a bellboy to walk into my bedroom and see Sarah Archer passed out on the bed and my lower half au naturel. I'll make it just fine with my legs.

Sarah buzzes to life again as I lean her over the bed and attempt to adjust her body into what should be a natural pose. "Wheereermmmmmeyee?"

I take this elongated syllable as an interrogative attempting to ascertain her location. "My bed," I say, and Sarah titters with delight. Her hands crawl up my arms like giant spiders, fingers grasping my shirt, tugging at my collar, trying to draw me down, down, into those sheets, into those pillows.

"Sarah, no." My tone is as firm as tofu. She tugs harder. "No." A little better, but not enough to deter her from pouting those lips, puckering them into two soft taffy mounds.

It would be so easy, so delicious, to say *what the hell it's just sex, who cares about species and nature and right and wrong,* to not just give in to temptation but throw myself bodily upon it, but whereas morality has taken a leave of absence, whatever superego I have left has stepped in to take up the slack. So though my heart and my loins are still pulling me down into the comfort of those arms, those lips, that wonderful mattress, my head knows enough to put down the comforter and back away with my hands up.

"I can't," I tell her. "I want to, but—I can't."

"Are you . . . married?" she asks.

"No—it's not—"

"Do you . . . do you have a girlfriend?"

"No, I don't. Listen—" The phone rings. I ignore it. "Listen," I repeat, and the phone rings again. The message indicator light is on, and has been since I came into the bedroom. Another ring. "Hold the thought," I say, and lift the handset.

"Holy shit, he's home! Rubio, where the hell you been?" It's Glenda.

"Glen, can this wait? I'm . . . busy."

"So you ask my help, then you're too friggin' busy for the answers, right? I can take a hint—"

"Wait! Wait—you found something?"

"Not with that attitude, I didn't." She's pouting now.

Sarah squirms across the bed, reaching for my arms, trying to pull me down. "Hang up the phone," she coos seductively. "Call them back."

Great, two dames to mollify. I hold up a finger to Sarah—one second, please, one second—and step into a darkened corner of the room. "Glen, I'm sorry, I'm just—there's a lot going on. But whatever you got, I'd love to hear."

"Not on the phone, you won't. We gotta meet up, Vincent."

"Last guy said that ended up dead."

"What?"

"Tell you later. We gotta meet now? You can't give me the basics?"

Glenda mulls it over, but her answer is firm. "I'd rather not. Can you get to the Worm Hole?"

"Now?"

"Now. You'll wanna see this."

"Yeah, yeah, sure. Gimme twenty minutes. And Glen—keep your guard up."

"Always."

I turn back to Sarah, already trying to formulate an excuse in my mind, a reason that I would have to leave her at so crucial a point in our . . . relationship, I guess. But as I turn around I can already hear the patterned breathing, the light snore, and I know I can put excuses off for another time. Sarah Archer is drifting off, one hand still clutched around the leg of my pants. "I'm sorry," I whisper. "I'm so sorry."

Her skin shines in the small glow cast from the living-room chandelier, creating a pale ivory surface so pure that it deserves a goodnight peck. As I lean down to kiss her cheek, Sarah's eyes creak open, and she looks up at me with growing wonder. A hand comes up to caress my face, warmth spreading throughout each feature she touches, and Sarah says, "You . . . you look like someone I knew once. A long time ago."

"Who was that?" I whisper.

But Sarah is finally asleep.

On this All Hallow's Eve, the dino bar in the back of the Worm Hole is probably much like it always is: herbs, noise, and drunken louts. But the mammal joint up front is rocking like I've never seen it rock before, packed to the brim with the filthy apes, each dressed in some moronic costume or another. I press my way through bumblebees and ninjas, cartoon characters and French maids, making my way toward the secret entrance behind the rest rooms.

Glenda's waiting for me at a back table, and as I casually stroll over, I run an olfactory scan of the room, checking for familiar scents. It's clean—at least it's clean as far as past assassins go. If someone's sent out new dinos to do me in, there's very little I can do about it at this stage of the game. I pull up a chair and order an iced tea. "No mint," I tell the waitress.

A puzzled look from Glenda. "No mint?" she asks. "You love mint."

I point to the three-ring binder tucked beneath her arm. "Whaddaya got for me?"

"This shit was hidden, and good."

"Deleted?"

"I think so. But whoever wiped the stuff out either did it in a hurry, or didn't think about the temp files. I used a file restorer to bring 'em up again, and most of the crap came through okay." Glenda's a whiz on the computer; at the very least, she's more of a whiz than I am. Ernie's dusty PC sits in my house, currently waiting to be reclaimed by the bank, but as it hasn't been used since he died except as another place to put my used dishes, the repo man might as well haul it away.

"Show me what we got."

The first few sheets are Ernie's handwritten interview notes, pages of them printed out in bold, dark ink. "He scanned them in as is," Glenda explains. "That's what we do at J&T—we got this crappy program that converts our handwriting into text, but it hadn't learned his writing yet, so it left it like this."

A lump forms in my throat as I stare at the loops, twists, and scrawls of Ernie's fractured script. His penmanship was horrendous, and it wasn't infrequent that he had to enlist my help in deciphering some indistinguishable part of his notes. It's almost as if he's sitting next to me now, passing me a pad he's just scribbled on, asking, "Vinnie—does that say *witness claims to have hugged victim* or *witness claims to have stabbed victim?*"

"From what I could figure out from his shitty handwriting, he'd talked to a bunch of the same folks you did— Mrs. McBride, that mammal nightclub singer, a few employees, even that coroner. You can check through it, see if you note any inconsistencies."

"I'll do that. What else?"

"Some of the usual stuff, filed expense accounts, time sheets, a few more scrawls I couldn't make out, appointment calendar—"

"Gimme that—the calendar."

Glenda searches through the printouts and hands over three pages that look to have been copied out of a personal organizer of some sort. Dates are preprinted at the top of the pages (in this case, January 9, 10, and 11), the section below divided into half-hour increments with space to write. The pages are mostly empty, but a number of appointments have been scribbled in.

On January 9, for example, he met with Judith McBride and four of the McBride Corporation's top executives. On the tenth, he saw Vallardo and Sarah, as well as a few others whose names don't ring a bell. But on the eleventh, on the day he was killed by a hit-and-run taxicab in some godforsaken back alley, at ten o'clock in the morning, just a few short hours before his head would crack wide open on a hard city street, Ernie had an appointment with Dr. Kevin Nadel. And only three days after that, when I flew out to New York in a drunken rage and burst into the morgue demanding to see my partner and best friend and the coroner who had so obviously pooched a simple homicide autopsy, Nadel was on a two-month vacation in the Bahamas, incommunicado.

A small, tight note is wedged in the corner of the ten o'-clock appointment date, too tiny and smushed to read with the naked eye. "You have a magnifying glass on you?" I ask Glenda.

"I have bifocals."

"Good enough." Glenda passes them over, and I hold the small lens at the bottom of the glasses above the handwriting. Now it's larger, still messy, but if I hold my eyes in just the right position and strain my ocular muscles to the point where they're about to snap and go whipping about the room, I can make out the note: Pickupphotos.

Pick Up Photos.

I look up at Glenda, and she holds out a black-and-white printout of a photo set sheet. "He must have meant these."

The McBride crime scene photos. The *real* McBride crime scene photos. No sanitary gunshot wounds, blood splattered in manageable portions along the floor—a nice, clean, wholesome death as multiple gunshot deaths go.

No, this is something else entirely. Blood fills each frame, covering the walls, the furniture, the carpeting, like an acetate tarp; beneath the crimson pools I can make out the vague shape of McBride, nearly torn beyond recognition, lying in a heap against a sofa set off to one corner, his aristocratic bearing shredded beneath what must have been a furious assault. I see bite marks, claw marks, tail lashings, and more, and I realize that what Judith McBride told me and what Dr. Nadel showed me earlier were the most bald-faced of lies.

Now I have proof: Raymond McBride was killed by a dinosaur.

"These were doctored," I tell Glenda.

"You've seen the other ones?"

"At the coroner's. He showed me one of these pictures, but most of the blood was gone, and the wounds had been . . . cleaned up, I guess. Made to look like gunshots, which is what Judith told me her husband died from. And the doc claimed that McBride had been hit with five different caliber weapons—"

"—which would explain the different sizes of the attack wounds," finishes Glenda.

"Goddamn."

"Goddamn."

"Somebody went through a lot of trouble to make it look

like a human pulled this off," I say. "And I bet you Ernie was on to it just before he got iced."

The waitress arrives with my iced tea, and I suck it down in one gulp. Glenda pulls her chair closer to mine, glancing nervously about the room. "I can burn these. You know that, don't you? We can go out back, pour some lighter fluid on these puppies, and torch up. If you're in, I'm in, but I want you to know we can walk away, and that'll be the end of it."

My answer is slow in coming. I want to be precise. "I watched Nadel get killed by a two-dino hit squad," I say. "I almost got killed by them myself. Before that, I was attacked by some freak of nature in a back alley and barely made it away with my hide, and way before *that* my partner was killed in an accident that couldn't have been an accident. I've been misled, laughed at, cheated—I've had my job, my life, my friends stripped away from me. I've been pushed around, and I've been lied to.

"And to be honest, you're right—I should get out now. We should go out to the alley and have ourselves a bonfire with marshmallows, and I should take the next flight to the Galápagos, find a few good trees, and chew myself into a stupor.

"I've got every reason to leave, and it's the smart money that runs through the open door and doesn't look back. But it's like Ernie used to say—it's always the dumbest son-ofabitch who finds himself sitting on top of the food chain when the meteors come crashing through.

"This time around that dumb sonofabitch is gonna be me."

During my little speech, a grin has crept its way onto Glenda's face. "Vincent Rubio," she says, "it's nice to see you again."

* * *

Tips from doormen come cheap, especially if they're not particularly fond of the building residents. Chet, the fellow who works the late shift at Judith McBride's Upper East Side home, gladly tells me where to find the missus after a fin has managed to work its way into his pocket.

"She's at a Halloween charity ball at the Four Seasons," he informs me, masking whatever dislike he feels for McBride with a smile. And then, still with that maddening grin, "The bitch wouldn't know charity if it rammed itself down her throat." I back away from Chet, into the taxi, and ask the driver to screech away as quickly as possible.

The Four Seasons Hotel is nice—if you like that sort of thing. Me, I'm a Plaza man. Glenda and I wander the opulent hallways, underdressed both for the hotel and the holiday, searching for the correct ballroom. We eventually break down and ask the concierge for directions, and he is neither as friendly nor as courteous as Alfonse, though he does lead us to the right place.

MASQUERADE FOR THE CHILDREN, reads a great flowing banner hanging proudly over the entrance. Behind a great set of double doors, fourteen feet high and gilded to the hilt, I can hear some band swinging it loud and clear— drums, trumpets, trombones, all in a steady 3/4 upbeat. A muted voice resonates through the hallway, crooning about ninety-nine women whom he'd loved in a lifetime.

"Hang back once we get inside," I say. "I'll get to Judith. You . . ."

"I'll steal some food."

I grab one door, Glenda grabs the other. We pull.

And the sound hits us like a shock wave, a blast of unadulterated music spilling past our bodies, pressing us

back into the open doorway. The band, the crowd, the incredible noise shuts down my thoughts for a moment, and
all I can do is stare. Three hundred, four hundred, five, a
thousand? How many creatures are mingling? However
many it is, a goodly number of them are dinos, as once the
wave of sound has subsided, the second wave of smells hit
me, and past the odor of sweat and alcohol, I can make out
the pine and the morning and the unmistakable drench of
herbs.

Glenda manages to shake off the daze and wander into
the ballroom in search of hors d'oeuvres. I set off in another direction, glancing around at the revelers, trying to
locate any familiar sight, sound, or smell.

The costumes here are more elaborate than they were at
the Worm Hole—these folks have the moola to spend on
nonsense like that—and I'm amazed at the intricacy and
craftsmanship on some of these outfits. A woman whose
breath is so laced with rum I can smell it thirty yards away
wobbles up to me and burps daintily in my face. She's
wearing what looks to be a large desk, with two drawers
where her stomach would be and a table just below her
chin upon which she props her arms. A Bible has been
glued to the bottom of one of the drawers, as have a pair of
reading glasses to the tabletop.

"Guess what I am!" she screams in my ear.

"I don't know."

"What?" she yells.

I'm forced to join in the shouting. "I said I don't know!"

"I'm a one-night stand! Get it? One nightstand. One—
night—stand!"

If I push her, she will fall down and cause a ruckus, so I
simply excuse myself and squeeze through an opening between two doughnuts in the crowd. Rhinoceroses surround

me, horns sticking rudely into my side, and I spin, looking for a way out. But now there's a contingent of aliens, black eyes wide set and menacing, reaching for me with their spindly arms and tumblers of gin and tonics. The other direction—Abbott and Costello, arguing, tumbling, pratfalling—Nixon, claiming over and over again to Abe Lincoln in a pitiful, high-pitched impression that he is not a crook—a piggy bank, replete with dollar bills pouring out of the top—

And a Carnotaur. A real, no-fooling-around, honest-to-goodness in-the-flesh Carnotaur. The rest of the ballroom drops away, falling into some visual abyss as every light swivels and fixates on the dino in the distance chatting it up with Marilyn Monroe. My first thought is that in the rush of Halloween, someone has forgotten to don their guise, much in the way that dino children, once costumed in human skin, will forget that they also need to wear clothing and walk out of the house buck naked, human naughty bits flapping in the breeze.

Without conscious effort, my feet have taken me across the room, and when I get within three yards of the dino, I can smell it—smell the oranges, smell the chlorine—smell *her*—smell Judith McBride. Unguised and chatting it up like it was the most natural thing in the world. I can understand the compulsion, the incredible *need* to be free of the girdles and the clamps and the belts, but not here, not now, not in front of mammals. Without thought as to consequences or social graces, I storm up to Judith and grab her by the crook of a well-muscled Carnotaur arm.

"She'll be right back," I explain to a startled Marilyn, who, I can see up close, is actually more like a Marvin, and pull Judith into one of the more nonpopulated areas of the ballroom, letting her have it all the way.

"What the hell are you doing, going out like that? Have you lost your mind?"

Judith, nonplussed, says, "This time, Mr. Rubio, I believe I will have you thrown out." She raises her hand—her forepaw—toward some unseen protector in the distance, but I grab it before the ascent is complete, holding the fingers in my kung fu grip.

"You can't do this—this is—this is violation number one, the big one—going out unguised—"

"It's Halloween."

"Screw the holiday, you can't risk security because some mammals want to make fools of themselves."

"I'm risking nothing, I assure you."

"You know what I'm talking about—"

"And you're not listening. It's Halloween. This—is—a—costume. A dinosaur costume. Nothing less."

My fingers unclench; the clawed forepaw drops back to her side. "That's not possible," I say. "The mouth—it moves when you talk. It's just like—the teeth—the tongue—"

Judith laughs, and the Carnotaur costume jiggles up and down. "I spent more on this costume than you probably did on your house, Mr. Rubio. I should hope it is realistic. As for its possibility . . . well, you should know better."

"This is . . . a guise?"

"I can promise you—I swear to you—that what I am wearing is the guise of a dinosaur."

Keeping my voice low, though on this night and in this place, no one would think twice if they overheard: "So you're a dino dressed as a human dressed as a dino."

"Something like that," she says, and to prove it to me, she carefully peels back a bit of skin just below her midsection, retracting from a seam I hadn't seen before. Beneath is a wash of pale human flesh, Mrs. McBride's "natural" guised-up skin tone.

"Good costume," I say lamely.

But I've got her laughing, and laughing is better than screaming at her bodyguards to throw me into the punch bowl. "Dance?" she asks, already stepping out toward the floor.

The song's a fox-trot, and I believe I remember the steps. "If you can forgive me," I say, "I would be honored." Casual dance-floor chatter might prove to be the perfect lead-in to my follow-up questions.

It does indeed begin that way, Judith and I talking about the weather, the city, the madness of the holiday as we slow-slow-quick-quick around the dance floor, my lead becoming stronger with every turn and promenade. She's an excellent dancer in her own right, following my moves with the slightest pull, the most delicate of touches. Soon I'm able to talk without counting the beats out in my head, and we fall into an easy patter.

"Are you done with whatever you came to find?" she asks.

"Yes and no."

"I assume you came tonight as you found something that couldn't wait. Isn't that what you people say? It couldn't wait?"

"Us people do say that sometimes, yes."

"And you'd like to ask me now."

"At some point in the evening."

"As we seem to have exhausted our stores of small talk," she suggests, "why don't we dispense with the rest of it and get down to business. I assume you've spoken with the Archer woman by now."

"I have."

"And the rest of Raymond's harem?"

"His harem?"

"Shocked? Don't be."

I was aware that Judith had known about her husband's affair with Sarah—I'd learned that tonight at dinner—but how many more of Raymond's dalliances was she privy to? "You knew about the affairs, then?" We spin around a slower couple, leaving them in our dust.

"Not at first, no. It took me a little bit to catch on, but not long. Raymond was a brilliant man, but in matters of the heart, my husband had long ago outlived his warranty.

"He started out low-key enough," Judith continues, "a girl from the office, I think, and for a while I thought it was cute. You know, he was taking this young thing under his wing, guiding her through the labyrinth of corporate existence."

"And then?" There's always a then.

"And then he started fucking her." The number picks up, the band climbing into a faster rhythm, and we escalate our steps to match.

"What did you do?" I ask.

"The only thing I could do: Deal with it. It happens all the time."

"What does?"

"Infidelity. There's not a friend of mine whose husband hasn't screwed around on her." Now *there's* a sewing circle to stay away from. "But it's not like us to get angry. Not openly, that is."

"Hit 'em when they're not looking?" I ask.

"Hit 'em *where* they're not looking. When you stake your life in the upper crust, the best revenge is always financial. So, in retaliation, we buy things. Furs, jewels, brownstones . . .

"I had one friend whose husband was such a recidivist that she was forced to purchase a small charter airline company and run it into the ground—often literally, mind you—just to get his attention."

"Did it work?"

"For a year. Then he was back at it, and she moved on to passenger trains."

I say, "But you didn't do anything like that, right? You were the good little girl of the group."

"Believe it or not, I was. For a while, at least. I took it all on the chin, accepted Raymond for what he was. Of course, those first few flings of his were . . . normal. Natural. He hadn't yet . . . switched species."

"And when did he jump ship?" I ask.

"Three years ago, maybe four, I don't remember."

"Was Sarah Archer the first one?"

Judith's laugh is humorless, a short bark of derision. "If you mean was she his first cross-species fling, no. Five, ten, twenty girls before her, all the same, all of them leggy and shaggy-haired and beautiful and dumb. Would you believe that some of them would call the house—*my* house—and leave messages for him?

"But if you mean to ask if Sarah Archer was the first one to possess my husband, to claim him as property, to latch on to him as if he were the dock and she were a boat in heavy chop, then yes, I would say she was."

"And that was when it started to grate on you."

"No," says Judith, "it troubled me long before that. There was a period of time when he spent perhaps two nights out of the entire month in my bed. And whereas Raymond and I hadn't . . . had relations in a while"—choice of words definitely less intense now—"there was still a void at night. When you are used to sleeping next to someone all your life, it becomes difficult to adjust to the empty space on the mattress. I believe it was then that I'd finally had enough.

"Money was out—he didn't care. And I couldn't reach him in the bedroom, not directly. So I got back at him the only way I could think of: I had an affair."

"With Donovan Burke," I say.

This does not discompose Judith as much as I would like, but it's a start. At the very least, her assured feet falter a bit, and I have to swing around to her side, shifting the move into an underarm turn, to accommodate the false step. "You know about it."

"I had my hunches from the start." Sarah's comments during dinner tonight only served to corroborate my earlier guess, but I choose not to let Judith in on this. "An affair to punish an affair. Very eye-for-an-eye of you."

"Are you judging me, Mr. Rubio?"

"I don't judge what I don't understand."

Judith accepts this with a wry smile and says, "It wasn't how it sounds."

"It never is."

"My affair with Donovan was not begun solely for revenge, you understand. If anything, it was for companionship. Raymond couldn't be there for me, and I was getting tired of shopping. Donovan was what I needed."

"In your bed?"

"In my bed, in my house, at the park, at the theater, wherever and whenever he could go. Companionship is more than sex, Mr. Rubio."

"And this affair with Donovan Burke—this was after Jaycee's disappearance, I take it?"

Silence from my dance partner, a telling pause. "You were having an affair with Donovan while he was still engaged to Jaycee Holden?"

The reply is meek, a mouse twitter, the first soft-spoken word I have heard out of Judith McBride's mouth: "Yes."

I don't want to be part of the Great Spiritual Oneness when the McBride family karma is finally added up; it's going to take a good portion of eternity to get all of their shit sorted out. "Back in your office the other day you claimed to like Jaycee Holden."

"I did."

"You called her a lovely girl, if I recall."

"I did."

"Then why would you choose to stab her in the back like that?" I hate to sound uppity, but all of this marital malfeasance is making me ill. Can't these people keep it in their guises? Of course, two hours ago I was ready to play amateur magician, rip the tablecloth out from under our Greek food, and throw Sarah onto the bare wood in a fit of passion, but that was two hours ago, and I have since found the control I almost lost.

"Jaycee was no saint," says Judith. "She had her faults."

Aside from a penchant for well-orchestrated disappearances and poorly orchestrated kidnappings, she'd seemed pleasant enough to me. "They had problems before you started seeing him, then?"

"Not that I know of," says Judith.

"Who started the affair?"

"It was mutual."

"Who started the affair?" I repeat. I feel like a father trying to discover which of his children broke the vase in the living room.

"I did," Judith finally admits.

"Did you seduce him?"

"If you want to call it that."

"Why Donovan? Why not someone who wasn't already involved in a relationship?"

Judith is unable to meet my gaze now. She stares off toward the bandleader, elongated Carnotaur snout propped against my shoulder. "Donovan and Raymond . . . they were very close."

"That's why you chose him—his friendship with your husband?"

"Yes. My intention was not to hurt Raymond, let me make that clear. But if he were to ever find out about the affair . . . a little pain might be in order. I chose a confidante of his so that he might feel betrayed as I had felt betrayed. It was a business decision, in many ways."

"I was under the impression that Donovan worked under you at the Pangea. That he had little contact with your husband."

"Professionally, he didn't. Donovan was an entertainment manager, nothing Raymond would have troubled himself with. But they'd been personal friends for a while. Golfing buddies. This was way back when we initially moved to New York."

"About fifteen years ago?"

"That's right."

"Where were you before that?"

"Kansas. Oh please, it was dreary, I don't want to talk about it."

Fair enough. I don't want to talk about Kansas, either. "Did Jaycee find out?"

"You know," Judith muses, "at the time I thought we'd done a pretty good job of keeping her in the dark."

"But you didn't."

She shakes her head. "No. We didn't. I know that now."

"Oh, yeah? And how's that?"

"I simply do. She disappeared two weeks later."

"And a few months after that . . ."

"I fired Donovan," she admits.

"Kind of you. Donovan must have been ecstatic. No woman, no job, no reason to go on."

"You don't understand," says Judith. "Without Jaycee, he was morose. The club was neglected, the books were a shambles. He—he was—"

"Useless?"

I don't get a response. The fox-trot ends, but the band gives us no respite. A sharp tango begins, and my body snaps to attention—the back going ramrod straight, knees flexing, arm curling around Judith's Carnotaur waist. "Can you tango?" I ask, and she answers by spinning into my arms for a perfectly timed dip. A number of other couples join the dance floor, and though it's getting crowded up here, Mrs. McBride and I are Fred and Ginger, swirling and stomping in all the right spots at all the right times.

"You move well," Judith says.

"Why did you tell me your husband was killed by gun-shots?"

"Because he was." Two three dip!

"I'll ask you again—"

Her hands disengage from mine, pushing against my chest as she struggles to move away. But I've got her tight around the waist; she's not going anywhere. I force her to continue the dance. "You think you understand every-thing," she sneers, "but you don't. You don't have clue one."

"Maybe you can help me. You can start by telling me why you lied."

"I didn't. I will show you the crime scene photos, Mr. Rubio, and you will see the bullet holes, you will see—"

"I've seen the crime scene photos," I say, and this shuts her up. "I've seen the real ones."

"I don't know what you mean."

"The undoctored ones. The originals." I'm right next to

her ear hole now, whispering harshly into the costume upon costume. "The ones with your husband almost torn in half by the claw marks, the bites running down his side—"

She stops dancing. Her arms drop away, begin to tremble. "Can we talk about this outside?"

"It'd be my pleasure."

I lead Mrs. McBride off the dance floor, and we receive polite applause for our efforts. It takes me a minute to locate a door to the outside, but we soon enter a small courtyard sporting a fountain, a few trees, and a bench. The sounds of the tango disappear behind another soundproof door. With a huff of air, Judith begins to remove the Carnotaur costume, exposing her head and torso to the cool autumn air. Now she's a human with fat green legs and a tail, looking like a drunken dino who's started to pull her guise on from the wrong end.

"Do you have any of those cigarettes?" she asks me. I toss her the entire pack, and she lights up. The smoke coalesces about her head, and she sucks it in deeply.

"Why did you doctor the photos? Why did you get Nadel to lie?"

"I didn't," she says. "I asked someone to do it."

"Who?"

She mumbles a name—"Who?" I say, standing over her. "Speak up."

"Vallardo. I asked Dr. Vallardo to take care of it."

Filling in all the blank spaces now—that's what the money was for, the deposits into Nadel's account. I can't believe it's come together this quickly. "Now, I can't arrest you," I say. "Not officially. But I can hear your confession, and I can make sure the cops treat you okay."

She's up again, pacing the courtyard. "Confession? What on earth would I confess to?"

"Murdering your husband is still a crime, Mrs. McBride."

"I did no such thing!" Indignation streams out of Judith like sunbursts, and I'm nearly singed by the blast.

"Fine, then—do you have an alibi?"

"Some investigator you are—did you even check with the police? I was the first person they came after, of course I have an alibi. I was running a charity event that night in front of two hundred people. Most of them are here this evening—would you like me to have someone fetch them so that you may accuse them of murder, too?"

Confused now. Not the way this was supposed to go. "But why would you cover it all up . . . ?"

Judith sighs and sits heavily on the bench. "Money. It's always money."

"You'll have to do better than that."

"I came back from my charity event, and there he was. On the floor, dead, just like I told you before. And I saw the wounds, I saw the bites, the slashes. And I knew that if word got out about it, the Council would be all over us."

I think I'm getting it now. "Dino on dino murder."

"Always brings up a Council investigation. They'd been looking for an excuse to bleed us dry for years—you know how the fines work. I don't know who killed my husband, Mr. Rubio, but I did know that there was a chance that whoever it was had . . . illicit dealings with my husband. Dealings his estate could be held accountable for. So, in order to forestall any official Council inquiry . . ."

"You had Vallardo and Nadel conspire to fix the photos and the autopsies to be consistent with a human cause of death. No dino murderer, no investigation, no fines."

"And now you know. Is that so horrible, wanting to protect my finances?"

I shake my head. "But what about Ernie? Why lie about him?"

"Who?"

"My partner. The one who came to see you—"

She brushes me off with a casual hand-flip. "That again. This time, I really don't know what you're talking about. Have you found some other imagined evidence to convict me?" Judith holds out her hands as if to be handcuffed, and I slap them away angrily, more because she's right than anything else. I don't have any proof that she was involved in Ernie's death, and the dearth of information is needling me.

"Nadel's dead," I tell her roughly.

"I know that."

"How?"

"Emil—Dr. Vallardo—found out earlier this evening, and he called me soon after. From what I gather, Nadel was found as a black woman in Central Park. Odd duck."

"I was there. He was killed—it was a hit."

"Are you accusing me again?"

"I'm not accusing anyone—"

"I'm sorry you seem to feel that I'm responsible for all deaths in Manhattan, but I'm just as nervous about this as you are. If you look on the other side of that door, you'll see two of my bodyguards ready to burst out here at a moment's notice." I glance at the closed door, but choose not to press the issue. "I'm prepared, Mr. Rubio. Are you?"

With theatrical timing, the door slams open, and I see Glenda pressed between the two beefy bodyguards who had greeted me in Judith's office yesterday morning. She's flailing, kicking, screaming: "—the fuck off me—I'll rip out your goddamned throats—" and inflicting as much damage as her legs and voice can muster.

"Friend of yours?" Judith asks, and I nod bashfully. "Let

her go," she tells the bodyguards, and they roughly body-check Glenda into the courtyard. I have to restrain her from following them back inside the ballroom, and it's not easy to hold back a hundred and fifty pounds of squirming Hadrosaur. She eases up, and I let go.

"Brought you some cocktail wieners," Glenda says, and dumps a heap of the appetizers into my hands. "Can we get outta here? I think the caterer's pissed at me."

"I think we're about done here," I say, and turn to Judith. "Unless there's anything else you'd like to tell me."

"Not unless there's anything else you'd like to accuse me of."

"Not right now, thanks. But I wouldn't leave the city if I were you."

Judith looks amused. "I'm not accustomed to taking orders."

"And I don't give suggestions." I shove a weenie in my mouth and masticate, the hot meat scalding the insides of my mouth. I had planned a few more parting volleys in Mrs. McBride's direction, but if I speak now, I just may spit up the wiener, and that wouldn't be good for anybody.

Grabbing Glenda firmly by the hand, I lead her out of the courtyard, through the ballroom, past the throng of drunken revelers, and toward the nearest subway stop. I give the token booth operator the last three dollars in my wallet, and we head for the southbound train.

Glenda has gone back to her apartment, and I have gone back to the lion's den. I stand outside the presidential suite, key card in hand, holding it just above the lock. Sarah is inside, maybe asleep, maybe not, and the stockpile of willpower I might have built up on the train ride over is ebbing out through some undiscovered leak. I've got people trying to kill me right and left, no money in my pocket, and no discernible future on the horizon, but it's the next five minutes that could prove to be my true salvation or my downfall. I swipe the card.

No snoring, I notice as I enter the suite, and the bedroom light is on. Sarah is no longer asleep. I make a snap deal with myself: If Sarah is reading, watching television, or just hanging out, I will order her up a pot of coffee from room service, beg a few bucks from the check-in staff, and send her back home in a cab, no funny business. If, on the other hand, I enter the bedroom to find her long, lithe body tucked beneath the covers—above the covers—around the covers—nude and waiting for me to return, I will close the shutters on whatever strands of rectitude remain in me and allow whatever primal instincts are left to guide my body as I leap headfirst into that luscious den of sin.

A note on the pillow. And no Sarah.

The note reads: *Dearest Vincent, I'm sorry for making you say you were sorry. Please think of me fondly. Sarah.*

I drop into the bed, note clutched tightly to my chest, and count the tiles in the ceiling. There will be no sleep tonight.

14

As expected, I did not reach dreamland even once. My evening was spent in the bathtub, alternately splashing freezing and scalding water onto my guiseless body. After each half hour of this, I would lurch back into the bedroom, toss on my guise in case the maids should break and enter, and attempt to drift off into slumber, which never came. The sandman is a lazy shiftabout. I hate him.

At eight o'clock this morning, the phone rings. It's Sally at TruTel back in LA, and she says that Teitelbaum would like to have a word with me.

"Put him through," I tell Sally, and he's there in an instant. I have a feeling he was there all along.

"You're off the case!" is the first thing he yells in my ear, and I have this sinking feeling it won't be the last.

"I'm—what the hell are you talking about?"

"Did we not have a discussion about Watson? Did we not have this goddamned discussion?"

"What discussion—you said don't mess around with Ernie's death, that's all—"

"And that's what you've been doing!" The tumbler in

my hand vibrates with the shout, ripples spreading across the water's surface. "You screwed me over, Rubio, and now I'm gonna screw you back."

"Calm down," I say, lowering my own voice so as to demonstrate. "I asked a few questions, just to get perspective on the McBride thing—"

"I ain't one of your suspects, Rubio. You can't pull this on me. I know all about your little friend at J&T—we know what she's been up to."

"Glenda?" Oh, crap—he knows about the computer files.

"And we know you put her up to it. That's industrial espionage, that's breaking and entering, that's theft, that's— that's way over the line. And that's it, it's over." I can hear Teitelbaum pacing the room, trinkets falling, crashing off the desk, and though it's amazing that he's finally made it out of that chair, he's winded, panting from the effort. "You're off the case, I'm cutting off your credit card, you're done. Finished."

"So . . . what?" I sulk. "You want me to come back to LA?"

"I don't give a fuck what you do any more, Rubio. I canceled your return flight back here, so stay in New York if you wanna, they got a nice homeless community under them subway tunnels. 'Cause I've got phone calls out to every firm in town, and the only PI job you're gonna get back here is tracking down where you left your last welfare check."

"I'm onto something here, Mr. Teitelbaum," I try to explain. "It's not bullshit this time, it's big, and I'm not gonna give it up just 'cause—"

But he's hung up. I call back and casually ask Sally to reconnect me to her boss.

A short pause, but Sally's soon back on the line. "He

won't come to the phone," she explains. "I'm sorry, Vincent. Is there anything I can do?"

I consider using Sally as my agent provocateur, asking her to sneak into the files, reinstate my credit card, messenger me a new ticket to LA, but I've already gotten Glenda in trouble, and I don't need to add another creature to my list of suffering friends. "Nothing," I tell her. "I fucked up, that's all."

"It's gonna be okay," she says.

"Sure. Sure it is." With no credit card and no cash of my own, I can't possibly afford to spend another day in the city. The room darkens perceptibly.

"You want me to mail your messages back home?"

"What messages?" I ask.

"You got a bunch, sitting right here. Mr. Teitelbaum didn't tell you?"

"Not exactly. Hell, I don't care. Are they important?"

"I don't know," she says. "They're all from some police sergeant, a Dan Patterson. Just wants you to call him. Says it's urgent, and there's four or five of them."

I'm off with Sally in half a heartbeat and connected to the Rampart division of LAPD. A quick, "Vincent Rubio for Dan Patterson, please," and he's soon on the other end.

"Dan Patterson."

"Dan, me. What's going on?"

"Are you home?" he asks.

"I'm in New York."

A pause, slightly stunned. "You're not—not again—"

"I am. In a way. Don't ask."

"Fine," he says, willing to drop the issue. Now that's a friend. "There's something we found in the back room of that nightclub—"

"The Evolution Club?"

"Yeah. Remember I told you I had some guys going

through the place? And that one box wasn't torched? Well, they found some mighty weird shit I thought you should know about, and it wasn't illegal skin mags."

"I assume this is something you can't tell me about over the phone," I say. A pattern has begun to emerge in my life, and it's getting tiring following it around the globe.

"It's more like a show-and-tell, and believe me, you wouldn't believe it or understand it unless you saw the damn things in person. I had to turn it all over to the Council, and they're having an emergency meeting right about now, but I made a photocopy of the paper goods for you."

"What if I told you I was off the Evolution Club case?" I ask.

"Easy—I'd still have a photocopy for you."

"And what if I told you that I had no money for a plane flight back to LA, that I'd just been officially banned from every firm in the city, that I don't give a good goddamn about Teitelbaum or his cases, that I'm about four-fifths of the way to getting myself killed out here, and that I'd probably need a heap of extra cash to come back here to New York after I saw you?"

He takes longer to think this one over, but not as long as I'd expected. "Then I'd walk down the street and send you some cash Western Union."

"It's that big?" I ask.

"It's that big," he says, and two hours later I'm standing in line at the airport with my trusty garment bag in tow.

Dateline: Los Angeles, five hours later. I was not upgraded to first class on my flight. The counter agent told me to talk to the desk agent, the desk agent told me to talk to the flight staff, the flight staff told me to walk back across the terminal and take it up with the counter agent again, and by the time I finally learned that yes, they would love to upgrade me, there were no more first-class seats available because everyone else had already gotten themselves bumped up an hour earlier. So I spent the bulk of the flight crushed between a dyspeptic software designer whose laptop and accompanying accessories encompassed all the available space on my tray table as well as his, and a six-year-old boy whose parents, the lucky shits, had landed seats in first class. Every two hours, his mother would walk back to us untouchables in economy and tell the child not to bother the nice man—me—next to him, and Timmy (or Tommy, or Jimmy, I can't remember) would solemnly swear upon all the cartoon characters he held holy to follow orders. Yet not ten seconds after his mother disappeared through the dividing curtain would he resume banging away on every surface possible, my body parts not excepted. He was a budding Buddy Rich, no doubt, but despite his talent, I was wholly prepared to risk life, limb, and the loss of a future jazz great by throwing him bodily out the nearest emergency exit.

When I could sleep, I dreamt about Sarah.

It takes some time to hail a cab in Los Angeles, even at the airport, but I eventually locate one willing to take me to Pasadena. The money Dan sent me is already going quickly, as the plane ticket cost over two thousand dollars due to the last-second purchase. I resolve to pay him back as soon as I get back on my feet again, whenever that may be. Right now, I'm just about on my chin and going down quickly.

A short swing up the 110 takes us to the Arroyo Vista Parkway and Dan's suburban house, where he was planning on spending most of his day off. Soon enough, we pull up in front of the blue-and-white ranch home, nearly slamming into the Ford pickup parked sideways in the driveway. I pay the cabbie and hop on out.

Spread across the front stoop of Dan's town house is today's *Los Angeles Times,* the open pages blowing in the warm Santa Anas coming up from the south. I gingerly step over this morning's headlines, being careful not to tread upon today's Sunday comics, and rap on the door. It's in dire need of fresh paint, the wood stain having long since been stripped by the omnipresent air pollutants, but it's still a nice chunk of oak that echoes my knock back to me.

I wait. Odds are, Dan's hanging out in the living room, plopped down in his La-Z-Boy imitation recliner, hooked into a virtual IV tube of Cheetos and Chunky Soups, squinting hard at his twenty-inch television because he's too darned stubborn to be fitted for contact lenses. "It's sad enough I've gotta wear makeup every day," he told me once. "Ain't no way I'm gonna mess around with contacts." Better not to even bring up the subject of glasses.

A minute passes with no response. I try again, pounding a little harder this time. "Danny boy!" I call out, mushing my lips as close to the door as possible without causing actual skin-wood contact. *"Abre la puerta!"* Dan knows the meaning of my words—he can say "Open the door!" in over sixteen different languages and four Asian dialects. Such are the spoils that come from being a police detective in Los Angeles.

Again, nothing. I notice that Dan's still got that door knocker up that I gave him last Christmas on a goof—an oversized, overpriced, overly gaudy gargoyle that would look out of place anywhere other than the Munsters' home—so I grab hold of the brass beast's nose and slam its feet onto the solid plate beneath. Now *this* is a Knock,

Knock, Knock, and the heavy thumps nearly throw me off the front stoop. The brass vibrates rapidly in my hand like an overcharged joy buzzer, and I quickly let go of the gargoyle before it has a chance to vibrate into animation.

A minute. Two. Silence. I listen in at the door, straining, pressing my false ear against the wood grain. Music, perhaps, a steady beat droning on and on. It's possible that he's asleep—deeply so, I would imagine, not to hear that gargoyle racket—but more likely he's out back in his small herb garden and has the music from his living room pumped up so he can hear it outside. I head around back.

Brambles and bushes try to stop me, extending their long, thorny claws to rip at my guise. Carefully avoiding the nastier barbs, I pick my way through the brush and eventually come to the tall wooden fence that defines Dan's modest yard. No space between these slats, but a knot in the wood provides an excellent peephole, and like a trained pervert, I set to peeping.

Oregano, basil, sage, and their culinary cohorts rise from the earth, making their way toward the sun, straining for its energy. Many a tipsy afternoon was spent sampling the delights of this well-kept piece of land. I see flowers to the left, what might be a carrot patch to the right, but there's no LAPD sergeant in sight. Balling my hand into a tight fist, I pound the fence and yell for Dan again.

Had I not seen his car in the driveway, had he not known that I was coming in today, on this very flight, at this precise time, I might think that Dan had taken a short hop out of the house or out of town, a quick get-away-from-it-all jaunt.

A quick whiff off a passing breeze . . .

Scents flowing in, piggybacking on the air, swirling through my nostrils, and I can pick up everything in the area, from the herbs to the flowers to the car down the street, the chemicals from a nearby one-hour photo, the messy diaper of a newborn four houses down, and the acrid vinegar odor of that bitter, bitter Stego widow who lives next door and always comes on to Dan after she's had a few too many.

But no Dan. Now I'm worried. Time to break and enter.

As I make my way toward the front door, I realize that there's no way I'm getting through that slab of oak short of a battle-ax; aside from the relative impossibility of knocking it in with my meager weight, Dan's job has taught him nothing if not to secure a house with multiple locks. Back to the garden.

Stepping off the porch, I nearly slip as my eye catches a small, dark stain on the ground and my body instinctively pirouettes to get a better look. It's blood. Three, four drops maximum, but definitely blood. Dried, but only recently. I would whip out my dissolution packet and run a quick chemical test to see if it's dino fluid, but I fear that I already know the answer. I downshift and leap for the fence.

The adrenaline rush bypasses my fatigue and I scale the wooden slats with as much skill and grace as my drained muscles will allow, my premiere fence-climbing days well behind me. As I reach the top and attempt to swing myself up and over, my left leg catches against an outcropping and down I go, end over end, toppling heavily into Dan's basil patch. The smell is overpowering, and I stumble to my feet and backpedal away as quickly as possible even as my mouth begins to work by itself, chomping at the air where the basil should be.

The back door is closed as well, bolted tight from the inside. I pound, I knock, I shake the door with all my might, but the only sounds I can hear from within are the swinging guitars and ruffled backbeat of Creedence Clearwater Revival, John Fogerty's tortured voice calling out to his

Susie Q. Fogerty, I recently learned, is an Ornithomimus, as are Joe Cocker and Tom Waits, so you can see from whence that vocal trait arises. Paul Simon, on the other hand, is a true-blue Velociraptor, and I don't think I've ever heard a better drug song than "Scarborough Fair," even though rosemary and thyme have never done much for me personally.

"Dan!" I scream, my voice cracking, register climbing into the stratosphere. "Open the goddamned door!"

John Fogerty answers. ". . . say that you'll be true . . ."

A window entrance, then, is my only option. Despite my growing paranoia, I'm still pushing myself to optimism: Dan cut himself while cooking dinner, didn't have bandages, ran to Rite Aid to grab a small first-aid kit, maybe took a trip over to the hospital for stitches, dripped some blood on the way out. Better yet, he was coming back from grocery shopping, dropped a container of lamb chops, the blood splattered a bit, and now he's at a friend's house barbecuing those babies up right this very minute. If I pretend hard enough, I can almost smell the charcoal . . .

The screen pops out in a flash with the help of my Swiss Army blade, and I'm soon faced with a solid, yet thin, window pane, easily breakable. I'm usually above such pedestrian entry techniques, but time is short so I smash away, using my elbow to splinter the glass. I'm not worried about Dan's security alarm—I know the code is 092474 from the time I house-sat for him last October, and if I remember correctly, I've got a generous forty-five seconds to turn it off.

But the alarm doesn't activate. I cannot hear the telltale BEEP BEEP BEEP that usually drives me so insane. I wish I could.

I pull up the window and slide inside, wriggling clear of the broken glass on the floor. Creedence is rocking louder now, the way Creedence should, emanating from the den, good old John still pining for his gal. "Anybody home?" I call out over the din. "Dan? Dan, you here?"

Dan's never been the tidiest of Brontosaurs, so I'm not surprised to see his clothing scattered about the living room in postapocalyptic fashion. A girdle here, a buckle there, a pair of guised-up underwear flopped atop the ottoman.

Though my earlier whiff on the front porch didn't pick it up, there is indeed a lingering trace of Dan's olive oil and motor engine scent, drifting in and out like a fading memory. I suspect it arises from the scattered clothing. Through the open wall in the living room I can see into the kitchen, over the low counter, across the breakfast table, past the Mount Olympus of dishes piled in the sink. No Dan.

His bedroom is located upstairs, and habit pulls in that direction. But Creedence beckons to me from the small den on the first floor, Fogerty having given up on Susie, now concentrating his efforts on doo, doo, doo, looking out his back door. Another rough circle of blood stains the carpet, stretching out into a long, tortured oval, leading beneath the den's door, trailing inside . . .

I open and enter.

Stereo speakers, canted, lying on the floor, blasting away, shoving the music into me, pressing me backward. Pictures, ripped to ribbons, frames smashed, glass shattered. A television tube lying five feet away from its cabinet, a bookcase torn and toppled. Drapes pulled down, lightbulbs popped, Lava lamps cracked and flowing slowly, slowly onto the carpet, their phosphorescence drooping like caterpillars through the light gray fibers.

And Dan, plopped in his favorite easy chair, guise half-shredded, hair half-matted, smidgen of tuna sandwich and overturned bowl of soup on the TV tray by his side, stab wounds covering his body, pocking his flesh, blood having long since seeped through his clothing and dried into carmine stains against his rough, brittle hide. Smiling, staring through the ceiling, to the sky . . .

"Dan, Dan, Dan . . . come on . . . don't . . . Dan . . ."

I'm muttering, I'm mumbling, I'm talking to myself without knowing what I'm saying as I run my hands over Dan's body, searching for any signs of life. I press my nose into his hide, I want to find a scent, I want to find some smell, anything! Working the snaps behind my neck, buttons popping off, carelessly pulling the guise mask up and off my head to get a better whiff, I try again, unencumbered this time, sniffing, snorting, locating his scent glands and drawing them as far in as I can . . .

Emptiness. No scent.

Sergeant Dan Patterson is dead.

I close his eyes, inner lids first, but I am loath to adjust the rest of his body. The police will have to be called in due time, and they're going to be upset enough that I broke in here, damaging their crime scene. Better to leave his body . . . better to leave everything unmolested.

Dan didn't go without a fight—the demolished state of the den says that much—but I don't know whether it's pride at Dan's courage, the sorrow at his passing, or both that spins a tight knot in my chest, pressing hard against my throat.

"There goes the fishing trip, huh?" I ask Dan's slumped body. "You sonofabitch, there goes the fishing trip."

The wounds are straight-on incisions, knife stabs, the occasional slash. I don't see the telltale markings of a dino attack like those I thought I picked up in the Raymond McBride photo—curved stabs resulting from claw jabs, parallel slashes from slices, conical depressions as a result of a biting attack, or the deep indentations of a tail spike.

According to the LED display on the front of the CD player, it's been playing the same disk over and over for the better part of four hours, which enables me to place Dan's demise within that time, unless the killer threw on Creedence after the murder in some sort of postslaughter uber-'60s ritual.

Dan's thick brown tail, I notice, has been freed from the G series of belts, but from its confined position beneath the overlapping torso girdle, I doubt he got a chance to utilize it during his defense. All indications—the defensive wounds on Dan's palms, the blood trail splattered across the room, evenly distributed, the lack of forced entry into the house other than my own recent intrusion, the undisturbed items everywhere but this den in particular—point to a surprise attack by someone Dan knew or thought he knew, someone he invited into his den, maybe to have a bite to eat, to catch a few tunes. And then—a stab, a slice, a quick filet, Dan stumbling backward, trying to defend himself, trying to rip off his guise, to free up his claws and his tail, but all of it too slow and too late. Then it was simply, quietly over.

On the air, a new odor drifting around, looking for some nose hairs to tickle. For a brief moment I delude myself into thinking that Dan has pulled a Lazarus on me, sprung back to life, and wants to grab a pizza, but though I soon realize it is not Dan's scent, it is somehow familiar. Nose leading the way, body following obediently behind, I search on the floor beneath Dan's easy chair, running my fingers across the carpet, the exposed tacks biting into my polyskin fingers.

There, within my grasp now, a square of what feels like cheesecloth, double-layered. I pull it out. It's a pouch, much like the disintegration packets I carry on me at all times. But this one doesn't radiate that terrible stench of decay, and there's no way the smell could have diminished over time; even empty disintegration pouches have to be burned, buried, and forgotten in some godforsaken landfill in order to conceal that rank odor.

Chlorine. That's it. I can't find any granules left in the pouch, but I've no doubt that it once held that very element. A few other scents are trying to make it into my sinuses, fighting with their stronger counterpart, but it's of no use; that first whiff has taken hold and won't relinquish control. I drop the pouch in the exact spot where I found it, scooting the cloth back beneath the chair in case the police should find some more meaning behind the evidence than I did.

The chaos and rampant destruction are even more evident from this lower vantage point; splintered wood and ripped wallpaper towering overhead, possessions crushed like empty soda cans. Nothing in this room was spared from the rampage, and I can only hope that Dan's eyes had glazed and darkened before he got a chance to see the destruction that had befallen his photos, paintings, and bowling trophies.

Consolation will be long and hard in coming, but at least I have this: Dan Patterson died in his favorite easy chair. He died in the heat of battle. He died while eating a hearty lunch. He died in his home, surrounded by pictures of those he loved. And he died while listening to Creedence Clearwater Revival, to Ornithomimus John Fogerty, which means that he passed into that great beyond borne on the kindred voice of a brother dinosaur. We should all be so lucky.

I want to keep on with my search, to comb the carpet for fiber samples. I want to grab a spare bag of flour from

Dan's kitchen and pat down the walls for fingerprints. I want to isolate those bloodstains on the front porch and scan through the DNA evidence. I want a clue, any clue, but there's no time. No time.

What I need is to find this all-important information that drew me back to Los Angeles in the first place, but an exhaustive search of the house turns up nothing interesting except for a drawer full of porn magazines like *Stegolicious* and *Double Diplodod Dames,* strictly soft-core all the way. Didn't know Dan went in for anything other than other Brontosaurs, but I'm the last dino in the world who should be moralizing right now.

Still, I can't find the photocopies Dan told me about, and there's no doubt in my mind that they are of the utmost importance, both to the Evolution Club case and everything else that's been going down the last few days. He did mention something about another set, though—the originals—and though I don't relish the thought of what I'll have to do in order to get my hands on those, I don't have much of a choice.

I return to the living room to place my call to the dino emergency line, a special branch of 911 manned solely by our kind for situations such as these. It's different from the ambulance line and cleanup crew line, but serves a similar function: bringing the proper authorities along at the proper time.

"What's your emergency?" asks the apathetic operator.

"There's an officer down," I say. "Very down." I give Dan's address, decline to tell the operator my name, and hang up quickly.

Back to the den, where I say my good-byes to my friend. They are short, succinct, and a moment after they leave my mouth I've forgotten what they were. It's better that way. If

I hang out any longer, wait for the cops to show up, they'll haul me downtown and stick me in some cell with an overblown, overfed T-Rex who'll try to question me until my ears bleed. I don't have time for that. I've got a Council meeting to crash.

15

arold Johnson is the current Brontosaur representative of the Council, and I know from the official Council calendar they forgot to take back when they kicked me off the board that any emergency meetings held during the autumn months are supposed to be held in his spacious wood-paneled basement. I cringe at the thought of another session with those bombastic buffoons, but it's my only chance if I want to get a look at those papers. That's assuming I can even get in to the meeting. I do have one plan in mind, and it might work as long as Harold hasn't changed from his usual anal, beastly self in the last nine months.

Traffic is light, and I make my way up the 405 with considerable speed. There are two velocities in Los Angeles: Rush Hour Halt and Warp Factor Nine. Due to the constant gridlock on our highways between the hours of seven and ten in the mornings and three to seven in the evenings, any chance we Angelenos have to duplicate Chuck Yeager's sound-barrier experiments during the less crowded moments are duly taken. Fifty-five is a joke, sixty a gas, sixty-five the actual minimum, seventy gaining respectability, and seventy-five the reality. Currently, I'm running about ninety. I've been trucking along these highways well over eighty-five miles an hour for all my automotive life—at least, when my car can handle it—and I've never once gotten a ticket.

Until now. Those lights flashing in my rearview mirror are not Christmas decorations, and that siren is not an air-raid drill. I pull over to the side of the road, stopping as quickly as possible.

What is the proper procedure here? I don't want to reach into my glove compartment to extract my registration—scurrying around and grabbing things is bound to make the officer nervous, and a nervous man with a gun in his hand is someone I'm not interested in meeting. Opening the door is probably a no-no as well, so I raise my arms above my head and spread my fingers wide. I probably look like a moose.

I watch in my side-view mirror as the officer, a portly gentleman in his midforties with a handlebar mustache—straight out of Central Casting—strolls cautiously up to my vehicle. He uses the butt of his nightstick to rap on my window, and I hurriedly roll it down, returning my hand to the air a moment later.

"You can put your hands down," he drawls. I follow orders. Saliva stretches between the officer's lips, a silvery strand glistening in the sunlight. It takes considerable effort to force my gaze away.

"Speeding, wasn't I?" No point in denying it.

"Ayup."

"And you're giving me a ticket, aren't you?"

"Ayup."

Naturally, I should argue it. Stick up for myself, for my reckless driving habits. Almost too late, I realize that this

isn't even my automobile—I've taken the liberty of steal-
ing Dan's Ford Explorer, as he no longer has a use for it,
and I no longer have any personal transportation—and I'm
gonna have my hands full trying to explain why I'm driving a car that belongs to a recently murdered police officer.

Things would be easier if this cop were a dino—his lack
of scent tells me he's human through and through—as I
could explain about the urgent, urgent Council meeting
and be done with it.

But as it is, he's looking at me strangely, head cocked to
one side, the movement reminiscent of Suarez and the tow
truck driver. "You're a Raptor, ain't ya? Don't meet many
of you fellas on the job."

Without thought, without wondering how this human
could have possibly learned of our existence, my instinct
kicks in—saliva floods my mouth as I prepare to rip out his
throat. One of the very first things a young dino learns is
that security leaks must be patched up, and quickly. Any
human who in any way suspects our presence must be
dealt with accordingly, which usually means a death sentence, swift and sure.

I glance up and down the freeway—the cars are coming
nonstop, and there is no visual protection along the shoulder. Even if I were able to take him down, I'd be spotted in
a moment. Need to find a safe place, a hidden location
where I can take care of business and—

"Raptor saved my life over in 'Nam," the cop says
proudly. "Best damn sonofabitch I ever did meet." He extends his hand through the car window. "Don Tuttle,
Triceratop. Good to meetcha." Stunned, I shake it.

"You . . . you're a dino?" I ask. My spit dries up as my
salivary glands go on a coffee break.

"Sure am," says the cop. Then, noting my surprise, he
slaps himself on the forehead and says, "Man—you

thought . . . the scent, right?" I nod. "That happens all the time. I know I should make a habit of pointing it out, but . . ."

Officer Tuttle turns his back to me, crouches down to window level, and pulls aside the wisps of hair adorning his guise. Working the camouflaged buttons with practiced dexterity, he flips the skin off his shoulders and displays for me the ranger green hide that covers the back of his head. A long, deep scar runs the length of his neck, stretching from ear to ear like a fleshy necklace, with two jagged triangles heading up either end.

"Bullet," he says. "Only time I ever been shot at, but I guess once is all it takes. Went in one side, straight out the other."

"Ouch."

"Nah, I didn't feel a thing. Took out a bundle of nerves on its way through." He covers his natural hide with the polysuit and snaps the covering back in place. "Also wrecked the hell outta my scent glands. Couple of dino docs over at County figured it was better to remove 'em than screw around tryin' to put 'em back in place.

"For a while I got these scent cushions, attached to a battery. Worked like potpourri simmer pots, you know them things? My wife has them all over. Doctors had some Diplodod pharmacist brew 'em up for me, says he does it pretty regular, but my wife said they smelled like old nickels. I didn't know what the hell she was talking about—old nickels? But I knew what she meant. They just didn't smell . . . right, you know? Better to go on without 'em, deal with it as it comes."

"I'm sorry," I tell him, not knowing the proper condolences for loss of pheromone production. I wonder if there's a Hallmark card.

"No big deal," he says nonchalantly. "Only thing is, I

gotta watch myself for dinos thinking I ain't what I ain't, you know?"

"Sure, sure." And now that we're on a more familiar basis . . . "Officer—Don—Officer Don, about my speed, I'm very sorry that—"

"Forget about it," he says, ripping the ticket into shreds. The newly formed confetti sinks into the ground, but I doubt he'll slap himself with a littering fine any time soon.

"Thank you," I say, grasping his paw and pumping it gratefully. "I was in such a hurry for the Council meeting that I—"

"You say Council meeting?"

"In the Valley. I'm late."

"How late?"

"'Bout a day. Give or take a minute."

"Well, hell!" he hollers. "We got to get you an escort!"

So it is that fifteen minutes later I arrive at Harold Johnson's rambling ranch house in Burbank, accompanied by three squad cars and two motorcycle units. It's a powerful feeling taking the streets by storm, sirens blaring, lights blazing, and I can understand how that adrenaline rush might lead to unsavory circumstances. I'm ready to crack heads right now, and there isn't a bona fide criminal in sight.

I thank the officers, dinos all, and bid them farewell as I maneuver my way across the cobblestone path leading to the Johnsons' front door. The welcome mat must have a pressure-sensitive plate beneath it, for long before my hand makes it to the doorbell I find myself standing across from the jittery Mrs. Johnson, all five foot four and 250 pounds squished down deep inside a guise constructed to handle no more than one eighty, tops. She needs a new guise, and soon—one more banana split, and the current one will burst under the strain. Her hands tremble in alarm, and she shoots worried glances about the yard, the street, her foyer.

"Go away," she pleads. "Harold won't like this one bit."

I say, "He doesn't have to like it. Just tell him I'm here."

She looks behind her, toward the door leading down to the basement. Even from here, I can make out the shouting and the incessant rumble of roars. "Please," she begs. "He gets so mad at me."

I put a hand on Mrs. Johnson's shoulder, the flesh beneath the fragile polysuit crying to be let out. "There's no reason for him to get mad at you—"

"But he does. He does. You know his temper—"

"Oh, I know it. But I want you to go down there and have him come up for me."

Another glance at the door, as if it's the wood itself she's frightened of. "Why don't you just go down? I'm sure they'd all like to see you."

"If I go down there unannounced, I'll be attacked faster than you can say trauma center, and then you'll have a dead Raptor on your hands. Now is that what you want, Mrs. Johnson?"

Slowly, gingerly, she turns and walks toward the basement door like an inmate walking that final mile. Mrs. Johnson disappears into the basement. I wait in the open doorway.

A crash, a scream, a contingent of bone-chilling growls. The plains of the Serengeti have been transported into the Johnsons' basement. As I stare about the foyer, soaking in the suburban lack of charm, the wooden door flies open, slams into the wall, and cracks into two pieces, falling off its hinges and onto the linoleum.

"Harold, I know what you're thinking—" I start, even before I see his hulking frame huddled in the open doorway, "and you have to give me a chance." He's out of guise, tail poised to strike, his massive body pulsating with anger, with hatred.

No human words that I have ever heard are coming out of this Brontosaur as he prepares to charge at me, head tucked into those powerful shoulders, arms clenched tightly by his sides. Steam should be pouring out of his nostrils. Behind him, I can see Mrs. Johnson scurry out of the basement and into the kitchen like a cockroach when the lights are turned on.

"Wait—wait—I have full right to be here," I announce.

"You—have—no—right."

"I'm a Council member."

"You—were—rectified." I don't like the way he's enunciating each word—he's never been one for stunning verbal intercourse, but the menace in his voice is palpable.

"Yes, yes, I was rectified, I saw the papers, we all know that. You kicked me off the Council, fine."

"Then leave—before I shove your tail down—your—throat."

Here's where I bring out my hidden ace. "But I never signed the papers."

"So what if you didn't?" he asks, and now I've got him speaking without pauses.

"Check the rules," I say. "If I didn't sign the papers in the presence of at least one other Council member, then it's not official."

"Bullcrap it's not official. We kicked Gingrich out three years ago—you were there—and he didn't sign squat."

"Then technically he's still in. No one enforces it anymore, but it's there since time immemorial. Go ahead, I'll wait."

And I do just that as Harold, a stickler for the rules if I've ever known one, retreats back into the basement to scrutinize some arcane rule I hope I didn't pull out of my ass. Ten minutes later, I hear his heavy footsteps clomping up the stairs. Heavy, slow—defeated.

"Come on down," he mutters, barely even sticking his head out of the stairway.

I am greeted by a chorus of catcalls and groans as the fourteen Southern California representatives from the remaining dinosaur species welcome me back with closed arms. They are fully unguised, and wander around the basement in a state of naked autonomy. Tails bat against one another as they swish freely about the floor, and I'm glad to see that there are no blood marks on the walls—yet. Harold has made a smart move and hung large plastic tarps across the sofas, the chairs, the coffee tables, in order to protect his furniture from stains once the stuff starts flying. And at Council meetings, it will always start flying, sooner or later.

There's Parsons, the Stegosaur, an accountant for a small firm downtown, and Seligman, the Allosaur rep, a big-shot attorney up in Century City. Oberst, the Iguanodon dentist, gives me a sidelong leer, and the T-Rex, Kurzban, some sort of evolutionary psych professor up at UCLA, chooses to ignore my presence altogether. But not everyone's a professional—Mrs. Nissenberg, our Coleo rep whose first name I can never remember, is a homemaker and quilter extraordinaire, and Rafael Colon—Hadrosaur—is a hopeless shiftabout who fancies himself an actor because he got a few bit parts back when *Miami Vice* needed scruffy criminals. And of course, there's Handleman, the representative for the Procompsognathus population, and a Council meeting wouldn't be complete without a Compy there to make it all the more excruciating.

"Why you here?" he chirps. "Huh, we kick you out!"

"It really isn't wise," mutters Seligman.

The new Raptor representative—Glasser, according to a name tag rudely affixed to his scaled chest, a tallish fellow with a nice tan hide—strolls up and sticks out his hand. "Thanks for screwing up, mate," he says with a hint of an Australian accent. "No ill will, eh?"

"No worries," I respond.

But the rest of them are mighty worried, screaming about how I abused their finances, abused their trust, abused the power of the Council for my own selfish motives, and I can't disagree with any of them. "You're right," I say. "All of you, one hundred percent correct."

But none of them are even willing to listen until Harold brings the full weight of his body and his power to the floor. His tail flops heavily behind him as he walks, and it clips Mrs. Nissenberg across the cheek. She yelps in pain, but nobody seems to notice or care.

"It's the rules, ladies and gentlemen. The Rules. We live by them here, and even though as individuals some of us choose to ignore them"—sharp glance in my direction—"this group as a whole cannot. If the rules say that the Raptor can stay, then the Raptor can stay."

Renewed arguments, heated debate, and I put up my hand for silence. I get none, so I shout over them. "Wait! Wait! I don't want to stay."

This quiets them down enough for me to issue my ultimatum. "I'll make you a deal. There's some information you now have in your possession, and I would like to be here when that information is presented."

A sharp glance from Harold—he knows what I'm talking about. "When were you going to go over that . . . stuff?" I ask.

"It's listed as new business, so . . . tomorrow sometime." And this is what they consider an *emergency* meeting.

"How's this: Get to it now—right now—let me stay here until it's over—and then I'll sign the papers, and you never have to see me again."

"Ever again?" they ask as one.

"Gone like I was a bad dream."

An electric murmur from the group. Harold asks, "Can we have a minute to think this over?"

"Thirty seconds," I respond. "I'm in a bit of a hurry."

This group couldn't figure out whether or not to breathe in only thirty seconds let alone process my request, but after a short series of motions and calls to order, my ulti-matum is answered. Harold walks to the bottom of the basement stairs and yells up at his loving partner.

"Maria!" And, after a few moments have passed with no response, "MARIA!"

"Yes, Harold?" comes the frightened reply.

"Send down Dr. Solomon." Harold turns back to the group, addressing us as one.

"Yesterday morning, I got some information I thought the Council might find interesting. Brings up some new questions about an old topic, adds in a twist I'm not quite sure whether or not to believe. I don't even know all the specifics yet, but we'll learn them together soon enough."

"What is it?" squawks Handleman, and we all tell him to shush.

"Before I share this with you, let me say that despite the potential implications this may have, everyone should re-main calm, and perhaps we can come to a solution in an appropriate amount of time." Hah! I'll be long gone before they've even decided the order in which they'll try to kill one another.

Harold Johnson heads over toward Oberst and Seligman, waddling like an oversized mallard. The two dinos flinch as he approaches, arranging themselves back to back, circling their wagons so as to defend their territory. Shooting the Allosaur and Iguanodon representatives a look of disgust, Johnson pushes past them, making for a file cabinet set beneath a rotted writing desk. I cannot see what he is doing, but I can hear a number of locks clicking open, granting him access to the treasures beyond.

He strides back into the middle of the room, a thick sheaf of papers bound by masses of colored rubber bands tucked beneath his arm. The edges of the individual pages have been singed, some to the point of ash. Black snowflakes flutter to the ground.

"This is only about one percent of the original stash," says Johnson, holding the bundle aloft for all to see. "The other ninety-nine percent has been lost to us. It burned in a nightclub fire sometime last week. Owner of the club died in the blast."

"He died?" I blurt out, unable to stop myself.

"This morning," says Johnson. "I got the call a few hours ago." I feel an odd sense of loss; though I never knew Burke personally, I have grown to understand the Raptor over these past few days. I have been privy to his likes, his dislikes, his relationships both moral and otherwise. I can only hope that Jaycee Holden has a strong shoulder nearby when she hears the news.

"But these papers"—and Johnson pretentiously waves the packet around like McCarthy holding his blacklist, crisped edges crackling in the air—"these are something altogether more important than any single dinosaur life. They were found in the bottom of a cardboard box that had been tucked away in the nightclub's storeroom.

"They appear to belong to Dr. Emil Vallardo, the dino geneticist working out of New York. They contain information regarding his . . . mixing experiments."

Eureka! I want to shout. That's why Judith McBride de-

nied ever funding Donovan's nightclub—it was Vallardo
who fronted the money all along! Still, funding a nightclub
clear across the country just so you could hide some papers
there seems like an awful length to go to in order to protect
an experiment that has already been heavily documented
by the Councils.

"And this," Johnson says, holding aloft a small glass
vial, his pudgy fingers spreading across the surface, "is
what they found in a hidden safe tucked beneath the floor-
boards."

Mrs. Nissenberg lifts her head. "What is it?"

Johnson's voice drops three notches. "This is one of his
experiments. This is a mixed embryo."

Chaos.

"We must disbar him!" screams Oberst.

"You can't disbar doctors," says Seligman. "That's
lawyers."

"We could have his license taken away—"

"The children, what about the children?"

As I lean back in my chair, using my tail as a balancing
mechanism, I tune out all of the commotion around me—
the harangues against Vallardo and his corruption of nature, the cries of *what shall become of us, we will all
become mongrels,* the gasping and the wheezing and the
whimpers over the destruction of our species. And despite
my congenital aversion to any type of whining whatsoever,
I can't say that I blame them. The Council members, like
all other dinos, are worried. They are worried about unity,
they are worried about the conflict of science and nature,
and they are worried about what is right and what is wrong
in a world in which we must hide ourselves away, in which
morals are topsy-turvy and positions can flip-flop from day
to day.

Most of all, they are worried that they will lose their

identity. But it is pointless to fret in this manner; we lost it a long time ago.

From the staircase, then: A clomp. Two thumps. Pause. A clomp. Two thumps. The sounds of a tired three-legged horse, of a body being dragged down a flight of stairs by reluctant murderers. A clomp. Two thumps.

The pounding is soon accompanied by a voice, insistent, crotchety: "Well? Are you helping or are you not helping?"

Harold bolts up the stairs—Brontos can haul when they need to—and, a minute later, reemerges holding an elderly man in one arm and a walker in the other. "Put me down," the old man grunts. "I can walk, I can walk. Stairs, no. Floor, yes."

"This is Dr. Otto Solomon," Johnson says, "a partner of Vallardo's from many, many years ago, and I think he may be able to shed a little light on the issue." The doctor—a Hadrosaur, if the scent hits me right—is still guised up in his human costume, and he's a curious little thing. Accent like an SS commandant, five feet high, face like a shar-pei, hair follicles clutching at the scalp, scrabbling for purchase but fighting a losing battle. It's a wonderful approximation of human deterioration, and I can't help but marvel at his choice of costume; I can only hope that when I reach his age I have the guts to so accurately depict my own physical decrepitude.

"What are you staring at?" he asks, and I chuckle, sorry for whomever he has caught in midgaze. "I said what are you staring at, Raptor?"

"Me?" Whoops.

"Are you done staring?"

"Yes."

"Yes, what?"

"Yes . . . Doctor?"

"That is more like it." Dr. Solomon snatches his walker from Johnson and gallops into the center of our circle—clop thump thump clop thump thump—zipping along with surprising speed for a dino of his age and infirmities.

"Before I give you my analysis of the situation," he says, each word a clipped command of Teutonic control, "is there anyone who has something important to say? Something that cannot wait?"

No hands are raised.

"Good," says Solomon. "Then you will kindly remember to shut up while I am speaking. I do not answer questions until I am done, and I do not entertain speculation at any time."

Again, we agree to his demand. Dr. Solomon pulls himself erect, stares each of us in the eye one by one, working the room. He begins with a short discussion of creation, of the primordial ooze and the single-celled organisms that had nothing better to do with their time than swim around, mutate, and divide. We work our way into early forms of multicellular life before the doctor starts babbling on about DNA, genetic codes, and long-strand proteins.

After nearly thirty minutes have gone by, during which time Mrs. Nissenberg has to poke me with her knitting needle just to keep me from falling asleep, I raise my hand high and ask, "Is there a layman's explanation for this?"

The doctor doesn't even glance over; he ignores me and continues with his speech. ". . . and so, with the ribosomes taking up the available material . . ."

But I'm determined to get to the bottom of this before dinner. "Excuse me, Dr. Solomon, but what does any of this have to do with Vallardo's papers?"

The doctor thunks over toward me, eyes blazing. "You want it so easy," he says. "All your generation, you want it now, you want it on a platter. You don't want to have to think about the answer—you want others to do the work for you. Is that it? Is that what you're looking for?"

"That's the situation in a nutshell, Doc." I look around the room, and the feeling, it seems, is mutual. "Now can you fork it over, please?"

Solomon sighs, shaking his head in pity for us poor unlearned masses. "Dr. Vallardo's papers, along with the once-frozen embryo inside that vial, indicate an experiment in cross-species mating," he says plainly.

"We already knew that!" cries Johnson. "We've known that for six months now."

"Six months!" yelps Handleman, anxious to exercise his vocal cords. "Six months!"

The others join in the harangue, blasting Solomon for wasting a half hour of our time on scientific fiddle-faddle, but the doctor claps his hands three times—smack smack smack—and comfortably commands silence in the basement once more.

"If you would stop your yapping," he says, each word tinged with ice, "maybe you would be able to listen to me as well as hear me. Listen. Dr. Vallardo has long been engaged in cross-*race* mating. But this is not what I just told you."

Handleman again—"Six months!"

"What I said," Solomon continues, "is that all of this evidence, if I am reading it correctly, shows that he has begun experiments in cross-*species* mating."

"Cross-species?" Colon repeats, unsure of the term's definition.

"Like what?" Oberst asks.

Colon steps up. "Like a . . . like a dog and a cat?"

"Or a mouse and a chicken?" asks Mrs. Nissenberg.

"A donkey and a fish!" yells Kurzban.

But I understand it all now, the whole thing, the big picture, the kit, the kaboodle, and motives to boot. Well, most of it, anyway. I step up.

"How about the mating of a dinosaur and a human?" I ask, already knowing I've got this one dead to rights. "Is that what Dr. Vallardo's been working on?"

Solomon smiles, a slow, wry grin he casually tosses in my direction. "See," he says, "some of you do know how to listen."

16

I was out of there just after the flesh started flying, but I managed to get nicked by a few stray claws and tails during my retreat. Chaos erupted the moment Solomon laid it out for us, made it clear that Vallardo was attempting to facilitate an interspecies birth, and it wasn't seconds later that scattered skirmishes broke out all throughout the basement, miniature battles of rage and confusion. Dr. Solomon, who certainly wasn't expecting the violent reaction in which the Council specializes, took a nasty club wound to the head before he was able to gather enough strength to pull himself up the basement stairs; Johnson, engaged in a no-holds-barred grudge match with Kurzban, sure wasn't going to help the elderly doctor this time.

So as blood, sweat, and bile splattered the basement walls, I grabbed Mrs. Nissenberg and dragged her into the far corner.

"You have to watch me sign this," I said, and pulled out a copy of the rectification papers. All the while, I was ducking tails, parrying claws, trying anything to remain unharmed and unmolested.

We went through the short motions of signing and notarizing, and then it was all over—I'd officially been kicked out of the Council for good. Mrs. Nissenberg wished me good luck, and I braved a few more swats and close calls on my way up the stairs.

Now, in the rush back to my apartment, no less than eight moving violations are committed by yours truly, including the running of a light that was a good ten seconds into its red cycle. Somebody up there likes me, or at least enjoys watching my shenanigans enough to let me live another day.

But how can I be blamed for breaking a few little traffic rules when my brain is occupied with so many other matters? I need to get back to the apartment, round up whatever valuables I can find, hock them for as much as I can get out of Pedro, the guy who runs the Cash 4 Crap store on Vermont, and get myself another plane ticket to New York. I need to confront Vallardo—I need to confront Judith—I need to find Sarah again, if only to take her out to dinner, squash any notions of this nonsensical relationship, and put an end to what was so unwittingly and unwisely begun.

Solomon's explanation of Vallardo's papers seals it—McBride's mind had indeed taken a long walk off a short pier, but the crazy apefucker had enough cash and enough similarly insane friends to pull off his delusion.

But what amazes me—what sickens me—is that his love for a human—his love for Sarah—was so great that he actually felt the need to father her children. If Sarah ever knew of the bestiality she'd been engaged in, I'm sure it would mortify her to death, but this new information—it might make that mortification literal.

A foreclosure notice has been tacked to the front door of my ground-level apartment, and I angrily rip it off, tear it into little bits, and scatter it along the dirt. The locks have been changed as well, but an overdrawn, otherwise useless credit card gains me quick entrance to my—*my,* damn it—home.

The power's off—I knew it would happen eventually—which means that the funky smell comes from the spoiled leftovers in my refrigerator. I stumble through the house, banging my shins in the darkness. The only good thing about the power outage is that the answering machine light is not blinking at me.

Microwave, blender—hey, the TV's still there. The appliances scattered around the apartment should be enough to score me a coach seat back to New York; even if I have to sit on the wing, I'll take it.

But there's no chance of me going back tonight. The sun's about to set, and even if I could somehow haul all of this crap into the car, I wouldn't make it to Pedro's before closing time.

I am in dire need of a nap. The last time I slept long enough to actually drop into a REM cycle was . . . let's see . . . two nights ago at the Plaza. Counting on my fingers—which are blurring, separating—makes it nearly forty hours I've gone without more than the occasional doze, and I'm amazed that I'm functioning at all. They haven't taken away my bed yet, so I decide to close the shades, lie down, and get in a few minutes of shut-eye.

The doorbell rings. I don't know how much later it is, but the sun has set and the streetlights have popped to life. The usually pleasant electronic chimes that I hooked up to my buzzer last Christmas tear away at my nerves, jangling my eardrums, as the battery-powered bell goes off again. I take a quick peek outside my window, toward the small parking lot in front of my apartment complex, but I don't see any cars other than those belonging to the humans and dinos who live nearby. Off to one side I can make out the hood of what might be a Lincoln parked just behind our Dumpster, but I can't be sure. Dragging my sluggish frame as quickly as I can, I move to the door and take a gander through the peephole, ready to whip off my gloves and bare my claws if need be. My tail twitches in involuntary anticipation, pulse revving at the starting gate.

It's Sarah. White silk blouse, short black skirt, legs, legs, legs.

The only thing I am thinking is that there is nothing that I am thinking. I've collared a few bad apples in my day who've stood stock solid as I dragged them downtown, and I always wondered why they had that deer-in-the-headlights look. Now I know—the brain shuts down when and where it wants to. It does not follow a schedule.

Sarah smiles at the door, at the peephole, expecting me to be watching her, and the walleye lens distorts her features, spreads her lips into a goldfish pucker, extends her teeth into great white monoliths, narrows her eyes. Horrifying. I throw open the door.

Without a word, we embrace, my arms encircling her body, pulling her close. If I could envelop her, I would. If I could make her a part of my body, suck her in, incorporate her, I would. She grasps my waist tightly, holding on as if to secure herself against a steady wind, her head pressed against my chest, her hair flung up, over, surrounding my nose, her artificial perfume beautiful to me despite its synthetic components.

We kiss. We've done it before, we'll do it again, and I can't help it so we kiss. It lingers. It sends flares shooting through my head. My hands move all about her body, outlining her curves, her exquisite lines, and I would like nothing more than to rip this guise off my skin so that I might feel her with my true hands, understand her with my real person.

I want to ask her why she's here, when she got in, where she's staying, but I know there will be time for that. Later. Later. Still silent, Sarah takes my hand, squeezes it, and I understand the question implicit in that grasp. I squeeze back and lead my human lover toward the bedroom.

Body is in full control, eyes and brain watching from the bleachers, cheering me on. Sarah undresses me—the outer me—slowly unbuttoning my shirt, pulling it off, tossing it carelessly on the floor. Hands rubbing against my chest, transferring the warm, firm touch to the real skin deep inside. I grab her breasts firmly, my first feel of a human, and she moans softly in response. Whatever I'm doing, it must be right. Sarah leans down and licks the hair on my chest, running her tongue past my nipples, down to my stomach. My guised-up torso is fair enough under human terms—not enough to land me in any of your finer ladies' magazines, mind you, but I've been told by those in the know that I have a passable chest and above-average abs. Still, with Sarah's gaze tickling every inch of my body, I do wish I had shelled out the cash for those pectoral attachments.

Sarah, smiling sweetly as we move to kiss each other yet again, doesn't seem to mind my "natural" body in the slightest, and she moves her attention below my waist, her hands gaining speed, moving from sensual to frantic as she works off my belt, cracking it through the air. Zippers sliding along now, buttons popping off, pants flying into the established heap on the ground, I go to town, being careful not to wrinkle, to crush, as I fumble with buttons and straps and hooks. Women's clothing, though a pain in the tail, is infinitely more delicate than our rough-and-tumble wear, and I have to force myself not to tear the fabric off her body in frustration and anticipation.

I am unaware of just how or when we made it to the bed itself, but as my eyes open in the aftermath of the deepest, most satisfying kiss these lips have ever had the honor of experiencing, I find myself cuddled up with Sarah atop my green and blue patchwork quilt, naked as the day I donned my first guise.

Sarah, too, is nude. And breathtaking. Literally—after a few moments of watching her lithe body squirm in anticipation of things to come, I am forced to slap myself in order to bring about a gasp of oxygen. Once again, Sarah brings my face to hers, cupping my cheeks in her two delicate hands, fingernails caressing my outer skin but still oh so delicious, and we roll together, moving as one as I prepare to betray my species in the most beautiful way I can possibly imagine.

A dino female—and most males, I should imagine—approaches sex in a very rational, practical fashion. The act itself is treated almost as an obligation, not to her mate, her partner, or her own intrinsic femininity, but to the species itself. It is as if we have been unable to work our way out from under the thumb of raw animalistic urges despite a good hundred million years of evolution. When the time comes to procreate (or at least go through the motions), the time comes to procreate, and woe betide the creature who tries to stop a dino female from having her way.

But there is a world beyond, I know now, a level deeper than any Tantric manual can provide. How could I have gone so long without this?

Of course, in the past, I had no experience outside of my own species, no clue that anything was absent from the equation. But now, as I move my body with Sarah's, my

costumed skin all but invisible to my hyperextended
senses, I realize that there is so much more to this act, an
element of sensuality that I have been missing all along.
With dinos, flesh grinds and gyrates, hide rubbing roughly
into a hot layer of friction. With humans—with Sarah—
flesh swells, billows, condenses, an undulation of one. As I
stroke myself in and out of her warmth, my engorged
member tight against the confines of the polysuit extension, tight within the confines of my new lover, she moves
with me, our energies coalescing into one great wave of
movement and heat. With dinos, the sounds are shrieks and
moans, howls to the religion of pleasure. With Sarah, there
are soft murmurs and syncopated heartbeats, delicate gasps
and whispers to the night.

I do not feel guilty in the least.

When it is over, when we are spent, when our arms fall
to our sides, exhausted from holding one another so close,
so tightly, I draw from the last remaining reserves of my
energy and place my forearm beneath Sarah's fragile body,
nestling her against my chest. It is not macho to cuddle, but
my usually ubiquitous sense of self-consciousness has left
the building, having been put out for the night like a
naughty cat.

Staring at each other, words still unspoken, eyes focus-
ing on eyes, pupils still dilating in the darkened bedroom,
her green irises set off beautifully against the shock of red
hair cascading across her cheek, I am unable to stop my
hands from roaming, searching out her body in their own
journey across the uncharted. I fondle her breast, teasing
the nipple with my fingertips. I have never touched a
human breast before this night, and I find it oddly firm,
sensually so.

We make love again. I do not know where I find the energy, but if I ever locate that source, I might be ready to set up shop with a perpetual-motion patent.

One of us must speak first. I suppose it's possible for her to silently dress herself, kiss me, and walk out of my town house without so much as a word the entire time; I suppose it would be romantic, fantastically so perhaps, but someone as garrulous as myself couldn't let that happen. And though I cringe as the PI who rents out space in my mind steps up and asks for a word with the landlord, I do indeed have a few questions to ask.

"How was the flight?" I begin. Sarah is still naked, splayed across the bed; I have covered my costumed body with the quilt. I am cold, my circulation poor. I really ought to see a physician.

She laughs, a high giggle that makes me want to leap up and start all over again despite the strange tingle emanating from my tail and lower extremities. I hope that those repetitive thrusting motions didn't damage my girdle; at the first possible moment I should run to the bathroom and check the apparatus out. A snapped girdle can cause serious circulation problems, which can, in turn, cause temporary and, in some cases, permanent loss of feeling in the affected areas.

"How was the flight?" Sarah repeats, tossing her hair away from her face. "That's what you want to ask me?"

"Figured I'd be asking you at some point, might as well make it now. Good a time as any." I give her nose a peck.

"The flight was fine," she said. "Would you like to know what movie we saw?"

"I'd be delighted to know."

"We saw *Spartacus*."

"Isn't that sort of an old movie?"

"It was an old plane. Besides, it took up most of the

flight." She yawns, stretches, and I watch her muscles strain with the effort. "So now you get to ask me what you really want to ask me, which is why I'm in Los Angeles."

"Well . . . now that you mention it . . ."

"A singing gig."

"A singing gig." I am skeptical.

Sarah lowers her eyes, runs a finger across my chest. "You don't believe me?"

"It's not that I don't believe you," I say. "It's that I figured, maybe . . ." Maybe she came all this way just to see me. I can't finish the sentence; it reeks of femininity.

"I found a message on my machine after I got back from your hotel. My agent got me a studio gig singing background on a B. B. King album. We've been recording all day."

"And then you decided to come in and see me? So I'm secondary?"

Sarah tickles me, a vicious blitzkrieg that sends me rolling across the bed before I'm able to mount my own counterattack. Soon enough, we're kissing once again like teenagers going at it on the living-room sofa before the parents get home.

We lie in silence for some time, holding each other, reveling in the perfect fit of our bodies. We are tailor-made for one another. "When do you go back to New York?" I ask.

"I've got an open-ended ticket," she says, "but the gig's supposed to be over the day after tomorrow." I feel a hand pressing against my costumed knee. It is moving up, toward that polyfiber mix that represents my thigh. My tail is really starting to tingle now, and I don't know if it's only from lack of circulation. "Of course, I could be persuaded to stay."

That's all the invitation I need to get me flowing yet

again. I am a dynamo today! Someone should bottle my sexual energy and use it to power India.

Nearly four hours and countless lovemaking sessions after Sarah first arrived at my apartment this afternoon, I invite her to stay the night. She accepts.

"Let me go back to the hotel, grab my stuff," she says.

"I'll drive you," I offer.

"I've got a rental."

"You don't know your way."

"I've got a map," she says, laughing. "Honey, I'm coming back this time, okay?" Sarah, now fully dressed, leans over the bed and plants a full kiss on my lips, her tongue searching out mine. I try to pull her back down onto the bed for another episode of playtime, but she backs away, shaking her finger. "Naughty boy," she snickers. "You'll just have to wait for it."

I nod; it will indeed be best if we separate for an hour or so. It will give Sarah time to pack, and give me time to adjust my costume and to the reality of what has just occurred. Now that my brain has been freed from the constant ecstasy of orgasmic highs, it has a chance to be concerned with the ongoing loss of sensation in my tail. Adjustments are in order.

Hopping out of the bed—yep, there's the tingle—I walk Sarah into the living room, toward the foyer. We embrace again, and I hide myself behind the front door as I let her out. I am not an exhibitionist, costume or no.

"An hour or so?" I say.

She laughs, obviously amused at my lack of pretense. I want her, she knows it, end of story. "As soon as possible, Vincent." She blows me a kiss and heads for her car. I shut the door and ensure that the blinds are drawn.

That tingle, that itch, has intensified, spread all across

my body. Something major must have quit functioning down in the nitty-gritty of my costume, and I can only hope that I caught it in time to prevent a major injury. I don't bother removing my mask or torso guise, as it's a pain in the rear to properly apply the epoxy in order to get that good, tight grip that will hold up under even the most intense bout of smooching, but I do remove the lower half of my outer layer. The polysuit slowly peels away from my hide, its already gummy backside positively slimy thanks to the buildup of sweat and other natural juices expelled during the last few hours.

Standing in my living room, across from the full-length decorative mirror hung on the far wall, I inspect my supportive trusses and girdles for any breaches in their superstructure. So far, I can see no flaws. Could this sensation, so near to my groin, be a purely psychosomatic one? A result of repressed guilt over what is sure to be the most unnatural act in which I have ever engaged? I certainly hope not, because if I have any say in the matter, I plan on being this unnatural again.

Wait, wait—there it is. Right beneath my G series, the clamp that always gives me the most trouble, a fabric strap has somehow managed to double over and work its way into a tight noose atop my tail. I can't imagine how it happened, but what with all of the interesting new postures Sarah and I got ourselves into, I'm not surprised at the result.

Grasping my tail with one still-costumed hand, I work the strap down and away, pulling it into a less offensive position; almost instantly, I can feel sensation, glorious sensation, rush back into my body like a river breaking free of its dam. It doesn't feel as nice as making love with Sarah, but it runs a close second.

Perhaps I should remove my entire guise and make whatever readjustments are necessary to keep this from happening again. I'm hoping Sarah and I will have an encore of our earlier performance once she returns to my town house, and I don't want any technical malfunctions to get in the way. The next time, that fabric strap could wrap around something a lot more vital than my tail.

I locate the hidden reverse buttons beneath my nipples and work them away from their confines, struggling to work my torso polysuit away from the hide below. Torsos always give me the most problems, perhaps because there are so few places to squirrel away the requisite attachments. Masks have countless hiding places—under the hair, inside the ear, the nose, etc. The lower half of the body allows for zipper and button placement in other, less socially acceptable areas, though it works out well in the end.

I've almost got that last Velcro strip unattached, reaching for it, reaching for it—

And Sarah walks in the front door.

"Vincent, I forgot to ask what street I—"

She freezes. I freeze. Only her eyes move, darting around my half-costumed body, taking in the spectacle before her. And I can project myself into Sarah's head, see myself as I must look through her eyes: a lizard draped with disembodied human skin, a beast who crawled up from the depths of prehistory to terrify and devour young, petite human women. A monster. A freak. Lust and passion and eroticism and, yes, love, are forgotten as my instinct, my damned instinct, orders martial law in my body and takes over all functions.

"Vincent—" she says, but I cut her off with my leap across the room, slamming the door closed with one exposed claw as I bounce off the far wall and pounce atop her chest. Sarah falls roughly to the floor, landing on her back with a surprised whoosh of air. My claws grab for her throat as my roar shatters the nearby mirror, glass spilling onto the carpet.

I know my duty. I have to kill her.

"I'm sorry, Sarah," I manage to say, even as I ready my claw for the final plunge into her beautiful, quivering neck. She's gasping in gulps of air, trying to say something, her breath still not coming—

"Vin . . . Vin . . ."

"I'm sorry," I repeat, and strike the death blow.

It is blocked. Her arm catches mine, holds it in place, the peaked edges of my claws inches from her throat. How is this possible? Perhaps in her fear she has gained strength. I strike out with the other hand, natural knives glinting—

Caught and captured yet again. Sarah struggles with my arms, holding her death at bay, face contorted in pain. "Vincent," she manages to say, her voice two octaves deeper than I have ever heard it before. "Wait."

But there's still that inborn sense of danger, of responsibility, telling me to *push it home, finish the job, kill the human before she lets it all out!* and I contract my muscles yet again, eager to get it all over with and start what is sure to be a prolonged mourning process.

"Wait," Sarah says again, and this time her word cuts through the din of instinct-driven insanity, halting the downward thrust of my arms. Is this foolishness on my part? Is this that human-bred habit of trying to *understand* everything rearing up again, costing me valuable time? In the dino world we do not overanalyze. We see, we react, and we conquer. With my interspecies coupling a mere half hour behind me, I find myself disgusted at whatever bits of humanity I have incorporated into my persona over the years. I should kill her now! But I find myself waiting to hear her out.

I sit back on my haunches, muscles still quivering, ready to pounce if she should try to run, to make a dash to the outside world. I love Sarah with whatever soul I have left in this body, but I cannot take the chance of trusting her. Not with this.

I expect her to try and beg for mercy, to explain that she will never ever tell a single living being about what she has seen in my apartment today, to plead clemency as others have done before her. But she doesn't even open her mouth, doesn't try to speak.

Instead, Sarah simply tosses her hair over her shoulders and reaches her hands up as if to bunch those long locks into a single ponytail. I hear a click, a familiar *zzzip,* and Sarah brings those beautiful arms forward again. I shall be sad to see them gone.

A shift of her features, an impossible slide to the left. Noses don't move like that. Chins don't move like that. At least, not without some major reconstructive surgery. Eyebrows are falling, rosy cheeks following, and what the hell is going on—

Sarah's mask falls off, skin drooping and sagging away from her face. A rich brown hide, a smooth sandpaper texture, peeks out from beneath. Contact lenses pop out of her eyes, green globules fluttering to the carpet. Stumbling backward, my body is no longer under my control as that false layer of flesh falls away, off her hide, onto the floor. I stare in disbelief as she stands and unfastens the rest of her guise.

Polysuit follows polysuit as Sarah Archer slowly and deliberately removes each flap of faux skin, every ounce of makeup, every inch of belt and girdle and truss from the real body beneath. I do not know how much time has passed. A minute, an hour, a day, it doesn't matter as I witness the gradual disappearance of Sarah Archer and the equally gradual unveiling of a very familiar Coleophysis.

"Vincent," she says softly, "I wanted to tell you."

I should have seen it coming, should have known it from the start. I'm a trained professional, for Chrissakes. It was there all along, of course, easy enough to detect if only I hadn't been blinded by my own lust for forbidden treasures:

Sarah Archer is Jaycee Holden. Jaycee Holden is Sarah Archer. Put it however you like it, the two women are one and the same, and I feel the increasingly unstable buttresses that support my world collapsing beneath me as the rest of my muscles give way. Someone, it seems, is dimming the lights . . .

17

We sit on the couch, three feet apart, miles away from each other. Every few minutes, she attempts to speak, but I hold up my hand, refusing to listen. Immature, perhaps, but I need some time to think. It has been almost an hour since I came to, and only now am I regaining enough control of my emotions to allow for rational conversation.

"Vincent, listen . . ." she pleads, tears welling in those soft brown eyes. Her green contact lenses soak in a spare case carried in her purse.

"I can't . . . How could . . ." I am not getting very far with speech, so I opt for a pained expression. It conveys the message properly.

"You don't think I didn't want to tell you? Right there in that Greek restaurant, I wanted to let it all out. Right in front of everyone if I had to, just let it fly, let you know that you and I . . . that we were the same."

I laugh sardonically, shaking my head. "We're not the same," I say.

"We're both dinos."

"Or so you say. Maybe this is a costume, too."

"Don't be childish, Vincent, of course it isn't."

"How the hell am I supposed to know?" I explode, and some part of me is glad to see her cringe. "I mean, Christ, Sarah . . . or is it Jaycee?"

"It's Jaycee."

"You sure? I could go for just about anything now. You want me to call you Bertha, I'll call you Bertha."

"It's Jaycee," she repeats meekly.

"Fine. You got anything left to hide, Jaycee? 'Cause I'm just about done playing around. You're missing, you're not missing, you're a human, you're a dino—"

"There's a reason," she interrupts.

"I would hope so. If you did this just for kicks I'd really be worried. So, you gonna tell me?"

"If you let me."

"I'm letting you."

"Good."

"Good. Now talk."

She begins slowly, shifting about the couch, unable to look me in the eyes. It was so damned easy before, wasn't it? "I don't know where to start," she says, and I suggest the beginning. "There isn't much of a beginning. It sort of . . . sprang up."

"Like a weed?"

"Five years ago," Jaycee continues, "I met Donovan on the streets of New York. Well, not on the streets—we were both at a deli counter down in Greenwich Village. And we were both single and we were both attractive and we were both ready for a relationship, though we didn't know it at the time. I smelled him the second he walked in, the strongest dino odor that's ever hit me. Do you remember his smell, Vincent? From your visit to the hospital?"

I remember the odors of barbecued meat, of roasted

Raptor, and though I feel Jaycee Holden deserves some pain for what she's put me through, I don't think divulging this information would represent a fair retaliation. "It was a hospital," I say. "You know how tough it is with those disinfectants."

She senses my tactful avoidance of the subject and nods gratefully. "He could light up a room with his odor. Like a wave of roses, a sea breeze. I used to call him my little sea dragon.

"I had corned beef on white with mayo, and he made fun of it. Said I didn't know how to eat properly. Those were the first words I ever heard him say—'Ma'am, I hate to intrude, but you don't know how to eat right.' "

How cute. "Is this nonsense going somewhere?" This is good old-fashioned jealousy talking, but I really don't care.

"You said to start from the beginning, I'm starting from the beginning. He was a great guy, Vincent, a lot like you. Not just because he was a Raptor, either. Your sense of humor, your style, the way you carry yourself—very similar. You would have liked him, I'm sure."

Flattery will get her everywhere; this helps to soften me up. "I'm sure I would have. Go on."

"It took some time to get Donovan over the concept of marriage, but once he warmed to the subject he really went at it with gusto. You know, planning our lives together, our futures . . . We had a place in the West Eighties, Donovan was still working for Raymond, I was occupied with the Council seat I'd won with his help, and we were what half the world would consider the perfect couple and the other half would consider the perfect Yuppie scum. Either way, we were happy. There was just the one little problem . . ."

"Kids."

"Yeah. Kids." Jaycee tucks her long, brown legs beneath

her body and slumps against a pillow, propping her tail along the side of the sofa. I remain rigid against the far armrest. "I wanted them, Donovan wanted them, but with our two different races . . . We could have adopted, I guess. I know there are enough egg donors in this world, but we wanted something we could call our own. Is that selfish? Donovan mentioned it once at work, I think, and Raymond put us in touch with Dr. Vallardo.

"We were an early case for him, actually. He'd been messing around with birds, some monitor lizards, frogs, snakes, but he'd only had a few dino patients before us. Things were still clandestine in his lab, and he had us come to the medical center at all hours of the night for tests and treatments. I still remember this one horrendous stew of chalk and zinc I had to suck down; even today, I can feel it rubbing against my tonsils."

"So you were guinea pigs," I say.

"We knew it going in. But if it was going to give us the chance to be parents, we would have gladly been boll weevils if that's what it took.

"A month went by, six months, a year, no luck. I kept donating my eggs, Donovan kept donating his seed, Dr. Vallardo kept mixing them together, toggling whatever genetic switches he had to toggle to get tab A to fit into slot B, but nothing ever came of it."

I shrug. "It happens all the time."

"Sure, but it doesn't make it any easier. It hit Donovan worse than it did me. He became despondent. Donovan was good at that, switching his happiness on and off. Most of his down times weren't long, and I'd gotten used to trudging through the doldrums along with him, the long days spent asleep, the somber mood music . . . but this one dragged on and on for weeks. He was sluggish, at home, at work, in bed. . . . The weeks turned into months, and soon enough I started noticing that he was avoiding things. Avoiding me."

"How?"

"Take the wedding. Half a year away, and Donovan, who'd been planning this event like it was the invasion at Normandy, didn't seem as . . . intense as he once was. It was like he was questioning things. Not me, not my motives, but himself.

"It was only a few weeks later that I realized he'd been sleeping with Judith McBride."

"Detective service?" I ask.

"Common sense," she replies. "It had been there all along, but I just hadn't bothered to see it." Sounds familiar. "In fact, I'd had my so-called friends—a wolf pack of society bitches who spent their time crooning over their fake human nails and new knitted hairdos—just about dropping it in my lap for over a month.

" 'Saw Judith and Donovan over lunch today,' one would tell me. 'Had a marvelous time.' And I would smile and nod and go through the motions of conversation, assuming that she'd seen them as employer and employee, negotiating perhaps a business deal.

"Well, I figured it out eventually, and can you blame me for being crushed? Five years of my life down the tubes, and all because of some withered old bag who didn't have anything better to do with her time than take advantage of an emotionally distraught Raptor."

I ask her if she said anything to Donovan, confronted him with her suspicions, and she shakes her head. "I meant to. Time and time again, I'd approach him, ask him to talk, but I couldn't bring myself to do it. It was like, if I didn't say it . . ."

"Maybe it wasn't true," I finish.

"Exactly. So I sat in the house, sat in Council meetings,

sat in restaurants, kept my mouth shut, and moped around just about as much as Donovan."

"And then?" I'm getting wrapped up in the story, despite that high level of resentment I'm trying to maintain, the narration weakening my resolve.

Jaycee glances around my darkened apartment. "Do you have any herbs?" she asks, moistening her lips with a flick of that luscious tongue.

"Fresh out. And if I'm not chewing, nobody is. What I wanna know is where does your little costume act come in?"

"I'm getting there," says Jaycee. "I was ready to break it off with Donovan, move out of the apartment, go on with my life. If not forgive, at least forget. And then we had an emergency Council meeting."

"I'm familiar with them."

"This one was about Raymond and his increasingly open relationships with human women. There was some concern among the group and, I admit, I was one of the most vocal. Raymond had been playing it up around town with a few of his secretaries, some acquaintances, even a professional or two from a popular human escort service, and the whole thing was just . . . wrong. Meanwhile, the Council was looking for a way to catch him in the act so they could levy some fines—and we're talking heavy. Forty, fifty million bucks in what amounted to extortion. I didn't know who to be more disgusted with—Raymond or the Council.

"Only question was how to catch him in the act. It was decided that we needed someone on the inside. Someone who could make him slip up and let us be there to get the physical evidence."

"Entrapment," I say.

She's about to correct me, then stops, nods. "Yes, entrapment."

"So that's when Jaycee Holden became Sarah Archer," I say, beginning to piece it all together.

"Very good, detective. And now you move into our bonus round."

Now that I think about it, certain elements of my investigation are coming together, making a little more sense. It's amazing I didn't see it all before, but it's like working a maze from finish to start—the twists and turns are there, but you can't see 'em until they've already passed you by.

"That's how you disappeared so easily," I say. "You had Council help."

"I had minimal Council help," Jaycee amends, "but they did manage to pull a few strings. Only two of the other Council members knew that I was the one . . . switching over, as it were. They thought I had disappeared, just like everyone else."

"But a simple costume switch wasn't enough, was it?" I say, thinking back to Officer Tuttle, the nice policeman who let me out of that nasty speeding ticket on the 405 that I so richly deserved. "You had to get rid of your scent glands, too."

Jaycee fingers the small scar on the side of her neck. A light, ragged river of skin tissue, it is barely visible on her ridged hide. "That was the hardest part for me," she admits. "I had a really kick-ass smell." She tries to grin, a wan, melancholy smile, and for the first time in more than an hour I find myself being drawn toward her again rather than repulsed by what I had considered her betrayal.

"Honey and gumdrops," I guess. "Light, airy."

"Jasmine," she says. "Sharp. I could walk into a florist's and you'd never find me. At least, not with your nose. But my desire for revenge was stronger than my desire to retain my scent, so we had our Diplodod representative extract my glands for the undercover work. He was a physician, and we had a little midnight rendezvous in his office, just him, me, a scalpel, and a lot of laughing gas."

"Can they be replaced?" I ask. "I might like to smell you sometime."

She shakes her head. "He kept them suffused with blood and whatever other vitamins they needed for as long as he could, but the tissues died out a few months into it. We didn't know how long my . . . seduction of Raymond would take. No one thought the whole affair would go on this long. He suggested mixing me up a chemical patch that could replicate the dino odor nicely, but I've . . . I've smelled them before. They say you can't tell the difference. What they say is wrong. It's metallic. Synthetic. And I don't like it in the least.

"So I was worried about my scent glands, yes, but the thought of bringing down Raymond, who I guess was pretty much the pawn in all this, was too tempting. Because if it brought down Raymond, it brought down Judith, too, and I couldn't wait to see her suffer like I had suffered. Was that wrong of me, Vincent, to want Judith McBride to suffer? Are those feelings wrong? I like to think I did the moral thing. Eye for an eye, man for a man."

I shake, I nod, I shrug—I've felt those pangs before, given birth to my own revenge fantasies, so I can't deny her those emotions. "And the singing? The gig out here?"

"True, every word of it. Here I am, my scent removed, my guise firmly in place, my past life a fabrication. We faked a place of birth, a few jobs, everything clean and neat, but when you can't come through with the qualifications . . . I couldn't type, couldn't take dictation, couldn't even use a computer." She holds up her fingers, wiggles them around. "Still can't. Pretty useless, I guess. Most of my professional life has been spent messing around in the swamp pits of dino politics, so there certainly wasn't a place for me in the human world."

"But you had your voice," I point out.

"That I did. I had my voice, and, more important, I had that fake body, and I had that fake face. And I gotta admit, it was damn good. We'd done a check of Raymond McBride's likes and dislikes before we guised me up—the goal was to present him with a willing partner who was his ideal human female. It just so happened that it worked in a nightclub setting, too.

"So there I am at this charity event that I've gotten my agent to take me to, and just before I'm about to be introduced to Raymond as Sarah Archer, I get cold feet. Nerves, tension, I don't know what came over me, but I suddenly decided I couldn't do it.

"I was all ready to tell my agent that I wanted to get the hell out of there when I heard a commotion from the kitchen. Bored with the conversation—I think we were babbling on about some opera or another—I wandered in to see what the fuss was about, and found Judith McBride and my Donovan spread out across the preparation counter, thigh-deep in salmon platters, kissing, groping, fondling each other." Sarah—damn it, Jaycee!—leans her head back and stares at the ceiling. I think she's chuckling.

"You okay?" I ask. "We can take a break."

"Please," says Jaycee. "I've had a long time to get over it. Where was I? Right, they're slobbering all over the kitchen counter and each other, and I let out a little gasp.

"Judith looks up and says, 'Do you mind?' No remorse, no guilt, no sense of chagrin at being caught. And that cold, eight-ball blackness in her eyes, that glare the bitch gave me . . . For a moment I thought I caught a glimpse of recognition in her eyes, but then I realized that this was how Judith acted to everyone. If only for that reason, she needed to be punished—if not for me, then for the countless others whose lives she'd made miserable. Well, my resolve was strengthened then and there, and I stared Judith down, then shot my own glance back at Donovan. At least he looked a tad embarrassed at the situation.

" 'You should be ashamed of yourselves,' I said to them. 'This is hardly sanitary.' And then I took my leave. Walked out of the kitchen, into the living room, had my agent introduce me to Raymond, and the rest is history."

"He fell for you quickly," I say.

"And hard. Natural charm, of course, but the guise didn't hurt, either."

"And then?"

"Then what?" she says, shrugging. "You know the rest—Donovan came out to the left coast a few weeks later, Raymond and I had our affair, I let the Council members in on when and where to instruct the detective agency to take pictures. You should have seen the trouble I went through to get Raymond to leave the blinds open when we had sex—I had to convince him that I was an exhibitionist, that it added something special with the windows uncovered. That got him moving . . ."

I say, "So the Council got their pictures, you got your revenge. Why didn't you break it off?"

"I was going to," says Jaycee, and once again I can sense her lachrymal glands preparing to spray their saltwater jets. "And then . . . then he died."

"He was killed," I clarify.

She nods, begins to tear up, and I find myself pulling her closer, into me, against my body, soothing her with long, full strokes across her back. I need to ask her about the murder, to ask her what she knows, what she thinks, what she suspects, but for now my foolish emotions are running things once again. "You loved him?" I ask.

"No," she sniffles. "I loved Donovan. But Raymond was a kind man, he was charming, he was intelligent. He didn't deserve . . . what I did."

"Setting him up?"

After a moment, Sarah nods, off and running on her crying fit once more. "And that's all," she says once she's regained control. "Since then, I've been too tired to make the change back to Jaycee. For that matter, there's no reason I should. With Donovan dead, I don't have anyone left for me in the dino world. I figured maybe I'd stay on as Sarah, see what I could make of myself as a human. I sure as heck screwed up as a dinosaur . . ."

"And that's everything?" I ask, curious why she left out what I consider to be a crucial piece to this puzzle.

"Everything."

"What about Vallardo?"

"What about him? I told you, Donovan and I stopped going after a few years." But Jaycee, who's managed a great deal of eye contact throughout her story, doesn't turn those baby browns to look at me when she says this, and I know it's a point I can press.

"But you've seen him since," I say. "Come on, Jaycee, no more hiding."

"Maybe at parties or something, but I don't know why you'd think I've seen—"

"The letter," I say plainly, and this quiets her up. "The letter that came to your apartment the night we met, the one that sent you into catatonia. It was from Vallardo, wasn't it?"

She doesn't try to deny it, nor to stall any longer. "How'd you know?" she asks me.

"Same way you knew without even having to pick the

thing up," I say. "The handwriting. Your name was scrawled all over the envelope. When I went to see Vallardo the next day, I noticed that he had a palsy in his left hand, yet he still used it for his daily functions. Didn't put the two together until a little bit ago. So you want to tell me why you wanted to have a kid with Raymond McBride?"

"Because I wanted a child, any child," she spits out. "And Raymond was a lech, but he would have been a hell of a dad. Not a *let's go in the yard and toss around the football* kind of dad, but a strong genetic type. I didn't care about the cross-race mixing. When I told Raymond I wanted a child he said 'wonderful!' and took me to Dr. Vallardo right away. Introduced him to me as the best obstetrician in New York."

"But Raymond thought you were human," I point out. "That's why he'd been funding the interspecies mix experiments."

"You know about those, too, eh?" she says, more than a hint of distaste curling the corners of her lips. "Well, Raymond had gone a little overboard with the . . . human element by this point."

"Dressler's Syndrome," I suggest.

Jaycee's guffaw is a violent bray that knocks me down a peg or two. "Let me assure you," she chuckles, "Raymond McBride did not have Dressler's Syndrome." She does not elaborate.

"But he wanted to mix with your 'human' eggs."

"He was interested in my species, you're right. And, to be frank about it, I wanted his Carnotaur seed. Only problem was Vallardo—once he started harvesting me, there wouldn't be much doubt that it wasn't a human egg he was dealing with."

"All those subtle differences," I say. "Hard shell, exterior gestation—"

"A thousand times bigger," she adds. "So you can see the difficulty. So I did what I had to do; I approached Vallardo, revealed myself as Jaycee, and told him to go ahead with our child but not to tell Raymond that I was a dino. I threatened him with every Council punishment I could think up, including complete excommunication from the community, which I think has only been approved once or twice. Napoleon got kicked out, I'm pretty sure."

"Camptosaur?" I ask, forgetting my fifth-grade history lessons.

"Raptor," she says, and shoots me a smile. "I had always planned to take my child and disappear back into the dino population once he or she was born, so Raymond need never find out that I wasn't what he thought I was. So I went through the process again, though by this time Vallardo had improved it somewhat. At the very least, I didn't have to ingest anything that would make my stomach do cartwheels, so for that I was happy.

"But before anything could come of it, Raymond was killed, and I was left alone. The experiment was over. Since then, I've been pretty much . . . treading water. When I saw that note from Vallardo, I was more worried about having to lie again, about delving back into the whole mess. And all this time I was thinking about calling Donovan, giving it a second try, but now with the fire . . . I knew what was in the Evolution Club, and I'm sure I wasn't the only one. Someone wanted those notes, that seed sample—Vallardo's, all of it—and I guess Donovan just got in the way."

Jaycee lapses into silence, and I'm not yet ready to take up the slack of conversation. There's too much to mentally digest. I choose, instead, to deal with more pressing, personal issues. "I understand why you did what you did," I tell her finally. "And I can accept it. But I'm still hurt that

you would do . . . what you did . . . with me . . ." I can't
come out and say it, say that she slept with me in order to
keep me quiet, or to gain inside information.

But she can say it easily enough. "You think I made love
with you as part of all this, don't you?" I turn away, and
she lifts my face to hers.

Have we fallen into the gender reversal zone somewhere
along the way?

"It's okay," I mutter, shuffling away from her touch.
"You do what you have to do."

"Vincent," she says. I do not look up. "Vincent, look at
me," she calls firmly, and I cannot disobey. "What I said
before holds true—I care for you. Like I said, in some
ways, you remind me of Donovan—"

"So I'm a substitute."

"No, you're not a substitute. You're not a replacement.
But when I'm attracted to a type, I'm attracted to a type."
She leers playfully, caresses my chest. "And lucky you,
you're that type."

"That's handy," I say, regaining my balance in the conversation. "You're my type, too."

"I'm glad," she says. "And no matter what happens, I
want you to always remember that, okay?"

"Sure."

"No matter what happens?"

"No matter what happens."

We make love again, this time as dinos, as nature intended it to be. Our hides rub against one another, rough
skin scratching with a sandpaper sizzle as we move back
and forth across the sofa, the floor, the bed, and the floor
again. There is nothing naughty about it, nothing forbidden, nothing adventurous or on the sly. And whereas that
sharpness, that just-below-the-surface buzz of danger, is no

longer with us, the act is somehow more beautiful, more real, than it was before.

At some point, after the sun has sunk below the horizon, we make our way to the bedroom and continue to discover one another well into the night. At some point, Jaycee tells me that she needs me, and I find myself saying it back. At some point, I drift off into sleep, hypnagogic images of lizards and jasmine dancing through my head.

At some point, I awaken into pitch black. A voice is whispering nearby, saying something like *catch the next flight* and *be there for the first crack.* In the meager light that has managed to make its way through my bedroom window, I can make out a silhouette of Jaycee on the phone by my nightstand. In my bleary-eyed stupor, the only thing I can think is that I'm amazed that they haven't shut off my phone line yet.

"Jaycee?" I mumble. "Sarah? Come to bed."

But even as I try to prop myself up on one arm, Jaycee has placed the receiver of the phone back on the hook and knelt down by my head. She caresses me gently, and plants two kisses upon my closed eyelids.

"I'm sorry," she says. "I think I could have loved you."

And before I can either respond in kind or ask her what the hell she means by I'm sorry, there's the glint of a syringe, a sharp poke in my arm, and everything fades into a beautiful, numb shade of black.

18

Glenda Wetzel's apartment in Hell's Kitchen is a lot like my old rental car in the sense that it is small, run-down, and probably infested with vermin. But she's been nice enough to let me crash on her living-room sofa—a pullout, with only six springs busted!—even though I managed to get her fired by J&T and somehow involved her in a no-longer-official case that has gotten no fewer than four dinos killed and a number of others, including myself, terrorized or harassed. My plan, carefully worked out over this morning's plane flight, is as follows: I will solve the case, I will find Jaycee, I will lift her into my arms much as Richard Gere did to Debra Winger at the end of *An Officer and a Gentleman,* and I will take her to Los Angeles. We will not go to the backseat of my car, due to the aforementioned vermin problem.

I woke up with a headache that could bring down Godzilla—whatever was in that syringe packed a wallop, and I wouldn't be surprised to find out it was some sort of concentrated herb. This reminds me of the hangovers I used to get back in my binge and binge days—my God, was it just a week ago?

Pedro turned my remaining furniture and appliances into nineteen hundred dollars in cash, and I thanked him profusely for bilking me out of the last of my worldly possessions. Twenty-dollar taxi to LAX, fifteen-hundred-dollar plane ticket, forty-dollar trip into Manhattan. I am currently as close to penniless as I've ever been in my life, and it's the furthest worry from my mind.

"I can't believe you're looking to bed down with the human," Glenda says as we prepare to hit the town. She's been fired from her job at J&T, but claims to enjoy the freedom of working freelance. I think it's bullshit concocted to keep me from feeling low at a time when I'm already only millimeters in height, but that's her story, and she's sticking to it. "I mean . . . a human, for Chrissakes."

"She's not a human," I explain for the tenth time. "She just looks and smells like a human."

"If it smells like a human . . ." Glenda mumbles, the age-old dino truism escaping her lips. "Okay, maybe she ain't a human, but she's a friggin' hussy."

"And she's not a hussy. She was doing it for the Council."

"I got the pictures, Rubio. Kodachrome and everything. The hussy was friggin' enjoying it."

" 'Course she was," I said. "They were both dinos. Now don't tell me two dinos can't enjoy being together . . . ?"

"Yeah, but—" This stops her, throwing her lower lip into a thoughtful pout. "Okay, you got me."

"Are you going to stop calling her the hussy?"

"Ooh, look at you," she teases. "You've really got the hots for this bimbo, don't you?"

Once we get that cleared up, I set about formulating a

plan of attack on the city. There is much to do and, if my hackles, slowly but steadily rising since I stepped off the plane, are any indication, little time in which to do it.

"First stop, McBride's apartment on the Upper East Side," I tell Glenda. "Can you stay here, make a few calls?"

"Shoot."

"Shoot as in *darn,* or shoot as in *fire away*?"

"Just tell me what to do," she says.

"Easy job—check with Pacific Bell and find out what calls were made from my house between six o'clock last night and eight o'clock this morning. Might have been collect, might have been calling card, but they should have the call sheet. Jaycee phoned someone from my house, I'm sure of it."

"And you think when you find that person, you'll find your little huss . . . Jaycee."

I smile at Glenda's attempt, however belated, to be respectful of my wishes. "She has to be somewhere," I say. "No one just disappears."

"Remember who you're talking about."

Grabbing my keys, my wallet, a few disintegration pouches on the off chance I should run into trouble, I say, "You'll get on it?"

"Right away, boss."

"Thanks." I peck Glenda on the cheek and she giggles. It's the first sign of femininity I've seen out of my new, temporary partner, but I think I liked her better when she cursed. This is too off-putting.

"Now get the fuck out of here," she commands, and all is right with the world.

"Lock the door," I suggest as I leave. "Lock it up tight."

Bolts slam into place behind me.

* * *

There is no comparison between, say, the Plaza and Mrs.
McBride's apartment building overlooking Central Park;
placing the hotel, however elegant it may seem, next to this
place would be like lining up Carmen Miranda next to
Queen Elizabeth for a group photo. What seemed so lush at
the Plaza now seems downright ostentatious compared to
the reserved elegance of this unnamed structure.

Talk about your exclusivity—the doorman, who is not
the same gentleman who gladly offered information on Judith the other day—won't even tell me *his* name, let alone
the name of the co-op complex. And there's no chance he's
letting me in that door. I explain to him that I have business
at the building, then switch it to a personal meeting with
Mrs. McBride. He doesn't bite. I try the intimidation tac-
tics that work so beautifully on most I encounter. No luck.

"Is there anything I can do for you to let me inside that
building?" I've run out of options.

"I don't think there is, sir." The doorman has remained
eminently polite, but considering he's not letting me do
anything I want to, it makes everything all the more frustrating.

"What if I ran past you? Ignored you and walked inside?"

His smile is chilling. Beneath his ridiculous doorman's
costume I can make out the shape of considerable muscles
dancing in powerful rhythm. "You don't want to do that,
sir."

Money. Money always works. I pull a twenty out of my
wallet and hand it to the man.

"What is this?" he says, looking at the bill in genuine
confusion.

"What's it look like?"

"It looks like twenty dollars," he replies.

"You win a Kewpie doll," I say, knowing that there's lit-

ERIC GARCIA

tle need for tact in a situation that turned tactless long ago. "I didn't need it anymore. Cluttering up my wallet."

"But twenty dollars . . ."

I throw my hands into the damp night sky—what is with this humidity? Has someone dumped an entire ocean into the air?—and say, "Fine, fine, fine! You don't want the money, you don't want the money!" I grab for my twenty back, but the doorman holds on tight.

"Whaddaya want from me?" I ask. "You don't want my money—"

"I didn't say that, sir."

"What?"

"I didn't say that I didn't want your money."

It hits me. "You . . . oh my Lord . . . you want more, don't you?" The laughter comes easily, rushing up from my diaphragm and spilling out of my mouth, covering the poor doorman in mirth. "This whole time I'm figuring I've got to have some magic word, and all I had to do from the beginning was bribe you!" I amend my earlier critiques of New York; I love this town!

The doorman does not flinch; to his credit, he remains straight-faced as a wooden nutcracker as he sidesteps me and issues a polite good evening to an elderly gentleman leaving the building. Afterward, he resumes his post and stares out into space, hand casually outstretched toward my wallet.

I gladly hold up a hundred for inspection and slip it into his pocket. There's more in my wallet if I have to lay it on him—if this guy wants a cash shower, I'll turn on the spigot. The $120 does the trick, though; the doorman nods once, grabs hold of the brass pull, and swings open the portal, granting me access to the vaulted hallways beyond.

"Welcome to Fifty-eight Park, sir."

I bow in gratitude. "Thank you ever so much . . . what did you say your name was?"

"That's another twenty," he says, poker face glued on tight.

Judith McBride isn't home. I suspect that such information would have been easier, and probably cheaper, to obtain, but the doorman, like everyone else, is in his racket for the bucks. Can't blame him. I would have scammed me over, too. I ring the doorbell over and over, knock a few times, whistle loudly, call out Judith's name, but there is no response.

I could break and enter, I guess—a credit card won't work on a door this solid, but I've got other tricks up my sleeve—but time is short, and I don't imagine that Judith will have left any wildly incriminating evidence lying around her apartment. I am about to take my leave, to return across town to Glenda's apartment and try to pick up the search for Jaycee where we left off, when I notice the corner of a yellow slip of paper sticking out from beneath Judith McBride's doorway. Actually, I'm only able to notice it after I've prostrated myself on the floor, shuttered up one eye, shoved a cheek against the plush carpet, and peeked through the crack, but the end results are the same, so what do the means matter?

There is no question as to whether or not it is moral of me to reach in and pick up the note—it is my civic duty to prevent littering, even in others' domiciles. Especially in others' domiciles. My costumed fingers, though, are too pudgy to fit beneath the door, so I am forced to bare a claw in order to get the job done.

Package notification. It means that the building manager or reception staff accepted a package for the tenant and is now holding it wherever such items are usually stored. I've heard of services like this, but never before witnessed it firsthand. When I was a renter, the closest my building managers ever came to accepting packages for me were angry notes shoved into my mailbox that read *If I gotta hear that UPS guy complain that you're not home one more time, I'm gonna rip down your front door and let him take a crap on your rug.* I've purchased stain-resistant carpets ever since.

I suppose I could locate Receiving, make a big fuss, try to claim the package as my own, but odds are whatever scam I pulled would either land me no useful evidence or a night in the county lockup.

But here's all the dirt I need, right on this slip of paper. Two separate packages are waiting downstairs, both addressed to Judith McBride. Package number one was sent from Martin & Company Copper Wiring Service and Supply in Kansas City and arrived early this morning according to the time stamped on the note.

Now what on earth could Judith McBride need copper wiring for? Science project? Too old. A bomb? Too rational. Do-it-yourself home improvements? Too prissy. I have a theory, but even as it springs to mind, I dismiss it as nonsense.

Package number two is equally curious, coming as it does from a pool supply company in Connecticut. There's nothing on the note to indicate what's actually in the box, but I can't imagine that Judith McBride has volunteered to spend her time cleaning out the facilities at the local YWCA.

I check it out. After another twenty dollars leaps from my wallet into the doorman's pocket, he tells me where to find Receiving, and I wend my way to the back of the building. There, another snob extraordinaire waits to rebuff me, but this time I don't have to worry about dealing with him. I just need to get close to the storage room.

"Can I . . . help you?" asks the clerk.

"No, no, just taking in the sights." I lean farther across his desk, and he backs away, startled at my proximity. "They keep the packages in there?" I ask, pointing toward the open space behind him, boxes neatly arranged in rows.

"Yes. . . . Are you a guest in the building?" he asks, knowing full well I am not.

I don't answer. I've got sniffing to do. I exhale quickly, expelling all my used, useless air into the clerk's ruffled face, and then begin a long, slow drag, my nostrils fluttering, my sinuses rumbling with the effort. Smells drift in from all over New York, my brain working on full power in an attempt to isolate and sort them out. I orient my nose toward the closed storage-room door and increase my suction. My chest expanding, my lungs filling, I wouldn't be surprised if I sucked all the available oxygen from the air, causing the clerk to faint dead away. That would make things easier.

And just as I think I can't inhale any more, just as the clerk, who has recovered from his confusion, is about to call Security down upon my sorry behind, I catch the slightest scintilla of the scent for which I am searching:

Chlorine. No doubt about it, the nose knows. A few cubes of chlorine tablets, wrapped within tissue paper, shrouded in Styrofoam, enclosed in cardboard, packed in a brown paper wrapper. Yes, I'm that good.

"Glenda, we gotta go." I have just paid a cabbie three times his fare in order to rush me back to Glenda's apartment and wait downstairs while I grab a few necessary items. He was more than happy to take my money, but I have serious doubts as to whether or not he was able to understand my instructions and actually remain in place. "Got a cab idling on the curb. Hopefully."

"You might wanna take a look at this," she says, and hands me a light, waxy sheet of fax paper three feet long, minuscule numbers and letters scrolling down and across every inch.

"What is it?"

"All the telephone calls from your house for the last month." She peeks over my shoulder, points to a singular 1-900 line. "Goddamn, Vincent, you got yourself a psychic friend?"

"Only once," I say absentmindedly, too concerned with this new evidence to defend myself.

There it is, the call I'm looking for—early this morning, four in the A.M. Collect, but still registered on this sheet, and it's to the 718 area code. "That's the one," I say, pointing it out to Glenda. "Right there."

"That's what I figured," she says. "So I checked it out already. You got three guesses where it goes."

"A child care clinic in the Bronx?"

"Hey . . ." she pouts. "You're not supposed to get it on the first try."

"I have some insider information," I tell her. "You get an address?"

"Sure did. Shit part of town and everything."

"Great. Come on, maybe we can get there before the floor show begins."

The cabbie has indeed waited downstairs, and fortunately for us, he doesn't want to practice his English with his customers tonight. I ask him to turn the radio up, and he puts on a charming Indian song that, by all indications, is

being sung by cats in heat. Perfect—I can tell Glenda my
story without worrying about having to whisper the whole
way to the clinic.

"Here goes," I say, and launch into the tale.

19

"That's gotta be the strangest shit I ever heard," says Glenda after I've laid it all out for her, piece by piece, theory by theory. I must admit, it's quite the doozy. We've pulled up just beyond that familiar alleyway in the Bronx, the child care clinic looming across the street. It waits for us, beckoning. I empty my wallet to pay the cabbie. "Bar none, weird city," she continues. "So that's it, right? No more surprises?"

"Well . . ." I hedge. "There's this one little thing I haven't exactly let you in on. But hey, a guy's gotta be sure before he goes blabbing to his friends. I'm not the kind of PI to investigate and tell. Hey, maybe I'm wrong."

"Yeah, well I hope you got your head up your ass on this one, 'cause if you're right about what's going down, I don't wanna think about what it's gonna do to us."

We step out of the cab, onto the street, and stare up at the clinic. Boards cover the windows like wooden eye-patches, the aluminum sliding bay doors clamped down tight. The crazies are out in full force this evening, and the occasional vagrant pinches Glenda's rump as we walk by. I have to restrain her from attacking anyone.

"Keep your nose open for danger," I say. "Last time I was here I ran into a little problem." A big, snarling, toothy problem is more like it. "You catch a whiff of barbecue, you let me know."

Casually, we move across the street, trying to look for all the world like two nonfelonious humans out for a nice stroll in the back alleyways of the Bronx at ten o'clock at night with no visible weapons or means of defense. "Move quickly," I caution, "but real natural-like."

The few lights on the outside of the clinic had been knocked out by vandals long ago, so we are able to take our first leg of the journey in darkness. We reach the front door. Closed. Locked. And once again, those sliding metal monstrosities off to each side would make too much noise in the stillness of the evening.

Glenda glances about the building, gauging its size. She says, "There's gotta be a back entrance around here. There's always a friggin' back entrance."

"I don't know. Last time I tried to find one, I got . . . side-tracked."

Glenda heads around the side of the building, and I follow, heart already thrashing away against my chest in anticipation of another attack. Great snorts of the surrounding air don't deliver any of that burning plastic scent to my olfactory nerves, but one can never be too careful. I continue my constant vigilance, glancing behind every corner and outcropping before stepping past.

There is no trace of my battle from last week, though the Dumpster has been moved, either by the cleanup crew once they arrived to take the skeleton away or by sanitation engineers whose truck was slightly out of alignment. We shuffle past the scene of my near demise.

A small metal fence bars our way to the back of the clinic, and Glenda prepares to climb it. Her hand reaches out—

"Wait!" I call, dropping my voice back to a whisper. "Test it."

Glenda turns, confused. "Test what?"

"The fence. They're not kidding around here; a stupid little wire fence like this one isn't going to do much good keeping out anyone who wants in. And I've seen the guard dogs they keep at this place." Tentatively, I reach out with an extended finger, nearing the metal diamonds . . .

Pressure, pulling finger down, trying to make me grasp the wire, drawing in my arm—I'm yanking it back, grimacing, fighting for my own appendage—

I win the battle and fly backward, slamming into Glenda's chest, both of us falling into a heap on the ground. Rolling off the Hadrosaur, I help her to her feet.

"What the hell . . ."

"Wired," I say, rubbing my arm, which is growing more sore by the second. "Electric fence, and from the way it grabbed hold I'd say we're dealing with some pretty lethal current."

No fuse box in sight, no way to short-circuit the fence, no breaches or holes in the structure itself. "Back around front?" Glenda suggests.

"No point. It's not going to open magically by itself." Unless . . . I look up, squinting through the darkness, and notice a small window ledge just above the top of the fence. "Glenda, can you hoist me up to that drainpipe?"

"I can hoist six of you up to that drainpipe. But how's that gonna get me in?"

"I'll work my way in through the back and open the front door. Come on, give me a lift."

After the requisite warnings to each other to play it safe, be careful, watch our backs, etc., Glenda lifts me onto her shoulders like a mother hoisting up her son to watch a parade, and I'm able to grab hold of the drainpipe. It's attached to the side of the clinic by some flimsy L-brackets that quiver as I let my full weight sink against the piping. Good thing I haven't had much time to eat recently; one burger in my belly might send the whole kaboodle crashing down. The brackets shake, shimmy, and shiver, but they hold.

A short climb—the pipe threatening to break away from the wall with every inch I gain—puts me in reach of the window ledge, and it is only after I have pulled myself up and onto it that I realize that much like the other windows in the clinic, this one, too, has been boarded up. Great wooden beams bar my way. And me without my buzz saw.

Glenda has already turned the corner, out of earshot, heading toward the front entrance to wait for me to open the door, so I won't be getting any help from that end. My only option at this point is to jump, but it's a good twenty-five feet down. If I could just unfurl my tail, the added muscular support might be enough to cushion the blow somewhat, but . . .

Well, heck, why can't I unfurl my tail? Rules are made to be broken, and if ever there's a time for rule-breaking, it's now. Grasping a knot in the wooden boards to steady myself, I quickly pull off my pants and my underwear, scrunch down the back of my polysuit, and release the upper portion of my G series.

Lord, it feels good to have my tail out in the open again!

The cool night air caresses my hide, bringing me back to last night with Jaycee, the way she rubbed me all over, using her body to . . . Okay, work, Vincent, there's work to be done. But this freedom does feel particularly nice, I have to admit, and I can only hope that I have the chance to frolic in the open air like this in some place other than the Eighteenth Street Child Health Care Clinic.

The specter of that long jump to the hard ground below is certainly helping to stall my efforts, but I have to get moving. Making a quick prayer to the gods above just in case I've been wrong my whole life about their nonexistence, I steel myself, take a baby step onto the edge, and hop.

As planned, my tail helps to soften the jolt, and I tuck into a roll, spinning along the ground, bringing myself to a halt only a few inches from the other side of the electric fence. Popping up as quickly as possible, I stand and brush myself off. "Piece of cake," I say to no one in particular, and my voice scrapes against the stillness of the night. I resolve to remain quiet if there's no one else around.

There's a scent of death, of decay, coming from a nearby corner, odors that should send me back into fighting mode, but it doesn't carry that tinge of danger, so I step closer to investigate, delving into a small niche. I peer around, my eyes taking time to adjust to even less light than before. From the long scrapes covering the roughly rounded walls, I'd say it looks almost scratched out, as if a feral beast had decided to carve out its den right here, concrete be damned.

Animal bones, cleared of their gristle, their surfaces cracked open and marrow sucked dry, lay in a two-foot-high pile around a bed made of tattered mattresses, newspapers, and old clothing. Blood cakes the walls in finger-painted murals, childish pictures of humans, of dogs, of dinosaurs . . .

I think I know who—what—lived in this den once upon a time. Before it attacked me. Before I killed it.

There's an entrance to the clinic within another small niche, and the locks on this one are easy enough to pick with the right tools. The credit card and soda can tricks are useful for the everyday door, but a job like this one requires a locksmith's set, which I was wise enough to bring along this time. Luckily for me, Ernie had a friend who had a nephew who had a pal whose mother worked at a manufacturing plant for such equipment, and he passed a kit on to me at cost. At least, he *told* me it was at cost.

I expect an alarm of some sort—and am relieved to find that none blares out at my arrival. The hallway I enter is dark and dismal, more so than outside due to the lack of ambient moonlight, and has the extra added attractions of mold spores and cobwebs dotting the walls. The corridors meet and converge in a haphazard, almost random pattern. The clinic didn't look nearly this large from the outside, and I wonder if there is some type of optical illusion involved.

I locate the front entrance quickly enough, and unlock the five dead bolts set in place on the inside.

"It's freaking cold out there," Glenda says, and I shush her with a finger.

Together, we move through the corridors, utilizing hand signals to suggest directions and courses of action. A continuous hum echoes through the building, and I imagine we'll find the power source sooner or later. And when we do, we'll see how right or how wrong I am about this whole mess.

"Psst!" I turn to find Glenda standing in front of a partially opened door. "I hear something—through here."

We make our way down a wide, darkened corridor, the walls lined with a metallic substance that picks up whatever electrical charge is running through this place; I can feel the tingle if I place my palm up against the wall. Small blue streaks of light shoot across the length of the walls at random intervals, and I can't help but wonder if we're approaching the center of the hub.

Another door, and behind it a low murmur, like a river pressing on a rusty water wheel, the mumble of an audience after a particularly bad film. "I think it's through here," Glenda says, and opens the door without caution. It's pitch black inside, and she slaps the inside wall in her search for a light switch.

"Wait a second," I whisper. "Take it easy—"

With a crash! a bank of fluorescent bulbs slam into life above our heads, illuminating a long rectangular room, a hundred feet long by at least forty feet wide, cage after cage after cage lining the walls and stacked three high. The curious babbling intensifies, and as we step inside the room, our mouths falling open involuntarily, we get a perfect view of what is making all the noise.

Each cage contains a . . . creature, for lack of a better term, a miniature version of the beast that attacked me three days ago, but that's not precisely correct. There are Stego genes and Diplodod genes and Raptor genes and Allosaur genes, and I can see the genetic traits of all the sixteen species of dinosaur in every single one of these things. Small, misshapen horns poke at odd angles out of large, misshapen heads atop twisted misshapen necks and disabled misshapen bodies. The sounds we hear are so odd to our ears precisely because no two mouths are alike—for those creatures who have been blessed with mouths. Some of these things have nothing but gaping holes in the sides of their heads, and the tiny, tortured whimpers that emanate from within are amplified by the horrible, empty cavity.

They're small. Two feet at the most. They're nothing but babies. But that's not all. Not by a long shot.

There are fingers. Honest-to-God fingers. And legs, real legs. And ears, and earlobes and noses and torsos, and the kicker about all these body parts is: they're human.

"He did it," Glenda says in a perfect blend of awe and revulsion. "Vallardo actually did it."

"It . . . it seems so . . ." I stutter.

"But what—what's wrong with them—"

"I think—I think they're the misfits," I explain.

"Misfits."

"Nothing gets accomplished without a few failures first. That's them."

As if on cue, they begin to cry out in small wailing tones. Kittens, puppies, babies in need of help and care. "But he's got them locked up, like . . . like animals."

I nod. "In a way, they are—"

"How can you say that?" Glenda nearly shouts, turning on me in anger. Great—Glenda Wetzel's mothering instincts have to make their debut at a time like this. "They're *babies,* Vincent."

In a daze, Glenda walks into the middle of the room, staring slack-jawed at the multitude of misfit monsters surrounding her. Before I can stop her, she reaches into one of the cages and scratches what looks to be a Hadrosaur/human mix behind a grotesque ear. It coos in delight.

"Look, Vincent," she says. "It needs to be loved, that's

all." Her face darkens, her tone growing angrier once again. "And that sonofabitch Vallardo locked them up like this."

"I agree, he's wrong and needs to be punished," I say, "but we don't have time for this. C'mon, Glen, step back."

Glenda doesn't seem to agree. She heads toward a console set into the far wall, running her fingers over the buttons, ire rising with each passing second. And a funny thing's happening—as Glenda gets angrier, the noise in the cages begins to increase.

"Apefucker thinks he can screw with nature and then lock babies up behind bars? Is this science? Does this amuse him?"

"Glen, I really think you should stop." The bars are rattling now, all of the creatures awake, alert, and banging at their confines. The whimpering has turned into hooting, and screaming's not far around the corner.

But Glenda doesn't hear my protestations or the rising racket. She's flipping switches left and right, and the console, once dead and quiet, lights up with a burst of energy. I trot over toward her, eager to stop whatever she thinks she's going to do.

"I'll show that sonofabitch what it is to screw with the gene pool," she's yelling. "I'll show him!" And now the menagerie of misfits is really letting loose, jumping up and down in their cages like a pack of monkeys, slamming their bodies against the bars, as if they know that escape is imminent, that a messiah has come to release them from their bondage.

"Glenda, don't—" I shout, just as she slams her palm into the button that pops open every cage at once.

With a wild group shriek that puts to shame Tarzan and all of his jungle friends, a hundred horrible creatures fall out of the sky, leaping into the room, onto Glenda, and onto my back. The attack is on.

My first thought is that I misjudged these things, that they're no more harmful than a flea, but that's over with as soon as the first one takes a nip out of my ear, ripping away a section of guise as well as a nice hunk of flesh. Without thinking, I reach behind me, grab it by the scruff of the neck—a ridged neck?—and toss it through the air, football style. It thwacks against a far wall and falls to the ground. Undaunted, it picks itself up and leaps back into the pile of writhing creatures.

But more are coming my way, jumping at me, using coiled, stunted tails to launch themselves into the air, crooked mouths wide open, razor-sharp teeth deadlocked at my eyes, my face, any soft tissue on my body. It's a deadly combination—those human fingers help some to grip on to my hide while their dino teeth do the dirty work. Through the clamor, I can see Glenda go down beneath a heap of the beasts, and I struggle to fight off as many as I can and make my way across the room.

My claws, poking through my guise like thorns on a rose, rake through any flesh they come in contact with as I use my hands to ward off attacks from the front. My tail, already freed up earlier, comes in handy taking out enemies that take a shot at me from behind, and though I've been bitten and clawed a hundred times in two minutes, I'm dishing out more than I'm taking. The majority of blood on the floor of the cage room is not mine.

"Glenda!" I call over the caterwaul of shrieks, and I hear a "Vincent!" in return.

"Are you okay?" I yell through another lance of pain, this time at my wrist, and I look down to find a set of teeth attached to a misshapen hunk of flesh planted firmly in my arm. I shake the arm up and down, curling the creature as I lift, but the teeth are caught tight, buried in my muscle. With the underclaw on my other hand, I reach out and spear the creature through the head; it issues a slight whimper of pain, then releases its grip and falls to the ground, dead.

And now Glenda's beside me, bloodied worse than I am, but we're both alive, and we're both standing up.

In a corner.

The creatures back off for a moment, at least seventy of the vicious little goblins, each no more than two feet high, horns included. They still cackle and shriek like a pack of mutated pigeons, but it's taken on a conversational tone, as if they are somehow communicating, deciding their next plan of attack.

"Okay, so I was wrong," Glenda admits. "They're not sweet little things."

I take a quick look around. The wall behind us is perfectly smooth, no room for hand- or footholds. "What now? They've got us cornered."

And they seem to know it. Glenda and I try a quick move to the left, and in unison, they shuffle over to block our escape. A quick move to the right produces similar results. "We're trapped."

The sounds are growing louder again, the creatures regaining their blood lust. In the back of the pack, two of them are going at it, little human fingers and little dino claws, fighting to the death, powerful jaws with stunted human teeth snapping instinctively toward unprotected necks and major arteries.

"Go," says Glenda.

"What?"

"You go, lock the door behind you. I'll take care of—of this."

"You'll be killed."

"Maybe not. Look, what you found is too fucked up not to stop. You started this investigation, and you have to be the one to finish it. I screwed this part up, I'll deal with the consequences."

"But I can't leave you—"

"Jesus fucking Christ, Rubio—go!" And then: "Find what's her name. Take her back to LA. Name a kid after me."

I don't have time to argue. Glenda calls out, "Hey, you ugly fucking leprechauns! Take a bite outta this!" and jumps to her left, kicking out with her legs as she flies through the air, claws raking at the tens of bodies already leaping toward her. Instantly, she disappears beneath a mass of improper flesh and disparate body parts.

A path opens in the chaos, and without looking back I take it, running at full speed down the corridor. One of the baby dino/man mixes breaks off from the pack and hops after me, making it out of the room as I slam the door closed and bolt it from the outside. The thing issues a feeble warning cry—cut off from its littermates, the sound is more pathetic than powerful—and makes a futile attempt to chomp down on my shin. I thrust my leg up and out, and the creature goes flying into the ceiling, landing on the floor below with a thud and a squish.

Good-bye, Glenda. Go quickly to wherever it is we go.

I stick to the right wall of the complex, utilizing an old maze-solving maneuver, and soon that hum grows in volume. Opening doors indiscriminately, I wander the clinic, keeping myself on high alert. The run-down sections of the building eventually give way to newer, decorated, *cleaner* areas, and I feel it's safe enough to remove my bloodied mask, free up my true nostrils, and take a good sniff around.

That chlorine scent again, this time mixed with the roses and oranges I had been expecting. Vallardo's scent of anisette, of pesticides, is present as well, and I assume emanating from the same location. Like a cartoon Country Mouse drawn by the aroma of a scrumptious city feast, I follow my nose up, up, and away.

I saunter into the "health clinic's" main laboratory five minutes later, tossing out smiles like so many free-trial magazine subscriptions. Technically one per customer, but I serve up a dozen each to Vallardo and Judith McBride. The two of them pale at the sight of me, Vallardo's naturally green Triceratops hide unable to hide the shock. He blanches into a yeti-white pallor; if I had my camera I could score ten thousand dollars from a national tabloid for offering proof of the creature.

Each of them—Vallardo, Judith, Jaycee (emerging from behind the good doctor)—sizes me up. I can feel the weight of their stares, of their unspoken questions. *How good is he with that stubby body? Can I take him solo? Can we take him together?*

I quench it all with a snap of my tail and a roar that manages to pierce even my own eardrums. They back away.

"You didn't even lock the laboratory door," I chastise, dropping from my growl into a conversational tone. "I'm disappointed in the lot of you."

Jaycee comes galloping up to me then, unsure of what to do with her body. Does she hug me? Does she push me out of the room? She opts for the safety of stopping a few yards outside my striking range and saying, "Vincent . . . you have to go."

"No," I respond. "I think I'm sticking around for this one."

I motion across the lab, toward the largest indoor water tank I've ever laid eyes on, bar none. Sea World has nothing on Dr. Emil Vallardo, M.D., Ph.D., OB-GYN. Glass-walled, over thirty feet high, its length and breadth encompassing a full half of this massive corporate-funded laboratory, they could dump the Indian Ocean into this thing and still have room for Lolita, the Killer Whale. But there is no Lolita in this tank. There are no fish lollygagging around in there, either, nothing to amuse the kiddies while the parents are getting toasted over at Busch Gardens.

There is only an egg in this artificial womb, a single, solitary egg, maybe a twenty-pounder, floating a few feet below the surface, suspended in the water by a mesh hammock. Brown and gray speckles dot its otherwise albino shell, each one leading to an electrode, a wire, terminating at a computer set up just outside the splash zone. Life signs flit across an enlarged CRT attached to the side of the tank, heart and brain functions beeping steadily.

There are cracks in the shell. Three of them, from my vantage point. I suspect there are more on the other side. Something wants out.

"When were you gonna tell me this part?" I ask Jaycee, knowing the answer is never.

"I . . . I couldn't," she admits, turning to Vallardo and Judith for support. "We . . . the three of us . . . we made the decision not to say anything."

"*We* didn't decide anything," Judith says caustically. "You decided, Jaycee."

"I did what I had to do," counters the Coleo, her claws snapping out, flicking into place.

"Before we start the floor show and you two go at it," I announce, "I'd like to get us all out in the open, okay? Anyone who needs to take off their guise, let's do so now." There's no reaction; they all stare at me as if I am speaking in tongues. Vallardo and Jaycee have shed their costumes a while ago; only Judith McBride remains in human form. I am not surprised.

"Here," I say, "I'll start you off, how's that?" Whipping off the rest of my remaining clothing with a stripper's panache, I casually unsnap my girdles and loosen my trusses, exposing the full length of my natural body. My claws click through the air, my tail swishes with contentment, and I roar my terrible roar and gnash my terrible teeth all for the fun of it.

"Now," I say, "hands up everyone who's a dino." I raise my own arm, just to get the tide moving. Soon, the three others have tentatively put their hands in the air.

I approach Judith McBride, her left cheek having taken on a delightfully humorous muscle spasm, and place my arm over hers, weighting it back down. "Come now, Mrs. McBride. Are you that confused as to your own identity?"

"I—I don't know what you mean," she stammers. "I'm a Carnotaur, you know that. You've heard the stories, you've seen the pictures."

"That's true, that's true," I say, making a big show of nodding, pacing around her body in an ever-tightening spiral. Ah, if I only had my hat, my trench coat. I spy a white lab coat hanging on a nearby hook, and ask Vallardo if I could borrow it for a minute. He's too confused to argue, so I slip into the long overcoat, feeling the comfortable weight upon my shoulders.

"I have seen the pictures, Mrs. McBride, of both you and your deceased husband. And you did make a fine Carnotaur couple. And yes, I've heard the stories. The rumors. The tales of Carnotaur Raymond McBride and his illustrious circle of dino friends. Entertainers, businessmen, heads of state. Very posh."

Jaycee's turn to interrupt. "Vincent, really, I don't think this is the time—"

"But I gotta tell you, I've had some injuries over the years, and I can't trust all my senses like I used to. I don't place too much stock in my ears, for example, ever since this little hunting trip I took with a band of humans 'round 'bout ten years ago. Gun-happy bastards were using heavy-gauge ammo on ten-point bucks, discharging those puppies right by my head. Three days and god knows how many shots later, boom, I've all but lost the high end of my hearing register. So you say I've heard the stories, yeah, I've heard 'em, but it doesn't mean I can *trust* what I've heard.

"My eyes? Forget about it. I was driving around with uncorrected vision for a while before I got wise and had my peepers checked, and lemme tell you that half the time I didn't know whether I was sitting at a red light or watching a really boring laser show. I've got Coke-bottle contact lenses, my vision is so bad. So those pictures I saw of you and Raymond all dressed up nice like the Carnotaurs you claim to be, hey, maybe I didn't see 'em like I should have seen 'em. I can't *trust* what I've seen.

"Taste? Don't get me started. I love spicy foods, it's a habit, but it knocks out my buds. After ten years of Aunt Marge's jambalaya, well . . . can't trust it any more. Touch? Well, you and I haven't gotten that close. But even so, there's saline in this world, there's silicone, there's this polyfiber we all know and love, so I can't trust my touch either, can I? So there's really only the one sense left to me, and as a result I've got to trust it above all else. I'm sure you understand that.

"My nose is my livelihood, Mrs. McBride, and a true dino never, ever forgets a scent. You can't fake it, though as you know, you sure can try. You can try real hard. But in the end . . ."

Ignoring her protests and pleas, her arms slapping me in the throat, in the face, I grab Judith McBride in a rough headlock and, with my free hand, reach behind her head, into the thick nest of hair just above the back of her neck. I quickly and easily find the device I'm looking for, secured to her scalp with a familiar epoxy glue, and rip it free. She shrieks in pain.

The pouch is filled with chlorine powder, with dried rose petals, with orange peels, the mixture emitting jets of manufactured dino odor via a steady electric current supplied by thin copper wires leading from a small lighter battery into the pouch itself.

Waving the odiferous cushion beneath her nose, holding it as if it contained a ripe, steaming turd, I growl, "This is your scent, the chemicals inside this pouch, and this is the only thing that ever made you remotely resemble one of us. I got a feeling that your husband was the same way, right, Mrs. McBride?

"You're no dino," I say, distaste swelling, puckering my mouth. "You're . . . you're nothing but a common human."

Enter the dramatic music, reprise.

My domination is total; Judith is unable to answer me, her mouth opening and closing, opening and closing. Her eyelids flutter uncontrollably. Goddamn human, I should kill her right now, out of not only duty but sheer principle alone. Lying to me like that, sending me back and forth across the country.

But Vallardo cuts us all off with a sharp gasp that commands attention from dinos and dino-fakers alike. "The egg," he whispers reverently. "It's time."

As one, our gazes pan across the laboratory, stopping on the lone inhabitant of that wide-open tank. The few cracks

I could make out before have spiderwebbed, fanning the full surface of the egg, new splinters forming every second. As Vallardo taps a few commands into the tank's computer, an external speaker buzzes on, amplifying those sounds bouncing around within the watery confines. A creaking, a crackling, and . . . could that be a wail?

"Come on, baby," murmurs Jaycee. "You can do it. Break out for Mama."

20

Rushing awkwardly to the side of the tank, Vallardo grabs hold of a series of pulleys, twisting the ropes down and around an anchor set into the floor. The left side of the egg's hammock lifts a little in the water, but now needs to be counterbalanced by a lift to the right. "The other side!" Vallardo yells across the room, and I do believe he's talking to me! I didn't come here to assist in a birth, but I guess if I have to do a little midwifery in the middle of my crime-solving, it wouldn't be the worst thing in the world.

"Now what?" I ask upon reaching the ropes. My angle into the tank is sharper, more acute, the water blurring the egg into a long ovoid blob. But I can still hear those splinters over the PA, so I know there's activity going on inside that shell.

"On the count of three," Vallardo yells to me, "pull down to the yellow markings on the rope!" I glance up—the band color shifts to a tawny tone ten feet away—and shout back that I'm ready. Vallardo gives the count, and we hoist. It comes up easier than I expected, my muscles having primed themselves for heavier exertion. My extra effort forces the right end of the hammock higher than the left, and the egg begins to slide—

"No!" screams Jaycee, launching herself at the ropes, at Vallardo.

Jaycee's added weight quickly hoists her end higher, which forces me to compensate in turn, and for a moment we are the Three Stooges meeting the Mad Scientist, wildly tugging on our ropes in an effort to stabilize the as-yet-unborn creature rolling around on that hammock.

"Careful," Vallardo warns, as if we didn't already know. "Don't let it slip!"

Jaycee anchors her rope and storms up to me, landing a good slap across my cheek. "You did that on purpose," she says. "You want it dead."

I say, "I want no such thing. The only thing I want is to bring Mrs. McBride in front of the National Council, let them decide how they want to handle her. I'm amazed you didn't kill her already."

"She almost did," says Judith. "But we came to a little arrangement, instead."

We turn to face the human interloper, and find that Judith has a gun. I knew she would; the bad ones always do. But I didn't expect a gun so . . . large. The monstrous revolver sags in her hand, her frail human wrist trembling with the effort to keep it upright. Judith uses the barrel to motion me away from the tank, and Jaycee and Vallardo reluctantly follow.

"The egg . . ." says the doctor. "We have to keep watch on it."

"I'll watch the egg," spits Judith. "It's my child, I can take care of it."

Jaycee snaps, a sudden burst of hatred propelling her across the room, tail whipping through the air, teeth bared;

as the blur streaks by so fast, all I can see is a brown streak of anger rushing by my face. Everything sinks into slow-motion replay, though without the color commentary: Judith's own reflexes burst into action, bringing up that revolver, the barrel the size of a Hula-Hoop, round, clearly chambered and ready to sear into flesh—my lungs paralyzed, refusing to deliver a breath so I can scream out the perfunctory No!—Vallardo throwing himself in front of the tank, ready to take a bullet, an arrow, a warhead, anything to protect the integrity of its structure—Judith's finger squeezing hard on the trigger, her lips tightening into a satisfied grimace—

And another blur, this one quite unexpected, as a vaguely Hadrosaur-shaped creature crashes through the laboratory door and into the easy target of Judith McBride. The gun reports, blasting its echo through my already-damaged ears.

Concrete chips fly out of the wall behind me, spraying sharp white shrapnel through the air. A shard imbeds itself in my tail. It is excruciating. I pay it no mind.

Glenda lifts herself off the ground, kicking Judith's gun into a far corner of the lab, her leg slamming into Mrs. McBride's rib cage. The human expels a gush of air and curls into a fetal ball.

"The hell's she got a gun for?" a bloodied Glenda says, turning to me. I shrug. Glenda whips back around to Judith, bends down, and grabs her cheeks, pulling the widow close. "The hell you got a gun for?"

Judith's best response is nothing more than a groan of pain.

"Glenda, you—you're okay."

"I'm hurtin', but I'm alive, yeah. Mean little apefuckers you got in them cages, Doc."

Vallardo's expression is constant; he's hard to read. "How's the egg, Doc?"

"It's stable," he says. "There is some time left."

"Then I'm gonna pick up where we left off. Anybody stop me if you get confused."

Ensuring that my lab/trench coat is buckled tight around my waist, I strut over to Jaycee and place an arm around her shoulder. "It must get tiring making things up all the time," I say. "Lying takes a lot out of you."

She tries to cut in with a "Vincent, I—" but as promised, I pay her no mind, running roughshod over her words. "Don't bother," I say. "I'm gonna tell it like it is, and even if you've heard it all before, don't stop me.

"Most of what you told me was true," I begin, keeping my comments directed toward my onetime (but five sessions!) lover. "You just left out a few key elements. Yes, Judith McBride had an affair with Donovan, and yes, you offered to impersonate a human in order to entrap Raymond for the Council. You probably even fell in lust with him, just like you said, and that's all fine and good.

"I'll tell you, I got into this case purely by accident, you know that? I was hired by the insurance company that was supposed to reimburse Donovan Burke for the fire at his Evolution Club. I had no idea it would lead to this, honestly, I didn't. And things were fishy there right from the start—fire trucks that were called before any of the witnesses actually saw the flames. Almost as if it was supposed to be a controlled fire, wiping out a section of the building without torching the entire place." I pause here, waiting for input from the accomplices.

"We didn't want to hurt anybody," Jaycee says eventually. "Especially Donovan."

"But you needed those papers gone, didn't you? And

that frozen embryo—now that you had this baby, you had to get rid of the extra evidence. Why couldn't you just ask Donovan for them back?"

"Yes, yes, well . . . He wouldn't give them to me," Vallardo says, stepping away from his computer and into the conversation. In the background, I can see the fragile eggshell continuing to disappear beneath the constant assault from the creature inside. It won't be long now. "Simple as that, yes? He thought I was being controlled," Vallardo continues, "and he wanted to protect me. Donovan was . . . very loyal."

"Ha!" snorts Jaycee, and says nothing more on the matter.

I turn back to Vallardo and say, "Loyal, sure. Especially after you funded his club in Los Angeles. You needed a place to keep a separate copy of your work, a safe haven, and he needed a new job. Who would ever think to look in an LA nightclub for such controversial work? Worst thing that goes on there would be a little hanky-panky in the restroom stalls.

"But the real question is why were you doing that work in the first place? And for this, we have to go back a little further." Stretching my fingers as if to crack my knuckles—I can't actually crack them, as my tight Raptor joints don't leak enough air—I walk up to Judith, still on the ground, and easily hoist her to her feet. She sags in my arms, but I know she can hear me, and I think she can talk.

"How long ago did you and your husband start pretending you were dinos?" I ask Judith, and Glenda nearly passes out.

"Pretending?" Glenda says. "You lost me."

"Like it sounds. We guise ourselves up as humans every day, she guised herself up as a dino when the need arose. Got away with it for at least fifteen years now, everyone thinking she's a Carnotaur costumed up as a matronly widow when she's really a cold piece of dirt costumed up as a Carnotaur." I grab a loose fold of flesh beneath Judith's arm and tug; it doesn't give, and the woman whimpers. Glenda, beginning to comprehend, takes a tug too, manhandling the flesh presented to her.

"So let me get this straight . . . this one here is a human pretending to be a dino pretending to be a human?"

"You got it," I say, and Glenda drops any pretenses of civility and charges toward Judith's throat, ripping off her guise mask with a practiced ease I have never witnessed before. This has got to be a Guinness record for disrobing. But I swing Judith around, away from the Hadrosaur's suddenly exposed elongated duckbill, pulling the human to safety alongside the far wall.

"Outta the way, Vincent!" snarls Glenda. "We gotta kill her, those are the rules. She's a human, she knows, she's gotta go."

"I know the rules, Glen, trust me. But this is a special situation. We're going to bring her up in front of the Council," I say. "They'll decide what to do with her." I catch Glenda's eyes with mine, pleading for temporary clemency. There are still gaps in my information sheet I need to have filled in. Reluctantly, Glenda backs off, wiping her drooling beak with a short brown arm. I'll have to watch her—she's still anxious to taste Judith's blood. "What I don't know is how she found out about us in the first place. Who let it slip." I spin Mrs. McBride around once again, stare into those vacant eyes. "You wanna enlighten me?"

"It was his Ba-Ba," says Jaycee, taking over the storytelling for a moment. "Raymond's Ba-Ba."

"What the hell is a Ba-Ba?"

"It's what he called his adopted mother. Kid talk for Barbara. Raymond's parents died when he was just a toddler, and he was sent to live with his mom's best friend, who happened to be a Carnotaur. He didn't talk about her much, but I know that she raised him as a dino, taught him how to make the scent pouches, how to act, how to guise up, how to present himself in the dino world.

"He found Judith here working as a waitress in Kansas, introduced her to the only life he really knew—that of a dino—and allowed her to make the choice as to how they would live their lives, as humans or as pseudohumans. They chose to act as dinos, and moved to New York City in order to find a greater population of their—of our—kind. The rest is pretty well documented if you look for it. Raymond's rise up the business ladder, Judith's rise up the social one, all because of their dino contacts. Jumping species can be very lucrative."

Thanking Jaycee for her additions to the evening's symposium, I take over once again, eager to display my crime-solving skills for all involved. "I knew there was something wrong from the moment I stepped into your office," I tell Judith, "but I couldn't figure out what it was. Your scent was odd, sure, but not odd enough to capture my immediate attention.

"I gave Donovan's name to your secretary, solely as a method to gain access to your inner sanctum, and I didn't expect it to last any longer than your first sniff of me. But we spent a good minute together—we even embraced!—and you *still* thought I was Donovan, guised up in a different human costume. And right there was the problem, my first inkling of suspicion, even though I didn't realize it until later—you couldn't smell me! Later in that same conversation, I asked you for Jaycee's scent, a clue to help me track her down, and once again you hemmed and hawed.

You couldn't tell me what she smelled like because you didn't know. Human noses, simply put, stink.

"I got another clue when I found a scent pouch at Dan Patterson's house. You remember Dan Patterson, right? The LAPD sergeant you had killed? Nice try, telling your hit men to use a knife to try and simulate dino marks, but even a rank forensics amateur like myself can tell a knife wound from a claw slash from ten feet away."

"She wasn't supposed to hurt him," Jaycee interjects. "She was just supposed to get the papers."

"And Nadel?"

"He was going to give you the photos. The real photos."

"And Ernie?" I ask. "Was she supposed to hurt Ernie?"

Jaycee's head turns away. "I didn't know about that 'til after."

"After she'd killed him?"

"Yes."

"How'd you do it?" I ask, and now I'm getting ready to take a bite out of Judith McBride. My grip on her neck grows stronger, and if I just press a little to the left, I could snap it in one easy blow. "How'd—you—do—it?"

Jaycee pipes up again. "She told me—"

"I'll deal with you in a second," I say plainly, keeping my growing anger below the high-water mark. "I'm dealing with the human now." Back to Judith—"Tell me, or you die right here, Council be damned."

"It was easy," Judith sighs. "A few hits on the head, a false witness report."

"Because?"

"Because he was getting too close. You got lucky with those two morons in the car, or you'd be in the same place."

I throw Judith to the ground, pacing back and forth

around her supine body. I need to return to the matter at hand. "So I found the pouch in Dan's den, the traces of chlorine, and matched it up with the pool supplies you received today at your apartment." I saunter over to my pants, lying in a crushed pile on the floor, and search through the pockets, emerging with a yellow note. I hand it to Judith, who mindlessly grips it, staring past the words on the page. "Two packages, down at Receiving," I tell her. "Open till nine.

"So what does all this mean?" I say rhetorically, addressing my rapt audience. "It means that Judith is a human, that Raymond was a human, and that the both of you were indeed fooling around with the other species, but that the other species were us dinos." Then, whipping around—"Judith here had her fling with Donovan, and she's really the one who funded your experiments, right, Doc? It was Judith, not her husband, who'd come down with Dressler's Syndrome. She was the one who wanted the dino/human mixed child."

Vallardo, defeated for once, nods. He says, "She's been looking for a way to have a child with the Raptor, yes? But it was not working."

"Why not?"

"Dinosaur seed, human egg. The fetal process was incorrect, it . . . The mixes are in need of the opposite situation if they are to grow properly during the dino ten-month gestation period, yes? Human sperm and dino egg, a hard exterior shell. Otherwise . . ."

"Otherwise they come out deformed. Like those things you keep in the cages. And the thing that attacked me outside the clinic."

A nod from Vallardo. "My earlier experiments. I did not have the heart to eliminate them."

"Oh yeah," says Glenda, "you're all heart, Doc."

"So when Judith realized she couldn't have a dino/human child of her own, she decided to have the good doctor here use Jaycee's eggs—which he'd already harvested and frozen from their earlier experiments with her and Donovan—and her husband's fertile sperm. It wouldn't be her genetic child, but it would be damned close enough. Vallardo would have made the kid, Judith would have raised it as her own, and no one would have been the wiser. And then—well, I can surmise and surmise all day, won't get us any closer to the truth. Why don't you tell it, Jaycee?"

"If you know it so well . . ." she says bitterly.

"I'd rather you fill us in. Firsthand accounts are always more enjoyable."

We all fix our gazes upon Jaycee, and I suppose that the pressure of silence overwhelms her desire to remain quiet. She begins. "I went to see Raymond to wish him happy holidays, that's all. The office was deserted—the whole building—because it was Christmas Eve, but Raymond was working as usual, finishing up some last-minute jobs here and there. I'd been bugging Raymond for a while, trying to get him to commit to some New Year's plans I had set up. He'd been having some troubles getting out of his party with the missus"—Judith and Jaycee's intense stares of hatred clash in the middle of the room and explode harmlessly—"and I was helping him come up with . . . excuses.

"I don't know what made me do it, but as we sat at his desk, me perched on his lap, laughing about the holidays and our baby and what a wonderful life we were going to have, I felt such . . . I don't want to say love, but closeness . . . Whatever it was, I had to tell him. The truth.

" 'I have to show you something,' I said to him, and he laughed and asked me if I was going to undress. 'In a way,' I said. So I stepped out into the middle of the room, took off all my clothes, and removed my guise. I stood there, a naked Coleo, and waited for his reaction.

"Raymond was quiet. Very quiet. I assumed he was furious with me for deceiving him, and was ready to throw me out, call Security . . . But I know now he was weighing his own options. Then he had me come back to the desk, he sat me down, and he told me his story. How he was raised. Where he came from. What he came from. And who he really was.

"He wanted to effect a settlement between the humans and the dinos, to introduce his kind to our kind in as peaceful a way as possible. He was so excited, he told me, that he could be the one to bring the dinosaur community out into the open. To bring us 'out of the closet,' as he put it, was his fondest dream, and he wanted me to be the figure under whom it could all take place.

"I don't know if he expected me to be happy, shocked, dismayed, and to be honest, I didn't know how I felt at the time. There was no time for me to think; you know how it is. I know you know how it is. All of us have been prey to instinct before, it's our species' cross to bear—Vincent, you tried to kill me when you thought I was a human and I had seen you in guise; we saw your partner's reaction to Judith just now. It's inbred, and what's more, it's what we're taught from day one: If a human knows, a human must die.

"I don't remember much about the attack. Honestly, I don't. I do remember coming to in a pool of blood that was not my own and seeing Raymond, who I had grown to care for, dead in the middle of it all. But that drive was still humming in me, and I cleaned myself up, sat down in Raymond's desk chair, and waited for Judith, who I knew would be arriving shortly.

"My plan was to kill her, leave the office, and disappear to another country: Jamaica, Barbados, the Philippines. I hear Costa Rica is fairly dino-intensive. The plan was to live anywhere that I didn't have to be around humans; they'd caused quite enough distress in my life."

Judith stirs to life then, dragging herself up from the floor, keeping a wary gaze on Glenda and me. "She attacked me when I came in. Threw herself at my throat."

"You're lucky I didn't kill you then and there," Jaycee says, then turns back to me. "But she got me to hold off for just a second, and she told me about the baby." Turning back to Judith now—"*My* baby. She said that she would continue to fund the experiment, that after we gave birth, I could raise him on my own.

"If I killed her, the experiment would die out. If I told the Council, they would surely destroy the egg and any of Dr. Vallardo's papers. So we had a deal."

Jaycee pauses, takes a long breath, glances around the room at the audience she has so competently held in the palm of her tanned fleshy hand. "And that's all there is to it. That first night, when you came to the nightclub and I got the letter from Dr. Vallardo—that was a false alarm."

"The egg was showing stresses on its lateral equator," says the doctor defensively. "I thought it best I should summon you."

"Whatever the case," Jaycee says, "it was a false alarm. But I kept in contact with Dr. Vallardo, and last night . . . well, last night was wonderful, Vincent. I wouldn't have traded it for the world. But when I called the doctor and he told me to come back to New York, that it was beginning . . . Can you blame me for not wanting to miss it?"

"Of course not," I say honestly. "But you didn't have to drug me."

"Necessary precautions," she explains.

I begin to pace the floor again. "Doctor, Jaycee, expect to be called up in front of the National Council within the next few weeks. I think they're gonna want to hear this one. And don't either of you make any sudden vacation plans.

"Mrs. McBride, I'm going to take you back to LA with me, and we'll see what the department wants to do with a cop killer. Glenda, a little help?" Glenda and I flank Judith McBride, each taking a firm grasp on her limp arms. She does not resist.

"It's happening!" Vallardo cries suddenly, his call echoing across the lab, accompanied by a gurgling squeal blasting out from the nearby speakers. The crackling has amplified as well, filling the air with hot white noise, drowning out Jaycee's subsequent shriek. Motherly delight? Phantom birthing pains?

"We must get it higher!" yells Vallardo, yanking the pulley attached to the egg's hammock. "It must break the surface of the water!" A strong tug—I run to the other rope, pulling with all my might—something's wrong, something's . . . creaking?

The rope snaps. The pulleys sink. The hammock collapses.

Jaycee screams, this time clearly not in happiness, and speeds toward the far end of the tank just as Vallardo regains his balance. The two of them launch themselves onto a ladder attached to the tank's glass wall and attempt to climb up and over; Jaycee, with her long Coleo legs, has more success than Vallardo, with his stout, stubby body, and she dives into the mini-ocean below. Vallardo struggles to the top a few seconds later and cannonballs in. Warm water splashes out of the tank and splatters against my feet, and the silky sensation reminds me of how much I like to swim.

Glenda, Judith, and I are awestruck as we watch Vallardo and Jaycee through the glass, witnessing their fantastic feats of water ballet. Vallardo dives beneath the surface, unhooking the hammock that has only managed to get in the way, and proceeds to hold the egg above his head, treading water as fast as he can, using his short, stubby tail to whip the water into a frenzy.

Grunts and moans mix with the sounds of splintering shell as the underwater microphones pick up the dinos' struggles. Jaycee helps Vallardo, clutching the egg with her long, brown fingers, doing all she can to keep her child afloat, and that wailing continues to grow and grow, a high-pitched warble somewhere between a human cry of pain and the mating call of a common canary.

And as we watch through that glass, as we listen through those speakers, Glenda Wetzel, Judith McBride, and I find ourselves as three speechless witnesses to the first successful interspecies birth this planet has ever seen.

With a final smack! the egg gives way, its proteins spilling out into the tank, clouding the water with their juices, the shell fragmenting into thousands of little pieces, drifting down through the water like ashes off a campfire.

"Can you see it?" I ask Glenda, not moving my eyes from the increasing obscurity of the tank.

"No," she replies, and I can only assume that she, too, is unable to look away. "Can you?"

"Uh-uh. Judith?" No response. "Judith, can you see the

baby?" Again, nothing. I turn to look at our captive, whose arm I find I have released some time within the last few minutes. She's gone.

"Glen, we lost—"

I am cut off by a piercing roar, a shrill banshee shriek the likes of which sends invisible spiders crawling all about my body. It is coming from the speakers, amplified tenfold, which means it is coming from the tank, which means—

It is coming from the baby. Water, splashing around, overcast with clouds of sandy afterbirth, obscures my vision, but through the waves I can make out Jaycee's lithe figure, still treading water, and as she lifts herself to the surface, I get a momentary glimpse of her newborn child. A moment is all I need.

Slight gray claws lance out from a pair of spindly arms, the webbing between dotted with tan lumps of flesh that wriggle and clutch at the unfamiliar air. They are fingers, stubby digits that have formed only as far as the claws jutting out from their sides have allowed them. Rough scaly patches meet with smooth, hairless pink, comprising an outer covering that is not quite skin, not quite hide. Its spine juts out, pressing against this thin covering, a Braille pattern of deformity, and I can make out individual vertebrae dropping up and down like a row of player-piano keys belting out a Dixieland tune. A single tail droops down and away at the end of that spine, no more than a thin strand of bones that effectively doubles the length of the child.

The torso is curved, a long, midnight-black stretch of burnt rubber, and the bloated potbelly, cresting, crashing, jiggling, carves a wake of flesh down the baby's side. Another set of claws, longer, darker, stick rudely out from stumps that might be five-toed feet, rapidly extending and withdrawing, extending and withdrawing.

And the head, that head, a frantic lottery of all conceivable features, nostrils indented, eyes wide yet yellow, ears practically nonexistent save for a single lobe dangling roughly off the left cheek, snout canted downward at an orthopedically undesirable angle, a few teeth already in and threatening to pop through the jawbone itself.

It is an amalgam of all I have ever seen, but somehow it is completely unlike the misfits we saw earlier. It is beautiful. I am horrified. I cannot look away.

And Jaycee Holden is happier than she has ever been; the haunted look in her eyes, the one that said *I don't want to be here anymore,* is gone, replaced with a mien of fulfillment, of purpose. Triumphantly, even as she continues to tread water, Jaycee holds her baby aloft, over her head, in what I can only assume to be a gesture of conquest.

A shot rings out—bangs out—overpowering the amplified sounds of postbirth exuberance—and a crack appears, webbing out from a rough hole on the very top of the tank, just above the water level. We spin toward the far side of the laboratory, toward the sound of the gunshot.

It's Judith. And she's got her gun back. She's aiming for the baby. Or Jaycee. It doesn't matter, because she's preparing to fire once more.

Now Glenda's got all the reason she needs to attack the human she was pulled away from before, and this time I'm sure not going to be the one to stop her. She leaps across the laboratory, her edged bill ready to sink into giving flesh. But Judith is lifting the revolver again—Jaycee, terrified for two lives, no other choice at hand, is ducking beneath the water, clutching the baby to her chest—Vallardo, too, engages his dive mechanism—and me? Ah, hell, I'm frozen in place.

I'm able to convince my throat to scream, "Watch her revolv—" before the second gunshot rocks the lab. A millisecond later, Glenda is on Judith like a crash-dieter given a one-hour reprieve at a Vegas buffet, sinking her teeth into the human's fleshy neck, searching out the precious arteries that will bring blood and end life.

I'd rush to help, I really would, but as I turn to make sure Jaycee and Vallardo haven't been hit, I find myself staring at the long cracks snaking all across the giant water tank, picking up speed, growing, growing, splintering out like fractal branches. Water is leaking, water is pushing, glass is bending beneath the pressure, and before I am able to convince my feet to *run you fools, save yourselves!* the walls shatter, releasing the floodgates.

I wanted to swim; now here's my chance. Glenda, Judith, Vallardo, Jaycee, the newborn, the lab—all of it disappears under the tidal cascade, as the tables bolted to the lab floor become artificial reefs in this brand-new ocean. I am buffeted against the breakers, thrown beneath the surface, breath bursting in my lungs, screaming to get out. I swim up—and hit my head on the floor. Wrong direction. I swim in the other up, and soon break into the open air, gasping for oxygen.

A second wave rolls by, tossing itself into my open mouth. I gag and fall beneath the surface again, struggling for purchase against the silken water around me. What do they say—three times and you're under? Then I'd better not plan on going down again. With a gargantuan effort, I flex my tail and launch myself out of the water yet again, barely avoiding the onslaught of another wave. Pieces of shell float by me like driftwood after a storm, and I struggle to keep my head above water as each new rush threatens to draw me to my death.

The door to the lab is open, and whatever water is able to escape through it quickly does so, making for a whirlpool of energy around the area. The swells pull me closer to this danger zone, the undertow threatening to overpower my meager swimming abilities, but I fight like a salmon and spawn upstream, grabbing on to whatever looks like it will help me in my struggle. I think I can see a limb flailing away on the other side of the lab, a wriggling similar to mine executed in an effort to stay afloat, but the sting of water in my eyes makes it difficult to make out an exact shape or color.

"Glenda!" I call, the water bubbling my words into "Blenbla!" but I receive no reply. It doesn't work for Blaybee, Bablarbo, or Bludibth, either. Locating a handhold beneath an installed Bunsen burner, I anchor myself in one area and wait for the storm to die down, using my energy to keep my head above water.

In time, the heaviest rush of water filters out of the laboratory, leaving me alone amid broken glass, broken eggshell, and calf-high tide pools. "Anybody here?" I try and call out, and am surprised to find that I don't make any noise. There's water stuck in my throat. It seems that I haven't been breathing for over a minute.

Upset that I should have realized this sort of thing sooner, I lean myself over a shattered desk chair and apply a self-Heimlich. Dino Heimlichs are administered much higher than their human counterparts, but I learned this a long time ago, the hard way—don't ask, don't ask. A spray of water shoots out, landing a good four feet away, adding a few more milliliters to the puddles, and I can breathe good, stale air once again.

"Anybody here?" I try again, my voice weaker than I would like but at least functioning. There is no response except for the sizzle of the PA speakers shorting out. It's a good thing they're mounted high on the wall, their sparks unable to contact this newly formed aquatic center, or I'd be lighting up like the Rockefeller Center Christmas tree.

Making sure to steer clear of any additional danger

areas, I tromp out of the laboratory, back into the damp clinic halls, which have been given a thorough cleansing via flood, the walls scraped of their debris by the rushing waters. I call out names as I go, and by the time I've searched a few empty rooms and have begun to worry that I was the only one who made it out alive, I hear a "Vincent?" calling to me from down a parallel hallway. I rush into action . . .

To find Glenda, lying on the floor in her own pool of water, smiling up at me, panting, her Hadro bill covered in a mixture of water and blood droplets.

Judith McBride is in this room as well, limp and lifeless atop a worn oak desk. Her arms are splayed to either side, her legs bent at an impossible angle, her head turned away from me. "Did the flood get her?" I ask Glenda.

"I got her," Glenda says, walking over to Judith and turning the widow's head in my direction. Three great bites mar the flesh across her neck, the gashes clearly visible to me, what with most of the blood having been washed away during the last few minutes. I'm sure there was little pain, and that it was over in a flash. "She knew, Vincent. The bitch had to go."

"You did good," I say, not wanting to cause Glenda any pangs of remorse. Killing someone, even a human, can be tough on the heart and the mind. Despite her easygoing attitude about it now, sleep won't come easy for Glenda anytime soon. "Come on," I say, patting her across the back. "Help me look for the others."

We search the building well into the night, leaving no room, no table, no desk, no beaker unturned. The clinic is tremendous, an ant colony of passages and cloistered rooms, water bearing the dead bodies of a hundred floating misfits—even those that Glenda left alive were washed clean in the tide.

At one in the morning, we find Dr. Vallardo, his hide purple, his body thick and bloated with water weight. Somehow, he had wound up inside a storage closet, unable to free himself from the rushing water. Perhaps his girth kept him down, or perhaps it was his ineffectual tail. Whatever the case, he's dead, and there's not much use in discussing it.

His mouth was stuffed with debris from the flood—yolk, eggshells, afterbirth—and we remove it all in order to simplify matters for outsiders. No need to get them confused, searching into matters at the clinic. There's been enough of that for some time, and the Council investigation that is sure to follow is going to dredge up enough sludge to fill ten of those tanks. We drag Vallardo's body into the room with Judith McBride's, laying them down side by side. This is a purely altruistic move; it's easier for the cleanup crews if all of the corpses are in the same location.

Two o'clock rolls by, then three, then four. Glenda and I have searched the entire building, top to bottom, left to right. "Let's split up and try it again," I suggest, and Glenda knows better than to argue with me.

Jaycee and her child are nowhere to be found. I am not frantic. I am not worried. I'm just an average Joe, doing his job. My throat hurts.

By the time dawn rolls around, we have made our run three times, and I have effectively shut myself down. This is the way I want to be. This is the only way that doesn't hurt.

After we drop a disintegration pouch on Vallardo's corpse, then do the same to Judith's despite the fact that she was never really a dino, Glenda convinces me that if we haven't found Jaycee inside the clinic yet, we will never find her. I'm sure she expects me to argue, to press the matter, to send her back out into the field, but I don't. I accept her decision, if only because it is the same one that the more rational parts of my mind have come up with on their own. If Jaycee is not here, Jaycee is not here. I can't think about what this could mean right now; I don't want to think about what it could mean.

"She must have made it out," Glenda suggests, her tones soft, rational, protective. Miraculously, she's not cursing— the flood must have washed her mouth out—but I'm barely able to register this victory for etiquette.

"Yeah," I answer. I hope she's right.

"She probably escaped, went back to her apartment. You can probably find her there."

"Yeah," I answer. I know she's wrong. Jaycee has skipped town, skipped the country, skipped the world for all I know. I will never see Jaycee Holden again.

"Let's go," says Glenda, and I allow her to dress me in my guise, then take me by the arm and lead me out of the room, out of the clinic, into the bright Bronx streets that are just beginning to wake up to a busy autumn morning. The sun sparkles off abandoned cars and broken traffic lights, making everything shine with its brilliance.

"See, Vincent," Glenda says as she leads me down the road, trying to inject a bounce into every step, a happy slide into every shuffle, "on a morning like today, even the Bronx is full of hope."

Epilogue

A year has passed, and the private investigation firm of Watson and Rubio has become the private investigation firm of Rubio and Wetzel. It took a few months, but I finally allowed the sign painters to take Ernie's name down from the outside window, though I made them leave it on the door to what was once his office. I look at it every day. Glenda and I are running at the top of our games, working overtime to get to all the cases that are thrown our way. We actually have to turn assignments away now, but each one we say *no thanks* to hits me sharp, like a hunger pang, as if reminding me that there was once a time when I had nothing in the fridge but a cherry tomato and a stack of basil.

Speaking of basil and its wicked cousins, I'm attending regular Herbaholic Anonymous meetings, and my sponsor, an Allosaur who used to be addicted to celery salt, of all things, is the shortstop for the Dodgers, so I'm always getting free seats behind home plate. It's been 213 days since my last herb, and I'm due to get my next gold star within

the week. Little goals, little steps, but that's the way to re-
build a life.

The so-called Council investigation into the McBride/
Vallardo/Burke/Holden affair was squelched by an order
from invisible higher-ups who were anxious to avoid a
full-scale catastrophe, and I wasn't about to go sticking my
skinny hide on the line for this crap yet again. The worry
was that the dino population wouldn't be able to handle the
implications of what had occurred—the idea that someone
so powerful had infiltrated their society at such an elevated
level—and might riot, commit suicide, or drive the stock
market down. Whatever the case, my dealings in the affair
before the National Council were brief, and I only had to
go to Cleveland twice to deliver my depositions.

Dan's funeral, held only a few days after I returned from
New York, was a lovely affair, with all of his buddies from
the force showing up to wish him farewell. We had ice
cream and Cheetos at the wake. I spent much of the time
drowning in my own sorrow, for any number of related reasons, so I guess I wasn't able to provide much comfort to
the other guests, but it was sure nice to have them around
to comfort me.

Privately, Teitelbaum eased up on the blacklisting once
he got the full story of my time in New York, and now
grudgingly contracts out some of his work to the firm. He
continues to bust my balls, and, if anything, has only in-
creased the size of his nutcracker. Probably had his secretary Cathy pick one up in Frankfurt. His public reaction to
my involvement with the McBride affair was to dock me
two weeks' pay for going outside the boundaries of my job
and then give me two weeks' worth of bonus money for
bringing recognition to TruTel. Let's hear it for treading
water.

I've got a new car and my town house is out of foreclosure, and there's enough money in the bank to last me through any rough spots I might hit, but still I come home every night, sit in front of the television set, eat a warmed-up piece of left-left-leftovers, and read my mail.

Bill—DWP. Bill—cable. Bill—spring water. Letter from a friend of mine in Oregon, asking me if I got the last letter he sent. Offer from MasterCard, a huge credit limit, all I have to do is sign on the dotted line. Another letter, this one from an old client, complaining that she can't get me on the phone at the office anymore, I'm so darn busy, and would I just call her already, she's got a case for me. Something about a reservoir and water rights for the LA basin. And a picture postcard, the vibrant colors poking out from the stack of mail, grabbing my attention. The photo is a long shot of a quiet, peaceful beach with soft, silken sand, an ocean of pure blue, and a sky to match. A GREETING FROM COSTA RICA, reads the flouncy yellow lettering printed in bas-relief across the top. I flip the card over.

There is nothing written on the back, save for my name and address, a heart over the *i*'s in Vincent and Rubio. Instead, in the box where the body of the letter should go, are some strange ink markings—three long vertical stripes, curving slowly, carefully up and around five smaller streaks, these dotted with what look to be half-formed fingerprints. I sniff the card, pressing it tightly against my nose, and believe that I can smell the sand, that I can smell the surf, that I can smell that fresh stroke of pine on a crisp autumn morning.

My gaze falls toward a full-length mirror situated at the end of the hallway. I am unguised, and I soak in a long look at my teeth, my hide, my ears. At my nose, my tail, my snout, my legs. At what makes me different from almost every other creature walking the face of this planet.

I let loose with my claws, flashing them out into the open. Long, curved, retractable.

Those are claw prints on the postcard, claw prints mixed with the early formation of some stubby human fingers. I can see it all so clearly now, these marks made by dipping a set of claws in ink and pressing them hard against the heavy stock paper. One set of adult prints, one set of baby prints. There is nothing else to clue me in, nothing else inscribed on the entire card, but this is all the message I need.

I throw the rest of my dinner in the garbage disposal, turn off the television, and head to the bedroom, unable to wipe away the smile that has crept, unannounced, onto my face.

About the Author

Eric Garcia is originally from Miami. He attended Cornell University and the University of Southern California, where he majored in creative writing and film. He lives in Los Angeles with his wife, Sabrina, daughter, Bailey, and their dachshund, Oliver, and is also the author of *Casual Rex*. He can be reached at www.anonymousrex.com.

He's just like a member of The Family...

THE DOGFATHER

by
Susan Conant

0-425-18838-8

Holly Winter gets an offer she can't refuse:
dog trainer to the Mob. Specifically, teaching an
Elkhound puppy to behave. Its owner is another
story—a wiseguy who's killed so many people even
the FBI's lost count. And now Holly's caught in the
middle of his newest vendetta.

Praise for the Dog Lovers' mysteries:

"Hilarious." —*Los Angeles Times*

"A real tail-wagger." —*Washington Post*